FRAGMENTS

A WIZARD'S WORK • BOOK TWO

Other Books By Mark Fassett

A Wizard's Work
Shattered
Fragments
* Bloodweave

Lords of Genova
Questioner's Shadow

Grim Repo Files
Grim Repo
* Parted Out

Other Titles
The Sacrifice of Mendleson Moony

Novellas
Dreams Of Earth
A Tower Without Doors
Zombies Ate My Mom!
* Zombies Bought The Farm

FRAGMENTS
A WIZARD'S WORK • BOOK TWO

MARK FASSETT

RAVENSTAR PRESS
MONROE, WA

Published 2013 by Ravenstar Press
Monroe, WA
http://www.ravenstarpress.com

For more information, contact Mark Fassett at
mark@markfassett.com

Designed by Mark Fassett
www.markfassett.com

Covert art by Joe Slucher
www.joeslucher.com

ISBN: 978-0615845333

For my Dad,
who kept asking,
"Where is it?"

Acknowledgements

I HAD QUITE a bit of help from several people on this book, even if they don't remember, or even know, that they were involved.

DeAnna Knippling read my first proposal for the book and told me to go back to the drawing board.

Michael Canfield, Michael Kingswood, David Michael, and Rebecca M. Senese provided needed feedback after I finished the manuscript and was at a point where I couldn't tell whether any of it was any good.

My wife, Wendy, hit me over the head several times, promoting good working habits, and my kids kept me on my toes as much of this book was written during summer vacation.

PROLOGUE

I N THE COLD of the deep of winter, Demetrius usually welcomed any warmth he could find, but the fire that warmed him now was as unwelcome as any midwinter freeze. His longtime friend and master, Monteous Roarke, lay burning upon a pyre of oak, dead at the hand of Orliss Kilore only days earlier.

Dead due to bad luck.

A shard of the Challenge Orb, shattered during a struggle for control of the Wizards' Guild, had sliced his throat wide open. No wizard had been able to kill him, but a piece of glass had done the deed with no ill intent.

He could hear the sniffles of Monteous's apprentices as they dealt with watching his body burn. Gerard stood to his left, stoic, his hand straying close to the redheaded girl next to him. Robert stood to his left, hand in hand with Angela, and the tears flowed freely from his eyes.

Robert had been with Monteous the longest, though nowhere near as long as Demetrius had been in the old wizard's employ. Monteous had become a father to the boy after Robert's own parents died during an uprising years earlier.

Demetrius wanted to reach out, pat Robert on the shoulder, tell him it would be all right.

But it wouldn't be.

The Guild was shattered just as the orb had been, its members scattering, though some still tried to hold it together.

Demetrius heard the crunch of feet stepping in the snow behind him and turned to see who it was.

Master Brin, one of the wizards with designs on holding the Guild together, was approaching. He wore a dark robe and propped himself up with his staff. His head had little more than a couple tufts of white hair sprouting from it. Demetrius didn't think it would be much longer before Master Brin's body lay upon a pyre of its own.

"May I have a word?" Master Brin asked, barely audible over the crackle of the fire.

"Now?" Demetrius asked, somewhat surprised.

"Please."

Demetrius glanced at Robert, but Robert wasn't paying attention to him. "Can't it wait?"

"I don't think so."

Demetrius exhaled, his breath emerging as fog, and then turned away from the pyre and his old master.

Master Brin led him toward the trees at the edge of the clearing, a ring of black oak as old and gnarled as the wizard.

When they reached the trees, Demetrius waited for Master Brin to speak.

"You worked for Monteous for many years," Master Brin said.

"Yes," Demetrius said.

"You were at the Conclave. You know the state of the Guild."

Demetrius pressed his lips together. Master Brin never failed to take his time getting to the point.

Master Brin smacked his own lips together once before continuing. "I was curious if you would consider taking employ with the Guild."

"I'm sorry, I can't," Demetrius said.

"But we would pay well," he said. "With the split, we need someone of your, ah, talents."

"It's not the pay," Demetrius said. "I am already under contract."

"So quickly? You have not left Ivron's estate. How could you have anything arranged?"

Demetrius would not, in a thousand years or fewer than a thousand tortures, ever tell Master Brin the truth. He did not like to think about the truth himself.

"Monteous asked me to watch over Robert, should anything ever happen to him. He paid me in advance." It was close enough to the truth.

Master Brin's eyes lit up.

"Then you can still help us," he said.

"I don't think so."

Master Brin smiled.

"You don't understand. That is exactly the job we had for you."

As he finished speaking, Master Brin looked around the clearing, then lifted his staff and waved it in a circle. Demetrius could not see the result, but he had once seen Monteous do a similar thing when trying to speak in confidence.

"I want you to watch over Robert. He will take his tests soon. We want to make certain he lives to take them."

"If that's all you want, why do you need me? Wizards are better equipped to protect against wizards." He protested only to lead Master Brin further from the truth.

"You have his trust, and we have other urgent business to attend to."

Demetrius knew what that had to be—preventing the Guild from coming even further apart.

"You mean you can't find any wizard willing to keep an eye on him."

"Oh, we'll have eyes on him, but you are wrong to think no one is willing."

Demetrius raised an eyebrow.

Master Brin glanced around, obviously looking to see if anyone could hear him.

"Many are willing," Master Brin said, "but there are few that I trust right now, and those few do not have the time."

Demetrius nodded.

"Thank you for telling me the truth, Master Brin. I'll watch over him. I'll stick to his side, whether he wants me there or not."

"Thank you, Demetrius. Now, if you'll excuse me, I should pay my respects to Monteous before he burns to a crisp."

Master Brin walked off toward the pyre, leaving Demetrius to stand under the trees, alone.

Out of the corner of his eye, Demetrius caught something move, but when he turned to look, it was only a branch shaking, its load of snow having just fallen off and cascaded to the ground.

Demetrius returned his gaze to where his long time employer and master was transforming into smoke. An end to a long chapter in his life, but it somehow didn't feel like it was quite over.

He let his gaze drift to Robert and Angela standing hand in hand, and thought about what he'd just agreed to do for Master Brin.

No, it's not over. Not over in the slightest.

THE FIRE ROARED in front of them, hot enough that Angela's face sweated despite the deep cold that still lingered after the snowstorm. Her backside felt the cold through her winter cloak. And then there was her hand. It was warm, though not warm for the same reason as her face. Her hand was warm because Robert held it.

He didn't talk, though. Neither of them did as they watched Monteous's body turn to ash and smoke in the flames. It didn't seem right to talk, and she didn't think Robert wanted to talk much, anyway.

He was barely out of bed after the injuries he had sustained battling Orliss. On their way out to the clearing, he rode behind her on the horse, still not quite strong enough to ride for himself.

Through his hand, she could feel the occasional sob as his body lurched. Out of the corner of her eye, she saw tears streaming down his face. Of all of them, he had been closest to Monteous, had lived with him the longest, and he had done the most to try to save him.

She heard the crunch of snow as someone took a step. She turned her head to see Demetrius, in his red coat and hat, walking away from the pyre on a path that would take him to Master Brin, her new master. Hers and Gerard's and Robert's. Maybe even Nina's.

The red-headed girl stood next to Gerard, braving the cold even though she had known Monteous only a little. She was there for Gerard, and hadn't left his side since they returned from the disastrous Conclave.

Angela wanted to talk to her, get to know her better, but Angela had spent most of her time in Robert's room with him, and the rest of it working with Master Brin.

She looked back at Robert, seeing his face in profile, and the tears still flowed.

She squeezed his hand, and he turned slightly to look at her. His gaze was full of sadness, but an undercurrent of determination ran beneath it.

"He would have been proud of you," she said in a quiet voice she hoped only he could hear.

"I like to think that," he said. "If only..."

He turned to look back at the fire, but she didn't, preferring to watch him instead.

She knew what his *if only* was. If only he had been faster, better, stronger. She'd told him many times since he woke that the shard of the orb that killed Monteous was a fluke and there was nothing he could have done.

They stood that way for a few minutes until she heard footsteps in the snow from behind her again.

Only, this time, it was her new master approaching, not Demetrius.

"He was a powerful wizard," Master Brin said, "may he now rest."

A few moments of silence passed, and for a moment, Angela thought Master Brin might not say anything else.

But he broke the silence.

"Robert," he said. "I have news."

Robert turned to look at him, but said nothing.

"Two weeks from today, provided you are sufficiently recovered, you will take the tests. Seeing as how you are standing, I think you will be in fine shape by then."

Robert nodded. "Thank you, Master Brin."

Master Brin turned toward her.

"Angela? Tomorrow, you, Gerard, and Nina ride out with me."

She saw Nina and Gerard turn to look their way after hearing their names mentioned.

"Where are we going?" Angela asked.

"We have settled on an estate that we will use for the Guild Academy. You three will go with me to help prepare the laboratories and return to your training. Other apprentices will come in as they are able."

"So soon?"

Robert squeezed her hand.

"Yes," Master Brin said. "We have decided we should not wait. A few apprentices are in situations like yours, with their masters dead due to that nasty business at the Conclave. The sooner we get to training you all, the sooner we can replenish our numbers. Say your goodbyes tonight. We shall leave in the morning."

Master Brin turned away from her, and back to the pyre.

"Goodbye my friend," he said, then turned and headed back to where the horses waited.

Angela could not believe it was happening so soon. She had thought the Academy would take months to set up, that she would have a few months with Robert before they had to separate.

"I'll come visit," Robert said. "I'll stay and help, if they'll let me."

"But..." She stopped. She couldn't articulate how she was feeling. She was excited to go, to learn from as many wizards as she could, but it meant leaving Robert so soon after they had come together.

"I'm not ready," she said.

"You're ready."

"No, I'm not ready to be away from you."

"It won't be for long," he said.

"You promise?"

"I promise. I'll pass my tests, and then they won't be able to keep me away from you."

She smiled, stood on her tip-toes, and kissed him. His lips tasted like tears, which reminded her again of why they were there.

"Why did he have to tell us now?" she asked.

Robert shook his head, then went back to watching Monteous burn.

FROM HIS PERCH in the branch of a snowbound black-oak tree, Trajon Jarl watched the body of Monteous Roarke, the most powerful wizard of the age, burn to ash on a pyre built taller than a man.

The flames and the blackening body held only a passing interest for him, though. It was the people who were in attendance that had brought him to the edge of the clearing in the middle of winter.

He came to take the measure of the man that had defeated Orliss Kilore in a duel, had come to kill him if necessary, and Trajon found him wanting.

The boy, mud brown hair standing just a shade taller than average, did have the strength to control large amounts of energie. It was obvious when Trajon slipped into the vew to take his measure. What the boy didn't have was experience or much knowledge. He wasn't even a master, yet.

It became clear as Trajon observed the boy, who had tears in his eyes for the recently deceased Monteous Roarke, that Orliss had died due to luck, as much as any specific skill of the boy's.

Killing the boy wouldn't serve any purpose right then. It likely wouldn't be any fun, either. And he was still young. Once Trajon's other plans came together, he might be able to take the boy and train him as he should have been trained.

No, it wasn't time to do anything about the boy, yet.

The others in the clearing were just as useless. Even that damnable Demetrius who had been a dagger at his neck for ages.

Demetrius stood close to the boy, protectively.

Trajon smiled.

It would be fun to bring the boy under my control while Demetrius frets and dances about. Without that old fool Thiobulus to help him, Demetrius won't stop me.

The smile faltered.

Thoughts of how Thiobulus and Demetrius had imprisoned him so long ago rarely left him for long, nor did they allow him much pleasure...

Unless he thought of his revenge.

Demetrius turned away from the pyre, and for a moment, Trajon Jarl thought he had been spotted.

But he was black-cloaked against a black-oak in the shadows of the forest.

And then Trajon noticed the doddering old wizard that had taken Monteous's place walking through the snow toward Demetrius. Trajon hadn't even bothered to learn the wizard's name. He was nothing.

The old wizard said something to Demetrius, and then the two of them walked away from the group, back to the treeline on the other side of the clearing.

Trajon's arm started to itch in the dry cold.

He looked down at it and saw the pale skin had started to show the spidery web of his veins beneath.

It was time to feed.

He fished a hand into his pocket and brought out his Telanderal, an oval shaped Work he carried with him everywhere. The stone bore a thin set of lines that crisscrossed near the thinner ends. He had carried it with him since the day he finished it, even through the dark days of his imprisonment.

If only I could have drawn the energie to use it while there.

He pushed the thought out of his head. He had seen what he came to see, and it was time to go. He didn't have time for anything but finding a meal.

He spun a thin thread of energie into the stone, drawing a pattern along the lines while thinking of his destination.

When Demetrius looked up to see the snow falling from the tree, it was already too late. Trajon Jarl was gone.

CHAPTER 1

"**D**O YOU KNOW what they said?" Robert asked Demetrius as soon as Demetrius met him outside the thick oak door of Monteous's laboratory. The morning summer sun still hung low in the sky with the day only a few hours old.

Demetrius, ever unflappable, and dressed, as always, in a red coat and hat, shook his head. "I can guess," he said.

"They said, 'Wait until the next Conclave. We will make our decision by then.' That's six months from now." Robert was trying to contain his anger, but he was losing the battle, and he knew it.

"The Guild has its rules and its methods."

Robert waved his intricately-carved, rosewood staff back and forth. "You see this?" he asked. "I finished this two weeks after Monteous died. I passed my tests. I learned everything I needed to know to qualify as a master in the two months after that. They should have made me a master three months ago, and now they want me to wait another half year?"

Demetrius sighed. Robert guessed Demetrius had to be frustrated with him, but Demetrius showed few signs of it. "You can't force them to make you a master, Robert."

"But I don't see the point of any delay."

"Do you really want to have this conversation outside?" Demetrius asked.

"No," Robert said, but he didn't move.

Demetrius pushed past him and opened the door. Robert was glad to let him do it. He hadn't yet come to terms with the idea that the laboratory belonged to him now.

"Are you coming?"

Robert peered through the open door and into the dark of the unlit room beyond. An overturned chair lay among the ruins of a number of Works and utensils, items Monteous and his apprentices had spent hours and days creating—all of it smashed by the treasonous wizard Orliss Kilore.

"I wonder how much is missing," Robert asked, delaying his entry.

"We won't find out unless we go inside. This was your idea."

Reluctantly, Robert moved past Demetrius and into the laboratory that was now his.

The door shut behind him. "At least they finally agreed that Monteous's order willing you his assets could not be set aside."

Robert nodded, sure that Demetrius could see it in the dim light that entered through the dirt encrusted windows.

Robert Weaved a light at the end of his staff, brightening the room a bit. The lamps were still in place, and he sent threads of energie to each of them until the laboratory was fully lit.

The light exposed destruction more thorough than Robert remembered, and it sent another wave of anger through him. The anger carried a hint of satisfaction, though, as the man responsible was dead.

"Orliss did not leave much," Demetrius said.

Robert picked his way through the remnants of the workbenches and shards of glass. He had to agree with Demetrius. The shelves were clear of the more expensive and difficult Works. The materials were mostly missing. The benches had all been emptied before being overturned.

He stepped onto the circular stone platform, the stage, as Monteous had called it. At his feet, he found an iron stand, bent and mangled. It appeared to be the only remnant of the portal he had opened during their search for Monteous—the portal that had proved to him that he could, and would, be a master. He reached down and picked it up.

"When Monteous died," he said as he turned the mangled iron over in his hand, "Master Brin told me I was to take the tests as soon as I was recovered. I was ready right then to become a master, to take Monteous's place. Then I passed the tests, and I made my staff. They were amazed at my skill and my ability, and they praised me for it. I thought for sure they would make me a master within the month."

He had been so sure, too. Nothing but praise and amazement, until they sent him away from Angela for more training. He had thought they would teach him of proscribed Works and Weaves, but they taught him nothing. When he returned, Master Brin barred him from the Academy and wouldn't allow him to see Angela, or even talk with her one last time.

"I've been so angry," he said, "ever since Monteous died. And when they wouldn't let me see Angela, I couldn't take it. I shouldn't have said those things. I shouldn't have threatened Master Brin and the others, but why did they have to take her from me, too?"

"You know why..."

"I know what they said. I know they said she needed to be free of my influence in order to complete her training, and I know they said I needed to concentrate on my own tasks, but that's a load of manure. I know there's something else going on. I've apologized, time after time, for my outburst and my threat."

Robert looked to Demetrius. "What are they trying to do to me?"

Demetrius stared back at him, silent.

"Dammit Demetrius, you know something, don't you."

Demetrius shook his head.

Robert dropped the unrepairable stand to the stone floor and walked off the stage. Robert surprised himself. He stood right up to Demetrius, grabbed Demetrius's red coat, and brought him in close.

Demetrius let him, even though Robert knew the man could probably kill him quicker than Robert could form a Weave.

"Tell me what you know," Robert demanded.

Demetrius shook his head, and then mouthed the words, "They're watching."

"AGAIN. PAY MORE attention to the pattern."

Angela sighed, but she started the Weave again, as she was instructed.

When she first heard that she was going to the estate the Guild was going to turn into the Academy, she despaired of ever seeing Robert again. Master Brin hardly even gave them time to say goodbye before he whisked her, Gerard, and Nina away, leaving Robert at Ivron's estate.

But on the ride to the new Academy, she grew more and more excited, despite her fear of losing Robert. The night before they left, the four of them had sat up and talked about what they might expect. The idea that they would learn from more than one wizard sounded exciting, and the prospect of additional apprentices to talk with sparked her interest. Robert told her not to worry, that he would come and visit as soon as his tests were done.

She knew that new apprentices and new masters wouldn't ease the ache she would feel at Robert's absence, but she had thought it would be infinitely better than sitting around listening to Master Brin drone on and on like he had during their time at Ivron's estate.

She had not, however, considered that the other wizards that had come to teach might actually be worse than Master Brin.

The new masters were introduced the first night after Angela and her friends arrived at the Academy. Master Brin was staying as the Headmaster, and three other wizards were chosen to join him.

Master Olimand was an obese man with night black hair and a beard that engulfed his face. He was fairly young, being only about ten years older than Robert.

Master Callalan was as thin as Master Olimand was round, but quite a bit shorter and older, though not as old as Master Brin. He didn't have any hair to speak of, either.

The third master, Master Brecious, was a woman, and Angela had looked forward to getting to know her. But it was quickly apparent that the woman had a heart of ice that matched her white hair and sharp features.

And it was Master Brecious that kept driving her to repeat the same Weave far past the point where Angela felt she could do it well. Master Brecious was never satisfied with anything Angela did, and her stare held all the understanding of a stone.

Angela tied off the threads, then sat back and examined the Weave. Flat, two feet square, and floating in the air.

She looked around to see what the other four students had accomplished. None of them were done yet, though one boy that had been a thorn in her side since the day she arrived was close to finishing.

He'd introduced himself the night of her arrival as Shane, and had immediately invited her to step around the side of the building to share a kiss. "You're the most beautiful wizard I have ever seen," he said. She had laughed, and told him she was already devoted to another.

"But is he a wizard?" he asked.

"Yes, and any time now, he'll be a master."

"Who is he?"

"His name is Robert."

Shane stepped back a bit and blinked his eyes. "He's not the apprentice that killed Orliss Kilore, is he?"

Angela smiled, and said, "The very same."

"My master said the Guild will never allow him to join."

Angela's anger got the better of her. "What does your master know? Is he a traitor like Orliss?"

Master Brin stepped between them and pushed Angela's arm down. She hadn't realized she'd been holding it up, and her wand with it.

"Apprentices, this is not the place to discuss politics," Master Brin said. Then he turned to Angela. "And we do not Weave against other apprentices unless instructed to."

"But..."

Master Brin leaned in close to her. "I heard what he said, and he is wrong. Ignore him. You are only a year or two away from taking the tests yourself. Don't waste it."

After that, Shane tried to best her at every opportunity, tried to prove himself to her, she thought.

"Angela," Master Brecious said.

She looked away from Shane to find the icy glare of the master directed at her Weave. "Yes?"

"Are you distracted by something? This one is worse than your last one."

Angela heard Shane snicker. She wanted to hit him, but didn't get the chance.

"You keep your thoughts on your Weave, Shane, or you will find it unraveling before you place the last thread."

Angela took a closer look at her own Weave, and saw that it was a little worse than the last one, but not much, and the last one had been the best she'd ever completed. "It still holds."

"Does it now? Would you be willing to stand on it?"

Angela sighed. "No." The physical Weaves were not her strong point. They never had been.

"When you do not have the strength in a particular area, you must be all the more precise. This Weave, when properly formed, should carry you no matter how little strength you have in the energie flows needed to create it. This is what comes of learning from a master like Monteous, who has all the control and power one could want."

Angela stood up, anger coursing through her over the comment about Monteous. "You take that back. Monteous was a great master. He was..."

"He was a master with a great deal of power in just about anything he tried. He didn't need to be as precise as you do, Angela. His strength overcame many weaknesses. If you ever want to be a match for a man like that, you must learn greater control and deal in precision, not strength.

"Now, sit back down and try it again," Master Brecious said while unraveling Angela's Weave.

Angela sat in her chair, but her body shook with anger. She stared straight ahead until the Weave disappeared. To do anything else risked the Ice Witch's wrath and Shane's smirks. She was not about to allow either.

She spared one last thought for Robert before raising her hands to form the Weave again.

I wish you would come and take me away from here.

GERARD KNELT IN the tall grass behind the stable, trying to stay hidden while he waited for Nina. He felt a bit silly hiding like he was, but the masters had frowned more than once upon his relationship with Nina, and today, he didn't want anything to interrupt his plans.

In the months since meeting Nina amidst their attempt to prevent Orliss from taking over the Guild, Gerard had come to see her as more than just a friend. She'd been his constant companion from the day they met until the day the masters separated them into different classes at the school.

It hadn't been all his idea, either. At first, when he had not yet understood what he felt about her, he tried to find slivers of time alone to think. Sometimes, he would try to get Master Brin to send him on an errand without her, but she always found a reason to go with him. Other times, he tried to sneak off into the woods alone, but she always found him.

He really did not have a moment to himself until they sent them to the school, and then he found the forced separation hard to bear. They spent every moment they were allowed together, and even moments they were not allowed.

And many of those moments they found back behind the stable.

He felt in his pocket for the band of gold it carried. He had spent weeks collecting the material for it, and then it took him another few days Working the ring in the spare moments he could find alone. It wasn't as detailed as he would like, but with the tools he'd been able to sneak off with, smooth was as good as he could do. He would add details later, his family's seal—hers, if she had one.

His parents would not approve, but it didn't matter. They had sent him away. He hadn't heard from them in years. He knew what they thought, too. Once Monteous had taken him, he had become Monteous's problem.

The dry grass crunched under the steps of someone approaching the stable. Gerard stood up and quickly brushed himself off, not wanting to appear like he was indulging in idleness, as Master Olimand—a master terribly familiar with idle indulgence, if his rotund figure were any measure—liked to say.

He need not have worried; Nina's redheaded face peeked around the corner.

Gerard both relaxed and grew exceptionally nervous at the same time. *This is it.*

She ran to him, threw her arms around him, and hugged him tight before lifting her chin up in demand of a kiss, which Gerard happily supplied.

When they broke off, Nina said, "I didn't think Master Olimand would let us out. He kept going on and on about diligence and details and hard work. Like he's ever done a bit of hard work in his life."

Gerard chuckled. "He did let you out, though, and I'm glad he did, because I've got a surprise."

Her eyes grew bright. "A surprise? What surprise?"

Gerard's heart fluttered, his hands broke out with sweat. *Do I really want to do this? Father will be apoplectic. No, I don't care. He sent me away.*

"Gerard? What's wrong? You look upset."

Gerard had not realized his emotions escaped his control. He forced a smile back onto his face. *This is supposed to be a happy time.* "Nothing's wrong," he said, reaching a hand up to brush a strand of crimson hair from her face and touch her cheek in the process. He reached his other hand into his pocket for the ring.

"It's been six months since you ignored your father and followed us."

"I didn't ignore him," she said, giggling.

Underneath her giggle, he thought he heard hoof beats coming up the road that ran past the estate. Whoever it was rode at a pretty good clip. He ignored it and continued on with his preface. "And in that time, you've made it pretty clear that I'm unavailable to the other girls."

She batted her eyes. "I don't know what you're talking about, Gerard. There's only two girls here worth having, and Angela is obviously not interested."

Angela. Nina liked to needle him about his poor treatment of Angela, and Gerard had no idea why. He'd long since apologized. He wanted to refute that he had any interest in her anymore, but held his tongue. Saying anything would only send the conversation down a different trail.

The hoof beats grew louder. The horse was right outside the gate.

Gerard pulled the ring out of his pocket. *Please don't come in the yard,* he asked silently, hoping to keep the rider away.

"In that time," he said, "I've grown fond of you, too."

She smiled and put her hand out to touch is chest using just her fingertips. "Fond?" she asked.

The clop of the hoof beats changed to the distinctive sound of horseshoes on stone. It had entered the courtyard, and Gerard knew he had run out of time. At least one master would come out to greet the visitor.

He shook his head. "Forget about that. Nina," he said, holding out his hand. "I..."

"Gerard Maracane," a voice called out. It belonged to the rider, Gerard was sure. It sounded vaguely familiar. Nina's head turned, even though they couldn't see the rider through the wall of the stable. "I'm looking for Gerard Maracane."

"I wonder what he wants?" Nina asked.

"I have no idea," Gerard said, but he had a hollow feeling in the pit of his stomach. No one rode that hard with good news.

"Excuse me," said another voice. This one belonged to Master Brecious. *She stepped out of her class quickly.*

"Would you mind telling me who you are and why you want to bother one of our students?"

"I'm sorry, Master Wizard," he said, his voice carrying an appropriate coloration of fear and respect. It sounded even more familiar, a memory from long past, but Gerard still couldn't place it. "I'm just a courier carrying a message from the boy's father."

"Your father?" Nina whispered.

"This can't be good news. I haven't heard from him since the first year after I became an apprentice, and honestly, I don't care what he has to say." But deep down, he knew that last was a lie.

"Don't be silly," Nina said. "You have to find out what it's about."

The choice was taken away from him by Master Brecious. "Come out Gerard, you too, Nina."

Gerard silently cursed the messenger's timing, but slipped the ring back in his pocket. He'd have to ask her later, though he hoped it would not be *much* later. "I guess I should find out what he wants," he said.

Before he could step away from her, Nina stood on her toes to give him a quick kiss. It wasn't enough for him, though.

"Gerard?" The master's voice had a way of penetrating the walls. Gerard swore it was louder than it should have been.

He stepped away from Nina, felt her fingers trace down his arm until her hand clasped his. They walked, hand in hand, around the corner, to face whoever had come for him.

When he saw the man, Gerard stopped in his tracks. The man atop the horse wore the typical summer clothing of Risuk: leather leggings, ram wool jacket, a metal band around his brow to keep his shoulder length hair from his face. Gerard didn't stop because the man was from Risuk. He stopped because he recognized the man on the horse and had not seen him since joining Monteous as an apprentice.

"Uncle?" Gerard asked, disbelieving.

Why would my uncle be here? Why not just a regular messenger? His heart raced. Whatever news his uncle carried could not be good.

"Come, Gerard. I have news from your father, and I think you would prefer to hear it in private."

"No, I don't think so. I don't think I want to hear it at all," Gerard said. *They left me here, they can just leave me alone.*

"What's going on, Gerard?" Nina asked from behind him.

"Shhh," he said.

"You must hear it," his uncle said. "Your father demands it."

"My father sent me away, and he hasn't sent even a message to me in the last six years. He has no right to make demands of me."

His uncle dismounted easily, dropping to the ground, and not showing any signs of the long ride, but his uncle wouldn't.

"He has every right, Gerard, he's your father. Come, let's find a quiet room in this place so that we can talk." He extended his hand, palm up, the ritual greeting of Risuk, an invitation for Gerard to step forward.

Gerard had no intention of doing so. His father had sent him away. His uncle could have prevented it.

"Just tell me now," said Gerard. He glanced at Master Brecious, then back at Nina. He didn't care if they heard anything the message from his father. "Whatever it is, I'm not going to do what he wants. He has no idea who I am. Neither do you. You had a chance to stop him, to take me in, and you didn't. I could have been your son, could have helped you, but you spurned me just like my father did."

"Gerard..."

"No, I don't want apologies. I'm happy here, and I'm going to finish my apprenticeship. Didn't my father always tell me to finish what I started? Well, I'm going to finish it."

His uncle dropped his hand. "Your way, then. I'm here to inform you that your brother is dead at the hands of brigands and that your father requests your presence at his funeral, to be held in two weeks time."

The message hit Gerard like a crossbow bolt to the chest.

"You are now the sole heir of the Maracane line, with the responsibilities your new position entails."

Eric, dead. It's not possible. Gerard sunk to his knees.

Nina came up behind him, put her arm around him. "Gerard? Are you all right?"

No. I'm not. "I dreamed of this when I first came to Monteous, I dreamed I was in my brother's shoes, but not this way, and not any more."

"You're going, aren't you?" she asked. He had no idea how she knew these things.

"I have to," he said. And that was the worst part. If it had been anyone else, he could have stayed.

"I'll come with you."

He looked up from the ground, looked into her green flecked eyes. "I want you to go," he said, "but you can't."

"Why not?"

"You need to become a wizard, join the guild, help Robert and Angela. That life is over for me."

"That's not what I want," she said. "I want to be with you."

"And I, with you."

He looked up at his uncle and saw Master Brecious standing behind him. The icy look she usually wore had melted, and Gerard realized she knew what this meant to him—what this meant for Nina.

"Please," he said. "You need to finish your studies."

"But..."

"No," he said, and decided to lie to her. "I'll come back, I promise. When your studies are done, I'll come back for you."

"That's such a long time," she said. "What if..."

"I love you, Nina. I'll come back, and I'll visit whenever my duties allow." *Which will be never.*

"If you promise. Write me," she said.

"I will."

He pulled her to him, hugged her, gave her a kiss that tasted of tears.

"When do we leave?" he asked, standing up and turning away from her. Her hand still held his, and he didn't pull it away just yet.

"Early tomorrow morning."

Gerard nodded. A quick break from Nina was better, anyway. His heart felt as heavy as a piece of granite, but the ring in his pocket felt heavier.

And then, in a moment of quiet defiance, he turned around to Nina one last time. He pulled the ring from his pocket, and then clasped her hand, slipping the ring to her. "Keep this for me," he said, and then strode off to his room to pack his things.

His betrothed, a responsibility of his new station, would never have that ring. *I'm sorry, my love.*

CHAPTER 2

THE WEAVE THAT had wrapped the doorway to Monteous's study for as long as Robert could remember was gone. Robert closed his eyes for a moment, shelving those memories in the back of his mind. Everything in this building reminded him of the man that he'd once thought of as a father as much as a master.

"Is something wrong?" Demetrius asked from behind him.

"No," Robert said, and opened his eyes.

He pushed the door open and was mildly surprised to find the study free of the disorder that had taken root throughout the rest of the laboratory. The Weave must have kept Orliss's henchmen out.

He stepped across the threshold, and a calm came over him, a feeling of solitude he experienced every time he had visited Monteous, a feeling he thought he would never experience again. The chaos of the outside world leaked past Demetrius and through the door.

"Demetrius, step in and shut the door."

When the door to the room shut, that last bit of chaos melted away.

"I always thought it was because of the Weave on the door," Robert said.

"What?"

Robert spun around, looking past the furniture, the shelves, and the books to the walls. He slipped into the *vew*, that trick of sight that let him see the threads of energie that ran through the world, and then down deeper, and he inspected the walls, looking for something, a telltale sign.

"What are you doing?" Demetrius asked.

There it is, he thought. He discerned a faint pattern of energie running through the walls, trapped forever until they were reworked.

"The walls, Demetrius. The walls are a Work. I never noticed before. I thought the effect was because of the Weave on the door, but the walls, the Work is so subtle."

"What effect?"

"Don't you feel it?" Robert asked. "Whoever you think is watching us, I doubt they can see us in here."

"I don't feel anything. What are you talking about?"

Robert faced Demetrius. "The energie that we use to Work and Weave surrounds us. I can always feel it, just a little, but it's more of an unconscious thing. I hardly ever notice it, unless I step in this room. There is less of it in this room. Only what you and I bring with us. I had always ascribed it to the Weave that Monteous kept across the door, but that's gone. The walls, Demetrius, the walls are a Work, a barrier to energie. They keep it out, and in effect, they will prevent any sort of attempts to spy on us."

Recognition spilled across Demetrius's face. "You think they can't hear us?"

"I know they can't. Please, Demetrius," Robert said, retreating from the confrontational stance he'd taken in the lab, "tell me what you know. Who is watching me?"

"You ought to be able to figure that out," Demetrius said.

"All right, the Guild is watching me. Why? What did I do?"

Demetrius sat down in a chair that Robert remembered sitting in more than once while he listened to lectures from Monteous. It left Robert standing, looking down at the man who had been Monteous's eyes and hands in the wider world. Robert glanced over at the chair in front of Monteous's desk. The plush pillow that sat atop its wooden seat beckoned him, but the idea of sitting in it just didn't feel right.

"You didn't do anything," Demetrius said. "They're trying to protect you."

"Protect me? From what? I'm a master in everything but title. I can protect myself."

Demetrius picked at his fingernails. "Do you think you could protect yourself from Monteous, if he were still with us?"

"Of course not."

"And there's your answer."

"That's hardly an answer," Robert said, his anger flaring. He wanted to throw something. "There's no one as powerful as Monteous."

"You are," Demetrius said. "And don't forget, not every wizard belongs to the Guild. Only the wizards in The Seven Kingdoms."

Robert immediately thought of the wizard that he had met right after the battle by the ferry, the old wizard that had created so complex a weave as to apparently stop time for everyone else but him and Robert. But Robert couldn't imagine that old man was a threat. He had asked Robert to find him, to become his student.

"You still haven't told me why."

"No, I haven't. But think about this—once you become a member of the Guild, you are strong enough that you are immediately a contender for Senior Wizard. Master Brin and others are concerned that should that happen, you might not survive the year."

"Haven't I already proved I could survive? I defeated Orliss."

"Using a staff that contained a proscribed Work, and that Work nearly killed you."

"But..."

"No, Robert. These are their arguments, and there isn't any way around them. I've tried."

Without thinking, Robert sat down in Monteous's chair, futility overwhelming his anger. "Then what do I do?"

"Clean this place, put it back in order, practice, become stronger. Prove to them that you can survive on your own."

"But that could be a long time, and I don't have much money for supplies." Robert imagined sitting in the middle of the laboratory, looking around at barren shelves, and waiting for a summons that would never come.

"You have more than you think. Everything that belonged to Monteous is now yours, and this room appears to be untouched."

Robert spun around, looking at Monteous's desk. It had several drawers. He slipped into the *vew* for a moment, but the Weaves that had protected the desk while Monteous lived were gone. He reached for the bottom drawer and pulled it open.

In the bottom of the drawer he found a lock box. Robert pulled it out. He'd seen it more than once as Monteous pulled it out to give them coins for use at the Festival. A smallish box, no more than the length of his forearm, and a hand and a half deep.

It had no key hole.

He didn't even have to slip into the *vew* to know that the box was a Work. "This will probably only open to Monteous's touch," he said.

"Try it."

Robert brushed his thumb against a metal plate on the front, like he'd seen Monteous do. The box clicked open.

"See?"

Robert lifted the lid. Atop the gleaming coins that nearly filled the box, he found a short note, written in Monteous's hand.

Robert,

It appears that something has gone wrong, and I no longer have the pleasure of living. Just by opening this box, you've undoubtedly learned that I have willed all that I have to you. Please take it knowing that I wish I could have done better by you.

You have the ability, but you must find it within yourself to focus that ability so that it can do you some good.

I write this, knowing that there is a faction in the guild that wishes me dead. I also suspect that if you ever pass your tests and are admitted to the guild, you could have a short life, especially now that I am not around to protect you.

Please, do not seek to join the guild just yet. Instead, seek out Thiobulus Soake and apprentice yourself to him. He will be hard to find, I suspect, as he has little love for the Guild and its members, but he will teach you what you must know to survive.

Do not delay. I fear The Seven Kingdoms are in grave danger, and there is little time to lose.

Monteous

Thoughts swirled in Robert's head. The first one that he was able to snag came to his lips. "How did he know?"

"He didn't know. He prepared. If he had come back, you would never have seen that letter."

Robert nodded. "He was talking about Orliss, right? The Seven Kingdoms aren't in danger any more, are they?"

"Who's to say? But I wouldn't be quick to dismiss the thought. A third of the wizards left or died that day. Where did they go? The orb they used to govern themselves is shattered. Now, they sit in a council and argue all day."

My status with the Guild is proof of that, Robert thought.

Demetrius sat up in his chair. "If they are watching you, protecting you, I would wager they still think there is a danger, beyond a personal threat to you."

Robert sifted through his thoughts. He wanted to see Angela, and he wanted to become a proper master. But neither of those were possibilities in the near future. He only had two other options. He could stay and clean up the laboratory, or...

"Demetrius, do you know where I might find Thiobulus Soake?"

ONLY MOMENTS AFTER Angela finally mastered the Weave such that it didn't fall apart when weight was set upon it, Master Brecious dismissed them all and left the room with a look of concern on her face and a quickness to her gait.

Angela practically raced out after her. She had no desire to endure Shane's smug looks.

She followed a corridor that ran along the back wall of the building, a guard barracks they had converted into a series of instruction laboratories. The corridor opened out into a laboratory complete with a stage, as Monteous had called it, where all of the apprentices could gather and watch a wizard Work.

This larger laboratory also served as a gathering place once the apprentices were let out for lunch, or after the day's lessons were complete. Angela found half a dozen students, mostly much younger than her, already gathered. Master Olimand must have let them out early.

Angela did not see Nina among them, and she smiled to herself. Nina had solved all Angela's problems with Gerard, and she became a good friend, as well, though they did not see each other much. If they weren't studying, Nina was usually off with Gerard somewhere. And she was probably with him now.

Someone had opened the windows in the room. The smell of the early summer grass wafted in on a slight breeze.

Also making its way through the open windows was the voice of a man shouting for Gerard. She did not recognize the voice.

Angela went to the window and looked out. A man, dressed in the fashion of Gerard's home kingdom of Risuk, sat atop a horse. Master Brecious was with him, and Angela heard her call for Gerard and Nina to come out.

Angela felt herself smirk. Everyone knew the spot behind the stable was Gerard and Nina's favorite place to meet. The Academy wasn't a place to hide secrets.

Moments after Master Brecious's call, Gerard and Nina emerged from behind the wooden building, both of them still wearing their gray apprentice robes. Angela noted surprise on Gerard's face, and then as the man atop the horse said something to Gerard that Angela could not quite catch, the look of surprise changed to one of defiance.

Angela ran to the laboratory building door. Shane opened it right as she arrived, and she bumped past him and out into the courtyard.

"Hey," he said.

"Sorry," she said without looking back.

She ran for the main house. Something was up. She knew it, and when Gerard finally made his way to his room, as she knew he would, she would press him for the details.

If Gerard was leaving, like she suspected he was—no one sent couriers for apprentice wizards—she had an errand for him to perform.

NINA STOOD IN the hot, dusty courtyard and watched Gerard's thick strong back as he walked away from her for the second time in her life, only this time she wasn't so sure she could find a way to follow him.

The first time had been easy. Her father knew she would leave and put up a fight only to appease Moma. The weather had not made for good travel, but the tracks were simple to follow.

Her whole life had changed the moment Gerard walked into their house in the middle of the storm. She just hadn't known by how much.

And now, *now*, just as she was starting to pick up some of the things the masters had been trying to teach her, now he was leaving again.

Despite what Gerard told her, she knew he wasn't coming back. The way he had pressed the ring into her hand, more of an apology than a promise, had made it clear.

"You should eat lunch, apprentice," Master Brecious said, penetrating Nina's focus for a moment. The master's voice was not full of cold judgment, as it usually was. Instead, it held something resembling compassion. "You will need your strength for the afternoon lessons."

Nina looked up at Master Brecious, then glanced at the man who had just ruined what she suspected was a marriage proposal. Gerard's uncle had already dismissed her.

"Yes, Master Brecious," Nina said, hoping she sounded resigned as she intended.

She was far from resigned.

She walked across the courtyard to the giant white building that had once been the primary residence of some lord, but was now the building where all of the apprentices and masters ate and slept. It was where the pair of cooks worked to feed them all. It was where they would be serving lunch.

Nina wasn't going to get lunch. She didn't have time.

Once she climbed the stone steps and entered the building, she looked behind her to be sure that Master Brecious wasn't following. She wasn't. The master was helping Gerard's uncle stable his horse.

Maybe she did have time, after all. Maybe she and Gerard had one more night together. She could use that night to get help from Angela, the one person she could trust to help her, the one person here, other than Gerard, that didn't look down on her because of her limited ability to Weave. Nina found the raven haired girl striking, taller than her and more beautiful than any of the other apprentices. She made her gray apprentice robe look like a ball gown. If Nina hadn't seen Angela Work, she would have had trouble believing that Angela was even an apprentice. Nina didn't know

Angela's past, they had never talked about it, but Angela carried herself much like a noble, and if she was from a noble family, or from a family aspiring to marry into nobility, Angela should have been betrothed long ago instead of toiling as an apprentice wizard.

When the door banged shut behind her, she slipped the ring from the palm of her hand and onto the finger she suspected it was meant for. It went on with ease, but she could feel that it would not easily come loose. She held her hand up in front of her to examine it. Plain, gold, but well made and shaped.

She smiled at the memory of his awkward proposal, even though he hadn't finished it. In the things that mattered to the outside world, he was decisive, but when it came to her, when it came to matters of the heart, he was like a child that had been burned one too many times. It melted her own heart, and it was one of the many reasons she loved him.

"If only he wasn't so stupid sometimes."

"What?" a female apprentice asked.

Nina looked up, saw the almond shaped eyes, the thin gold hair. Nina could not remember the girl's name, but knew she was of Gerard's rank, several years ahead of Nina.

"Sorry, nothing. I didn't realize I spoke aloud."

"That's a pretty ring," the girl said. "Did Gerard give that to you?"

Nina clenched her fist and put it in her pocket. The girl obviously knew who *she* was. Nina had to stomp on the jealousy that threatened to rear its head. She could not afford to get into fights with the other apprentices. She wasn't strong enough, or experienced enough, to survive. She could barely create enough of a spark to get a campfire lit.

But it did not stop her from feeling proud. "Yes," she said. "He did."

"You're so lucky," the girl said, and Nina thought for a moment that the girl wasn't like the other apprentices who were more powerful and looked down on the apprentices like her who had a bit of ability, but no strength.

But Nina's hopes died when the girl continued. "I don't know what he sees in you. You'll never be his equal."

Nina's fist threatened to come out of her pocket, but she held it there. Moma would have been proud at her restraint.

"I don't have to be his equal," Nina said. "I just have to be better than the alternatives."

Then she stalked off to find Angela, leaving the girl behind her.

She made her way upstairs without running into another apprentice. They were all eating, she suspected, or they had not yet been let out of their morning instruction.

She followed the long hallway past a number of apprentice bedrooms, past her own that she shared with a much younger apprentice, hoping that Angela would be in her room instead of downstairs with the others. Angela didn't make a habit of eating with everyone else.

Nina smirked as she thought about it. None of the three of them really fit in with the rest. Her own part had been small, but Gerard and Angela had gone through so much that it seemed they felt uncomfortable around the other apprentices. And Nina never would.

Monteous's sentiment and desire to have everyone with any ability trained were things she had desired for herself. But the reality paled in comparison with her imagination. The other wizards didn't really see her as anything but a waste of time.

Just as Nina was passing Gerard's door, where she knew he would be packing, it opened and Angela stepped out.

Angela shut the door behind her, then turned and nearly collided with Nina.

The collision quickly turned into a hug as Angela wrapped her arms around Nina and squeezed tight.

"I'm so sorry," Angela said into her ear.

"Sorry for what?" she asked. "He hasn't left, yet."

"But he will, and..." Angela trailed off.

Nina stood back from her. "I know he's not coming back. That's why I was looking for you."

"You were looking for me?"

Nina looked around. Except for the two of them, the hall appeared empty, but that didn't mean there weren't watchers.

"Let's go to your room." She took Angela's slim-fingered hand and pulled her down the hallway.

When they reached Angela's door, Angela opened it, and the two of them slipped through. Angela shut the door behind them.

"Could you put up a Weave?" Nina asked.

Angela nodded without hesitation and went to work, despite the possibility of extra chores if she was caught.

With some difficulty, Nina slipped into the *vew*, the trick of sight that let wizard's watch the threads of energie as they were Weaved. She watched Angela direct the threads into a Weave that surrounded them. Nina marveled at the complexity of the Weave. She barely understood what Angela was doing. Three separate threads, at least. Nina could only imagine being able to control three threads. One thread was, at times, almost more than she could handle.

When the Weave was complete, Angela said, "Now, tell me why you were looking for me."

"I want your help. I'm not letting him leave me here."

Angela sat down on her bed and gestured to a rickety chair that owned one corner of the tiny room. It was another thing Nina envied Angela. The room was too small to house two apprentices, so Angela had it to herself.

Nina sat on the chair with little hesitation. Though it looked rickety, she knew from experience that it was strong as any other piece of furniture in the academy.

"You know," Angela said, "that the masters won't let you go. Not until you've completed your apprenticeship."

"That's why I need your help."

"I thought being a wizard was important to you."

Nina looked out the hazy window. Someone needed to clean it, but there weren't any servants here anymore. Through it, the sun appeared hidden behind a bank of thick clouds.

"It *is* important to me, but it's not more important than Gerard. I'll never be a full master, anyway."

"You've just started. You don't know what you can be."

Nina brought her attention back into the room, back to Angela.

"You're trying to keep me from leaving."

Angela didn't move or say anything.

"Why... why would you keep me from following him?"

Nina saw the first tear in Angela's eye, perhaps before Angela even realized it was there. The tear told Nina everything she needed to know, and she thought back to what Gerard's uncle had said. *You are now the sole heir of the Maracane line, with the responsibilities your new position entails.*

Angela knew what those duties were, and Nina wanted to beat herself about the head, because she should have known what that meant, too.

"They expect him to take a wife," Nina said.

Angela nodded.

"They probably have one picked out for him, and she's waiting for him to arrive."

Angela closed her eyes, and nodded again.

Nina felt so stupid.

But she didn't let the feeling last long.

Nina got out of the chair, and then knelt down in front of Angela like a supplicant. Angela's tears flowed from her eyes. She lifted her gray sleeve to her face to try to wipe them away.

"Please, Angela, why won't you help me?"

Softly, in between her tears, Angela said, "I don't want to see you hurt any more than he's already hurt you. Families always get what they want, and if they don't..."

"What do they do if they don't get what they want?" Nina asked.

"They send you away."

Nina stood up and hugged Angela, pulled her sobbing head to her breast. She didn't know what had happened in Angela's past, but now she knew it had something to do with her family and their expectations, and whatever had happened, it hadn't been anything good. And they had abandoned her. It was fine for the masters to say that the past is passed, and that none of it matters in their lives as wizards, but you couldn't just forget about it.

"You want him to go, don't you. You want him to get what you want."

Angela stood up, pushing Nina away. "Don't you say that. Don't you ever say that. I don't want to go home . . . ever."

"Then why?"

"He's already made his decision, Nina. Can't you see?" Angela glanced down to the ring on Nina's finger. "That ring he gave you, if there was any doubt in his mind what was more important, he wouldn't have given that to you. He's giving you up for his family. In his room, I pleaded for him to stay. He wouldn't hear of it. He thinks it's his duty, his responsibility, no matter how poorly they treated him."

For a moment, Angela's words rang through Nina's mind and almost convinced her that Angela was right. If Gerard could give up being a wizard, if he could make that ring and then press it in her hand and say goodbye and lie to her about coming back, then why would she even want to follow him? She should be angry at him for lying to her. She should be angry at him for leaving her.

But the moment passed. She wasn't angry at him at all. She was ready to fight for him, no matter the odds, no matter the cost.

And then she wondered why she was even talking to Angela, instead of in Gerard's room convincing him not to go. She had until morning to convince him to stay.

But the answer to that came too easily. She didn't want him to stay. She didn't want to stay.

And then she did get angry, at herself. She was willing to fight for Gerard, but she wasn't willing to fight the perceptions of the other apprentices, of the masters.

She reached out and wiped at Angela's tears. "I'm sorry, Angela, you're right. Following him isn't the answer at all."

"What do you mean?"

"I shouldn't be in here asking for your help. I should be in his room fighting with him to stay."

Which would mean she would have to stay and fight to change their perceptions of what she could be. *I can fight that fight, too.*

TRAJON JARL WAITED until after sundown before approaching the estate, what the Guild now called the Academy. The low wall surrounding the half dozen buildings would not keep him out, nor would the feeble wooden gate. There weren't any guards on the squat towers that marked every turn in the wall. There weren't any watchers at all.

He slipped into the vew as easily as taking a breath and noted the Weaves that surrounded the estate, crossing each other, warding, guarding. The wizards thought they were safe.

And they were—from almost anyone but him.

Six months. Six months of waiting and planning, pushing and prodding. The end of the Guild, and The Seven Kingdoms, began six months ago with the destruction of the orb and the death of that pompous fool Monteous.

Tonight would begin the final, crushing stroke that would sever the guild from The Seven Kingdoms. First, the masters, including that old fool Brin who had taken control of the Guild, and then the apprentices, the future of the Guild. All here, all in one place, except the one who had killed Orliss. If only he could find that one, but the Guild had hidden him well.

No matter. When the Guild was no more, when the wizards were scattered, frightened, or dead, the final door would be open. A door that had remained shut because Surotta had refused to lead Mrongil against The Seven Kingdoms while even the semblance of a Guild existed.

He wished he could have just taken control of Mrongil himself, but having his name come out might have galvanized the Guild against him.

Trajon reached into his night-black cloak and withdrew a small vial, the contents of which had recently belonged to a farmer that had lived only a few miles to the south. He unstoppered the vial, dipped his little finger into its contents, and put the finger to his tongue. The tangy iron taste of the farmer's blood energized him, and he closed his eyes to savor it.

He licked his finger clean, then held his hand out in front of him. He poured a bit of the blood over the hand and began to draw the energie from it and the other elements around him. He directed the energies into a Weave that he wrapped around his body.

No one would see him. No one would hear him, and their Weaves would not detect him.

When his Weave was complete, Trajon licked the blood from his hand until it was clean. *No reason to let it go to waste.* He stoppered the vial and stuck it back into the folds of his cloak.

He took a deep breath.

The air tasted clean, like summer.

He smiled at the thought that it would soon taste entirely different.

He took his first step toward the Weaves that protected the estate and the wizards inside from everyone but him.

CHAPTER 3

*T*HIOBULUS SOAKE. THIOBULUS *Soake.*

The name went through Robert's head again and again. He repeated it as he rode his horse, with Demetrius following, down the road that would lead them to the Academy. The low brush at the edge of the road still held most of its green, though it would soon turn brown as summer advanced. The sun, still overhead, was about to dip toward the horizon. They would have to stop for the night in the next town.

Thiobulus Soake. Thiobulus Soake.

He hoped that the repetition would lead to an insight that would help him find the reclusive wizard. He hoped the repetition would keep him from thinking about Angela.

Demetrius hadn't known much beyond the name and who Thiobulus was.

"He's an old wizard," Demetrius had said while they still stood in Monteous's laboratory, "a legend, really, who held the Senior Wizard position when Monteous was still an apprentice. He's supposed to be an extremely powerful wizard, but I don't know of anyone who has seen him since he left the Guild."

"Why did he leave the Guild?" Robert asked.

"I've never heard. The Guild doesn't give up those secrets to men like me."

"Then who might know where to find him?"

"You can't go there," Demetrius said.

"Go where?"

"To the Academy."

Robert didn't even have to ask who might be at the Academy that would know. Master Brin was the only Master there old enough to have known Thiobulus.

"I'm going," he had said.

"They won't let you in."

"I don't have to go in. I just have to get Master Brin to come out and talk to me."

Which led them directly to the road they were now on, its dust floating up and coating his tongue. Demetrius hadn't been able to dissuade him, and when Robert asked if Demetrius had any other ideas on how to find Thiobulus and pointed out that Monteous had told Robert to find him, Demetrius gave in.

Robert couldn't help hoping they might let him in, might let him see Angela, but he knew it was unlikely; they had turned him away before. Which was why he kept repeating Thiobulus's name.

Two day's ride. That's all it was, but it seemed to be taking forever. Keeping thoughts of Angela out of his head was a constant struggle as they rode past the fields and farms that surrounded the City.

As they rode into the small town where they would stay the night, Robert looked up to see that the sun, with only a sliver of sky between it and the horizon, had turned a deep dark red. His parents would have called it an ominous sign, were they still alive, and it gave Robert a chill that threatened to take hold around his heart.

He turned to Demetrius. "The evening before my parents died, before the uprising, they saw a sun like that," he said.

Demetrius nodded. "Some do believe that a red sun on the horizon means death."

"Do you?"

Demetrius shook his head. His red coat was covered with dust. "There is always death, somewhere," he said. "I don't think it means much at all."

They brought the horses to a stop in front of the single story inn. He could hear a harpist plucking away inside.

They tied the horses to the hitching post to wait while they bargained for a room.

Demetrius set one foot inside the inn, and held the door for Robert. Before Robert entered, he took one last look at the setting red sun.

Maybe Demetrius is right. Superstitions and portents are the province of failed wizards.

He stepped inside, and the door shut behind him, but he couldn't shake the chill around his heart.

GERARD LAY ON his bed pretending to read the book that Master Brin had given him. The old wizard had pulled him aside in the hallway and put the book in his hands.

"I heard about your brother. I am sorry you must leave. Take this and study it while you are gone."

Then Master Brin had walked away without another word.

The book was a thick, leather-bound tome of instruction in the art of manipulating the more delicate Weaves, an invitation, as Gerard saw it, to return and continue to work toward becoming a master.

He looked surreptitiously over its edge, hoping that Nina had given up and left, but she still sat cross-legged on his roommate's bed. Her robe pillowed out around her, hiding her athletic shape from him. Her hands rested in her lap, her left hand atop her right, the ring he had given her prominently displayed.

He had managed to avoid her for most of the afternoon.

First, he attended the afternoon instruction conducted by Master Brin. Over the months he had been at the Academy, Gerard noticed that he was slowly increasing his ability with the more delicate Weaves, and Master Brin had been instrumental in that. Master Brin had a way of describing the processes that made far more sense to Gerard than anything Monteous had ever said. Gerard began to think he might reach Master status in all the disciplines, a far more desirable result than being deemed only an elementalist.

Then, upon seeing his uncle seated to eat at one of the long tables in the main hall, he had taken his dinner to one of the study rooms and eaten it there. He would have a lot of time to talk to his uncle on the road back, and at the moment, he still wasn't sure how he felt about the man. Gerard still struggled with the idea that his brother was dead. It didn't fit in with what he knew of the world. He couldn't believe it.

But the fact that his uncle had come to retrieve him could mean nothing else but that it was true.

When Gerard was done, he had returned to his room to finish packing and get some sleep before he had to ride out in the morning.

He opened the door, stepped inside, and found Nina sitting on his roommate's bed. She didn't say a word as he entered. She didn't move anything but her eyes and her head. Those followed him wherever he went.

Since she didn't speak, he didn't either. He didn't know what to say.

He finished his packing, stuffing what he could into the duffel his horse would have to carry. It wasn't a lot, but he didn't have much, either. All the time, he could feel her eyes on him. With his back turned, they felt accusatory, but if he caught them out of the corner of his eye, or even directly, they appeared patient and understanding, which was almost worse.

He tied the last lace, picked up the book, lay back against the headboard of his bed, and cracked the book open.

At first, he had tried to read, but it was useless. Just her presence distracted him.

They sat that way, him reading, her watching, until Gerard looked out the window, which was cracked open to let some air in the room. The sun, big, red, and angry, had started to dip below the horizon—appropriate on the day he learned his brother died.

He turned away from the sun, set the book down beside him, and sat up so he could look at her directly.

"Aren't you going to say anything?" he asked.

"What is there to say? You've already made up your mind."

"Then why are you here?"

She blinked, slow and measured. "Gerard, you know why I'm here."

The worst part of it was that he did know why she was there.

"You can't come along," he said.

A hint of a smile crossed her face. "I thought about coming along, but then Angela made me realize it would be easier to convince you to stay."

Angela? She talked to Angela?

"I have to go," he said.

"Who says you have to go?"

"My father, my uncle."

She snorted, derision palpable on her face. It was one of the things he loved about her. If she wanted to do something, she did it.

"You don't owe them any sort of loyalty. They don't have a claim on you anymore. You're an apprentice wizard, and a good one."

He wanted to pick the book back up and hide from her again. He was ready to face anger from her, had expected it, but instead she was still the same, calm Nina that never backed down from anything.

"I have a duty. My family needs me."

"They didn't need you when they sent you off to become a wizard," she said, a bit of anger showing through. He thought the anger might not be directed at him.

"No," he said, looking down at the dark floorboards that ran perpendicular to the bed. "It doesn't matter what happened in the past. They need me now."

Nina unfolded her legs and moved to the edge of the bed to dangle them just above the floor.

"Gerard," she said using a softer voice, "what would happen if you didn't go?"

"I'm the sole heir, now. If I don't go home and help my father..."

"Then what? Your father makes a living as a merchant, running caravans from province to province. Is that what you really want?"

No, I want you. I want to stay.

"If I don't go," he said, "I will be outcast, outlawed. My father's holdings will be taken and divided among the other landholders."

"I don't understand," she said.

"In Risuk, you don't own land. It is given into the care of a family, and if that family can no longer care for the land, the family will lose the land, and the standing that comes with it."

"What does that matter to you? They sent you away."

He looked away from her, toward the window. He didn't have an answer to that question. It mattered, but he couldn't put his finger on just why. Even though he wanted to stay, to have Nina as his wife, his duty to his family mattered more, and he couldn't have both.

He heard her move, but didn't turn back until she pulled at his chin with her fingers so that he had to look her in the eye.

"You don't know," she said. "You think you have a responsibility to them."

He nodded. He did have a responsibility. But he also had a desire. He had always wanted to be his brother, but Nina was so close, he could smell the jasmine that she applied to her neck each morning, that she applied for him.

If only I could have both.

But that wasn't a possibility.

Nina smiled. "Since nothing I can say to you will convince you to stay," she said, "then I'm going with you."

Right. He should have known. The thought that she would give up her dream of becoming a wizard for him brought a warmth to his heart, but he knew what awaited him. His parents would never accept her, and he was sure they already had someone else in mind. Someone with money, or connections. Someone hand-picked to further his father's goals.

"You can't go with me," he said. "The masters won't let you."

"You think they'll have a choice?"

She smiled. It was the same sort of smile he remembered seeing on her the first night he met her. Predatory, but inviting.

An incoherent shout echoed through the open window, and Gerard turned just in time to see a white flash of lightning light up the courtyard, and the room. The crack of thunder was immediate and shook the walls.

"What in the..." he said, before another blast of lightning interrupted him.

Gerard jumped from the bed and ran to the window.

He looked out on the courtyard. A pair of wizards stood facing each other across the solid dirt of the yard, their staves held erect. One he recognized as Master Olimand from his rotund figure. The other stood straight as his staff, a hood covering his head. He held the fingers of his free hand splayed out in front of him. Gerard did not recognize him.

An arc of bluish lightning flashed out from Master Olimand's staff and crashed into a barrier that sprung up in front of the hooded wizard. The lightning exploded in a hundred directions.

Nina came up to stand next to Gerard.

"What's going on?" she asked.

"I don't know." He found himself whispering. "Master Olimand is fighting someone in the courtyard."

But it seemed a strangely one sided battle from what he could see. Gerard slipped into the vew to see what was happening. He could see Olimand's threads, the ropes of energie he was directing. But he could not see any of the other wizard's energie. Nor could he see any energie feeding the barrier. It was just there.

Master Olimand dropped his staff, and his hand went to his throat. Gerard still could not see any sort of energie coming from the wizard Master Olimand had been fighting.

Master Olimand fell to the ground, and the other wizard stepped toward him until he stood over the top of the fallen wizard. Nina's breath hissed through her teeth.

A chill raced through Gerard.

He had not seen what happened six months ago when Wallace, Monteous's youngest apprentice, had met his end while trying to unravel a proscribed Weave, but Robert had described it. Robert had told him he had not been able to see the threads until it was too late. Angela, who had been sitting at the same table while Robert talked about it, said she hadn't seen anything at all.

What Gerard had just seen was too close to what Robert and Angela had described to be a coincidence. The wizard outside was using proscribed Weaves, Weaves derived from energie drawn from blood, and he had just killed a master.

The wizard tapped at Master Olimand's now inert bulk with the butt of his staff. The master didn't move.

The wizard, his cloak billowing out behind him, turned toward the manor-house. His head tilted up, his eyes, which would have been black pits in the darkness, were easily discerned in the vew, the pattern of the energies behind them moved in complex swirls. Those eyes looked up, through the window and pierced the fogged glass.

Gerard gripped the sill with his hands, ignoring the pain in his fingers. A smile formed on the wizard's face, a knowing smile, as if he knew Gerard. Gerard could not think for a moment who the wizard might be. Robert had killed Orliss, the only wizard Gerard knew would have been able to kill Master Olimand so easily while using proscribed Weaves. No. This man was too short by a head.

The wizard's hand flicked forward, igniting a giant ball of fire and flinging it toward the window.

Gerard reached out, not thinking, and dragged Nina away from the window. "Down!" he said, pulling her with him as he tried to duck out of the way. His knees hadn't even hit the floor before the fireball crashed through the window to scorch his head and shoulders with the heat of the sun and set the room ablaze.

The heat from the fire was intense, and the pain of his burns erupted through him. *I'm dying! I'm sorry Nina!* He wanted to scream, but the heat seared the air he tried to breath in.

"No!" he heard Nina shout through the wall of pain.

And just before he could take it no longer, the pain of his wounds seemed to fade a little, and he slipped into the blackness of sleep.

AFTER HER UNEXPECTED outburst in front of Nina, which had been almost as upsetting as the memories that had come storming through the walls she tried to keep in place, Angela had skipped lunch and had wanted to skip the afternoon sessions. But the masters did not allow any sort of indigence. Getting upset by a memory would not rank anywhere on their list of acceptable excuses.

"Masters do not let emotions get in the way of what must be done."

She had heard that phrase from the lips of Monteous Roarke, and had heard it again more than once in the past six months from the lips of every master at the academy. Of course, when Monteous said it, the phrase had almost always been directed at Robert.

"An uncontrolled mind results in uncontrolled Weaves."

Another master favorite.

It turned out, however, that the afternoon session, an exercise in defense against divination, proved to help her shove those memories back and rebuild the walls that kept them contained.

The sessions didn't help so much with her hopes for Gerard's ability to get a letter to Robert, or her desire to run back to her room and compose it. In fact, as she rebuilt the walls around her undesirable memories, her desire to write the letter grew. Gerard had promised he would send it as soon as he left.

When the sessions ended, she wasted no time talking with her fellow apprentices. She escaped the end of the day activities in the instruction laboratories, and returned to the manor house, intending to go right to her room and compose the letter.

But when her stomach growled and reminded her that she had missed eating lunch, she made a quick detour to the dining room where she knew she would find food set out for them. She put a slice of bread on a plate, along with a large pile of a mixed potato and meat dish—she couldn't figure out what the meat actually was—and returned with it to her room.

She sat down at the small writing desk in her room and set the plate off to one side. She pulled out a sheet of parchment, ink, and a pen. She removed the stopper from the ink, dipped the nib of the pen, and wrote "Dearest Robert," at the top of the parchment.

Then she stopped. What would she say?

Despite her earlier hasty wish for Robert to come and take her away, she had little desire to actually leave. She wanted him with her, and she would do just about anything to be with him, but she wouldn't leave before she was a full master, like she knew he must be.

Master Brin wouldn't let her quit, anyway. He would come find her, or send someone for her.

No, she couldn't ask him to take her away. Not yet. But she could ask him to visit, to spend a few days with her.

She spent the rest of the evening working on the words she hoped would bring Robert to see her. Her dinner grew cold, and the sun dipped below the horizon by the time she signed her name to the letter.

She rolled up the parchment, tied a ribbon around it, and stood up. Her back ached from sitting crouched over the parchment for so long, and she rubbed at it and stretched. The stretch helped ease the pain a bit.

She took the parchment from the desk, looked down at the still full plate of food, and decided it could wait until after she'd given the letter to Gerard.

The first crack of thunder boomed through the hallway as she shut her door.

The second crack of thunder came when she was about half-way to Gerard's door.

She had her hand up, her fingers tucked into her palm, ready to knock when fire exploded through Gerard's room. The door flew open from the force of the blast and threw Angela into the wall behind her. The back of her head cracked against a wall sconce and sent an eruption of fire through her skull.

She dropped the parchment, put her hands to the back of her head, and slipped to the floor while scrunching her eyes shut against the agony.

A few seconds passed before the pain subsided enough that she could smell the acrid smoke and feel the heat of the fire from the room. She heard shouts in the hallway, other apprentices stepping out of their rooms.

She opened her eyes. The hallway, and the room beyond the door, swam in her vision. She couldn't tell if it was because of the blow to her head or the heat of the fire.

Beyond the door, the walls were ablaze, an orange-yellow glow illuminating everything. The wood crackled and popped as it burned.

On the floor near the foot of the bed, Gerard lay to the left of Nina, his arm over her back, protectively. Neither of them were moving.

"Gerard," Angela cried out. "Nina!"

Her shout did not bring a reaction from either of them. A sudden fear that they were dead wrenched at her, quickened her heart.

She tried to slip into the vew, thinking about the platform she had mastered earlier in the day, thinking she could somehow use that to weave a barrier around them to protect them from the flames, but she couldn't get her eyes to focus. The swimming world she saw was not because of the heat.

She pushed herself up to her knees in an attempt to crawl forward. She would drag them out if she had to.

A hand on her shoulder held her in place.

"Angela, are you all right? We've got to get out of here."

She knew the voice, but could not place it right away.

"Angela?"

Then she had it. Shane. Of all the people she wouldn't want to help her...

"Angela!"

"Don't help me," she said, and pointed into the room. "Help them."

"But..."

She turned to look up at him. He was looking down at her, concern written across a face that still held on to the roundness of youth.

"Please help them." she said.

His eyes somehow coalesced, sharpening, despite the fact that the rest of him was still fuzzy. He turned away from her to face the room, held his hand out.

Angela turned to see what he was doing. She tried again to slip into the vew, but it just wouldn't come.

It didn't take but a moment, though, before she could see that Shane *was* helping. Shane had Weaved the platform underneath Gerard and Nina, and lifted them from the ground. He was pulling the two of them out of the room, out of the fire.

When she saw that they were nearly out of danger, she let her attention drift to the rest of her surroundings. A half dozen apprentices stood around her. One girl with short brown hair and a single overlarge hoop earring looked like she would kneel next to her. Angela couldn't remember her name.

More shouting echoed through the hallway. Then screams. Someone was hurt, frightened.

The girl looked up.

Angela did, too. The sudden movement intensified the pain in her head.

A loud explosion ripped at some other part of the manor. The whole building shook, jostling the girl over on top of Angela. The girl's knee slammed into the small of Angela's back.

More screams.

"What was that?" Angela asked, though she knew no one around her would know.

"I told you," Shane said. "We have to leave."

Angela looked up, saw that Gerard and Nina were out of the room.

"What do you mean?"

The girl that had fallen on her was scrambling up.

"I saw someone out in the courtyard. He killed Master Olimand without touching him. I swear he was Weaving something, but I couldn't see the threads."

Proscribed Weaves. She had seen them before, or actually not seen them, when Wallace had died.

The fear that gripped her served to numb the pain. She knew what they could do, and she had no defense against it. And if Master Olimand had fallen as easily as Shane described, the wizard using them had to be a powerful wizard. Perhaps even as strong as Monteous had been.

She pushed herself to her knees. The pain was still there, but she could get up. She had to. Even if there wasn't the threat of another monster like Orliss, the fire in the room was out of control. It would burn the manor to the ground.

Another explosion rocked the building. This one, it seemed, was closer to the stairwell. Screams echoed from that direction.

"What do we do?" a boy asked. His voice sounded frightened.

"Shane's right," Angela said while pushing herself to her feet. "We have to leave. We have no defense against proscribed Weaves."

A collective gasp came from the apprentices around her, and a frightened babble followed it.

"Quiet," she said, and put her hands to the back of her head. There was a lump, and wetness. She was bleeding. Her fingers touched the open gash, and the sting of it caused her to gasp.

The smoke from the fire seeped out into the hallway. She could smell it.

"How? The stairwell is blocked!" A girl, this time, her round eyes wide with fright. She had the olive skin and sharp nose that indicated she was from Aretria, on the southern coast.

Angela looked toward the stairwell, and found the girl was right. Orange flames licked the walls there, too. Probably from the last explosion.

She surveyed the others. Seven of them, not including Gerard and Nina, who both lay motionless on the floor. They were all younger than her, all lesser wizards. Even Shane, who tried to compete with her and succeeded sometimes at beating her, could not yet be called her better.

And none of them had been through anything like this before.

She thought about it, tried to figure out how they could get out, and then remembered the small roof that jutted out above a lower level entry way, right below her window.

"My room," she said. "We'll go out the window."

"But..." She seemed to hear it from all of them.

"Go!" she shouted, causing another burst of pain to rip through her skull.

But the apprentices went in a hurry.

"What about them?" Shane asked.

Gerard's back and shoulders were black and blistered, the hair on the back of his head singed nearly off, but he seemed to have protected Nina from the worst of it. Most important, they were both breathing. "They're not dead. Bring them."

"I don't know how much longer I can hold up the platform," he said.

"You just have to do it long enough to get them out of the building. You can do that."

Shane nodded. "Of course."

Gerard and Nina, their bodies on an invisible pallet, moved down the hallway toward her room. Shane followed, and Angela trailed behind him.

She coughed. The smoke was growing thick.

Another clap of thunder rocked the building. The masters were still fighting whoever had killed Master Olimand. They would not be able to help their apprentices.

A feeling of dread stole over her.

"Hurry," she said to Shane, and he picked up his pace.

She did too, despite the throbbing in her skull that occurred with every movement, every footstep. She needed a healer. Gerard and Nina needed one, too. There was a healer at the academy, but Angela feared the woman was dead. She feared all the Masters were dead, and that the wizard would be coming for them.

Shane maneuvered Angela's injured friends through her door with the help of the girl that had fallen on Angela. Angela couldn't remember the girl's name. She didn't know any of their names.

Then Angela herself was in the room.

The apprentices were already climbing through the window.

The smoke had grown thick in the hallway, causing Angela to cough.

She turned to the door to shut it, and looked out into the hallway to see if anyone had been left.

The hallway was empty, but a movement at the top of the stairs at the far end caught her eye.

A dark-robed figure, tall and thin, ascended them with deliberate, tired steps.

"Master Brin!" Angela called out.

A stray flareup of flame illuminated the hooded face, and Angela realized it was not Master Brin at all. It was someone she did not recognize, but who had an aura of darkness and age that she could almost feel. A smile crept onto that face, almost as if the man knew her.

The figure raised his staff. Frightened, Angela shut the door behind her and barred it.

"Out! Out!" she screamed at the apprentices that were left in the room, fear taking over.

Angela raced over and helped Shane get Nina and Gerard through the window and down to the ground. Sweat poured off Shane. He was spent.

Angela had expected the apprentices who had gone through the window to help them, but they all scattered.

Just above the ground, Shane let the platform go, and Gerard and Nina thumped down on the hard-packed earth. Angela cringed, but she could do nothing about it.

"Get down there," she said.

Shane climbed through the window, and onto the roof, then slipped over the edge to the ground where he fell in a heap. He got up, though, and reformed the Weave underneath Gerard and Nina.

Angela looked around her room one last time, thinking she might have time to grab something she would need, and she remembered the letter. She had left it on the floor in the hall.

Something slammed against the door, hard and solid. The bar on it buckled, but the door didn't fall open. It would with one more blow.

She had run out of time.

She climbed out on the roof, and then jumped from the roof to the ground. The collision made her eyes blur again with pain.

"To the trees," she said, fighting through it. "Run!"

That wizard, she was sure, wanted to kill them all.

CHAPTER 4

ROBERT WOKE EARLY, his head clear, but with an irrational gnawing fear in his gut. The red of the last evening's sunset still burned fresh in his mind.

His room was dark, but the sky outside his window had lost the black of the deep night. It couldn't be more than an hour before full dawn.

He Weaved a thread of energie into the wick of the lamp at his bedside and sat up.

Today, he would see Angela again for the first time in months. He thought that perhaps it wasn't really fear that had his stomach tied in knots, but nervousness and excitement at seeing her again.

She was all he had left, unless he counted Demetrius or the varied properties that Monteous had left him, and he didn't. Sure, he had means, now, a way to support himself. He would never be a beggar. He would never have a worry about where his next meal would come from. But that didn't mean much to him with everyone he'd ever loved dead, everyone but Angela.

And she was close. Three, four hours at most.

He swung his feet out from under the covers and placed them on the thin bedside rug that kept bare feet from the chill of the polished oak floors.

Demetrius wouldn't appreciate it, but it was time to get moving, time to be on the road.

Robert dragged his clothes on, picking out the best he had from his pack. He stuffed everything else back in, extinguished the lamp, and went to wake Demetrius.

Robert knocked on Demetrius's door, and was not surprised to find the man already up, packed, and ready to go. Demetrius had his pack slung over his shoulder.

"You're anxious to see her," Demetrius said.

"It's been a long time."

"They might not allow it, you know."

"So you've said before, but they'll let me see her. Master Brin will understand." *He has to.*

"Just remember why we're going in the first place," Demetrius said as they walked down the hallway together.

"I remember. But I can see her, too."

The innkeep was already up and bustling around the common room. Robert didn't want to waste the time on breakfast, but Demetrius refused to leave without food in his belly.

"I don't have any desire to ride for hours on an empty stomach," he said.

Robert hardly paid any attention to the eggs and cakes they were served, wolfing them down while thinking of Angela. He finished before Demetrius was even half done.

"You're going to get cramps," Demetrius said.

"Just hurry." Robert's foot was involuntarily twitching, eager to move on.

"She'll be there," Demetrius said.

"She hasn't sent me any letters. I've sent her a dozen."

"You know they probably didn't let her see them," Demetrius said between bites. "They want her to focus on her learning. There's a lot at stake."

Robert glanced over at the fire that burned in the hearth. The innkeep would let it go out before long, after the day grew hotter than the fire could possibly match. "I know. But I still don't see why. It would hardly take long to read. They can give her that time."

"Distractions, Robert."

Robert knew. Distractions had been the thing that kept him from completing his apprenticeship with Monteous. If he hadn't allowed himself to be distracted, if he had been able to focus, he'd be a full master right now. He would have stood at Monteous's side at the Conclave. He would have been able to see the threads of the proscribed weave that killed Wallace before Wallace had even learned to use a wand.

"I keep thinking," he said, "that if I had been a better student, if I had been able to focus, I would have been a master when Monteous was taken. Wallace wouldn't have had to die."

Demetrius set his fork down, the last bite of his eggs still on it. "Robert, if you had been a master, you would not have been there to help. Wallace may have lived, but Monteous would likely still be dead, and Orliss would have succeeded."

"Still..." He didn't finish the thought. Demetrius was right, no matter how little Robert liked it.

Demetrius stood. "I can see we should be on the road. It is you that needs the distraction."

Robert snorted at the irony, but got up and followed Demetrius to the stable.

THE SUN CAME up hot, and the ride was dusty, almost from the outset. The grasses to the side of the road were just starting to take on their summer shade of brown.

The landscape around them was mostly farmland that lay atop rolling hills. The farmers were out in the fields working their land. Here and there, trees sprung up from the hills like lonely sentinels.

Robert wished they could hurry. Every mile set more nerves alight within him. He wanted to push his horse to a gallop to get there, to convince Master Brin to let him see Angela.

But it wouldn't do for the horse to run in the heat that already had sweat dripping from his brow, and it wouldn't do to look anything but a wizard in control of himself when he met Master Brin.

So he kept to the pace that Demetrius set, even when they finally drew close to the academy.

The two of them topped a rise in the rippled landscape. In the distance, right near where the Academy was nestled between the hills and a sparse forest of elm and ash, a dark haze hung over the land like a cloak.

A slight breath of wind brought the stink of smoke to his nose.

It wasn't a haze.

"Something's burning," Robert said.

"Be calm, it's probably just the forest."

Robert looked at Demetrius, trying to gauge if the man really believed what he said. At the best of times, Demetrius was hard to read. Now, his face was inscrutable.

Robert loosened his staff from the bindings that held it tight to the horse. "You don't really believe that," he said in the hopes that it would trigger a reaction.

Demetrius reached out and put a hand on Robert's arm, an effort to keep him calm, Robert knew. It wouldn't work, though.

"If something happened, rushing in might only get you killed. There are four masters and thirty apprentices at that school. If they couldn't handle whatever happened, what makes you think you can handle it on your own?"

"But I might be able to help."

"Look, Robert, the smoke is just a cloud, now. It's been there for a while. Whatever happened already happened. You can't stop it. Rushing in might only get you killed."

But the agitation in Robert's bones and his fear for Angela ate at him, spurred him into action. He kicked his horse into a gallop and raced toward the academy, ignoring Demetrius's cries and pleas until they faded with distance.

As he rode, the muscles of his horse shifting powerfully underneath him, the smell of the smoke grew stronger, and a gritty layer began to coat his tongue. There was still ash in the air. Something still burned. He tried to tell himself that it was just the forest, but he knew otherwise. He couldn't believe it. The red sun had presaged his parents' deaths, and whether it was superstition or not, he could not keep himself from flashing back to those nights. The smoke had been thick, then, too.

When he reached the top of the last hill between him and the Academy, the smoke was so thick he could not see more than thirty feet in front of him. He had to slow the horse for fear of having it trip over something that it couldn't see.

He slipped into the vew, hoping to see the wards that the masters kept over the academy. They were either missing or obscured by the smoke.

Hoof beats came up from behind him, fast. Robert turned to see Demetrius join him, and Demetrius slowed to match Robert's pace. Demetrius coughed. His horse didn't sound well, either. Robert's own horse seemed nervous.

Robert reached out for energie, taking it from the smoke and the air around him, directed it through his staff, then created a barrier against the smoke, pushed it all back in a large circle that surrounded them. It didn't remove the smell, but he could breathe easier. He looked at Demetrius and found that he and his horse also seemed to be having less trouble.

"Thanks," said Demetrius.

"I should have thought of it sooner."

Robert urged his horse forward again, and together, they made their way to where the front gate of the Academy should be.

When they reached the gate, it seemed intact, but they could not see much beyond it. The smoke obscured everything. He still could not see the wards. They were definitely down, and it worried him. He gripped his reins tightly in one fist, his staff even tighter in the other.

"Master Brin!" Robert called out as they rode into the courtyard. "Angela! Gerard!"

No answer. Not even from someone else.

Then his horse suddenly shied away from a shape on the ground, startling Robert. He looked down to see what spooked his horse and found the lifeless body of Master Olimand, eyes open wide in death. Robert's breath caught in his throat, and for a moment, he couldn't breathe. It wasn't the sight of the dead body, for he had seen death before, but the crushing knowledge that his worries were true.

He took a moment and calmed himself, forced himself to breathe slower and easier.

It doesn't mean they're all dead. She could have escaped. She could have escaped.

"Demetrius," he said, and then pointed to the ground.

"Master Olimand."

Demetrius jumped down from his horse and went to the dead master's side. He checked over the expansive body for a few moments then looked up.

"There are no wounds. This was wizardry."

And then, as if by Work and Weave, a breeze kicked up and thinned the smoke enough that they could see the entirety of the Academy.

It was a ruin. The manor had burned to the ground but for the chimneys and a few walls that were made of stone. Those walls looked on the verge of toppling in. The laboratories had met a similar fate, though some of the walls had blown outward.

Bodies littered the courtyard. Apprentices, servants, and two more masters. Master Brecious, and Master Brin. A staff was jammed into the ground near Master Brin's body, a piece of parchment nailed to it.

Robert ignored the parchment and slid down from his horse. He ran over to the closest bodies and searched for the face he hoped would not be among them.

He checked face after face, their robes making them look similar until he came close. He even recognized a few of them, though he did not know their names. And after he checked them all, he had not found a sign of Angela, Gerard, or Nina.

"Where are they?" he asked aloud, not expecting an answer, afraid of any he might receive. If they had died in one of the buildings, he might never recognize them. He might never know.

But he had to check.

He ran to the manor house. Parts of it still burned within the rubble.

He scanned the ruins as best he could, but all he found was ash, stone, and charred wood. The bodies of his friends, if they were in there, were buried, and the rubble was still too hot to search.

He wanted to cry, tears threatened to come, but he wouldn't allow them. He did not want to believe that Angela had died as his parents had, trapped in a burning building until her flesh turned black, unable to escape the lumber and stone that would ultimately collapse on her. He wanted to believe that she had escaped.

"Robert," Demetrius said from behind him. "Look at this."

Robert turned. Demetrius was holding a parchment, the one that had been nailed to Master Brin's staff.

"What is it?"

"You need to come read this."

Robert went to Demetrius and took the parchment from him. He read.

Dearest Robert,

Every day in this place without you is almost more than I can bear. I've tried writing you, and Master Brin claims he sent the letters, but you haven't replied to any of them. I worry that you have forgotten me, but I don't want to believe it. I prefer to believe that they just aren't sending them to you.

"You can read that later," Demetrius interrupted. "Read the back."

Robert flipped it over.

There was a different message on the back, written in a different hand, written with a reddish brown ink. The message started out the same, but it was much shorter.

Dear Robert,

Know that the end of the Guild is nigh. It began tonight.
You have a chance to join me, to become one of the masters of a new world.
I look forward to our meeting.

Trajon Jarl

"What does this mean?" Robert asked, "and why was it addressed to me?"

"It's clear the writer is looking for you. He knows who you are. So far, the Guild has been successful at hiding you."

"But who is he? I don't recognize the name."

Demetrius reached out for the parchment, and Robert let him take it. Demetrius held it close to his eyes, looking for what, Robert did not know.

"This is meant to be an announcement, and a warning. And though I could be wrong, and this could be someone who has assumed the name, I don't think so."

"What do you mean?"

"You don't recognize the name because it was stricken from most of the official histories. Trajon Jarl was a founding member of the Guild, but he is also the reason the Guild proscribed the use of blood as a source of energie."

"But that would mean that he's over two-hundred years old!"

"At least. Which is why I think that it's possible someone is trying to scare us by assuming his name." Demetrius shook his head as he spoke.

"But you don't believe it."

"No. The name has been shrouded by time and intention. It's not a name that would inspire anyone, anymore. No one remembers it."

"But you do. How is that?"

Demetrius didn't answer for several moments, as if he was deciding how much to tell Robert. Eventually, he said, "It is given to the Senior Wizard to know these things. It is passed among them in case Trajon Jarl ever returns. Monteous, one night over a few cups of ale, told me of him."

"So why do you think he's looking for me?" Robert asked, returning to his original question.

Demetrius gave him a disbelieving look. "You should be able to figure that out for yourself, Robert."

Robert looked away from him, toward the pile of rubble. He did know. Everyone told him, even mysterious old wizards that he had never previously met. He could be the most powerful wizard in more than an age.

"What do we do now?" Robert asked.

"We have to tell the Guild."

"But..." Robert started to protest.

Demetrius seemed to read his mind.

"But, we will wait until the smoke clears so that we can see if anyone still lives . . . including Angela."

Robert sighed with relief that Demetrius wouldn't force him to choose between riding to alert the Guild and searching for Angela.

He held his hand out and Demetrius placed the parchment in it. Robert found a stone to sit on, a place to read Angela's letter while he waited.

CHAPTER 5

NGELA REACHED THE treeline, gasping for air, and stuck out an arm to catch one of the thin ash trees to steady herself. Each breath was a labor, her head was still spinning from the blow in the hallway, and every shadowed tree counted double or triple in her sight.

The other apprentices were ahead of her somewhere, scattered deep into the sparse forest. Even Shane, with his burden of supporting Gerard and Nina, had entered the forest before her.

She looked back, down the slight grade that she had just climbed, to where the Academy was, where it had been. Flames shot twenty, thirty feet above the buildings, lighting up the area in angry red and gold.

Other than the flame, nothing moved.

She expected to see, at the least, the shadow of the man that had destroyed the Academy and killed Master Olimand and the others. She expected he would follow her, follow the rest of them so he could complete his task.

But no one followed that she could see.

What now? Where do I go? Where are you, Robert?

A thousand more questions filled her mind, and she had answers for none of them.

She put her hand to the back of her head, and the pain ratcheted up. *Gerard and Nina need a healer, and I probably do, too. But where do we go?*

Dry brush crackled behind her, and she spun toward it, sending a wave of nausea through her, forcing her to clutch at the tree again.

"It's just me."

A flicker of light from the burning Academy lit up a face for a moment, giving it a somewhat haunted quality.

"Shane."

He had come back, dragging Gerard and Nina with him.

"Why are you still here?" he asked.

Angela turned back to the fire with a deliberate movement, trying to keep the nausea at bay.

"I'm watching."

"For what?"

"The man that did this, the wizard, he was in the hallway right before I shut the door. I saw him. I think he knew me."

"Do you know who he is?"

"I've never seen him before."

"Then how could he know you? You're just an apprentice."

Anger rose in her, and she didn't know why. But instead of forcing it down, she held onto it. It seemed to help fight the nausea.

"I was there, Shane," she said. "I was there when Orliss shattered the Challenge Orb. I was there when Robert killed Orliss. They know who I am. What if he's one of them?"

"One of who?"

Angela turned back to him, incredulous. "Do you really not know? The Guild split nearly in half, and you don't know why?"

"What are you talking about? The Guild hasn't split."

Angela stared into his eyes, looking for some sort of recognition, but only the fire of the Academy danced there.

She turned away from him.

That's why we're different. The other apprentices don't know.

Which made sense. The Guild would want to keep any sort of split secret. They wouldn't want their enemies to know they were weakened. They wouldn't want their apprentices to know that either.

But it didn't make sense why the wizards who split off would not trumpet the split, would not go out of their way to make sure everyone knew.

"Last winter, at the Conclave, Orliss destroyed the Challenge Orb."

"What's the Challenge Orb?"

"It's what the Guild used to settle disputes and choose the Senior Wizard. I'm not sure what else it's used for, but it basically kept all the wizards working toward the same goal."

"And with it gone?"

"With it gone, the Guild split. Those who thought the same as Orliss were driven out, or they left when they realized they would no longer be trusted."

"Why don't they just create a new Orb?"

"I don't know."

Smoke stung her eyes.

She closed her eyes tight, trying to clear the sting away.

When she opened them, she thought she saw a shadow move down near the Academy, a shadow that had previously been stationary.

"Look," she said, pointing to the shadow and unsure of her own vision. "Do you see any movement?"

She couldn't see it anymore.

Shane waited several moments before finally answering, "No, I don't see anything."

And then it moved again, and it looked like it moved toward them. It was crouched down a bit, following something, Angela thought.

"Wait," said Shane. "I see it. And it looks like it's coming toward us. Could it be one of the masters?"

Angela reflexively shook her head, and wished she hadn't as the pain bloomed again. "I don't think we should stick around to find out. I have a feeling they're all dead."

"You think it's..."

She nodded. "I do. We should go."

"Where?"

"We'll figure that out after we've lost him."

Angela turned away from the fire, and the shadow, and moved deeper into the forest, hoping she could find some other apprentices to help her, hoping she could find anyone at all that could help.

BY LATE AFTERNOON, Robert was sifting through the rubble, looking for clues to Angela's fate, hoping he wouldn't find her body among the burnt timbers.

Demetrius worked along with him, their hands and feet black from the charred wood, their noses and lungs rough and painful from the inhaled smoke that still drifted up from hotspots.

They found the other three masters among the dead in the courtyard. Within the rubble of the Manor, the first of the buildings they searched, they found several more bodies, mostly those of apprentices that had not made it out of the burning building. Not a one of them was Angela, Gerard, or Nina.

Then they searched the ruins of the laboratory, but they did not find any trace of his friends there, either.

When they were finished, Robert stood up amidst the ruins of the laboratory and heaved a sigh of relief. "They escaped," he said.

"Possibly. We could have missed them."

Robert shook his head, unwilling to believe that. "We would have found something of at least one of them."

"Perhaps you are right."

"I am right."

He stood up and glanced around the ruins again. Most of the building was destroyed, and everything was blackened. Many of the Works were melted beyond recognition or cracked and broken while falling from shelves that burned out from underneath them.

He toed through some of them, half lost in thought, half looking for something still useful.

He hoped he was right. He hoped they had escaped, but he worried that if they had escaped, they were right at that very moment being chased by that fiend, Trajon Jarl. There was no other word for him, either. Well, monster, perhaps.

"Why the Academy," Robert asked. "Why not..."

"Why not some other place? The Guild Hall, perhaps?"

"Right."

Demetrius bent down and picked up a scrying bowl. It had a chip in the lip, and was black with soot, like everything else, but seemed otherwise intact.

"The Guild Hall is not very assailable. Those portals won't open for you if you are not a Guild member. The actual location is not known..."

"Someone has to know it. If Trajon Jarl was a founding member of the Guild, wouldn't you think he might know it?"

"It's possible," Demetrius said while delicately brushing the soot from the bowl. "But the hall does not see much use except for during the Conclave. There's no one there."

"What about some other place?" Robert asked. "Why go after people who don't even belong to the Guild?"

"What other place is there, Robert? Where else could Trajon Jarl attack to make a statement? Other than the Guild Hall, the only other option is to go after each master individually. There were four masters here.

"And, you're forgetting one thing."

"What would that be?"

"That letter you stuffed in your pocket. Trajon Jarl wasn't just here to make a statement. My guess is that he was searching for you."

Demetrius finished wiping the bowl clean and held it up to look at it.

It was a beautiful Work. The glass was a translucent blue color, rimmed with gold, except for where it had lost the chip.

"If only I had something of Angela's to use in that bowl," he said.

Then he reached up and grabbed his hair and pulled in disbelief at his slow-wittedness.

The letter.

THE MORNING DAWNED bright and clear ahead of Angela and Shane. Behind her, the morning light was filtered by a haze of smoke that had infiltrated the trees. They were well out of that smoke, but she thought she could still smell its stink. She could not be sure it wasn't in her clothes.

The light brought a new hope to her, a feeling of success that gave a little life to legs that threatened to give out with exhaustion at every step.

The pain in her head had not subsided so much as it had changed from a sharp ache to a dull throb. Some time during the night, her vision had resolved itself so that not everything looked like it had a twin standing only a foot away.

This alone had allowed her to take a turn hauling Gerard and Nina through the forest on a platform.

Still, holding that Weave, moving it through the forest without dropping Gerard and Nina to the ground, was tiring. Shane looked just as tired as she felt. They could have used another hand, but she had yet to see any of the other scattered apprentices. She feared she wouldn't see any of them again.

Angela's stomach growled. It knew what time it was, it seemed, and if they were back at the Academy, she would be heading down for breakfast, with Gerard and Nina on her heals.

Yet, here, among these trees, they had nothing.

"Shane," she said, "let's take a break. Five minutes, maybe ten."

Shane agreed by slipping to the floor of the forest and leaning back against a tree.

"Don't fall asleep," Angela said.

Shane closed his eyes, anyway.

She let the platform drop to the ground and released the weave. She would have to make it again, but she needed the rest. She intended to keep moving, but keeping the weave intact while they weren't moving was wasted energie.

A glance at Gerard told her his condition hadn't changed, though he would need to get to a healer soon to keep it from worsening. Nina—she couldn't tell what was wrong with Nina at all. Maybe just a solid knock to the head like her own.

Not for the first time, she wished she could heal. It would have made things so much easier.

But she had been told time and again that wizard's don't heal. Monteous had never offered an explanation as to why, nor had any other master she had ever asked about it.

And the answer was always "wizards don't heal" —not "wizards can't heal" —almost like a wizard could heal if he wanted to but it just wasn't done.

It didn't matter right then. She couldn't heal, and neither could Shane.

Angela sat down next to Nina and Gerard. They were both still breathing, slow and even, as if they were just sleeping.

Angela put her fingers on Nina's head, felt around for bumps or cuts or anything that might explain why she hadn't awakened.

"What are you doing?" Shane asked. He had opened his eyes.

"I'm trying to figure out why she's not awake. She doesn't look hurt at all."

Angela felt around the back of Nina's head, and found nothing to explain why her friend would not wake.

Finally, she gave up.

"I don't understand," she said.

"Does it matter?"

"She was in that room, too," Angela said. "Yet there's not a burn on her. I would think she would have some burns, even if Gerard managed to shelter her from most of it."

Nina's robe was just as soot stained and charred in places as Gerard's, too. It just didn't make sense.

"So what are we going to do?" Shane asked, sounding defeated.

She looked at him, really looked at him. Dark rings shadowed his eyes, his shoulders hung slumped from fatigue. She realized he was pushing himself too hard. Despite his grasp of the Weaves, he was still younger than her and had less experience.

He was on the verge of draining himself, and if that happened, she would have three bodies to carry. She could not carry them all.

"I want you to skip your next turn carrying them," she said. "I'll take it."

"You can't do that. You just had your turn."

"And I'm older and stronger than you, and we both know it. You practically fell to the ground when we stopped, and I'm willing to bet that you're on the edge of draining yourself, and if that happens, you'll be one more body I have to carry."

"But you're hurt." It seemed a half-hearted protest.

"We didn't even start taking turns until well after midnight, and the pain has mostly subsided." The last bit was a lie, but it didn't matter.

"You're lying," he said. "I'm taking my turn."

But she knew he couldn't take his turn. He wouldn't make it.

Though, she *was* tired.

If only Robert was here. He could move this platform for hours.

But he wasn't, and she knew if the four of them were to survive, she would have to make it happen, and she could not do that if she could not keep her eyes open. She could not do that if they drained themselves.

"All right, I've changed my mind," she said. "Two hours. Take a nap. Get some rest. Then I'll take my turn." She hoped she was making the right decision. She hoped Gerard would not get worse while they rested, but it would not be any better for him if they drained themselves and couldn't move him at all.

Shane looked at her through his shadowed eyes, then let them shut.

"Where are we going after we wake up?" Shane asked without opening his eyes.

"We need to find a healer. I figure if we go north from here, we'll run into the road, and can head west to the next town."

"And then?"

"We'll figure that out later."

She sat up, weaved a ward around the four of them that she hoped would give them enough warning, then lay back against a tree.

She couldn't sleep, though. Every time she closed her eyes, she saw fire, and the shadow of the man that had set everything alight.

CHAPTER 6

ROBERT RAN TO the well at the center of the courtyard, carrying the scrying bowl with him. He pulled up a bucket of water, which he promptly dumped into the bowl.

The water was not as clean as he would have wished, ash and soot having fallen into it. He used his hand to remove the worst of it, the bigger bits, but the water itself retained a clouded quality. It would do, though.

"What are you doing?" Demetrius asked.

"I'm going to scrye for Angela."

Robert set the bowl on the ground, and then sat cross-legged in front of it.

"Don't you need something of hers?"

"I have something," Robert said. "I have the letter."

"I thought it had to be something she'd had for a long time."

Robert shook his head. "It doesn't only have to be that. It can be something that the person has great emotion toward, even if it only belonged to them for a short time. The best is something they had on their person for a long time that they loved or hated greatly. A wedding ring, or some other precious item. The letter, though, should be enough, especially since she won't be that far away."

He pulled the letter from his pocket and unfolded it.

He turned it over, from the side Angela wrote on to the side Trajon Jarl had defaced and back again, looking for the perfect bit that he could tear off. It would be best if it had some of her writing on it, but none of Trajon Jarl's. Having Trajon Jarl's writing would introduce a greater chance of finding him instead of Angela.

But Trajon had written large enough that nearly every bit of Angela's writing had something of Trajon Jarl's behind it.

Eventually, he decided to tear off the part where Angela had written *With all my love, Angela*. It had a few bits of Trajon's script on it, but it was the best he could do. He hoped the emotion he imagined her investing in it would be enough.

He slipped into the vew and drew threads of energie from the water in the bowl and the air around him, then Weaved those threads across the top of the water until they formed an intricate web.

When it was done, he held the paper above the bowl until he found the traces of energie Angela's possession and emotion had left on the paper, traces that were intermixed with the energie of two others.

"Maybe..." he said.

"Maybe what?" Demetrius asked.

Robert bit back the words that had run through his head. *Maybe this isn't a good idea.* But he had to know where Angela was.

He dropped the scrap.

It floated down through the web of energie he had drawn atop the scrying bowl to land in the water below.

The energie coalesced into an image of Angela sitting in a chair in a small room, eating. Nina lay on a bed, Gerard on another, apparently hurt. With them, a man and a woman. A healer.

"She's alive."

Tension flowed out of him. She was alive and safe, and he could find her. Gerard and Nina looked hurt, but they were with a healer. They would be fine.

"Where?"

"At a healer's, somewhere to the west of here." There was always a sense of direction and distance that filtered up from the threads of the Weave. "I don't think it's far."

Robert watched her in the image, the way her raven hair flowed over her shoulders, and the way her eyes flashed in the light. He ached to speak to her, but it was enough for now to know that she had survived, that he could find her before the night was through, as long as she remained at the healer's.

The bowl shook; the scene wavered and grew black.

"What the..."

"What's wrong, Robert?"

Robert blinked his eyes a couple times, but the scene the scrying bowl showed him remained black, like the light had gone out. But that couldn't be. Even if Angela was in the dark, he should still see her like it was day.

"I don't know. I saw her, and then it went black. Like..."

A voice entered his head through the Weaves he was holding. *Well, hello, Robert. It is good to hear from you. You must have received my message.*

It was almost as if the speaker was standing next to him. He looked up from the bowl for an instant, but only he and Demetrius were in the courtyard. He looked back to the bowl, and the water was still black, a deep dark pool that seemed to swallow everything.

"Your message?" Robert said aloud.

The one I wrote on the back of the letter your woman left behind.

"What are you talking about, Robert?" Demetrius asked. His voice was loud and present, but still seemed distant and not wholly there.

"Trajon Jarl." Robert's heart thumped in his chest. He was communicating with this man, this myth, and he didn't know how.

Have you considered my offer?

"This shouldn't be possible," he whispered to himself.

Oh, it is possible. They don't teach you the better arts these days.

"Robert?" Demetrius's voice had palpable concern in it.

"How?" Robert had to know.

About my offer. I'll only hold a place for you at my side for a short while, so you had better choose soon. I'll even let you bring along your lover. She'll be safe from what is to come, then.

"What's to come?" Robert felt like an idiot for even asking the question, but he just couldn't grasp how he was speaking to a man through the scrying bowl, speaking to a man that should be rightly dead a hundred years past.

The complete destruction of the Guild, the ruination of The Seven Kingdoms and the lands surrounding it. At the end, I will construct a new world order where men like you and I are in our proper place.

Robert held his breath. He wanted to let it out, but he couldn't. The idea that Trajon had just expressed meant changes to the world, to his world, on a scale he was having trouble grasping. The end of The Seven Kingdoms? What would come after? An empire ruled by Jarl?

I know you're wondering why I'm making you this offer, and the answer is simple. You are potentially the most powerful wizard of the past century. Your old master Monteous knew it, Orliss knew it, and now I know it. I want you at my side, Robert.

"You made this offer to Orliss."

The voice in his head chuckled. *No, I did not make this offer to Orliss. If he had succeeded, I might have, but you proved his better even without having completed your apprenticeship. No. Orliss was not who I wanted at my side. I want you.*

"But..."

Did Monteous ever tell you what really happened to your parents?

"They died in the uprising, their inn burned to the ground."

No, I'm afraid not.

A tremor ran through Robert's hand.

"What do you mean?"

The Guild is not all that you think it is, Robert, and I can offer you more than you could ever get from them. You didn't even know that a scrying bowl could be used to communicate, did you.

"Tell me about my parents! Are you saying they're alive?"

No. You're not ready. Think about it and contact me again. All it takes is a scrying bowl and a drop of blood.

Robert didn't even think as he stood up and kicked the bowl away from him. It flipped end over end, spilling its water across the parched courtyard dirt. The Weave snapped and sent a spike of pain through his head as the energie all collapsed into him.

He shut his eyes as tight as he could to try to ease the pain, but it helped only a little. This was the danger, the quick release of energies bound up in the Weave. But fortunately, it had only been a small amount of energie, enough to make the bowl work. Enough to find Angela, and to activate...

He didn't even want to think about it.

"Robert!" Demetrius shouted. "What's going on, what happened? Are you hurt?"

Demetrius's hand came to rest on Robert's shoulder, but Robert ignored it. The pain was too intense.

He opened his eyes enough to see the well, then walked over to it, away from Demetrius, and sat on the edge.

"Who were you talking to? How?"

"Please," Robert said. "Wait a minute."

"Are you all right?"

"I will be. Just wait."

He mulled the whole conversation over in his mind and tried to figure out what it meant, and what he was going to do about it. He kept coming back to two things that he wished he could stop thinking about: the blood on the letter and his parents' real fate.

When the pain ebbed, Robert opened his eyes and looked out past the destruction to the fields and the sparse forest beyond, not as much an act of looking for something as it was an act of not looking at Demetrius.

"So tell me what happened," Demetrius said, breaking the silence.

Robert's gaze snapped back to Demetrius. Demetrius had a look of concern on his face, an intensity to his eyes that was always there, but was not focused entirely on Robert.

Robert searched those eyes, and for the first time since he had come to know the man, since Demetrius had helped save his friends, Robert wondered if he could really trust him. He wondered if he could really trust anyone in the Guild.

"My parents. How did they die?"

Robert's chest felt tight.

"What happened, Robert? What does that have to do with this?"

"Please, tell me."

"They died in a fire during the uprising in Vanarth."

"Were you there?"

Demetrius shook his head a little. "No."

"So you only know what Monteous told you."

"Why are you asking about this?"

Robert stood up, the movement causing a bit of extra pain behind his forehead, but he ignored it.

"The ink Trajon Jarl wrote his message with was blood. It—it let me talk with him."

Demetrius's eyes opened wide and he took a half step back. "How?"

"I don't know. The blood made some sort of connection between us."

"What did he say then?"

"He said he intended to destroy the Guild, and The Seven Kingdoms." Robert was stalling, and he knew it. He didn't really want to believe that Monteous had lied to him, that Trajon Jarl wasn't lying, especially not after he had seen what Trajon Jarl was capable of.

"I understand that," Demetrius said. "What about your parents? Why are you asking about them."

"He told me that they didn't die like Monteous claimed."

"You can't believe him, Robert. I have never known Monteous to lie, but the stories of what Trajon Jarl did, what you've seen that he can do even here—you can't believe that he would be telling the truth about it. How would he even know?"

Demetrius was right. Trajon Jarl could not be trusted.

But he had planted a seed, and Robert felt that seed take root in the soil the Guild had tilled within him by not admitting him as a full master.

And Trajon Jarl wasn't even the first to suggest the Guild could not be trusted. There was that wizard by the river who had seemed to stop time itself. And Monteous had written that letter imploring him not to seek membership in the Guild.

"It doesn't matter how he would know. All that matters is that I don't know who to trust, anymore."

Demetrius stepped forward, put one hand on each of Robert's shoulders, and looked Robert straight in the eye.

"You can trust me," he said.

THE FIRST TIME she woke up, Nina opened her eyes just enough to see the tops of trees above her. They were moving through a deep blue sky. She tried to lift her head to look around, but she felt like she had been awake for three days. She had no strength in her and couldn't raise it even an inch.

She closed her eyes and went back to sleep.

The next time, she felt a bit better, but still exhausted. The sky had changed, though. She could see the sun. Clouds were absent.

She was able to move her head a bit, this time, though it was more of a roll to the side, giving in to its desire to fall that way, and she saw Gerard sleeping next to her. Something about the color of his skin bothered her, but she couldn't place her finger on it. She was too tired, and her mind refused to work.

The third time, the sky was tinged with orange. The sounds of a small town assaulted her ears—farmers, merchants, children running in the streets. Someone was taking her somewhere.

Gerard was still laying next to her. Her fatigue was less than it had been, though still weighed heavily. Gerard. His color was off, even for the late evening. And there was something else . . . burns on his arms and face.

A dream came to her, then. Looking out the window, a big fireball coming closer, closer. Gerard grabbing her. She reaching down inside her, trying to form a shield with everything she had.

Not a dream, then. Something real. But what had she done?

She knew what she had done, what she had been warned about doing, especially with her limited ability. She had overreached, took too much energie from herself, drained everything she had, or very nearly. It felt like everything. She had been warned doing so could kill her, or make it impossible to tap the energies ever again.

But she knew she hadn't thought, in that moment, about anything more than protecting herself, protecting Gerard.

And she had failed. The proof was in the burns, the blackened clothes and skin.

She noticed his breathing—shallow, but still pulling air in, still alive.

"At least you're not dead," she said. Her voice sounded weak to her ears.

"Nina?"

The movement stopped. Nina turned and found Angela standing next to her. Angela had a strained look on her face, mixed with fatigue. Her eyes were dull, her shoulders slumped, but there was a lift to the corners of her mouth.

"You're awake!"

"What happened? Is Gerard..."

Angela knelt until they were face to face. Nina tried to push herself up, but the effort sapped what little energy she had.

"Don't get up. Gerard will be fine. We're taking the two of you to a healer. We're almost there. I'm just glad you woke up. I couldn't figure out what was wrong with you."

Nina thought back to her dream, the dream that wasn't. "I think I tried to save us, to put up a barrier."

"You drained yourself."

"I didn't succeed, did I."

"You aren't hurt anywhere that I could find—not like Gerard."

"Who was that? Why did he kill Master Olimand?"

Angela blinked her eyes, and her lips thinned. She patted Nina on the arm and stood up. "Rest," she said. "I'll tell you after you've recovered."

"But..."

"No. Rest. We're not far from the healer."

The sky above her started moving again, and when she looked down, she saw the ground moving beneath her, as if she were floating just above it.

She lay back. Angela was right. She still needed rest.

She took one last look at Gerard before she let her eyes close again.

I won't fail you next time. Not ever.

CHAPTER 7

THE FIRES WERE mostly out. All that was left was a blackened ruin and a pile of bodies that Robert didn't want to look at anymore.

He heaved himself off the well wall and strode to his horse. Despite Demetrius's assertion that he could be trusted, Robert could not trust him. Demetrius had known what the Guild was doing in keeping Robert from becoming a full master, and he hadn't told Robert until he was forced to. And when Robert asked about how his parents had died, Demetrius fed him the story he had heard all his life. Then, Demetrius ignored the followup question Robert asked.

There was more to Demetrius, more to his loyalties, than Demetrius was willing to tell, and at the moment, Robert had no desire to listen to any more lies.

"Where are you going?" Demetrius asked.

"I'm going to find Angela."

"No, we have to warn the Guild. We must warn the king."

"We must?" He spun to face Demetrius. "What duty do I have to the Guild, Demetrius? What duty?"

"They need to know."

"If they've been watching me, they know already. If they wanted my help, they could have made me a master months ago. I did everything they asked, and then they left me to dangle like a broken thread."

Demetrius took a step toward him, and held his hands out in front in supplication.

"But Robert, the king needs to know, too. This wasn't just a blow to the Guild, it was an attack on The Seven Kingdoms."

"Then go tell him. I need to find Angela, make sure she's safe."

"She won't be safe if you go to her."

"She's already in danger, Demetrius. He knows who she is. He knows who I am. If we hurry, I know where she is. We can find her before Trajon Jarl gets to her."

Demetrius took another step forward.

"Please, Robert. Think. You need protection from Jarl. He will be coming for you, and the only people that can protect you are the guild."

"Protect me? Look around, Demetrius. Look what one man did to four of the most accomplished masters in the Guild! I only know of one wizard who might be able to protect me from Jarl. He told me to come find him; he told me that he would teach me what Monteous could not. And I think the wizard Monteous mentioned in that letter is the same wizard."

"He's dangerous, Robert," said Demetrius, a warning, and perhaps a little fear, in his voice. Not fear. Something else Robert couldn't place.

"Why are you trying so hard to keep me from doing what Monteous asked me to do? He's dangerous? Monteous all but told me in the letter that the Guild was dangerous."

"That letter was written before he died, before the Guild split. The wizards that are left..."

"Are untrustworthy. They made you follow me, they watch over me, and they don't even tell me they're doing it. No. Even if Monteous lied to me about my parents, I still trust him in this."

He turned and continued toward his horse.

Without looking over his shoulder, he said, "You can come with me and help, or you can run to the Guild and the king and tell them what happened, but you and I both know they're watching. They already know what happened here."

He patted the white stripe on his horse's forehead, then stuck his foot in the stirrup and mounted.

He looked at Demetrius for what he thought might be the last time. He didn't really think Demetrius would come with him. He wasn't even sure if he wanted Demetrius along, but he had to ask anyway.

"Are you coming?"

In answer, Demetrius strode to his horse, mounted it, and pulled up behind Robert.

"Lead on."

WHEN THEY FOUND the healer's house, Angela walked up to the door and knocked while Shane collapsed in the dirt at the side of the road. For the last two hours, Shane had barely been able to walk at her side. He was finished. He could not maintain the platform any more, let alone move it. The burden of carrying her friends had fallen solely to her.

She didn't mind. She would carry them as far as needed.

Fortunately, she did not need to carry them any farther, and with luck, Gerard would be up and able to help her figure out what to do within hours.

Angela wished she could sit down and rest like Shane, but she couldn't let her friends down. Whenever she felt herself flagging, all she had to do was look at them and think about how they were depending on her to keep herself going.

The town itself was not very large. About a half mile after they passed the inn, they found the post that marked the healer's residence. It was as tall as a man, and a carving of a pair of cupped hands adorned the top.

Angela's eyelids drooped while she waited, the darkening sky telling her exhausted body that it was time for rest. Just about the time her eyes shut completely, the door swung open.

The woman answering the door wasn't old, nor was she young anymore. Her hair, pulled back in a bun, was still a dark, rich brown free from streaks of gray, but she had lines on her face and near her eyes that suggested she'd seen at least twice Angela's years.

And the woman's eyes, brown and deep, had seen their share of tragedies. They evinced no surprise at finding the four of them at her door.

"Mommy, mommy, who is it?"

The tiny voice asking the question belonged to a young boy that popped out from between the woman's legs. He was only a little larger than his voice. He had the same color hair as she did, but his eyes were alive, bright, and full of expectation.

The woman grabbed the little boy by the wrist and pulled him up before he could run headlong into Angela.

"Go inside, Briton. Tell your Pa to stoke the fire."

"But who are they?" he asked.

"People who need my help. Now go," she said, spinning the child around and shooing him back inside the house.

Once the child was gone, running through the house yelling "Pa," at the top of his lungs, the woman turned back to Angela.

"I have never seen this many young wizard apprentices in one place, let alone at my door, exhausted and injured. It is a strange sight, I tell you. Where are your masters?"

Then she put a finger up to prevent Angela from answering.

"I am a fool. You are all from that wizard Academy down the road. I thought Maghda was there to take care of you."

Angela could barely bring herself to whisper the answer. "They're all dead."

This brought shock to the woman's eyes, and she took a step back. "Dead? What happened?"

She looked around the group again, letting her eyes fall to Gerard and Nina at the last.

"No," she said, "Don't answer. You can tell me after I've helped these two and you have rested a little." She stepped out of the doorway.

"Please, come in."

Shane went inside without saying a word, but Angela waited while the healer bent down and first put her hands on Gerard, then on Nina.

"He will need my help," she said under her breath. "She just needs rest."

Then she looked up. "Why are you still standing here? Get inside."

"I was going to help you bring them in," Angela said.

The woman chuckled. "Pa will help. Now get inside before you fall over and split open your skull and I have to fix that, too."

Angela took her advice and stepped through the door, only to find herself having to squeeze past one of the largest men she'd ever seen—easily a head and a half taller than Robert and muscled like a blacksmith. He smelled of iron and sweat.

She followed a short hallway that opened onto a large room where she found Shane sprawled out on a thick cushioned blue couch. A space next to Shane looked inviting, but before she moved to sit down, she turned and saw Pa carry Gerard into another room. The healer, with Nina in her arms, followed her husband into the room.

Angela went to the door they had disappeared through and looked inside. A pair of beds were in the room, along with a small stove and shelves lined with jars of herbs and devices that looked much like the Works that wizards used.

Pa had already laid Gerard on one of the beds and was intently stoking the fire in the stove. The healer was busy laying Nina down on the other.

When she stood up, she turned and saw Angela in the doorway.

"You're not going to take my advice, are you," the healer said.

Angela knew she should, but she didn't want to. She wanted to know that Gerard and Nina would be all right.

"No, I didn't think so." The healer continued when Angela did not respond. She motioned to a chair near the stove. "Well, come in and sit down at least. If you fall asleep, try not to snore."

Angela took the chair gratefully.

"Briton!" the healer called out.

The little boy appeared at the door as if he had been waiting for her to call for him.

"Yes, Ma?"

"Fetch water and bread for our guest. Make sure you give some to that other boy, too. They shouldn't be sleeping on empty stomachs."

Briton smiled and looked at Angela. "You're wizards, aren't you. I want to be a wizard, too," he said.

"Briton," said the healer, "Go!"

"Yes, Ma."

The boy left the room, but Angela knew he would be back. He wanted an answer. It was probably the most exciting thing to happen to him in a long time.

"Pa, make up a vegetable broth for this one," she said, pointing at Nina. "Put a bunch of honey in it, too. We'll need to wake her up and make her drink it, but it will get her moving around faster than anything else."

Then the woman moved to Gerard's side and began to examine him. She brushed her fingers lightly over Gerard's wounds, but he didn't stir. She clucked her tongue a couple times, then stood up and went to her wall of herbs. She sorted through them, picked out a pair of dissimilar bottles, and went to stand next to her husband, who was already stirring up the broth for Nina.

She removed a bowl from a shelf above the stove, then poured the entire contents of the bottles into the bowl. She added some water from a pitcher that sat nearby, stirred up the mixture, then set it onto the stove next to the broth.

"Excuse me..." Angela began, but realized she didn't know the healer's name. "I'm afraid I don't know your name."

The woman looked up. "You can call me Nendra," she said.

Angela nodded. "How does healing work?"

Nendra hissed and a spark flashed through her eyes, and then she calmed down, all in the space of a heartbeat. "I cannot tell you. It would be the end of me were I to be discovered giving our secrets to a wizard. You should know that."

Angela shook her head. "I have only ever been told that wizards can't heal. You make it sound like that is not true."

"I don't know if that is true or not, but we have rules against it, and I will not break them."

"I was only curious. When we were walking through the forest, I was wishing there was a way I could heal my friends. I didn't mean to..."

"It is no problem. I understand your curiosity. Now, if you will excuse me, I must tend to your friend."

Nendra reached for her bowl with a bare hand and pulled it from the stove. Steam escaped the top of the bowl, but the bowl itself appeared miraculously cool. A Work, not just a bowl.

Briton came back just then with a plate of bread and a cup of water. He set them on a small oak table that was next to her, and then opened his mouth as if to ask a question.

Nendra forestalled him. "Is the boy taken care of?" she asked.

"Yes, Ma."

"Good, then off to bed with you."

"But Ma, I want to talk with the wizards!"

"No, Briton. You must let them rest. They have had a hard day. Perhaps they will speak with you in the morning."

The boy turned his face to Angela, his eyes lighting up. "Will you?"

Angela nodded. "If we are here when you wake, I'll tell you a story or two."

"Oh, thank you!" He turned and bolted out the door.

Nendra sighed.

"He's no bother," Angela said as she picked up the bread. It was warm, had a dollop of butter spread on it, and smelled fresh baked—no more than a day or two old. She took a bite, and discovered it was as fresh as her nose had suggested.

"It's not that," Nendra said as she crossed the room to Gerard.

"What is it then?"

Nendra held the steaming cup to her nose and inhaled.

"It's you and your friends, showing up at my house, one of you injured, the rest of you exhausted and frightened. Do you think I want my son to enter that world?"

"It's not..." *like that,* she wanted to protest.

But it was like that, at least, it was like that now. Now that the Guild was broken. Now that the academy, Monteous's vision, had been destroyed in an evening.

"You don't think we know the Guild has had troubles. Maybe you don't know it, but we hear things, and your appearance on my doorstep only gives proof to those rumors."

I know it. I know what happened. She wanted to tell Nendra what had happened, she wanted to tell someone, but she had promised Master Brin—*he's dead*—that she wouldn't tell anyone about the events at the Conclave. She had broken that promise when she told Shane, but he was a fellow apprentice. He needed to know.

Nendra looked at her as if she could read Angela's thoughts. Angela looked away and took another bite of the bread.

When Angela looked back again, Nendra was sipping from the cup.

"Why are you drinking that?" Angela asked. She'd seen healers give their patients concoctions to drink before, and she'd seen healers drink themselves, but she'd never really been curious about it, not before.

Nendra paused for a moment in her sipping, as if she thought about answering, but then continued without saying a word.

Angela took the hint. She was not to ask questions, so she settled back in her chair, popped the last bit of bread into her mouth. She would watch and see if she could learn something.

Nendra finished her drink and set the cup aside, then bent over Gerard and started to work.

Angela slipped into the vew, hoping to see something that might help her understand how to heal, or at least how it was done.

Nendra's energies were organized much like a wizard. Gerard's were chaotic, especially around his wounds. He was hurting, maybe even dying, and Angela felt tension creep back in. But then whatever Nendra was doing began to work, and Gerard's energies began to coalesce into the more familiar patterns of someone who was not seriously injured.

But Angela could not see how Nendra was doing it. There weren't any threads between them. She wasn't putting her energie into him, or removing any from him, nor was she taking energie from the world around her.

Angela tried harder, thinking her fatigue was causing a lapse in her concentration, but it did not change a thing. If anything, it compounded her fatigue, and her eyelids began to droop.

She tried to keep them open, but after a few more minutes of watching, trying, she failed and closed her eyes.

She had one last thought, one last insight that threatened to break through her fatigue, but she couldn't coalesce the thought into a memory before she fell asleep.

CHAPTER 8

I N THE MIDDLE of the night, only a little past the turning of the day, Demetrius followed his young master into the tiny little town where Robert said they would find Angela.

Bird.

A silly name for a town, but then, he wouldn't know the name if he hadn't passed through it a thousand times, stopped at the inn almost as many, had more glasses of wine than he could count with the innkeep, Mason.

But they would not be stopping there this time, at least, not this night.

The trouble with wizards, Mason would say over their third or fourth glass of wine, *is that they think they know everything.*

Demetrius would usually nod his head, despite knowing that Monteous was different, had been different, at least until his contract had been handed, along with everything else, to the young wizard that rode ahead of him.

Not that he had let Robert know that little fact. He kept it from Robert as best he could. It gave him more freedom to protect the boy, and he had thought it might give him some help in guiding Robert along the path Monteous had wanted.

But things had not gone as Monteous planned, and Monteous's instructions in his letter to the boy were counter to the instructions he had given Demetrius. Monteous had always told him, *I may be your master, and I may be a member of the Guild, but my first duty is to The Seven Kingdoms, thus your first duty is to The Seven Kingdoms.*

Which Demetrius concluded would mean that he should steer Robert toward the same loyalties.

But he had not been very successful steering the young wizard, and Monteous's letter to the boy had not helped one bit.

If only he had known about the letter, about what it contained, before Robert had read it. If only Monteous had told him, given him any idea what he would ask the boy to do. If Monteous was not dead, Demetrius would have had strong words for him. Loyalty was important, more important than just about anything, but Monteous had gone too far in sending Robert to Thiobulus Soake.

And now, for the first time in a long time, Demetrius knew his loyalties were conflicted.

He had a duty to stay with Robert, but he had a duty to The Seven Kingdoms—and no desire at all to see Thiobulus again.

They came upon the darkened inn, closed up for the night like every other building in the tiny town. He wanted to go up to the door, bang on it, wake Mason up and drink with him until he forgot about everything. He could tell Mason what had happened, and Mason would make sure that the king knew about the disaster at the academy, but he couldn't leave Robert alone. Not while Jarl was out there watching him.

And if Jarl had not been able to find him before, Demetrius was under no illusion that Jarl could not find him now. Whatever Robert had done must have established some sort of connection between them. Demetrius would bet on it—even if one third of the masters that had been protecting Robert had died at the Academy.

If he had to admit it, sending Robert to Thiobulus really did make sense. Of any wizard that Demetrius knew, only Thiobulus could truly protect Robert, and possibly teach him enough to survive. It still didn't mean he had to like it.

As they passed the inn, the clop of their horses' hooves the only sound, Demetrius looked back.

No. He had to admit that he could easily inform the king. He could slip over to visit Mason early in the morning. He just pushed Robert so hard to take a different direction because he didn't want to see Thiobulus Soake at all; he didn't want to face the man who had made him what he was.

The inn receded. As he turned to face forward again, before he had turned even a little, his eyes caught a shadow in the distance. A shadow shaped too much like a man. A man watching them.

It could be someone from the town standing guard, or someone awake and about because they couldn't sleep, but Demetrius discounted that, especially with what had happened the previous night. Trajon Jarl could be anywhere, even here.

He cursed under his breath, making no sound. If it *was* Trajon Jarl, the man knew he had been discovered. Demetrius should not have paused to look, but recent events had him out of sorts and jumpy.

He forced himself to face forward, to pretend he had not seen the shadow. He would not tell Robert about it, just on the chance that the shadow did not realize it had been noticed.

But he could listen. He would hear movement. If they hadn't been riding horses, he could have heard the shadow breathe. One of the *gifts* of Thiobulus.

He would listen until they reached the healer's, and then he would see Robert inside. And when the wizard and his friends slept, he would slip outside and figure out just who was behind that shadow.

FINDING THE HEALER was easier than Robert had imagined. The town was tiny, even smaller than Ferrytown. One main road—the one passing through—and one crossroad. A couple dozen homes and shops at most, with the inn sitting on the corner of the two roads.

The healer's home was the second to last building before the far edge of town, the pole that marked it sticking straight up next to the road. From the front, the home did not seem at all very large, a lightly sloped roof, a window in front. No light from within.

Robert dismounted and gave the reins of his horse to Demetrius. By the light of the moon, it was difficult to read the man's face, but Robert did not imagine he was any happier now than he had been when they left the Academy.

But Robert didn't care. Angela was inside.

He walked up to the door and knocked lightly. In the silence that had descended after they stopped riding, his light knocks sounded like hammer blows.

Of course, they were probably all asleep. He would be if he wasn't so anxious to find Angela.

He knocked again, a little louder. It was thunder in his ears.

He looked behind him, toward Demetrius, and saw that the man wasn't looking him at all, but was looking back down the street from where they came. Curious. Of course, Demetrius was always looking behind him, but he seemed to be spending extra effort this time.

"Did you see something?" Robert asked, trying to keep his voice just above audible.

Demetrius shook his head, but did not turn away from whatever he was looking at.

Robert turned back to the door and was about to knock again when he heard footsteps from the other side.

The door opened, and a smallish woman stood behind it, her hair up in a bun, a lamp held at her side. The healer he had seen in the scrying bowl, before Jarl twisted it.

"Can I help you, young wizard?" she asked.

"I'm looking for some friends. They are . . . wait. How did you know I was a wizard?"

"The staff on your horse gives you away," she said.

"It's just a walking stick."

"Then why aren't you using it for walking? I can see the carving, young man, and I know what a wizard's staff looks like. Why are you here?"

"Like I said, I'm looking for some friends. A woman a little younger than me with long black hair named Angela, and another woman and a man, both a bit younger still."

"I haven't seen them," she said. "Is that why you woke me up?"

Robert stared at her for a moment. They had to be here. He had seen it, seen her.

"Please," he said. "I saw them here. I know you've seen them. I saw you with them."

In the lamplight, she did not look the least flustered.

"I do not know what you saw, or how you saw it, but you are wrong. I haven't seen anyone like you describe."

"Nendra," Demetrius called from behind him, "Let the boy in and send your husband to help me with these horses. I want to get out of the street."

Then the woman looked startled. Robert was startled, too. He hadn't realized that Demetrius would know the woman.

I shouldn't be surprised. He's probably met all the wizards and healers in The Seven Kingdoms.

"Demetrius? What are you doing here? I didn't recognize you with you turned away from me, and all."

Then she stepped out of the way, leaving an opening for Robert to enter.

"First door on your left, son," she said. "They're all asleep."

Robert stepped through into the dark hallway.

The door Nendra mentioned was not far down. He opened it and went in, shutting the door behind him.

A lamp burned low, casting just enough light to see where he was, but it hid many of the details. He could tell that there were shelves on the walls, but the contents were difficult to discern among the shadows.

Against the far wall, Nina and Gerard slept on separate beds. In the low light, Robert could not tell how badly they were hurt. Even if they were completely healed, Robert suspected it would be days before the two of them felt like normal. From Robert's own experience after a laboratory mishap in his early days as Monteous's apprentice, Robert knew healing took a lot out of the person being healed.

There was a small stove that still gave off some heat, and nearby, Angela slept in a wooden chair. Only the high arms of the chair kept her from falling out of it.

He sighed in relief that he had found her, that she was safe and unharmed. He almost felt giddy, his stomach and shoulders tingling with energy, that he would get to talk to her again, to hold her tight and protect her.

He went to her side and knelt, then put his hand up to the side of her head, hovering it there for a moment before letting it touch her. At his touch, she started to wake.

"Angela, it's Robert."

She came fully awake, alert in the instant.

"Robert!"

The excitement in her voice struck him in every nerve. He had missed that sound, the silk sound that came from her when she spoke.

"I'm here," he said.

She stood up—he stood up with her—flung her arms around him and pulled herself tight to him, hugged him like he'd imagined she would, like he had imagined hugging her when they could finally be together again.

"How did you find me?"

"I received your letter," he said. "I used it to scrye for you."

"Then you know..."

He nodded, put his head down to hers.

"About the academy? Yes, I saw it. I was coming to ask Master Brin a..." She looked up at him, her eyes glowing and wet in the low light. "He's dead."

"I know. I found his body. The other masters are dead, too."

"It was awful. One man, one man did it, killed them all, burned the place down. He took my..." A tremble ran through her. "How did you find my letter? He took it."

"Demetrius found it. The man who took it wrote a note for me on the back."

"For you?"

Robert reached up behind her and put his hand to the back of her neck. He pulled her head down to his chest before he answered.

"He knows who I am, Angela, he knows about what I did to Orliss, he knows about the Guild." He stopped there, not knowing if he should tell her the rest.

"Are we safe here?" Angela asked.

He kissed the top of her head. "For now."

"For now? What do you mean? What was the message?"

"I'll show you tomorrow."

"But..."

He heard a noise from behind him.

"Yes," said Nendra, "Tomorrow would be a better time. She still needs her rest. Come with me, I've got space for the two of you to sleep proper. We don't want you waking your friends."

Robert said a silent thanks to Nendra for interrupting. He wasn't ready to tell Angela what the note had said. He wasn't sure if he would ever be.

CHAPTER 9

A BALL OF fire, shooting toward him. Then, searing pain across his chest, shoulders, back, head. It went on forever, every moment unbearable. He couldn't even remember what had caused it.

Until it all changed, and the pain was gone. He didn't know how long it took, maybe an instant, maybe much longer, but eventually, he recognized that he hadn't felt the burning pain in a long time.

Gerard's eyes popped open. He lay on his side facing a room he did not recognize. Early morning light streamed in through a window above him.

Across from him sat a stove with a tea kettle resting on it. Next to the stove, a chair. Shelves lined the walls, much like Monteous's laboratory, but the items on them seemed different.

It wasn't Monteous's laboratory. He hadn't been there in six months. He'd been at the Academy, but the room wasn't any room at the Academy. He'd seen them all.

The Academy.

He wanted to sit up, but his body still held memories of pain. It didn't want to move at all.

"Don't get up. Just lay still," said a woman's husky voice from a corner of the room he hadn't examined.

He looked that direction and saw a woman, hair pulled up and out of her face. She wore a bright yellow blouse, or it would be if there were more light, and dark brown skirts that hung to the floor.

"Where am I?" His voice croaked.

"In my house, of course," she said. "You sound like you need some tea to soothe that throat."

His mind did not seem to be working correctly. She acted like he should know who she was.

"Who are you?"

"I'm a healer. My name is Nendra, if you need such."

The woman, the healer, pulled a bottle from her wall, and a cup. She unstoppered the bottle, poured some of the contents into the cup, then put the bottle away again. She took the tea kettle from the stove and poured hot water over the contents of the cup. She sniffed at it, then stepped over to Gerard's bedside.

"Sit up," she said.

He did so, slowly. His muscles ached, and there were places on his body that felt like they'd been rubbed raw. He only recognized them as the blanket that had been covering him fell away. His robe was missing. He quickly grabbed ahold of the blanket and pulled it across his midsection to keep from embarrassing himself.

"Where..." he stopped as his voice cracked.

Nendra held the cup to his lips. "Drink this," she said.

She tilted the cup, and he sipped at it. It wasn't all that hot after all. He took more and more. Honeyed tea with mint. The tea wet his tongue, slid down his throat and soothed as it passed.

"Your friends brought you here," Nendra said as he drank. "Do you remember what happened?"

He was still drinking. He reached up and took the cup from her so that she wouldn't take it away. He tried to think back, but he couldn't remember anything more than something about fire, fire and pain. He said as much between sips.

"Not surprising. Your body took quite a shock."

"What *did* happen?"

"I don't know. Your friends can tell you when you see them. They brought you here. Most of your upper body was covered in burns."

Gerard reached up and touched himself where it felt raw. His touch stung a bit, but the skin was smooth.

The sting of his touch unlocked a memory, a ball of fire flying toward him from outside his window. Nina stood with him. He ducked, pulled her down to the floor. The fireball broke through, bathed the room in red-orange light and heat, so much heat.

He looked around the room and couldn't find her. There was another bed in the room, but it was empty.

"Nina... where is she?" he asked, setting the cup down.

"She stepped out a few minutes ago," Nendra said. "She seems to care a lot about you."

Gerard bowed his head and stared at his knees, which had become uncovered as he looked for Nina.

I care for her, too.

And he had protected her.

"You know," Nendra said, "I don't know what she did, but she saved your life."

Gerard looked up. The healer stood in front of him, looking down at him as if she was scolding a child.

"Why do you say that?" he asked.

"She came here asleep and utterly spent, drained. She's a nice girl, and once she had some food in her, she told me all about you."

Nendra took the cup from him.

"What did she say?"

"She didn't have to say very much. It's obvious when a girl is in love, when she does not think of herself, but only of the man she's given her affection to. When she said she was in your room to try to get you to take her home with you, it became clear to me."

"I don't understand."

Nendra set the cup down on a side table and turned to face him. "That girl is utterly besotted with you, and she risked her life to save yours. I don't know why you're trying to leave her behind, but I have my suspicions, and I think if you keep on the path you are on, you are making a mistake. She's a treasure."

How much did she tell you?

He kept his mouth shut, figuring he could only make the conversation worse.

Behind Nendra, the door opened, and Nina stepped into the room.

She stopped just inside the door, peeked around Nendra, then rushed over and threw her arms around him, knocking him backward and freeing the blanket from his waist so that it slipped to the floor. She pulled him tight to her.

"You're awake," she said into his ear.

She pulled her head back so that he could see into her eyes.

"I thought we were both dead," she said.

She put her lips to his, warm and soft and wet, and kissed him.

After a minute, she pulled away, and then looked down. A smile crossed her face.

He looked down and discovered she could see everything. He covered what he could with his hands.

Nendra held out the blanket to him and he took it and pushed it in between him and Nina.

"He still needs to rest, young woman," Nendra said.

She pretended to pout, but she climbed off him all the same.

He pushed himself back on the bed and spread the blanket out a little better.

"What happened?" he asked.

"I'm not sure. I did something, Angela tells me, that saved both of us from the worst of the fire, but after that, I don't remember a thing. She says I drained myself."

"How did we get here?"

"Angela brought us," she said.

He had more questions than he could ask at one time, so he started with the obvious. "How did the masters let us out of the Academy? Is one of them here?"

Nina shook her head. "Angela says the Academy is gone, burned to the ground. Robert confirmed it."

"Robert? He's here?"

Nina nodded. "He arrived with Demetrius late last night while we slept."

Gerard stopped asking questions. There were too many things to sift through. Too many things had happened. It was like last winter all over again. Someone was ripping apart everything he knew, between the Academy, Nina, his uncle.

He'd completely forgotten about his uncle, his brother, and his duty to return home.

"Have you heard from my uncle?"

Nina shook her head. "You could ask Robert and Demetrius. They might have seen him."

Gerard started to push himself up from the bed, but Nendra's hand jumped at him like a snake and pushed him back.

"You stay there," she said. "I won't have you opening up those wounds just yet."

"Aren't they healed?" he asked.

"Not yet. You can move around tomorrow."

Great. Another day he would have to weather Nina and her insistence that she was going to come with him. And now, with the Academy gone, she wouldn't even have to get permission to leave.

He shunted aside the questions he had about his duty to the Guild. He'd already left it. Just because he was still there when the Academy was destroyed didn't mean he owed them anything.

No. He would spend another day trying to convince Nina not to come, and then he would go home.

DEMETRIUS STOOD IN the same place he'd been standing since he returned from investigating the shadow man—just outside the healer's home, off to the left of the building, among the morning shadows. It was still early, the sun just cresting the horizon to spread its warmth around. The day promised to be hot.

A pair of homes, each constructed of wood and stone with the same lightly sloped roofs as Nendra's place, faced him from across the road. One was well kept. The other looked like it had been vacant for some time—a shutter hung loose from the lone window, and the brush had crept into its yard, hiding all traces of the walkway that should have been there.

Down the road, where he knew the inn lay, he could see some activity, but no one had yet passed the healer's home. The silence wouldn't last. Merchants and farmers would be on the road soon, making it hard for him to distinguish who might be watching them like the shadow from the previous night.

The shadow still bothered him. Something about it didn't feel right. He'd spent most of the night looking for a sign of the shadow and found nothing. Whoever had been watching them was gone by the time Demetrius returned. He found footprints in the dirt, but they could have been from anyone. The shadow could have been anyone, a patron of the inn out for a breath of the night air.

He didn't think so.

Which was why, when Mason opened the doors of the inn, Demetrius left his place at the side of Nendra's home and went to see his old friend.

Demetrius pushed the door to the inn aside and entered Mason's demesne. It didn't take his eyes long at all to adjust. Wide windows let the sun stream through to light the main room.

The tables were sparsely populated. An older man with a beak for a nose sat talking with a younger man that sported the same facial feature. A largish man with a beard that extended below his breast sat alone spooning oatmeal into his mouth, somehow keeping his beard free of any drips.

And then, seated behind the bar to the left of the entrance, was a mountain of a man, clean shaven with sharp green eyes. Rolls of fat extended beyond the suspenders that held up his pants. His round face seemed perpetually on the verge of a smile.

And he was already waving Demetrius to him.

"Demetrius," he said, and then did smile for true. "I didn't expect to see you here, but then you always show up at the oddest times."

Demetrius could not keep from smiling, himself. He went to the bar.

"The whims of wizards," he said.

Mason's smile fell. "I heard about Monteous. You still working for those bastards?"

Demetrius spread his hands wide and shrugged. Mason would never understand. He blamed them for nearly everything wrong with The Seven Kingdoms. People starving? Blame the wizards for not helping with the harvest. Locusts? Blame the wizards. A summer that burns hot or a winter that just doesn't know when to end? Must be the fault of wizards.

"I don't have much choice," he replied.

"I thought Monteous was dead. Wouldn't that terminate your contract with him?"

Demetrius shook his head.

"Never trust a contract written by a wizard," Mason said. "So what is it that you're doing here, then?"

"In Bird? You know I can't tell you that," Demetrius said.

Mason's laugh boomed around the room. "No, what are you doing coming to my inn for breakfast?"

Demetrius glanced around the room behind him, but nothing had changed. The few patrons were still involved in their own conversations.

"I'm not here for breakfast. I'm looking for someone."

"Got a name?"

"No name. I saw him standing outside your inn last night as I came into town."

"You came into town last night and didn't stop in?"

"Not my choice. Did you see anyone that seemed out of place? Did a man check in here yesterday, alone? Perhaps he might have reminded you of a wizard?"

"A man somewhat like you describe asked for a room yesterday, but he was no wizard. Seemed like one of those mountain men from Risuk. Didn't talk much. Kept to himself."

It didn't sound like the man he sought. The men of Risuk did not become shadows. They were more apt to charge at you while bellowing at the top of their lungs.

"Is he still here?"

"I haven't seen him leave."

Demetrius smiled. "Then get me a table and breakfast. I need to see if you've improved your cooking."

Mason laughed. "With a request like that, you're more likely to discover just how much my poisoning skills have improved."

Mason stepped out from behind the bar and led Demetrius to a table that would give him a good view of the room. It also gave him a view of the stairs and the hallway that lead to the guest rooms. Unless the fellow jumped out a window, Demetrius would see him before he could leave the building.

"You try to poison me every time I eat here." Demetrius said. "I should hope they've improved by now. They couldn't get any worse."

Mason's booming laugh echoed throughout the room again, and the rolls of fat jiggled with it. "Eggs and bread good enough for you?"

"It'll work."

"You just sit there, and I'll be right back."

Mason lumbered off toward the kitchen, and Demetrius allowed his gaze to wander toward the stairs.

Mason returned far sooner than Demetrius anticipated. He carried, in one hand, a pair of plates, steaming eggs and a slice of bread on each. He had topped the eggs with cheese. The other hand held two cups of tea, the smell of mint escaping them.

"That didn't take long."

Mason's eyes lit up. "I've got help, now. Anna, she's a much better cook than I."

"Anna?" Demetrius asked. "I've never known you to have kitchen help."

Mason set the food on the table, then sat down across from Demetrius. Mason's bulk blocked Demetrius's view of the door, but he could still see the stairs, and anyone who might descend them.

"She came to work for me about nine months ago."

There was something about the way Mason didn't quite look him straight in the eye as he spoke about her that prompted a question.

"Mason, you didn't." Demetrius said.

"Didn't?"

"You did. She doesn't just work for you."

Mason's smile grew wider than Demetrius had thought possible. "We married last fall. I would have sent you a letter, had I any idea where to send it."

Demetrius took Mason's hand across the table and clasped it. "Congratulations. It's about time you got help with this place. When do I get to meet her?"

"What?" The grin disappeared from his face. "I can't let her meet you. I told her about you."

Demetrius chuckled, and clapped his friend's wrist before withdrawing. "She must share your opinion of my employers."

"She's worse."

The clump-clump sound of boots echoed down the stairwell, and Demetrius turned to look.

The man from Risuk that Mason had described appeared bit by bit with each step. His boots were not Risuk make, but the rest of his clothing was, and well made, too. Black goat-leather riding pants trimmed in fur, a thin—for Risuk—shirt, and a metal circlet holding his hair back. He had a blue ram-wool jacket slung over his right shoulder and a pack dangling from his left hand. The man's face was weathered, having seen years on the road, his dark brows thick as his long hair, and now tinged with gray.

Demetrius forgot about the eggs sitting in front of him, and stood up. "Bryce?" he said, quietly he thought.

The man looked over quick, like he'd been caught for a thief, then squinted before opening his eyes in surprise. "Demetrius?"

"You know him?" Mason asked.

Demetrius answered without looking away from Bryce Maracane. "He's the uncle of one of Monteous's apprentices. I wonder what he's doing here."

Demetrius left Mason behind and went to clasp hands with a man he hadn't seen since he and Monteous had traveled to collect Gerard. He didn't think the man was the shadow from the previous night, but even so, he couldn't fathom a reason for the man to be in Bird, and he wanted to know why Bryce looked so startled when Demetrius said his name.

But when they clasped hands, he voiced none of those thoughts.

"It is good to see you Bryce," he said. He would discover the rest later.

ANGELA WOKE FROM a jumbled mess of dreams to find that Robert was not still next to her, sleeping on the floor of Nendra's sitting room. For a panicked moment, she thought even he had been one of her dreams.

And then she heard his voice as he spoke to someone in the next room, and she relaxed. It wasn't a dream after all. He really was there with her.

She pushed herself up and tiptoed over Shane, who had rolled off the couch and continued to sleep on the floor, and entered the other room. The first three people she saw sitting around the table were Robert, Demetrius, and Nendra's husband, though she could not remember what his name was to save her life.

The fourth person seated at the table surprised her. She'd only seen him from a distance, before, but she knew Gerard's uncle.

"What's he doing here?"

The four of them looked up.

"I found him at the inn, this morning," Demetrius said. "You know him?"

"I know he's Gerard's uncle and he's trying to make Gerard give up becoming a wizard." She couldn't quite figure out why she was so upset that he was there.

She looked at him directly. She couldn't find even a hint of soot on his clothing. "I thought you died with everybody else."

He stood up. He was tall. Not quite as tall as Robert, but with the strength in his shoulders visible through his shirt, he was imposing. He smiled and stepped around the table.

"I escaped through a window just before the building went up in flames. A dreadful shame what happened," he said.

She took a step back as he approached.

"Why didn't you come for Gerard?"

He extended his hand. "Bryce Maracane," he said. "I haven't had the pleasure of meeting you."

She refused to take the hand. Something about him didn't feel right, and she didn't think it was just her anger at his attempt to separate Gerard from Nina.

"Why didn't you come for Gerard?"

He let his hand fall. "I thought him dead. I was surprised and glad, actually, when Demetrius told me he still lived."

"You're going to make him go back," she said.

"It's his duty."

"After what happened, you think it's more important that he run home?"

A hint of steel crossed the man's eyes. "Even more so. It's folly for him to stay when four wizards can't protect the apprentices in their charge."

Robert got up from his chair, distracting both her and Gerard's uncle. He came to her, took her hand, and pulled her out of the room. She went with him, but did not take her eyes from Bryce Maracane until Robert dragged her around a corner so that she could no longer see through the doorway.

"What?" she asked.

"Why are you so angry with him?" Robert asked, his voice low.

"If Gerard goes with him, he'll have to marry some girl he doesn't know, and Nina..."

Robert laughed. "Is that all this is about?"

It only made her more angry. "All this is about? Robert, he was going to propose to Nina until that man showed up. He made a ring. He *gave* it to her."

"All right, I agree that you have a point, but that's a bit unimportant right now."

"Unimportant?" She knew he was right. She knew she should be concerned about what happened at the Academy, but she didn't want to think about it. The images of the fire and the wizard in the hallway still stained her eyelids whenever she closed them. She had thought nothing could be worse than what they had gone through to save Monteous. She had thought it was all over then.

"I didn't mean unimportant..."

She put a finger to his lips. "No, I know what you mean, and you're right. I just don't want to think about it. I can still smell the smoke."

He pulled her to him and hugged her, kissed the top of her head.

"I'm glad you're alive," he said. "I don't know what I'd do if..."

She waited for him to finish his thought. When it became clear he wouldn't finish, she said, "If what?"

He remained silent.

She pulled back from his embrace and looked into his eyes. They seemed at once full of love for her, but also haunted. He wasn't looking at her, but at some vision in his own head.

"If what?"

He still did not answer, but he did focus his eyes to look at her.

"Robert, what's going on?"

His features set, apparently decided on something.

"We must leave," he said.

Something about his tone frightened her. "Why?"

"I think the wizard that destroyed the Academy will come after me."

"After you? Why? You weren't even there."

"He knew I would be." He ran his fingers through his hair. "He wrote on your letter. He knew I would find it."

"You were supposed to tell me his message."

Robert took a deep breath. She almost did, too, but found her throat constricted in anticipation.

"He wants me to join him."

It felt like a knife in her heart. She could only imagine what it felt like to him. The wizard had come to the Academy looking for Robert, or he knew that its destruction would draw him there. And if Robert was right, if the wizard knew everything about Robert, then he knew about her. If she hadn't been there, everyone that was dead would still be alive.

Her knees gave out on her. She would have fallen to the floor, but Robert reached out and caught her.

"Are you all right?" he asked.

"If I hadn't been there..."

"No," he whispered. "No. He would have destroyed the Academy all the same. And it wasn't you he wanted. He was after me."

His words weren't very comforting. While he might be right, probably *was* right, about the wizard's intentions to destroy the Academy, she couldn't keep her own involvement out of her head. But she forced those thoughts into the corner of her mind where she kept all her despair. She had to deal with the problem that was in front of her, focus on the thread she could control.

She got her feet back under her, and stood up, but she didn't pull herself away from Robert. His arms felt too protective and safe for her to want to leave them.

"What do we do, then?" she asked.

"Monteous wanted me to find Thiobulus Soake."

"Thiobulus who?"

"Soake. Monteous left me a letter that warned me against trusting the Guild. In it, he said I should find Thiobulus and learn what I can from him. Remember just after the fight when we crossed into Ferrytown, and there was that confusion about the wizard that was there, and then wasn't?"

Angela nodded.

"I think that was Thiobulus Soake."

Angela's eyes went wide. "Where is he?"

"I don't know. I went to the Academy to ask Master Brin, but..."

Shane stepped out from behind a corner, rubbing his eyes, still wearing his soot stained apprentice robe. "My master might know where to find him," he said.

Robert spun around, leaving Angela to stand alone.

"Who are you?" Robert asked. He sounded wary.

"I'm Shane. I was with her at the Academy," Shane said, his finger pointing at Angela.

"Of course," Robert said. "I'm sorry, I should have realized from your robe. Who was your master?"

"Master Wendell."

Wendell. The name stirred a memory in her mind. An old, stooped, balding wizard she and Robert had met at the Conclave before Orliss destroyed the orb. She hadn't liked him at all, but the reason why confounded her.

Robert's shoulders slumped. "Master Wendell. He won't be any help. He hasn't liked me from the first time he saw me."

Angela remembered. Master Wendell had thought Robert stole the staff he used to defeat Orliss. He had not believed that an apprentice could beat a master.

And then Angela remembered something else, something Shane said. She stepped up beside Robert.

"You told me that your master would never allow Robert to join the Guild. What makes you think he would help him?"

Shane's eyes flicked up to look past her. She and Robert both turned around to find Demetrius in the hallway behind them.

"He'll help because I'll be there with you," Demetrius said. "He is one of the wizards helping to protect you, Robert, and going to him is a good idea. It's on the way to Risuk, which is where we'll need to go if he can't help."

"Why would we need to go to Risuk?" Robert asked.

Demetrius went to Robert and put his hands on Robert's shoulders. "Because, Robert, Risuk is the last place I saw Thiobulus Soake."

CHAPTER 10

ROBERT WASN'T SURE what to think about Demetrius's announcement. He had thought Demetrius would continue to argue for telling the Guild what happened, and for telling the king as well, but instead Demetrius was suggesting that they go to Risuk to pick up Thiobulus's trail.

By way of Wendell, who Monteous had all but accused of having ulterior motives.

It would solve the problem of telling the Guild. Demetrius had also pointed out that they could leave Shane with him. Robert hadn't even thought about it, but Demetrius was right. Shane was too young to be left on his own.

Even as the impromptu meeting in the hallway broke apart, Robert pondered Demetrius's motives. Why hadn't Demetrius told him before that he might know where to find Thiobulus? Why had he let him go to Master Brin? Was he hiding something?

Robert wanted to ask him, but decided that answers to his questions would have to wait. The obvious answer was that Demetrius thought Master Brin might have been able to pinpoint Thiobulus's exact whereabouts, but that didn't feel right. No. Robert suspected Demetrius was hiding something. Demetrius had seen Thiobulus, perhaps even talked to him. Demetrius knew something about the old wizard that he didn't want to tell Robert. But he would have to wait to find out what it was. He was sure Demetrius wouldn't discuss it with the others around.

The rest of the morning passed slowly for Robert. He went to visit Gerard, who was awake, but still stuck in bed. Nendra refused to let him leave it until his wounds were fully healed—another day at least. Nina sat across the room from him, and tension filled the air between them for no reason that Robert could discern. After a while, Robert had to escape. He had no desire to get stuck in the middle of a fight between them.

Every time he tried to get Demetrius alone, Demetrius was busy with either Nendra or Gerard's uncle, or just not anywhere to be found at all. Robert suspected Demetrius knew what he would ask and was making it as difficult as possible.

And Angela had gone back to sleep. She was exhausted from her ordeal and still hadn't recovered. Even that Shane kid, who seemed to have some sort of obsession with Angela, slept. He hadn't left her side while she remained awake. The exasperated looks on Angela's face when she thought Shane wasn't looking did make Robert smile, however.

Eventually, the inaction proved too much for Robert to bear. His mind kept alternating between dwelling on what Demetrius wasn't telling him and wondering when Trajon Jarl would contact him again.

To try to quell his worries, he took his staff out behind Nendra's home and went to find a place to practice, to focus on something other than the multitude of problems that beset him, at least for a little while.

Behind Nendra's home, horses grazed in a large, fenced in pasture. Robert's horse caught sight of him and came over to the fence. Robert put out his hand for her to nuzzle.

Robert patted her, scratched her neck. "Go eat," he said. "We'll have a long road ahead, I think."

Then he left her and walked beyond the pasture, over a small rise, and into a hidden, bowl-like depression. A pond rested at the bottom of the depression, mostly depleted of water by the dry weather, its surface marred only by a few ripples. Desiccated cat-tails lined the edge of the pond where the water had receded. Cut stones of various sizes lined the far side of the pond, like someone had built a wall which had subsequently been knocked over and kicked apart. A single tree with a smallish canopy of leaves overlooked the pond, providing the only shade from the sun that rode high in the sky.

It would work for what he needed.

He skirted the pond and put himself within the scant shade of the tree. *I'll start with the stones.*

Robert slipped into the vew. The energie of the place sprang into his sight. The water of the pond, the few frogs and other organisms living within its confines became a dance of intermingled energie, all of it subject to his will. The stones had their own energie, harder to work with, not quite as flexible, but for certain uses, far more powerful.

He buried the tip of his staff in the ground and reached out to the energie that ran through it.

He pulled on that energie, formed it into threads, and weaved those threads around the largest of the stones.

He caused the stone to rise into the air, six feet above its original resting place.

He spun out another thread to another stone, the next largest, and made it join its sibling.

Again and again, he raised stones from the ground until he had eighteen of them in the air. Maintaining his control over them was easier than it had been only months ago, but it still required that he work to keep his focus.

He wasn't practicing the Weave. He practiced his control over himself.

The stones fell to the ground, the threads severed like someone had sliced through them with a knife.

Robert tried to spin around to look for the wizard that had somehow destroyed his Weave, but he found himself bound in place, unable to move. He reached through his staff and into the earth for more energie to weave against his attacker, but he couldn't grasp it.

"I'm impressed."

Robert knew the voice. Trajon Jarl.

"Not many wizards can manage that many threads at one time. You've gained quite a bit of control since last winter."

Robert still could not see him. Trajon had to be behind him.

"Where are you? Show yourself." Robert said. At least he could speak.

"Oh, no. I think not. It is enough for you to know that I am nearby. Have you put any thought into my offer?"

Robert struggled against his invisible bonds, but still couldn't move. He couldn't even nod. "Yes," he said.

"And have you decided?"

Robert thought about telling him no, but decided against it. If Trajon was close enough, if he angered Trajon, the wizard could destroy every one of his friends and Robert could do nothing to stop it.

"No, I haven't," he said, even though he realized that he had decided if there was any way he could avoid joining the wizard, he would.

"Ah, that is good. I wouldn't want it to be too easy a decision for you. Easy decisions are easy to change."

Robert chose not to respond.

"I suppose you want some proof that I am acting in good faith. Well, here it is. You have three days to make your decision. In those three days, I think you should watch your friend Demetrius closely. He is keeping secrets from you."

"I know that," Robert said.

"Have you wondered what he is hiding? I, you see, am hiding nothing."

"You're hiding yourself."

Trajon laughed, and it chilled Robert. "I hide myself because not doing so would be folly. I have not hidden my intentions."

"How did you break my threads so easily?" Robert asked.

"Ah, that I can not answer, not until you agree to my proposition. But you can be sure that I will teach you that, and more, once you agree. Decide quickly, Robert. You have three days."

The bonds that trapped him fell away, and Robert could move again. He reached out through his staff, and energie flooded into him.

He spun around, but could see no one.

He raced out of the depression and looked in every direction. Near the back of Nendra's home, he saw Gerard's uncle standing with the horses. In every other direction, the land bore nothing but browning grasses and a few lone trees.

He broke into a sprint, and ran back to the house. He passed Gerard's uncle and dashed through the door and into the living room where Angela and two of the other apprentices still slept.

The noise of his arrival woke Angela.

"What's wrong?" she asked while wiping at her eyes.

Robert was breathing too hard and too fast to speak. He took deep breaths to calm himself. When he felt he could speak again, he said, "I need to find Demetrius."

"I'm right here, Robert," Demetrius said, stepping into the room. "What's the matter?"

"Trajon Jarl is here," Robert said. "We must leave, now."

GERARD WATCHED HIS uncle's face turn bright red in anger.

"She's *not* coming with us!"

The shout reverberated off the walls, and Gerard had a momentary impulse to cover his ears, but he managed to keep his hands at his side and not react. He suspected his ability to remain stoic had as much to do with his general level of exhaustion as any force of will.

Gerard glanced at Nina, who was sitting on the other bed in the room, her back flagstaff straight, her chin slowly moving in circles. Gerard imagined he could hear her teeth grinding, but she held her tongue. She was much better at that than he was, even when she wasn't exhausted.

She had her arms folded, her left hand on top of her upper arm, the ring he had given her prominently displayed.

Gerard turned back to his uncle and looked him straight in the eye, where the blood vessels looked near to bursting. He summoned his best impression of an angry, stubborn Monteous Roarke.

"She saved my life," he said without raising his voice. "She is going home with me."

He had decided to take her with him soon after she came into the room and told him what had happened. With the Academy destroyed, he had no real argument against her leaving. He still had an argument against taking her with him; his father's plans for him would not leave out an *appropriate* marriage, and he would spare Nina that pain.

But she knew the risk, and after she had saved him, he could not deny her.

"Your father will not be happy." He glanced over at Nina. "And that ring she's wearing? You two are not married. You had no right to give that to her."

Gerard tried to leash his anger. It helped that his uncle's statement sparked the germ of an idea. He looked at Nina, caught her eyes when she noticed his movement.

"I had every right to give that to her. I made it for her, and for no one else."

He had a duty. He knew it. He would have to become the heir, but that would not be formal until he returned home, until he went through the ceremony. Until that time, anything could happen.

"She is *not* coming," his uncle said. "I will brook no more argument."

He turned away from them and stalked out of the room, slamming the door behind him.

"I'm glad he's not your father," Nina said.

Gerard shook his head. "They are of the same mind, much of the time. My father will not like your presence there at all."

Nina got up from her bed and came over to sit next to him. She put her arms around him and hugged him. When she pulled away, she left one arm around his shoulders. One of her fingers traced the edges of the new skin that was growing where his burns had been.

"You know I won't care what your father thinks," she said. "I'll stay by you, no matter what, if you'll let me."

"I'm sorry," he said. "I shouldn't have tried to make you stay."

She smiled. "No, you shouldn't have."

They sat that way for quite a while, neither of them speaking. He was glad to have her there, and the germ of the idea continued to grow.

There had to be a chapel somewhere along the road where he could marry her, a lord that would do the honor. It made him think of Lord Ivron, the lord they had spent so much time with during the search for Monteous. But Lord Ivron was not on their way to Risuk. It didn't matter. He would find someone.

He took her left hand and held it in his, separating out the finger that wore his ring. It fit perfectly.

"I wish I would have had Lord Ivron marry us before we left for the Academy," he said. But he had been so unsure, so surprised at what Nina had brought to his life. It was far different than the relationship his mother and father had.

"Yes," Nina said. "You should have." She wore a smug little grin.

"There must be a lord somewhere along the way that would marry us," he said.

Nina nodded. "There must." Her breath was coming in short little bursts.

"We'd have to escape my uncle, somehow."

She leaned in closer to him.

"Would you?" he asked.

She blinked, sat back, and the smug grin came back. She took her right hand from his shoulder, slipped off the ring, and held it above his lap.

"Not without a proper proposal, Gerard."

Gerard took a deep breath, and then held his hand out, palm up. She dropped the ring into it. The ring still held her warmth.

He wrapped his hand around it, then slid off the bed, taking his blankets with him. Nendra had yet to supply him with any clothes, he suspected in a bid to keep him in bed until she was satisfied he was healed.

He made sure the blankets covered the important parts, and then knelt in front of Nina. He looked down again, he told himself it was to be sure he was covered, but more than that, he wanted to hide his nervousness. Of a sudden, his muscles had all lost whatever strength he had managed to gain back that morning.

He gathered his courage and made himself look up at her, her red hair framing her freckled face like a piece of art. He was amazed the fireball hadn't even touched it.

"Nina," he said after a few deep breaths. "I had a whole speech planned out when I thought I would do this back at the Academy, but it has escaped my mind. Know this, though. In my heart, I never wanted you to stay at the Academy. I only sought to spare you the suffering that would come from my father."

Nina nodded. He thought he saw a tear in her eye, but she blinked and it was gone.

"Whatever happens, I would be your husband. Will you have me?" he said, and held out the ring, palm up.

Nina sniffed, her nose wrinkling up just a little before she composed herself. "That has always been my intention," she said, and put her hand atop his, covering the ring.

He took her hand with his left, and pulled the ring out from under it. Then, slowly, he slid it onto her finger for real.

Heavy footsteps pounded in the hall outside, and then the door flew open.

Gerard turned to find Robert standing in the doorway. Robert's eyes took everything in, and Gerard prepared for a comment on the scene before him, but Robert surprised him, and drove a spike of fear through his heart.

"Nina," he said. "If he is well enough, find Gerard some clothes and get him ready to leave."

"Why?" she asked.

"The wizard who destroyed the Academy is nearby," he said. "We are all in danger."

CHAPTER 11

THE THOUGHTS WHIRLED around in Nina's head, much like a dozen dust devils fighting over the same ground, and did not come close to settling down until it was near dark. The thoughts helped her ignore the dust and the ruts in the road they traveled, they helped her ignore the sun as it beat down on her, and they helped her ignore the fact that she felt naked on the road without her bow.

Gerard proposed.

They were in danger from a powerful wizard.

Gerard is going to marry me.

They were running away from everything she knew, and Gerard's parents might not be happy with his decision.

Gerard proposed.

She wanted to shout and scream how happy she was, but the constant looks from Gerard's uncle kept her from saying anything. She knew he would be unhappy if he were aware that Gerard had proposed. He was already unhappy that she was riding with them.

Ever since Robert had poked his head into the room while Gerard knelt at her feet and announced they were leaving, the group had worked in a frenzy amidst a string of arguments.

By the time she found clothes for Gerard and had him dressed, Nendra was objecting to his leaving.

"He's not ready for travel," the healer said. Her hair was a mess, and she seemed quite flustered at all the panic in the air. "Another day, at least!"

Demetrius settled her down. "If he stays, he's putting you in danger."

"But he'll need protection from the sun," she said.

"I'll take care of it."

And then Demetrius strode out of the house.

While Demetrius was gone, Gerard's uncle entered the room, all bluster and anger, and told Gerard that Nina would not be coming with them.

Nina worried at that moment that Gerard would give in to his uncle, as he had back at the Academy. She felt so proud and happy when he stood, a little wobbly, but strong, and said, "She's coming with us, Uncle. It's not your decision."

The two went back and forth for a couple minutes, until Nendra walked in on them and shooed Gerard's uncle out. Gerard stood strong until his uncle left, and then he sat down unsteadily on the bed, and Nina rushed to his side to steady him.

When Demetrius returned, he helped Nina bring Gerard outside. Demetrius had found a merchant's covered wagon and a pair of horses to draw it.

"You can drive it, can't you Nina?"

She had nodded. Of course she could.

They loaded Gerard into it and made sure the sun would not touch him. Nina climbed up onto the bench, and Angela climbed up next to her, which forced Shane to ride in the back with Gerard. Robert, Demetrius and Gerard's uncle rode their horses.

The group left only a little after the sun reached its zenith. Nina drove the wagon, following behind Demetrius and Gerard's uncle who was still furious she was along, but had ended the majority of his complaining. Robert rode next to the wagon on Angela's side, holding his staff up and maintaining a Weave he said should keep them from being observed.

Robert and Angela kept their voices low enough that she could only hear a little of what they said, but she heard enough to know how much they had missed each other and did not want to be separated.

All the while, she kept glancing back to peek at Gerard. Each time, the thoughts of her marriage to him ran wild in her head.

The next town was about a day's ride from Bird. If they kept on, Demetrius thought they would arrive sometime after midnight. Nina was not looking forward to driving the horses after dark, but it seemed she had little choice. Demetrius and Robert intended that they drive on until they reach their destination, the home of a wizard named Wendell.

When Robert rode ahead, just as the sun started to dip beyond the horizon, Nina spit the dust out of her mouth, then leaned over to Angela.

"I haven't had a chance to tell you," Nina said.

Angela leaned in close. "Tell me?"

"Gerard proposed this morning." She could not keep her giddiness out of her voice.

Angela reached around her and hugged her.

"I'm so happy for you," she said. "Does his uncle know?"

"No. We're not telling him either. Not until we're married."

"How are you going to do that without him knowing?"

The horses started to drift, and she pulled on the reins, bringing them back to the center of the road.

"There must be a lord we can impose upon to marry us. I don't know how we'll sneak off quite yet..."

"I can hide you," Angela said, winking. "He won't see you leave, though I don't know how long we'll be on the road together."

"What do you mean?"

"Robert said we might separate from you once we reach Master Wendell's. Robert is looking for someone, and if Master Wendell can help us find him, we'll be leaving."

"Who is he looking for?"

"A wizard named Thiobulus Soake. Monteous thought Robert could learn from him."

The comment, for some reason, brought all the thoughts about why they were even on the road back to Nina, and some of the horror she had experienced as the fireball came toward her. She was glad she hadn't seen the Academy afterward. She could imagine it, and even that made her shiver.

"The wizard we're running from. Does Robert know who he is?"

Angela didn't answer for a moment. She seemed lost in thought.

"Angela?"

"Robert mentioned a name to Demetrius. Trajon Jarl. I've never heard the name, but Robert knows who he is."

"How did Robert meet him?"

"I'm not sure if Robert has actually met him, but the wizard left a note for Robert on the back of the letter I wrote him."

Nina sucked in her breath, the implications obvious. "The wizard was looking for Robert?"

It was hard to tell if Angela nodded, or if her head dipped forward due to a bump in the road.

And then another thought occurred to Nina.

"He knows who you are."

"Yes," Angela said. "He probably knows who you and Gerard are, too."

"How?"

"I can only guess it's because of the Conclave."

It made sense. Nina hadn't been there, but she'd been around them before and after. She'd been seen at Gerard's side at the king's table—an event which still amazed her—and outside Orliss's estate before it erupted in flame.

"What's it all about?" Nina asked.

Just then, Robert started to fall back from his talk with Demetrius.

"I don't know," Angela said. "I think Robert might know, but he hasn't talked about it much."

The wagon came even with Robert and he looked toward them.

"Demetrius says there's a stream just beyond the rise ahead. We'll stop there to water the horses and eat before the sun sets completely."

"We're not stopping for the night?" Angela asked.

"No. We need to see Master Wendell as soon as we can."

"Why?"

A cloud seemed to cross Robert's face.

"Not here," he said.

"Why not? Look around. Who will hear?"

Robert pointed to the back of the wagon, leading Nina to think of Shane and Gerard.

He can't mean Gerard.

And then the wagon topped the rise, and Nina found herself looking down a gentle slope to a stream that she could jump across without getting wet. From the rocks surrounding it, the stream was quite a bit larger during the cold months, but still easy to ford.

Nina drove the wagon down to the edge of the stream and stopped it there. Robert, Demetrius and Gerard's uncle were already leading their horses to the stream.

Angela jumped down from the wagon and ran after Robert, Nina assumed to hound him further about why they had to hurry. Nina jumped down, too.

"Can we get out?" Shane asked from within the wagon.

"Yes, for a few minutes while we water the horses."

Shane jumped down from the back of the wagon, and Gerard climbed out onto the bench.

Nina went to unhitch the horses. She didn't want to be dragging the wagon through all the stones.

"Do you need my help?" Gerard asked.

"It will go faster, if you're up to it," she said.

Gerard climbed out of the wagon and came to help her. He brushed her shoulder with his hand as he walked past, causing her to shiver.

Together, they unhitched the horses. He took one, she took the other, and they led them to the water.

She tried to get as close as she could to Robert and Angela. She wanted to hear what he told her, if he told her anything.

But when she got there, they weren't saying anything to each other. Angela was scowling and looking out across the water, leading Nina to think Robert hadn't told her what she wanted to hear. Robert's face was stoic. He seemed to be trying to keep himself under control.

The horses lowered their heads to the stream to drink. The waters were clear, and must not have run past any villages upstream.

"If we followed this stream," she said, "I wonder if it would lead us to Risuk."

Gerard looked upstream, north. She knew the mountains of Risuk were up there somewhere, his home, eventually her home.

"It might. Risuk is still quite a distance. I can't even see the mountains from here."

"When do we turn north?"

She heard a snort from where Gerard's uncle was standing. It could have been his horse, but she didn't think so.

"Just after this next town," Demetrius said. "We'll take Ravenhead Road until it crosses Sundered River. After that, we'll be in Risuk, and we'll climb into the mountains."

"If we're all going," Robert said, barely above a whisper.

Nina heard footsteps behind her and turned to see Shane walking toward them. He rubbed at his left thigh as if massaging out a cramp.

"How long are we going to be here?" he asked.

"Long enough to hitch the horses back up," Robert said.

Nina glanced back at her horse. She'd had her fill of the stream. Gerard's horse was done, too.

"Dammit, Robert! What's the hurry?" Angela said.

Robert's control slipped, finally, and it wasn't anger that he was holding back, it was fear. He turned to face Angela.

"He will kill you if I don't do what he wants!"

They all collectively held their breath except for Demetrius. Of course he knew.

Nina knew without asking who Robert was talking about. They all did. The wizard that had destroyed the Academy.

She looked at Angela, but couldn't get a read on what she was thinking. Beyond her, Gerard's uncle turned away, and led his horse up the slope.

ROBERT RODE HIS horse at the head of their little caravan, avoiding everyone. He did not want to talk about his outburst at all. He had not intended Gerard and Nina to learn that Jarl was threatening him, that they were in danger because of him. He had wanted to keep them as safe as he could.

Which was why he was still maintaining the ward over the group. It would keep most other wizards from finding them via scrying. He hoped it would work on Trajon Jarl, too.

He had been cursing himself for not putting up the Weave after leaving the Academy ever since discovering early that morning that Jarl knew where he was. He had relied on Demetrius's assertion that the Guild was watching out for him, protecting him, and that Jarl had only found him through an indirect route, a note that he had left.

Obviously, something had changed.

Jarl could either see through the protection the Guild had set up, or Jarl had someone close by watching him, following him. But Robert had not seen evidence of that at all during their ride, and when asked, Demetrius had also been unable to discover a spy.

So Robert had done the only thing he could think of and put up the concealing Weave.

Every now and again, he glanced back toward the wagon, looking for Angela. In the moonlight, she was only a shadow against the wagon's cover. She had been so angry with him for not telling her earlier. She had refused to talk to him since his announcement. And he hadn't even told her what Jarl wanted him to do.

But he was angry with himself, too. He had lost control and shouted it out. He had not lost control like that since he learned Monteous died. He didn't want to go back to losing focus whenever something distracted him. He could not afford to return to the Robert he had been as an apprentice.

Not now.

Not with Angela's life at stake.

He had three days left, two and a half, really. Two and a half days to find Thiobulus and appeal to him for help, or to at least learn where the wizard was and hope he could outrun Jarl.

He could not wait to get to Master Wendell's and drop off the wagon and Shane. They were slowing him down. And if Master Wendell knew where to find Thiobulus, and Robert had only himself, Demetrius, and Angela along on the ride, he had little trouble imagining he could reach the wizard in time.

And maybe Master Wendell would let Angela borrow a wand. Robert wouldn't feel quite so vulnerable, then, with another wizard to take over the wards.

Demetrius would not even have to come along. Demetrius could go warn the king, or do whatever he felt necessary. Demetrius had been looking at him out of the corner of his eye since they left the stream. Robert didn't have to see him do it to know. He could feel Demetrius's eyes on him. Robert was sure Demetrius was wondering why Robert hadn't told him that Jarl had threatened Angela.

Of course, Demetrius had his own secrets, among them was the answer to why the man had so readily agreed to help Robert after fighting so hard to head him in a different direction. It didn't make any sense at all.

He couldn't trust Jarl, he couldn't trust Demetrius, and now Angela was angry at him, and his own anger at himself boiled deep within.

As the road brought them through a thicket, Demetrius pulled up along side him.

"How long?" Demetrius asked.

Robert knew what he was asking. "Three days. Two and a half, now."

"That's not enough time. It could take weeks to find Thiobulus. If we have to travel to Risuk, it could take longer."

They passed out of the thicket. Stone fences lined the road, farmland beyond them. In the distance, the moonlight highlighted the rooftops of the town. They were getting close to Wendell's.

"Master Wendell will know, won't he?"

"He might, but you can't count on that. Thiobulus has often been hard to track down."

Robert didn't want to think about what would happen if Master Wendell did not know how to find Thiobulus. He tried to ignore the thought that Master Wendell just might not choose to tell him.

"How far to Master Wendell's?"

"Not far at all. Just the other side of town."

Robert waited a bit before asking his next question. He didn't really want to know the answer.

But he asked it anyway. "What can we do if Master Wendell won't help us?"

Demetrius's head turned his way, and Robert could feel Demetrius's eyes on him. "That depends on you, Robert. It seems you don't trust me. How can I trust that you won't give in to him to save Angela?"

Robert recoiled in his saddle, and then his anger rose up.

"Who is to say I shouldn't?"

"Look what Jarl did at the Academy, Robert."

"If he's right and the Guild murdered my parents to get me, does that make the Guild any better than him? How am I supposed to determine which side is right if I can't trust either of them?"

"Trust me, Robert. Trajon Jarl has done more unspeakable things than you can imagine."

"Trust you? Can I? You still have secrets you haven't told me."

"I've never lied to you."

Their horses' hooves started to clop as they transitioned from the mostly dirt road to the cobblestone of the town.

"I'll find that out when we talk to Master Wendell," Robert said.

He turned away from Demetrius and forced his gaze straight ahead, down the street.

Demetrius was right. He knew what Jarl would do, knew that joining Jarl was the wrong thing to do, but if it came down to choosing between saving Angela or doing the right thing, he knew he would probably choose Angela. With Monteous gone, and his parents long dead no matter who was at fault, Angela was all he had.

If only there was another way. If only they could find Thiobulus before his three days were up.

They passed through the rest of the town in silence until Demetrius pointed down a crossroad to the left.

"This way," he said and led them in that direction.

A few minutes later, they came upon a fenced estate. Not as large as the one that the Guild had chosen for the Academy, but certainly out of place in the small town.

All the windows were dark, which wasn't unexpected. But to Robert, the shadows around the door were all wrong. Moonlight illuminated the entire front of the building, but where the door should have been, there was only black, as if the door wasn't even there.

Robert Weaved a light from the top of his staff and directed it at the door.

It was gone.

Robert dismounted and ran to the gate. It stood open, wide enough to have let a man through. Robert saw all his hopes evaporating. He would have to go to Risuk and somehow protect them all from Trajon Jarl.

"Wait Robert," Demetrius said.

Robert ignored his call. He had to know if Master Wendell still lived.

He pushed open the gate. Its hinges squealed as if it had been neglected for months. It sent a shiver down his spine.

He wanted to rush. His whole body ached to run to the doorway and look inside, but Demetrius's call for him to wait had done one thing. It reminded him that he was entering a wizard's property.

He slipped into the vew and looked for Weaves.

There weren't any visible Weaves of any kind. It surprised Robert. There should have been something, but they were all gone, if they had ever been there in the first place. But he did not know a wizard that didn't protect their home and their laboratories with Weaves.

He moved forward.

Footsteps rushed up to him, and he caught the sound of steel being drawn. He looked behind him and found Demetrius with his sword out.

Demetrius nodded to him.

When they reached the door, Robert stopped.

There were scorch marks on the stone around the doorway. Shards of the door littered the floor inside.

Robert already knew Master Wendell had died, and he knew who killed him. He didn't know when.

"It will be dangerous to go in," Demetrius said.

"I know."

Robert looked out past the fence. Angela and Nina were watching. Gerard had climbed down from the wagon. Gerard's uncle seemed to be looking on with interest.

Shane jumped down from the back of the wagon, looked at them for a moment, then at the door. He burst into a run toward the gate.

Gerard got in his way and held him back. Nina jumped down to help.

"We have to go in, though," Robert said.

"Why?"

"None of the others have a staff or a wand. We must at least find them something to use, or they will be useless if we have to face him."

"You can't face him," Demetrius said. "You won't survive it."

Robert stepped through the door.

"We certainly won't if they don't have staves."

Robert tweaked the Weave that gave off light, and it widened to show the room beyond the doorway. He didn't have to look far to find Master Wendell's crumpled body. Its head faced the doorway, and bore only a slight resemblance to the wizard he had met at the Conclave the previous winter. It looked like a piece of dried fruit, the skin shrunken tight around the skull. The hands bore the same look as the face, tight skin around bones. The wizard's staff rested on the open right hand.

Robert scanned the rest of the room. A fireplace on one end, cold. A rocking chair next to it, a small table with a book resting on its top. A crystal glass lay on the floor beside the table.

Robert walked over to the glass and picked it up. He rubbed a finger inside and it came away dry. The floor where it had fallen was also dry.

Did it mean anything?

Shane burst into the room, followed quickly by Nina.

"We couldn't stop him," Nina said.

Shane ran to Wendell's body and bent down over him. His body started to shake. Shane took Wendell's staff and clutched it to his chest.

"This doesn't appear to have happened very long ago," Demetrius said.

"The glass is dry."

"A day, two. No more."

"The same night as the Academy?" Robert asked.

"Maybe, maybe not."

"He couldn't have made it here in one night. Not without a portal."

Demetrius put a hand on his shoulder. "Don't forget that Trajon has abilities at his disposal that the Guild does not allow."

How could he forget? The evidence was on the floor in front of him.

"This could be how he found you," Demetrius said.

Robert looked up from the body into Demetrius's eyes. The light from his staff gave the pupils a gold quality.

"How is that possible?"

"I told you earlier. Master Wendell was one of the wizards maintaining the protections over you."

Robert shivered.

"How many others were there?"

"Master Brin was one. There were three others that I know of."

Two out of five were dead. How many were needed to hide him from Trajon Jarl? How many were dead?

"What do we do now?"

"You look for your staves and wands and anything else you think we'll need, then we'll camp outside town until morning."

"Then we move on to Risuk?"

Demetrius nodded. Robert had never noticed Demetrius looking despondent about anything, but Demetrius looked decidedly unhappy about their upcoming journey.

"You don't like it," Robert said. "Why?"

"I'll tell you some other time," he said. "We should get moving."

"We won't be able to take the wagon," Robert said.

"We'll take care of that in the morning, unless you keep dragging your feet. Go find what you need."

Robert took one more look at the desiccated corpse on the floor and then went looking for the laboratory. He knew Demetrius was right. If they had to face Trajon Jarl, they would lose. But if Angela and Gerard had staves, they might be able to hide themselves well enough to keep from having to face him.

CHAPTER 12

TRAJON PULLED A circular Work of iron and bone from his pocket. The iron, a smallish round piece the size of a coin, polished smooth, sat at the center of a frame made from bone and sinew. In all, it was no bigger than the palm of his hand.

He sat on the lumpy bed that had been given to him when he took a room at Bird's only inn. It had not been hard to make the innkeep forget, an act he'd found necessary when he thought Thiobulus's creation might have spotted him.

Thiobulus. The wizard's name sparked ages of ire within him. A thorn in his side since the early days of the Guild, and after, when Thiobulus had expelled and imprisoned him.

Trajon took a vial of blood from another pocket, opened it, and spilled a drop on the surface of the polished iron. He went about spreading the drop with his thumb so that it covered the whole of the surface while he slipped the vial back into his pocket with his other hand.

The vew came easily to him, as it always did. The energie in the blood, still connected to the man. He could feel that connection in him. He put the Work to his forehead, blood to skin, and drew the energie within himself.

And then he sent it out, searching along the connection, the thread that linked the blood to the man.

Master. It was a thought, not a sound.

Tell me of them. Where are they? Trajon sent.

They have discovered Master Wendell.

Trajon allowed himself a smile. They were on the path.

Have they discussed their plans?

I know they will continue on to Risuk.

All of them?

I think so. Will you really take the apprentice for your own?

That is none of your concern.

They talk of finding someone named Thiobulus, as if he would offer safety from you.

Trajon smiled. It was as he'd hoped. With the Guild in a shambles, Thiobulus's construct would lead Robert right to him.

Do what you must to keep them on that path.

He thinks he has only a couple days.

Because that was what I told him. Do not trouble yourself over it. Just be sure to contact me should he be on the verge of finding Thiobulus.

I will. But I won't be able to leave Risuk with them.

You must find a way.

But...

This was the thing he hated about working with normals. When they thought they were doing well, they presumed too much.

Do you need more motivation?

No, Master!

Find a way. And if Robert seems to think he has escaped me, disabuse him of that notion.

How?

Be creative, but you must leave Robert and his protector alone.

Yes, Master.

Trajon removed the Work from his forehead, severing the connection. It would do no good to let the fool know that Robert had effectively hidden himself. He might think Robert's protection might extend to him.

And that wouldn't do.

In the end, they would all have to go, especially him. A man who would turn on his own family could not be trusted.

And Robert, he would accept Robert if Robert truly wanted to join him. But even in the search for Thiobulus, Robert had provided his answer. Any change of heart would be suspect.

And any wizard that could hide himself as well as Robert had managed was a danger he could not accept without complete commitment.

No. They would all die as soon as Thiobulus was found, at the latest.

He gathered the few things he had with him, reached into his pocket for his Telanderal, closed his hand around it and fed it his energie. He had more wizards to visit before they realized just what he intended.

ANGELA'S SLEEP THAT night was anything but solid. She woke up to nightmares on at least three occasions, and only one of them had anything to do with the Academy's destruction.

The other two showed her scenes of Trajon Jarl fighting Robert, fireballs and lightning and enormous amounts of energie flung about, until Robert eventually succumbed and failed. And then Trajon Jarl stood over her. The first time, he said to her, "It's your turn," and she woke up. The second time he stood over her and said, "You are mine."

She warred within herself over which dream frightened her most.

When she woke the third time, she picked up her newly acquired staff, courtesy of the deceased Master Wendell, and started out across the tiny little camp they had made within a copse of white blossomed angel trees

Nina and Gerard slept next to each other, her head snug in his shoulder. Angela could not help smiling for them. Shane slept near Demetrius on one side of their hastily made fire pit, Bryce on the other.

She stepped gingerly around them and made her way to where Robert sat alone in the wagon, looking out over the camp, his staff held up and ready. She knew if she slipped into the vew, she'd see the Weave of protection he maintained while the rest of them slept.

He looked at her as she approached.

"It's not your turn yet," he said.

"I can't sleep."

She climbed up next to him. It was warm enough that she didn't need a blanket, but she snuggled up to his warmth, anyway.

"You're not angry at me, anymore?" he asked.

"I'm still angry," she said, "but I'm not going to let that keep us apart."

She stared out through the trees at the road. She tried not to let the trees remind her of her run from the Academy. The trees were different, but the shadows still provoked memories. She glanced up through a hole in the canopy of blossoms and saw a few stars, but she could not see enough of them to make out the constellations. At least they weren't obscured by a pall of smoke.

"I didn't want you to be afraid. I thought..."

Angela waited for him to finish his thought. When no more words came, she looked at him and saw him staring out through the trees.

"You thought Master Wendell would know how to find Thiobulus, and you wouldn't ever have to tell me."

His head bent down.

"You don't have to protect me, Robert. I can protect myself, and you haven't seen what he can do. I don't think you could protect me, not from him, not by yourself."

He looked up. His eyes were nearly black pools in the darkness. Only a hint of glint from the stars showed them for what they were.

"I have seen what he can do. He cut through the threads I Weaved without any effort. He held me in place and I could do nothing. I've only seen one other wizard capable of that. I even thought about accepting his offer, just to keep you safe."

She put her free arm around him and pulled him tight to her.

"You can't do that, Robert. He's a monster. How could you trust him?"

"Who am I supposed to trust anymore?" The struggle within him came out in the tightening of his voice. "Monteous told me not to trust the Guild. Trajon is telling me I can't trust what Monteous told me about my parents."

"You told me they died in the uprising."

"That's what I've always believed. Trajon told me that Monteous lied to me."

"Did he tell you what happened to them?"

Robert hung his head.

"No. He wouldn't tell me."

Angela slipped her hand up to his neck and started massaging it. His skin seemed cool, his muscles tense.

"Robert," she said. "He's deceiving you. He doesn't want you to trust Monteous. But a man that could kill four wizards, kill all those apprentices, try to kill Gerard and Nina, he can't be trusted. He's a monster, Robert."

His eyes came back up to lock with hers.

"Then what do I do?"

"You pass the Weave to me and get your rest," she said. "You're tired and not thinking straight."

"But..."

"Robert, please. There are only a few hours before daybreak. I can handle it. You can't keep it up all day and night."

"I don't even know if the Weave will work."

Angela slipped into the vew and followed the threads to the Weave that formed a blanket over them. It was a little more complex than the one she might have chosen, a little harder to keep in place, but provided more protection, too. And, it was expertly done. She could not have done a better job, and these were the Weaves she was good at.

"If he can find us through that, then he would have been able to find you anywhere, at any time," she said. "He wouldn't have needed to leave a note for you."

"But..."

"He's just a wizard, Robert. He knows more than us, has more experience, but he still must follow the same rules."

"What I'm worried about is that there are rules we've never been taught."

She had no answer for that.

"Pass me the Weave, Robert."

"All right," he said.

The threads detached from Robert's staff and hung in the air for just a moment before she reached out for them and bound them to her own staff. The burden on her would not be slight, but she could handle it. She would have to.

Robert's shoulders slumped with the release. She pulled his head to hers, and kissed him on the cheek. She wanted to kiss him other places, but he was too tired, and she worried she might lose control of the Weave. Already she could feel the strain.

"Go to sleep," she said.

He climbed down from the wagon, then turned to face her.

"Thank you," he said.

"For what?"

"For being someone I can trust."

He turned and walked over to the blanket she had been sleeping on and lay down. She kept her eyes on him for long minutes until he rolled on his side and she could only see his back.

CHAPTER 13

ROBERT FELT BETTER when he woke and the seven of them were once again on the road. He didn't get much sleep, but it was enough to allow him to feel more normal and less like he was carrying the world. Angela was smiling at him again, too.

Demetrius had gone into town and traded the wagon and its horses for a pair of horses better suited to riding. He bought two more, as well as packs full of supplies for them all.

Master Wendell's laboratory had been good to them. Even Nina had a wand that was better than the one most apprentices were given to use.

Gerard had stuffed his new staff through the top of the saddle pack. It appeared to have been an old castoff staff. Better than the ones that Gerard would have been used to at the Academy, but not, Robert thought, as good as the one he carried.

Shane refused to let go of Master Wendell's staff and kept it cradled in his free arm. Angela held her own new staff upright, the tip stuck on top of her boot. She had refused to give up the Weave when Robert woke.

The group made good time, he thought, now that they weren't burdened with the wagon. He kept an eye on Gerard. The healer had said he should be fine by now, but he still appeared weak. From time to time, when Robert turned Nina's way, he caught a look of concern on her face. She too didn't trust that Gerard was really ready to ride.

But they didn't have any time.

It would take them a week to get to the border of Risuk, and they didn't have a week.

Angela was right. Robert knew it in his head.

The Weave should keep them hidden. Monteous himself had taught them this Weave. But Robert still had trouble accepting that they would be safe from Trajon Jarl. Not with the way the man seemed to jump around from place to place with little effort. The Academy, Master Wendell's, the healer's. It was all too easy.

Robert wished he could do the same thing. It would make finding Thiobulus that much easier.

But they were stuck riding horses.

While searching for staves, he'd also looked through Wendell's stores, thinking he might be able to create a portal to take them to Risuk. It would have saved them days.

But Wendell hadn't had enough of the right ingredients, nor had he the book that would have helped Robert figure the right alignment of metals in the focus. Robert took what materials he could fit into his pack, but the Works were too bulky. Even the scrying bowl.

He had thought deeply about bringing that along, despite its bulk, but after his conversation overnight with Angela, Robert was glad he hadn't given in to the urge. He might be far too tempted to use it in the end.

Demetrius called a halt for a quick lunch. He led them off to the side of the road and into a small clearing in the dry brush. He pulled plums and smoked pork from his pack and passed them around.

"Demetrius," Robert said after swallowing a juicy bit of plum. "Are there any other wizards on our way to Risuk?"

Robert reached up and wiped at the juice dribbling down his chin.

"There's one. Master Lamen. He's not high in the Guild, however. He's one of Lord Taren's retainers."

That dashed Robert's hopes of finding the book he wanted, and without it, he wouldn't be creating a portal. No wizard who could open a portal would deign to work on retainer.

"Will we be stopping there?" Robert asked.

"I hadn't thought about it, but perhaps we should look in on him. He should at least be able to deliver a message to the Guild."

If he's not dead.

Robert couldn't keep the thought out of his head.

"When will we reach Lord Taren's?" Nina asked.

Robert wondered why it would matter to her.

"Tomorrow afternoon, I should think," Demetrius said.

The answer brought a smile to her face. She glanced at Gerard, but quickly looked away.

It seemed odd behavior until, out of the corner of his eye, he caught Gerard's uncle grimacing.

Bryce hadn't at all liked the idea of Shane and Nina continuing on with them. That morning, he had argued for Nina and Shane to stay behind, to go back to the Guild.

Bryce had spluttered and shouted in anger when Demetrius said he would not send them back to uncertainty. Eventually, his anger had run down, or at least his volume did, and he grew silent. If he continued to fume, Robert had not heard him.

After they finished eating, Robert noticed Angela's eyelids drooping and took the Weave from her. She hadn't let the threads shift even a little bit, despite her obvious exhaustion. He'd have to watch her. He decided she might not be fully recovered from carrying Gerard and Nina from the Academy.

He caught Shane looking between them.

"I can help," Shane said.

"Can you?" Robert asked

"I carried Gerard most of the way through the forest," he said.

"This Weave is quite a bit more complex than that."

"I can do it," he said.

Shane's voice carried a hint of desperation that Robert could understand, a need to be useful. Robert had felt that need himself after Monteous died and left him with no one.

Robert glanced at Angela, who he saw had an eye on the two of them. *Well, not no one.*

But the past six months had left him feeling pretty useless.

"Tonight," he said, "after we've stopped. Better to see if you can hold it while we're not moving around, first."

Shane nodded, eagerly. His yellow hair fell into his eyes, and he pushed it aside.

"Thank you," he said.

And for a moment, Shane reminded Robert of another eager, young, apprentice. One he had watched die from inexperience.

He pushed the thought aside. Wallace's death was different, and Robert knew better now, no matter how much his mistake had hurt at the time.

But this time, if Shane made a mistake, they might all die.

Shane looked so grateful that Robert forced himself not to dwell on it as they all mounted and resumed their journey.

Demetrius and Bryce took the lead, Gerard and Nina the rear. Shane had somehow maneuvered his horse next to Angela's before Robert could, forcing Robert to follow after them.

Robert didn't let it bother him. There were too many currents running through the group that he had to understand, too many secrets he felt might threaten them all. He had to sort them out, at least in his own head, before they became distractions too large to handle.

❄ ❄ ❄

GERARD FELT BETTER as the day wore on, despite having spent the entire time in the saddle. Toward evening, his legs and back were sore, but his skin no longer felt like it would peel off with the slightest touch.

They entered the rolling hills of Northern Dominand in the late afternoon. Wooden fences rolled along with them, keeping people out, or animals in. The sheep they saw were pale imitations of the mountain rams in Risuk, lacking horns and any minimal sense of self-preservation. The occasional tree poked up from the grassy terrain, a reminder of the more southerly forests they had left, and a harbinger of what they would face on the lower slopes of Risuk.

Gerard knew there were still two or three days before he could see the mountain slopes and the blanket of trees that clothed them, but the hills gave him the first sign he was heading home.

A home he hadn't seen in seven years.

As they passed the first set of hills, Gerard found himself feeling ambivalent about going home. He couldn't wait to see the familiar landscape, the majestic shoulders of the giant mountains, and he knew he had his duty to his family, but since he proposed yesterday, even before that, he had little desire to see his father. He knew his father would find fault with Nina, knew his father would erupt in anger, whether he had a right or not, and Gerard had no desire to buffer the inevitable storm.

He wanted to curse his brother for dying.

"I wish my parents could be with us," Nina said.

"What?" Gerard asked.

"I wish my parents could be with us, you know, when we get married."

As if on cue, Uncle Bryce turned and looked back at them, a scowl on his face. He couldn't have heard, though. He was too far ahead of them, three horse lengths at least and the same number of horses between. On top of that, the breeze was blowing the wrong direction. There was no chance he heard.

But it wasn't worth taking the chance.

"I agree," he said, "but I don't think we should discuss it, right now."

"How many more days until we see the mountains?" Nina asked as if they had been talking about the travel all along.

"Three, I would think," he said. "We'll see the tops in the distance, and then we'll see more and more trees, until eventually we can see nothing but trees most of the time. By then, we'll be in Risuk."

"And then?"

"We'll go through Blisterwind Pass, and then we'll be home. Another two days, I would think."

"Will it be cold?"

Gerard laughed. "No, not during the summer. It's not hot like it is here, but the sun is warm."

"Will we be staying?"

Gerard looked sideways at her.

"I will have to stay," he said.

Her shoulders sagged, and she gazed straight ahead.

"Is there something wrong?" Gerard asked, worried he had upset her.

"No," she said, then sighed. "It's just that these hills are different. We're going farther than I've ever traveled and it reminded me how long it has been since I've seen my home. I feel like I won't see it again."

A desire to reach out and pull her close, wrap her in his arms, overcame him, but the horses made it impossible.

"You'll see them again," he said. "We'll visit, I swear."

She looked at him. "You promise?"

"I promise," he said, holding a fist over his heart in the Risuk traditional gesture of oath-taking.

Her shoulders came up, a smile crossed her face. She readjusted her new bow, which she wore slung over her shoulder. She looked again like the Nina that had chased out after him in defiance of her father's command.

"Good. If you break it," she said, "I shall break you."

"Fair enough," he laughed, drawing another scowling look from his uncle.

Gerard couldn't wait to return home and lose that man's dark looks. There was something about him that was different than the man Gerard had grown up chasing through the trees. He just couldn't put his finger on it.

AT DUSK, DEMETRIUS signaled for the apprentices to follow him off the road at the bottom of a valley. He led them alongside a stream that ran through the valley until he found a spot that would give them enough cover for the night, but would provide them enough room to let the horses graze on the thick grass.

He really didn't like this portion of Dominand. The grass wasn't tall enough, and the trees weren't thick enough, to provide real cover. The best he could do was get as far off the road as he could and hope some farmer didn't come after them in the middle of the night for camping in his field.

But Demetrius didn't think anyone claimed this part of Dominand for their own. He hadn't seen a farmhouse in several miles.

He was glad Robert's Weave appeared to be working. There hadn't been any hint of Trajon Jarl during the day. Robert wasn't at all ready to take on Trajon, even if Robert thought he was, even if Demetrius stood with him.

They all spent time taking care of the horses, grooming them, removing the saddles and the packs before setting them out to graze.

When that was done, Demetrius built up a low stack of wood and had Gerard light it with a Weave. He took out a travel pot, filled it with water from the stream and set it upon the fire. He cut up the potatoes, threw them in the water to boil, and added a few other vegetables he purchased along with their supplies that morning.

And then he sat and let it cook. He turned so that he could watch Robert work with the young apprentice, Shane. Robert was trying to help him duplicate the Weave Robert had held all day.

Demetrius wondered if it had something to do with Robert's guilt over Wallace's death. He knew Robert still carried that burden in his heart. The pain was obvious on his face every time Wallace's name came up.

In any case, it couldn't hurt to have a third person capable of maintaining the Weave. Stealth would serve them far better than confrontation.

Bryce sat down next to Demetrius and stared into the flames that licked at the travel pot.

Demetrius still wasn't sure about the man. He seemed different than when Demetrius met him those years ago, more guarded than the jovial merchant and occasional mercenary Demetrius had come to know on his trips through Blisterwind Pass to research Gerard.

But losing a nephew might do that to a man, especially if some people thought to lay the nephew's death at the man's feet.

"Do you think to come with us through Blisterwind, Demetrius," Bryce asked. "I'm sure Gentran would welcome you."

Gentran. Gerard's father.

"He never welcomed me before," said Demetrius. "He wouldn't let me even enter his home."

"He thought you were intent on Eric."

"Gerard's brother was never our focus," Demetrius said.

"Well, Gentran will be glad that you are bringing Gerard home, in any case."

Demetrius leaned forward and stirred the soup.

"I'm not bringing him home. That's your doing. If I had my way, he would not go home at all. There are duties far more important in this world than a son's duty to his father's mercantile business. The Seven Kingdoms has need of Gerard's talent. It should not be wasted trading in furs and iron."

Bryce snorted. "Wizards only care about themselves and the size of their coffers. Gentran is a lord, Demetrius. When that boy gets home and marries the girl that's waiting for him, it will unite two of the most important families in Risuk and it will keep him out of the hands of those wizards who can't even keep themselves safe."

Demetrius quickly searched the camp with his eyes for Gerard and Nina, hoping they weren't close enough to have heard his uncle. He found them sitting by the stream, too far distant to hear Bryce's statement. He could safely continue pretending he hadn't heard their plans to marry the following night. Bryce and Gentran would be in for a surprise.

"Wizards," Demetrius said, "care far more about the affairs of the land than they do about their coffers. Without the Guild, The Seven Kingdoms would have been at war for most of the last two centuries."

"You only say that because you work for them."

"Look at those five apprentices, Bryce. Do you really think they would stand for hearing your opinion right now? They lost friends, mentors, all to men who would destroy The Seven Kingdoms, to men who would see The Seven Kingdoms become a province of Mrongil. The Seven Kingdoms are already at war, Bryce. Gentran would take a weapon from us."

Bryce did raise his gaze from the fire, but he only sniffed, clearing his nose.

"It's not war, Demetrius. It's just wizards fighting, like they always do."

Bryce turned to face Demetrius giving Demetrius a look straight into the man's eyes, lit as they were by the fire.

"Gerard will *not* be a part of it, Demetrius."

Demetrius decided not to respond. Bryce was different now, and so was Gerard. Demetrius suspected Bryce was in for a surprise at the end of the journey when Gerard decided what he would, and would not, do.

He stirred the stew again, spooned a steaming bit out and put it to his tongue. Hot, spiced how he liked it. Done.

He called out to the others, then turned to Bryce.

"Would you like a bowl?"

To this, Demetrius knew the man could not say no. Bryce had never turned down a meal.

CHAPTER 14

A S THEY APPROACHED the gate of Lord Taren's estate, Robert could see a large manor house and a tower over the top of the walls. The walls, constructed from a local blue-gray stone, stood ten feet high or more. A wide ditch, dry from the summer heat, encircled the estate, with only a thin bridge for them to cross.

To get there, they had ridden through the town of Andsdale, most of which was built from the same blue-gray stone. Trees were sparse, but the stone seemed to be everywhere.

Demetrius mentioned, as they rode through Andsdale, that the locals quarried it from the banks of the river that flowed from the mountains of Risuk.

Robert didn't see the river until they rode past Andsdale and into the farmland beyond. The road ran along the river's edge for a mile or more until the river turned northwest, away from it. The road continued straight north through land that was home to a number of farms, and ultimately led right past Lord Taren's estate.

A large, thick gate barred their entry to the estate, but after Demetrius spoke a few quiet words with the guard on the other side, the gate swung open.

Demetrius led them into a courtyard, again paved with the same blue-gray stone. Men rushed up to take their horses, and a portly, balding man nearly rolled down the steps of the manor house to come greet them.

"Demetrius," he said through heavy breaths. "We haven't seen you in some time."

"It has been a while, Jergin. Is Lord Taren in?"

"He's taken a meeting with Andsdale's Mayor. He should be finished within the half-hour, I think. What brings you here?"

Robert dismounted as three young boys came to take their horses. The boy that came for his horse, no older than twelve, tried to take Robert's staff from him, but Robert shook his head.

"I'll keep this," he said, and then turned away from the boy as the boy led his horse away.

"Ah, I understand," said Jergin.

Robert wondered what Demetrius had told the man and silently cursed the timing of the stable-boy.

"Well, we should like to speak with Master Lamen, if he is about, while we wait."

"Of course. I'll send for him once we settle you down for refreshments. I'm certain Lord Taren would want you to accept our hospitality for the night."

The portly man turned away and waddled back to the manor house at a much slower pace than the one he had come to meet them with.

Demetrius jerked his head, indicating that they should follow the steward, then started after Jergin, himself.

Robert took Angela's hand and fell in behind Demetrius.

The front doors opened onto a great hall that had a raised dais to the right and a monstrous fireplace, its flanks carved into the likeness of a pair of charging horses, on the far wall. Two long tables ran the length of the room, and the walls were entirely clad in a dark reddish-colored wood that had to have been brought in at great cost.

Robert couldn't decide which was more impressive: the wood on the walls or the carved horses on the fireplace.

Jergin led them to the left through a door which opened into a room that was not so large as the great hall, but still had seats enough for the seven of them. This room was also clad in wood, but of a lighter color than that of the great hall.

"Have a seat while I bring refreshments and find Master Lamen," Jergin said.

Robert would have preferred to find the wizard himself and ask him whether he had a copy of the book about portals. He couldn't help but feel the time slipping away from him.

But he took a cushioned chair, anyway. It was a great improvement over the saddle he inhabited the past few days, and he told himself Jergin would have a better chance of quickly finding the wizard.

Angela took the seat next to him and reached out for his hand. The warmth of her skin calmed him.

The others found seats around the room and fell into an uncomfortable silence. Gerard stole glances every now and then at his uncle. Nina did, too, but not nearly as often. She spent most of their wait staring at a large tapestry that depicted a scene from the formation of The Seven Kingdoms. It showed the lords gathered around the Founding Tree, with King Enselme addressing them, his bloody sword thrust into the ground next to him.

Demetrius sat, still as a stone until Robert looked his way.

And then a maid with gray hair and a stoop entered the room burdened by a tray and seven glasses of gold wine. Lord Taren didn't spare expenses anywhere, not even with uninvited guests.

Just as Robert took his glass, an older man stepped into the room. He had a crooked beak of a nose and wispy white hair. The black robe he wore had gold stripes running down the seams of the sleeves and around the cuffs and the hem. His eyes darted quickly around the room, taking the measure of everyone there. They seemed to widen a bit when they landed on Robert, but he looked away before Robert could study them.

Demetrius stood, stepped around the maid and went to shake his hand.

"Master Lamen," Demetrius said.

Master Lamen did not take Demetrius's hand.

"Demetrius. It is surprising to see you here."

Demetrius pulled his hand back and let it fall to his side. His eye twitched once.

"Surprising?"

"Especially so with five apprentices trailing you. Shouldn't they all be at the Academy?"

Robert slipped into the vew and focused on Master Lamen, assessing the wizard's strength. He blinked and looked again. But his second look only confirmed the first. Master Lamen stood near the bottom of the Guild. Of the five of them, Master Lamen's strength bested only Nina's.

"The Academy was destroyed."

The old wizard let out a cracked laugh.

"I'm not surprised by that," he said. "Too many apprentices in one place. Dangerous."

"Trajon Jarl killed all but these," Demetrius said, sweeping his hand backward. "He also killed Masters Brin, Brecious, Olimand, Callalan, and Wendell. It would not surprise me if others were dead by his hand, since."

Master Lamen took the news without faltering. Based on his ability and the apparent frailty of the man, Robert had expected him to quail at the news.

"Trajon Jarl. You are certain?"

"He spoke with me," Robert said.

The old man doddered forward until he stood in front of Robert. Robert desperately wanted to drink from his wine, now, but left the glass at his side.

"You are the one from the Conclave, the one that killed Orliss."

"Yes."

"I remember you." He looked around at the rest of them. "You and your friends. You seem to be at the center of things again, if Trajon Jarl is speaking to you. Why would he speak to you?"

Robert tried to think of a response. He was not certain telling Master Lamen how Trajon Jarl wanted Robert to join him was a good idea.

Fortunately, Demetrius stepped in between them at that moment.

"That's really not important, Master Lamen. What *is* important is that we need you to send a message to the Guild. Warn them that Trajon Jarl is alive and is seeking revenge against the Guild. He has plans for The Seven Kingdoms, too."

"You know this how?"

"He told me," Robert said.

Demetrius looked at Robert and frowned.

"Why would he tell you? You are a strange young man. I can see your power. You could squish me underfoot with hardly a thought, but you aren't even a Guild member..."

Master Lamen blinked a couple times, looked to Angela, then back at Robert.

"Oh, I understand, now. Trajon thinks you might hold a grudge against the Guild. He seeks to bring you to his side."

"How..." Robert started to ask.

"I don't have much power, young wizard, but I'm not stupid."

Robert looked down in an attempt to avoid the old wizard's gaze. A pair of worn leather sandals adorned the wizard's feet. His toenails stuck out, yellow and gnarled from having seen too many summers.

"I'm sorry."

"You are not the only wizard to make that mistake with me. Don't feel too poorly, and remember this. Don't ever think your ability is what makes you the kind of wizard your late master was."

He turned back to Demetrius.

"So what are your plans? You and Monteous never lacked for those."

"Thiobulus Soake."

Master Lamen grunted. "You think that pompous fool will help you? If there was ever a wizard that took himself far to seriously, Robert, it was Thiobulus Soake."

"Robert had an encounter with him last year," said Demetrius, "in which Thiobulus indicated Robert should find him."

"He likely warned you off the Guild, too, didn't he."

Robert nodded. But Monteous had, too.

"Well, I haven't the least idea where he is. He keeps to himself, and I've always thought that was for the best. He will be your best chance against Trajon Jarl. I'm having a difficult time believing he is even alive, but then, the Guild exiled him for a reason."

He may not be stupid, but Robert thought the man wandered quite a bit in his thought.

Just then, a knock on the wall brought everyone's attention to the doorway, where another old man stood. The lines on his face were not as deep as the ones Master Lamen wore, but his head was bald and covered in liver spots. The lines at the corners of his eyes turned up more than down, as did the ones at the corners of his mouth.

"Demetrius," he said, smiling. "Good to see you. I see you are already conducting business and consuming my wine."

"Lord Taren. Your wine is, as always, impossible not to consume," Demetrius said before raising the glass to his lips and taking a few sips.

Master Lamen took hold of Robert's robe with one clawed hand and pulled Robert close. "I'll send your message," he said. "You just keep that Weave over the top of us, you hear?"

"I will. Thank you."

Lord Taren strode across the room, his posture not bent at all with his age. "Message, Lamen? What news is this?"

"Find a glass or two of wine for yourself, Lord, and take a seat. It's not news to hear standing up."

WHILE DEMETRIUS TOLD their tale, Gerard sipped his wine, though he had no intention of finishing it. He didn't care much for how dry it felt sliding across his tongue. He would have much preferred the ale brewed in Risuk.

Lord Taren's eyes grew wider with every revelation until Gerard thought the old man's eyes might just pop out of his head. They didn't, of course, but when Demetrius was done, Lord Taren sat for long moments in a stunned silence.

But Gerard couldn't keep his mind on any of Demetrius's troubles, even if they belonged to him, too. He had missed so much of it, they seemed remote compared to the imminence of his return to his home.

And across the room from him, holding a forgotten glass of wine, was his only chance to interrupt his father's plans for him.

"I'll have to inform the other lords, and the king, of course," Lord Taren said once he'd come out of his shock. "Is there anything else to be done?"

"Ready yourself for war," said Demetrius. "I can't predict when or from where it will come, but it will come. My bet is on Mrongil, after the spring thaw next year. We think Mrongil's Emperor was behind the strife within the Guild last winter, and ultimately responsible for the death of Monteous Roarke..."

"I heard about his loss. Dreadful."

"If Mrongil and Trajon Jarl are not in league, and Trajon is on his own, Mrongil will take advantage of any weakening of the Guild."

Lord Taren downed the contents of his goblet, then pushed himself up.

"I must see to writing letters, it seems. Jergin will find you rooms for the night. We'll talk more at supper."

When Lord Taren went for the doorway, Gerard put his half-full goblet down and went after the old man.

"Lord Taren," Gerard said, "may I speak with you?"

Lord Taren turned before he got out the door. "What is it, young wizard?"

Gerard looked around, saw that everyone was watching him, including his uncle. Gerard gestured to the door. "Out there?" he asked.

"Of course."

Uncle Bryce scowled, but he didn't get up to follow. He had to have some idea, though. Uncle Bryce had never lacked for wit.

They entered a short hallway that seemed to pass along the back wall of the great hall, and had doors that Gerard suspected would lead to the kitchen.

They were alone.

"All right, what is this about?" Lord Taren asked.

"I..." Gerard stumbled over the words. His tongue didn't want to work. By asking, he would be setting himself against his father's wishes. Though the memories were old, Gerard's memories of his father's fury still sprang vividly to life in his head when he thought about them.

But when he thought about Nina, her devotion to him, how she had never wavered and saved his life—even when he had chosen to leave her—he couldn't imagine being without her. She turned his guts over and over, and spun his brain about more times than he could count.

"What is it, son?"

Spit it out fast, before you have a chance to stumble.

In a low voice, Gerard said, "My betrothed and I would like you to marry us. Tonight, if you would."

Lord Taren blinked his eyes rapidly.

"Tonight? That's hardly enough time to prepare a proper ceremony," he said. "Why me? Why so urgent?"

"I... We would like to be wed before I go home to see my father."

"I suspect you think your father would not approve." Lord Taren's eyes had stopped blinking. No longer surprised, Gerard could tell he was thinking it through.

"My uncle would not approve, either."

"I see. So you want this done without his knowledge?"

"I just don't want him to stop us."

Lord Taren ran his hand over his bald pate and sighed.

"Why should I do this for you? And don't give me any blather about love."

Gerard's heart beat faster. He had not thought that he would have to convince Lord Taren.

"Hurry, young wizard. I must write those letters and get them sent off."

"Nina has been there for me, at my side, while we tried to save Monteous, and again when Trajon Jarl attacked the Academy. She saved my life from Jarl, even after I had told her I was leaving, after I had given her up."

"Why were you leaving?"

"My older brother died. My father wants me to come home to take my brother's place running the caravans. He has a wife already planned for me. I do love Nina, and I don't want her to suffer because of my father."

A few seconds passed before Lord Taren responded. Gerard could feel sweat rolling down his cheek.

"I said I didn't want to hear any blather about love."

Gerard slumped back against the wall.

"What would your father do if you went home with a wife?"

"I don't know. He would probably rage and yell, and he might throw me out again."

"Would you rather be a wizard or drive a caravan?"

"My duty to my family…"

"Answer my question."

When put in those terms, a caravan driver versus the life of a wizard and all that came with it, he knew he would choose being a wizard every time. But he had always wished he had been firstborn, wished he had his father's eye and well wishes.

"It's a simple question, young wizard."

"I always wanted to be first, and now…"

"Do you think your father will treat you any different?"

It was Gerard's dream, but he knew it would be unlikely to happen. Before Gerard had left with Monteous, he had fought with his father, as they always had. The threat of his leaving hadn't changed a thing, and neither had the long absence.

Gerard shook his head. "No. I don't think he will ever change."

"So answer the first question."

"Wizard." It was so easy when he thought about his relationship with his father. He still hoped it would be different, but he had to admit the chance was slim. His father had sent his uncle, and not even a personal letter.

"Well then," said Lord Taren with a twinkle in his eye and a slight smirk. "I think it is my duty to marry you and your young lass this evening, especially in light of the tidings I received today."

"I thought..."

Lord Taren chuckled. "We can't be losing our best young wizards to the very plain task of driving a caravan, now, can we."

"Thank you," Gerard said. "Thank you."

"After supper, and after I've written these letters. You will need witnesses."

Gerard nodded. He knew Angela and Robert would witness.

"It is set then. I will send Jergin for you when it is time."

"Thank you," Gerard said again. They seemed to be the only two words that he could utter.

Lord Taren wagged a finger in his face. "Don't thank me, young man. You may think you know what you're doing, but in my experience, young men eager to marry their loves find out that the other side of the door is quite different than they anticipated. Yes. Quite different.

"Now, I must go draft my letters. If you will excuse me."

The old lord turned and walked away before Gerard could say thank you one more time.

Gerard waited until Lord Taren disappeared through a door at the far end of the hallway before reentering the sitting room.

He only had to keep it from his uncle for a few more hours.

As he entered the room and saw the dark cloud of his uncle's face, Gerard hoped his uncle did not already know. He comforted himself thinking that if his uncle already knew, he would have said something already.

Gerard picked up his goblet and sat next to Nina, but he didn't take her hand, as much as he wanted to. His uncle watched him through anger-slitted eyes.

"What was that about?" his uncle asked.

"Nothing," Gerard lied. "I just wanted to ask him about something for Mother. I'd like to bring her a gift when I return."

His uncle grunted something unintelligible and returned to his wine.

Gerard put his own goblet to his lips and turned it up, consuming the rest, hoping it would take the edge off his nervousness.

He yearned to take Nina's hand and squeeze it in some fashion that would let her know their wedding would happen that night, but he didn't dare.

Only a few more hours, and it will all be over.

✸ ✸ ✸

ROBERT ENTERED THE room he would share with Gerard and Shane. Two large beds with stark white covers dominated the room. A chest of drawers supported a vase with a bouquet of white-petaled flowers. The walls were just as ostentatiously ornamented with wood as every other wall in the place, only the wood in this room had white streaks running through a deep red wine color. He had never seen the like. The flowers and bed covers were obviously meant to compliment the streaks in the wood.

"I wonder what kind of wood this is," he said.

"Goldvein," said Gerard. "It comes from the northern slopes of Risuk."

"You talk about Risuk as if it's a mountain range and not a kingdom."

Gerard laughed. Once they had left the cold stares of Gerard's uncle, Gerard's demeanor had changed drastically. He seemed happier than he had in days, but an undercurrent of fear, or something else, ran through it.

"Risuk *is* a mountain range. There is no part of Risuk that is not mountain."

Robert found his pack just inside the door where one of the servants had left it. He tossed it on the bed nearest the window. He wasn't looking forward to the night.

At first, when Jergin brought them to their rooms, he had wanted to give each a separate room, which would have spread them out around the Manor. They would have been too far apart for his Weave to cover them all.

In the end, Jergin had put Demetrius and Bryce into one room, the girls into a second room on the other side of the Manor. Robert and the other apprentices were put into a room next door to the older men. Angela would maintain a Weave over her and Nina, and Robert would cover the rest of them.

He wasn't looking forward to it, but there wasn't much choice. Shane couldn't quite get the hang of keeping the Weave intact, and Master Lamen, well, Robert suspected the old master would be unable to stay awake for more than an hour.

Shane slipped in behind Gerard and fell back onto the other bed.

"This will be nice," he said. "I'm tired of sleeping on the ground."

"Get off," Gerard said, pushing him to the floor. "This one is mine."

"Who says it's yours?" Shane said from the floor.

"I do," Robert said. "You sleep on this one."

"I thought that was yours."

Robert shook his head. "I'm not sleeping tonight."

Shane scrambled up from the floor.

"I'm sorry. I'm trying, I'm really trying. I don't know why I can't keep the Weave together."

Gerard lay back on the bed and laughed.

Shane spun on him.

"Why are you laughing?"

Robert started to chuckle, understanding why Gerard was laughing.

"Why are you both laughing?"

Shane didn't seem to know which one of them to look at. His head kept flipping back and forth as if it were a flapping shutter in the wind.

Robert hadn't realized it, but now that Gerard had made him think of it, he knew exactly what Shane's problem was, besides being too young for what they were involved in.

"I know exactly why you are having trouble keeping the Weave in one piece," Robert said.

"Please?"

"What are you thinking about when you are holding the Weave?"

"I'm thinking about the Weave."

"The entire time?"

"Yes. Mostly."

"What else are you thinking about?"

Shane looked down. His hair fell forward to cover his eyes. "I don't know. Sometimes..."

"Sometimes you get distracted."

"Yes," he said and then looked up. "But you walk around and talk to people all day."

"Yes, I do. I keep myself focused on the Weave, a part of my mind devoted to it at all times."

"How do you do that?"

"First, you have to learn how avoid the distractions. You must focus on the task, and only the task. Block everything else out, even your own random thoughts. Until you can learn to do that, control over things like this Weave will elude you."

"Fine. It's something I need to work on. So why were you laughing?"

Robert chuckled again, and caught Gerard trying to stifle another laugh.

"Do you want to tell him, Gerard?"

Gerard laughed and sat up.

"The reason we're laughing is because Robert could not keep his concentration for more than five minutes before something distracted him. We all despaired of him ever finishing his apprenticeship."

"Oh," Shane said, then turned back to Robert. "Then how did you learn to focus?"

The mirth went out of the room like someone had opened a window to let the heat out.

"I had no choice," Robert said, thinking back to the hours and days after

Monteous disappeared through the portal, only to be abducted. He wondered what his life would be like had he failed to reopen the portal that allowed Demetrius into the laboratory, had Orliss succeeded in his plans.

"What do you mean?" Shane asked.

Robert looked at the kid, only a couple years older than Wallace had been when he died. The kid in front of him had already lost his master and any number of friends. Shane almost seemed oblivious to it, except that Robert remembered him weeping over Master Wendell's body.

"I'll tell you later," Robert finally said. He didn't want to bring up memories for Shane right now. Robert didn't want to deal with his own.

Just to calm himself, Robert slipped into the vew and checked his Weave. It was still in good shape, protecting them, hiding them from Trajon Jarl. Once he had learned to focus, splitting his focus into parts had come easy. He only wished learning to focus had not come with such a heavy price.

CHAPTER 15

SUPPER SEEMED TO take forever. By the time it was over, Nina thought she had endured as many dark looks from Gerard's uncle as she could possibly stand. His presence at the table made her uneasy. She had wanted to run away from the table as soon as she finished, but that would have been rude and unwise. She needed Angela with her wherever she went. She didn't want to expose them to Trajon Jarl.

While they ate, Angela took over the duties of their protective Weave from Robert. Robert had held it most of the day, and would have to maintain it all night, too, probably without sleep. She knew Angela would have to do the same.

She couldn't understand why that old man Jergin could not find them rooms on the same side of the Manor so that Robert and Angela could trade like they had the last couple of nights. They could all have slept in the great hall, too.

But the bed had looked soft, and if Angela and Robert weren't complaining, Nina would not complain, either.

There was one other thing that kept her at the table.

She simply had to find out what Lord Taren and Gerard had discussed. Nina thought she knew, despite the story Gerard had given about getting something for his mother. She thought Gerard must have asked him to marry them, but if he had, Gerard hadn't given her the answer. He hadn't had a chance. His uncle had hardly left his side while she was around.

It took a while, but eventually, Demetrius distracted Gerard's uncle with a question, and Gerard caught her eye. He pointed at his finger where his ring would be if she had one to give him, and nodded slightly.

Her heart skipped and then took off racing. She felt the heat of excitement reach her face. She had to be turning red.

Nina looked at Angela's plate, and saw that it was empty.

"Angela," she said, "I need to go back to our room."

Her voice brought the dark stare from Gerard's uncle again.

"I... I'm not feeling well," she said, hoping that would explain it all.

"Should we have Lord Taren call for a healer?"

Lord Taren looked her direction. "Is something wrong?" he asked. Nina wasn't sure, but there seemed to be some real concern in his voice.

"No, my stomach is just a bit upset. I think I just need to rest," she said.

"By all means," he said. "You should rest. I'll send Jergin to look in on you in a little while to see if you need anything."

"Thank you," she said and stood up.

Angela stood with her and came to her aid.

Nina didn't have to feign her weak knees. She was going to marry Gerard tonight. He would be hers, and whatever his uncle and his parents had in mind for him, they wouldn't be able to change that.

Angela took up her staff with one arm and put the other arm around Nina and helped hold her up, almost carried her out of the room.

When they were on the stairs that led to their room, Angela looked around quickly. Nina did, too. The stairway was empty.

"What is going on? I saw Gerard do something, and then you flushed. I know you're not feeling ill," Angela said.

Nina couldn't help giggling.

"Lord Taren agreed. I'm going to marry Gerard tonight."

Angela crushed her in a hug.

"I'm so happy for you," Angela said into Nina's ear. "We must get you ready. See if we can get you a bath."

Nina took a deep breath. A bath sounded so relaxing.

They continued up the stairs, arm in arm, around a corner and down the hallway that led to their room.

When they reached the door, Nina stopped.

"I don't have a ring for him," she said in a panic. "I don't even have a dress."

Angela stood back from her for a moment, examining her.

"The robe will do," she said. "It's fitting, I think, seeing as you are an apprentice."

"But a ring?"

"We'll figure something out," Angela said. "Maybe Lord Taren will have something you can borrow for the ceremony."

"But it won't be the same." Nina couldn't imagine telling Gerard he'd have to give a borrowed ring back.

"Does it matter?"

"It's a symbol that says…"

Angela put up a finger to stop her.

"It's just a symbol, Nina. It's not the marriage. It won't change the way you feel about each other, will it?"

Nina pondered that for a long moment, and then gave in. "I suppose not," she said. "I just wish I had something to give him."

"You're giving yourself to him. You already saved his life. What else could he want?"

Nina could imagine more than one thing he could want, things she would be more than happy to give him.

Nina turned and pushed open the door, then stopped dead in the doorway.

Jergin sat on the bed closest to the door, his bulk putting a deep dent in the mattress. Spread out next to him on the dark blue bedding lay a pale yellow gown.

"Lord Taren wished that I bring this to you. It is the gown his wife wore when the two of them married."

"His wife?" Nina asked. It was all she could get out. From the doorway, the gown looked wonderful.

Jergin pushed himself up with a hefty heave which was almost not enough to get him standing.

"Sadly, she passed away a few years ago, but Lord Taren thinks she would have wanted you to wear it tonight."

Nina couldn't help herself. She ran over to the bed, picked up the dress, and held it out in front of her. It had pale blue flowers stitched along the neckline and around the cuffs.

She flipped it around and held it against her. The hem barely scraped the floor.

"What do you think?" she asked Angela. Of the two of them, Angela would know better whether the gown was appropriate.

"I think it looks beautiful, Nina, though I think we need to get you washed before you try it on."

"There is a bath just down the hall," Jergin said. "It is already drawn and waiting."

Nina laid the gown back on the bed, then turned and stretched her arms wide to hug the chamberlain. "Thank you," she said.

"You mustn't thank me. Thank Lord Taren. He won't admit it, but he loves these affairs."

"I'll be sure to thank him, too. How long do we have?"

"I've been told you should expect to hear from me about an hour after sundown. I don't know why you're all being secretive, but Lord Taren assured me it was important."

Nina looked out through the window. The sun still had a hand or two between it and the horizon. Two hours, at least. Enough time. If only her parents could see her. Her father would probably faint at the news.

"We should hurry, then," Angela said. "We don't have much time."

Jergin started toward the door.

"Oh," Angela said, "Jergin. Would you happen to know of a ring that Nina might borrow for the ceremony? We haven't had time to find..."

"I will look into it," he said, and smiled. "I'm sure I can find something."

"Thank you, thank you," Nina said.

Then Jergin stepped back and looked Angela up and down. "I think I might be able to find an outfit for you, as well."

Nina glanced at Angela's apprentice robe, and realized that it wouldn't do to have her best friend wearing a travel stained outfit to her wedding.

"Oh, that would be wonderful," Angela said.

"Yes, yes. Thank you so much!" Nina said.

Is this really happening?

She would be married to Gerard that night, and it didn't seem quite real. As Jergin led the two of them to the bath, Nina whispered to herself, "This is happening. This is happening."

GERARD STOOD AT the door to the great room, his fingers nervously twitching while fingering the cuffs of the coat Jergin had loaned him. The black material had as fine a weave as any Gerard had ever worn, even before his father exiled him.

Robert stood at his side, his staff in hand as it had been for the last few days. Robert looked ever more the wizard, and not the apprentice. It probably helped that Robert wasn't wearing apprentice robes, but clothes that were more suited to someone of greater means. A dark blue coat with brass buttons, a white shirt, and pants that matched the coat. Gerard had been unable to keep the surprise off his face when Robert pulled them from one of his packs and handed them to Jergin.

Earlier, Robert had given Gerard a hug when Gerard first whispered the news to him in their room. Gerard hadn't expected that, either. They hadn't ever been the closest of friends, especially during their duel for Angela's affections. And after, they hadn't seen much of each other.

"I'd like you to witness," Gerard had said.

"I'm honored," Robert said.

And then Robert went to his pack and pulled out those clothes. "Demetrius made me bring these along," he said.

A knock on the door froze the two of them for a moment. Robert gripped his staff.

Shane went to the door and opened it. Outside stood Jergin, and he had a bundle of clothes draped over his arm.

"May I come in?"

"Please," said Gerard.

Jergin entered and Shane shut the door behind him.

"Lord Taren suggested that you might need these," he said, extending the clothes toward Gerard.

Gerard took them. He held them out, and they were finer even than the ones Robert had pulled from his pack. The coat was black, with silver trim on the tails and buttons. The rest were tailored to match. "Tell him I said thank you."

"I'll be certain to," said Jergin. He turned to Robert. "Would you like me to have those pressed?"

Robert seemed unsure how to answer.

"Yes, please," Gerard said for him.

Jergin had then taken the clothes from Robert. "Dinner will be served soon. I will have these back just after."

And then the portly chamberlain had left.

"Lord Taren must like you," Robert said.

Gerard laughed. "Or maybe he couldn't stand these clothes Nendra found for me," he said, pulling at the road stained shirt he was wearing.

Then supper had come, and Gerard found an opening to signal Nina the wedding was on. Her skin flushed red immediately, and Gerard worried that she would give it away, but she had been quick to cover for her distress.

And his uncle had not noticed anything out of the ordinary, he hoped. Just a girl with an upset stomach.

The remainder of supper had frustrated him. He was forced to sit there and listen to Demetrius and Lord Taren talk. Uncle Bryce occasionally provided some input, but he mostly sat and scowled like he had done ever since he lost the battle to keep Nina from coming along. Robert discussed their future plans with Lord Taren and the old wizard, but Gerard had stayed silent. He couldn't even think about the dangers ahead of them. He couldn't think about his father and what battles bringing Nina home to meet him might provoke. He only had room in his mind for his impending wedding.

"When do we go in?" Shane asked, breaking Gerard's reverie.

Robert turned around to look at Shane, who stood behind them. Robert insisted Shane had to come along because they couldn't be sure what Trajon Jarl knew about him.

"We go in when they open the door, now be quiet," said Robert.

Gerard had asked about hiding Demetrius and his uncle. Gerard wanted Demetrius there, but there hadn't been an opportunity to inform him.

Robert had solved the problem by asking for Master Lamen to visit them. Master Lamen assured Robert that he could hide the two men until Robert returned.

Jergin had eventually tapped on their door just after dusk. He gave Gerard some instructions, then bade them come to the great hall, but not to enter until the door opened.

"When will they open the door?" Gerard asked.

"You too?" Robert asked.

"Why are you the one that sounds nervous?"

"I'm not nervous, just..."

Gerard didn't have to see the bags that had formed under Robert's eyes to understand.

"I wish I could help you," Gerard said.

"I know. I wish you could, too. Maybe with another couple years training..."

Gerard slipped into the vew for a moment. He could see the Weave. He could see the energie used to create it. He could, if Robert asked, even help provide some of his own energie to Robert. He had done it before, back when they created the portal to try to find Monteous. But even with the eight years of tutelage he'd had under Monteous, he had never been able to grasp any of the Weaves designed to protect or find. His only strength lay in creating Weaves that could destroy.

"You know that will never happen," Gerard said. "I may not even get more time as an apprentice."

"You might."

That, for some reason, struck Gerard as funny. He couldn't contain his laughter.

"Why are you laughing."

"Because you're right. After my father finds out what I'm about to do, he will probably kick me out of Risuk."

"That's funny?"

"Not really, but..." Another bout of laughter overcame him. He bent over, trying to tame it. It wouldn't do to have them open the door with him laughing like a madman.

But the door swung open while he was doubled over, and in his attempt to stifle his laughter, he caused himself to choke for a second, which brought on a bout of coughing.

Jergin stood to the side of the door. "Are you all right, Master Gerard?"

Gerard coughed a couple more times to clear his throat, then stood straight. "I'm fine. Just a fly in my throat."

"Good. Then we shall proceed."

He held out his right hand discretely and spoke in a whisper. "Take the ring Master Gerard."

Gerard looked down and saw the ring he had made for Nina sitting in Jergin's open palm. Gerard reached out and plucked it from Jergin's hand.

Holding the ring again brought back everything that had happened, and reminded him of why they were standing in the doorway.

He looked up and saw Nina at the other end of the hall, standing just below the dais, Angela at her side holding her staff. Lord Taren stood on the Dais, holding the *Book of Lords.* The long tables had been pushed to the wings.

Nina wore a pale yellow dress that he had never seen before. He guessed it was a loan from Lord Taren just like his own outfit. Someone, Angela, had put Nina's hair up, piled it on top of her head, and held it there with a silver comb. Nina looked as regal as any woman he had ever seen.

"Take a step, Gerard," said Robert.

Right.

Gerard put his right foot forward and entered the room, his laughter forgotten.

ROBERT HAD NO idea how Demetrius managed to get to the great hall without alerting Gerard's uncle to the event, but there he was, sitting on a bench toward the side of the room. Robert only hoped Master Lamen was still outside the room keeping the Weave in place.

Demetrius had his sword with him, as if he expected trouble, but Robert knew Demetrius always expected trouble.

Robert expected trouble, too.

From the time he learned of Gerard's plans, and knowing something about his father's plans for Gerard's future, Robert had kept an eye on Gerard's uncle. The man had seemed to grow more and more irritated and less friendly with each day they spent on the road, especially when Nina was near.

But it wasn't Robert's battle to fight, and he was truly glad to see his friend had found Nina. She seemed to have done some good for him.

He watched Gerard for a moment and wondered just when he had become a friend. Robert certainly wouldn't have used that term for Gerard back when they were under Monteous's instruction. They had been rivals, and both of them knew it.

But even though they hadn't shared the exact same experiences, Gerard was the only person, other than Angela, who knew what Robert had been through last winter.

He decided it didn't really matter when, as he looked at his friend with his face flushed from either nervousness or excitement. It was true now.

They ended their walk down the center of the room just short of the dais.

Nina, in her pale yellow dress and silver comb that kept her hair up, no longer looked like the farm girl she had been when he met her.

But it was Angela that caught his eye. She wore a blue dress instead of the apprentice robe he was used to seeing her in. A pair of silver clips that looked to match Nina's comb held her hair back from her face. Someone had provided her with makeup, too, and it seemed she hadn't forgotten how to use it through all her days as an apprentice.

She looked like the lady she would have grown up to be had her family not thrown her out.

Robert glanced down at his own outfit, newly pressed, and then back up at Angela.

She winked and smiled at him. Apparently, his looks met her approval.

"We're all here, it seems," said Lord Taren.

The lord had dressed in the blue and gold that Robert remembered seeing fly on a flag above the mansion. His house colors. The thick *Book of Lords* did not seem to strain him too much. His did not smile, but the hint of a twinkle flashed in the corner of his eye.

Lord Taren lifted the book up as if he would read from it, but Robert saw that the lord's eyes hardly even glanced at the text.

"In times of prosper as well as times of strife, the duty of a lord requires him to see to all of his subjects with an eye toward improving the lot of all. In this, the duty of performing a marriage between a man and a woman is more than just the binding of those two to each other, but the affirmation that such union will benefit all of the lord's subjects, and ultimately, The Seven Kingdoms as a whole."

"The duty of the husband is to..."

Demetrius turned his head sharply, looking toward the far end of the hall in the direction of their rooms, and Robert stopped listening to Lord Taren.

The others, immersed in the ceremony, did not look.

Demetrius put his hand on his sword, as if he expected trouble.

Had he heard something?

Robert wanted to turn around and look, but he didn't want to interrupt the ceremony.

"It is time for the rings," said Lord Taren.

Gerard reached in and pulled the ring from his pocket. Robert had not seen it up close, but it was gold, and though its surface was plain, it was shaped in such a way that it could be marked later.

Nina turned to Angela, and Angela dropped a silver ring into Nina's palm. Nina couldn't have had the time to make one herself.

The two of them held their rings out for Lord Taren to examine. He took a close look at the ring Gerard proffered. When he looked at the one Nina held, Robert thought he saw a tear form in the lord's eye.

"It is not often that wizards choose to marry. Their duties often conflict with the duties of marriage. But when they do, we celebrate it all the more for it means the strengthening of our lands beyond what we might normally expect."

Demetrius stood up and faced the rear of the hall. Robert wanted desperately to turn around and see what Demetrius was looking at, but he refrained.

Robert missed what Lord Taren said next, but Gerard reached out, took Nina's hand, and slid his ring on her finger.

When he was done, Nina slipped her ring onto Gerard's finger.

"Do the two of you agree to uphold the laws of our land, and the laws of your marriage, until death takes you both?"

"I do," said Nina and Gerard simultaneously.

"Then..."

The loud crash of a door opening sounded from the back of the room.

"By the power vested in me through my..."

Robert spun around.

"I now pronounce you..."

"Stop," Bryce Maracane shouted from the back of the hall. His clothes were disheveled, as if he had just woken up. He had a dark smear of something across his face.

"...husband..." The interruption did not seem to bother Lord Taren.

"You can not do this!" Bryce said.

"...and wife."

Bryce ran toward them. Only then did Robert notice he held a long knife in his hand, its blade stained red and dripping.

Demetrius stepped in front of the raging man, and with the speed that Robert had come to take for granted, punched him on the chin, knocking the bigger man to the ground.

Robert heard the *Book of Lords* slam shut behind him.

Lord Taren stepped off the dais and walked toward the fallen man.

Once Lord Taren stood over Gerard's uncle, he spat on the ground. "You do not tell me what I can not do in my own house or on my land."

Robert's eyes drifted to the blade that had fallen from Bryce's hand and skittered across the floor.

It was covered in blood.

A tremor ran through Robert.

"Master Lamen," Robert said.

He didn't even think before he dashed out of the room to find Master Lamen, in the hope that the old wizard still lived. If he was dead, Gerard's uncle might not live through the night.

Robert wasn't sure the idea bothered him.

CHAPTER 16

ROBERT RUSHED THROUGH the hallways of the manor, panicked about what he would find. He knew, he knew, but he hoped he was wrong. He took the stairs two steps at a time.

At the top, far down the hallway, just outside the room Demetrius was sharing with Bryce, Master Lamen's body lay crumpled on the floor.

Robert rushed to him and barely stopped before he stepped in the puddle of blood that had seeped from the long, ugly slit across Master Lamen's throat. He lay on his side, back toward Robert, but it was all too obvious the wizard was dead. No healer could help him.

The sound of footsteps, slower and lighter than his own had been, echoed down the hallway. Lord Taren hurried as quick as his old bones would let him.

Robert bent down to listen for a breath, any breath, on the off chance he was wrong, but he felt none. He put his hand to Master Lamen's cheek. The heat had already left Master Lamen's flesh.

Another wizard dead, though not by Trajon Jarl's hand, this time, but by one of their own.

Lord Taren knelt, tears spilling down his cheeks, and put his fingers to Master Lamen's dead eyes, closing them. He rolled the body onto its back, exposing another knife wound to the chest.

Gerard's uncle had not just stabbed Master Lamen, he had made sure the wizard would die.

"I'm sorry," Robert said. He felt uneasy being that close to Lord Taren and his grief.

"There's no need for you to be sorry," said Lord Taren. "That man will pay for the murder he committed."

A pair of Lord Taren's guards ran up behind them, their mail shirts jingling. "Master Lamen?" asked one of them.

"Dead. There is a man in the great hall. He will be in the custody of this young wizard's friends. Take him into ours. He shall see trial in the morning, a hanging in the evening."

Robert suspected the trial would not be long.

The guards ran off, leaving Robert alone with Lord Taren.

"Will we have to stay?" Robert asked.

"No. I saw what you saw, and while some might question why the rest of you are not tried with him, it is clear to me that you were not involved."

Robert stood with Lord Taren until Jergin arrived with a pair of men to take care of the body and clean up the blood.

Robert returned to the great hall where he found the others gathered near the dais. A guard stood near the door, dressed in Lord Taren's colors, but Gerard's uncle was gone.

When Robert told them what Lord Taren said, there was little reaction from anyone, not even Gerard. It had been obvious to Robert that the two of them didn't get along, but he had never asked why, and it didn't seem appropriate to ask after what had happened.

"Should we leave now?" Robert asked.

Demetrius shook his head. "No. We have to think about what to do with Shane."

"What?" Shane asked.

"I was going to leave you here with Master Lamen," Demetrius said.

"Why?"

Robert didn't wait for Demetrius to answer. "He can still stay. Lord Taren will see that he finds his way to the Guild."

"But I don't want to stay," Shane said, standing up to come face to face with Robert.

Robert shook his head. "There's no need for you to risk your life with us. Trajon Jarl is not after you."

"Not yet."

"If I have my way," Robert said, "not ever. Trajon Jarl is looking for me. He knows who Gerard and Angela are. I think he even knows about Nina, but there's no reason he would think you are anyone important. You could stay behind, and he wouldn't even notice."

"I don't want to stay behind. Where would I go?"

Demetrius stepped between them. "We are all tired, and with the events of the evening, we have a lot to think about. Go back to your rooms and sleep. We'll figure it out in the morning."

"Could we change the sleeping arrangements?" Gerard asked.

"Why?"

"With everything that's happened, I don't want Nina so far away, tonight."

Robert did not want Angela so far away, either.

"If Nina and I took your room, Demetrius," Angela said, "Robert and I could split the time holding the shield."

"You can sleep in our room, Demetrius," Robert said. Suddenly, the idea of half a night's sleep sounded good to him.

A look on Gerard's face, a slight lessening of the excitement in his eyes, made Robert believe his friend had had different arrangements in mind.

"We'll get our stuff," Nina said, then took Angela by the hand and led her from the hall.

There was little other discussion before the four of them tramped up to their rooms.

They found Jergin still watching over his charges as they scrubbed the floor. The stain was almost gone.

Jergin helped Demetrius move his things between the two rooms, and then went about preparing it for the girls' arrival.

Eventually, Robert sat alone by the window, staring out at a starlit night and listening to the snores of his friends while trying to wipe away the memory of another wizard lying dead on the floor. He had seen too many in the last few months.

The first hour passed slowly. The next two, even slower. He could not stop thinking that there was more to Master Lamen's death than just Gerard's uncle losing his mind.

"You're contemplating something," said Demetrius, making Robert jump.

Robert turned away from the window. Demetrius stood next to him.

"You don't think this was related to Trajon Jarl, do you? I mean, Master Lamen, dead."

"I don't think so. Gerard's uncle killed him. If he had any connection to Trajon Jarl, we'd all be dead now, don't you think? No. Master Lamen was just in Bryce's way, and who his nephew married was more important to him than one old wizard's life."

"How do you think he knew?"

"Bryce wasn't stupid, Robert. Anyone could see the looks those two were exchanging. And when Gerard left the room to talk to Lord Taren in private, his lie when he returned was hardly convincing."

"But I didn't know."

"You've had other things on your mind. Bryce had only this one thing on his mind: getting Gerard home so he could marry the girl his father arranged for him."

"Why would Bryce care enough to murder someone?"

"Duty to the family is terribly important in Risuk. Everything is done for the family. In the dead of winter, they are all you've got to trust. From what I've gathered, Gerard had already left Nina once, at the Academy, when his uncle came for him. I don't know what changed Gerard's mind, but somewhere between then and the time we left Nendra's, Gerard decided to devote himself to Nina. Bryce would see that as a slap in his face, an insult to Bryce's place and Bryce's own duty to bring Gerard back."

"How do you know?"

"I've spent a few of my years in Risuk, including time spent speaking with Gerard's parents."

"Monteous sent you to look in on Gerard?"

"He did."

Robert thought back to the moments and days after Monteous disappeared. They had found a piece of parchment with Demetrius's name on it. But Gerard told them he didn't recognize the name.

"Did Gerard lie when he told us he didn't know you last winter?"

"No. I never met Gerard directly. I asked around about him, including having discussions with Bryce and Gerard's mother and father, but Monteous did not want any of you learning of me. It wouldn't have mattered. Gerard's father wouldn't let me near him, especially after I mentioned the possibility of Gerard becoming a wizard. He wouldn't hear of it, even though second sons in Risuk are generally sent away from home."

"Then how did Gerard become an apprentice?"

"You should ask him."

Feeling properly admonished, Robert held his tongue. Demetrius was right. This was Gerard's story from here on, and it was Gerard's to tell, if he wished.

Robert heard rustling sheets. Gerard sat up in his bed.

"You don't have to ask me," Gerard said. "I'll tell you."

"Did we wake you?" Robert asked.

"No. I haven't been able to sleep at all."

Robert slipped into the vew and checked the Weave while he waited. It was about time to wake Angela for her turn, but he wanted to hear Gerard's story first.

"Like Demetrius said, second sons often have no place at home. They are sent to work with others. I know it sounds contradictory to the family duty that Demetrius mentioned, but it's not. We're sent away, usually to work for friends of the family, or families that we'd like to be friends with. In this way, a web of familial duty is created which sustains all of Risuk.

"But my father and I never got along, and when he sent me away, he sent me to work for a man who would have had me work in the mines. He thought it would tame me, make me more pliable."

Robert chuckled. "I don't think it would have worked."

Gerard laughed. "I didn't think so either. I went to my uncle and begged him to take me in, but he sided with my father and sent me away."

"Then how did you end up with Monteous?"

"Toward the end of that winter, just after my father had told me where he was sending me, an old man came to the door and asked if I would like to go with him to become an apprentice wizard. He knew what my father had decided."

"The old man was Monteous?"

"Yes, though he didn't tell me his name."

"And you went with him, then?"

"No. I told him no. I didn't want to leave Risuk. My feeling that I owed a duty to my family still ran strong, I just didn't think working in the mines benefited my family in any way.

"But when my uncle refused to take me in, I had nowhere else to go. I could go work in the mines and probably die within ten years..."

"Or you could apprentice yourself to Monteous," Robert finished for him.

"I wish I knew then how likely it was that I would die in ten years."

"You're not dead yet," Robert said.

"I've still got a couple years left."

Robert picked up his staff, swung the tip of it in little circles, and watched the shadow created by the starlight streaming through the window.

"And now you're going home again," Robert said.

"I am," Gerard said. "But I'm not going home for duty, anymore. It's something Lord Taren helped me see before he would agree to marry Nina and I. I'm going home to tell my father that I've got a new family, and a new duty."

"You do have a new family, now," Robert said.

"No. Not just Nina. You, too. You and Angela and Demetrius. The whole of The Seven Kingdoms."

Robert set the staff down with a hard thump.

"I had thought to leave you and Nina at your home, so that you could be out of it," Robert said. "He doesn't want you, just me."

"From what I understand, he wants all of us connected to the Guild either dead or in his control. I will not submit to that," Gerard said.

"What about Nina?"

"Nina can take care of herself, Robert," said Angela.

Robert looked up and saw Angela in the doorway, holding her staff. He wondered how long she had stood there listening. It didn't matter. She'd heard enough.

"Nina could never stand against Trajon Jarl," he said.

"An arrow will go through his neck just as easily as it will go through yours. Now, isn't it my turn to take the Weave? You sound like you're about to fall asleep in that chair."

GERARD COULDN'T REMEMBER falling asleep, but it had happened sometime after his conversation with Robert. He knew this because the sunlight woke him when a beam slashed through the window and landed on his face.

He still hadn't come to terms with what Uncle Bryce had done. He hadn't seen the body, but he didn't need to. The blood on the knife was enough to condemn the man.

He didn't look forward to bringing that news to his father. Bringing Nina to him would be bad enough, but he couldn't take that back, and wouldn't if he could.

But his father would be devastated.

He slipped into the vew and stared at the Weave that protected him and the rest of his companions from Trajon Jarl. He wished he could control the energie needed to make the threads of the Weave, but the ethereal energies always felt slippery to him. He couldn't control them unless he bound them with fire or air or water.

But he could be a weapon.

He could do that.

He slipped his legs out from under the thin blanket that had kept him warm overnight, trying not to disturb Shane, who had slept next to him.

Once the sunlight no longer blinded him, he saw Demetrius standing at the window.

"Don't you ever sleep?" Gerard asked, quietly.

"I do not need as much sleep as the rest of you. I..."

Demetrius went silent.

After a few seconds, Gerard couldn't stand it any more.

"You what?"

"I trained it out of myself. When you do what I do, sleep is dangerous."

Right.

Gerard looked at the outfit he had worn for his wedding, wishing he could keep it. Of course, he'd have to give it back, and there wasn't any use for it where they were going.

He put his hand out to pick up the clothes he'd received from Nendra's husband, and caught the flash of silver from the ring on his finger.

It looked to be pure silver, an intricate pattern that resembled the scales of a fish or a drake. He wondered if he'd have to give that back, too. Nina did not have time to make the ring, and she certainly couldn't have afforded it, even if they had passed a shop that would stock a ring like it. They hadn't.

He figured it must belong to Lord Taren.

He would wear it until they were about to leave, and then he would give it back.

He put his clothes on, then stood up and went to stand by Demetrius at the window.

"When do you think we'll be leaving?" he asked.

"We'll give Robert another hour or so to sleep," Demetrius said.

"I want to have a talk with my uncle before we leave."

"Why?"

"He never told me how my brother died. I'd like to know before I go home to face my father and tell him he's lost his brother, too."

"I'm sure Lord Taren would let you see him, but we can't stay long. We need to be on the road."

Gerard understood that.

"It won't take long."

Gerard busied himself with packing his things, not that he had that much to pack. When he finished, he sat down and stared out the window into the courtyard.

He hadn't seen many guards on their way in, but a whole troop of men stood at attention, swords at their sides, all wrapped in Lord Taren's colors. The Lord wasn't taking Master Lamen's death lightly.

Gerard wondered at his own lack of anguish over the impending trial and execution of his uncle. He was family, after all, and Gerard had a duty to him. He should have felt something, but there was nothing. In fact, he realized that he wasn't upset his uncle would be executed. He was upset at his uncle for killing Master Lamen.

By the time Robert started stirring awake, Gerard concluded that the reason he felt nothing for his uncle was that his uncle had already forsaken his family duty to Gerard years ago by refusing to take him in.

"How long have you been awake," Robert asked as he sat up.

"Not long."

"We let you sleep," Demetrius said. "You needed it."

Robert looked over and saw Shane still asleep. "And him?"

"What was the point of waking him up when you were still sleeping?"

"Right."

Someone knocked on the door, and Gerard went to open it.

Jergin stood outside.

"Lord Taren would like to have you come down for breakfast," Jergin said.

"Could I have a chance to talk with my uncle, first?" Gerard asked.

"I shall ask Lord Taren."

"Thank you."

Jergin turned away, and Gerard noticed that Nina and Angela were already standing in the hallway. Jergin must have informed them first.

Robert reached over and woke Shane up, and within a couple minutes, they were all making their way down to the great room.

Gerard held Nina's hand. Her fingers played with the ring he wore.

As he entered the hall, Gerard detected the aroma of fresh bread and eggs and several other foods. One table was laden with plates of pastries, meats, plums, and grapes. Lord Taren sat at the head of the table, patiently waiting.

Jergin met Gerard at the door.

"Lord Taren agreed that you may talk with your uncle, but he thinks you should eat, first. He doesn't want your talk to ruin your appetite. He also says there is business you need to attend to."

Gerard's mouth was watering already, and he wondered what Lord Taren wanted from him. His uncle could wait.

As they approached the table, Lord Taren stood up.

"My friends, it grieves me that such an evil tragedy overshadowed what should have been a festive occasion. Thus, I've ordered a much richer breakfast than I normally would, in the hopes that you will forgive my failings."

"Your failings?" Gerard asked. "It was my uncle at fault."

"Ah, young Gerard. I am the host, and I knew the circumstance. I should have foreseen that a guard should have been in place outside your uncle's room. As angry as I am at your uncle, I am as angry with myself."

Lord Taren seemed to catch himself. He cleared his throat quietly, and then spoke again.

"Forgive me. I did not mean to sour the mood this morning. I meant to raise spirits. First, however, there is one bit of business that we should have attended to last night, but for the events that interrupted us."

He motioned to Jergin, who went to a small table near the wall and picked up a pen, an inkwell, and a parchment.

"What didn't we do?" Nina asked.

"We need to make your marriage official. You must sign the document, and a copy of the document. Your witnesses must sign, and then we will record one in the library, and the other you will keep. You will have something official to show your father when you see him next. He knows me. He will not question it."

Gerard felt gratitude well up in him. He had wondered how he would convince his father he had married for true.

He pulled Nina over to the small table and looked down at the documents. They were identical. Each had a declaration that they had been married by the will of Lord Taren, as well as blank lines for every necessary signature.

He'd never been very good with a pen, but he managed to put his name to both documents without too much blotting. Surprisingly, Nina's signature was better than his. He wondered at how quickly she had learned her letters at the Academy.

Robert and Angela came next, and when they were done, Lord Taren stepped up and affixed his own signature.

"We'll let these dry while we eat, and then, Gerard, you can visit your uncle. I'm assuming you will want to be away before the trial starts."

"We must," Demetrius said. "We need to get these two home, and then we need to find Thiobulus. The longer we stay, the more we put you in danger."

"You think so?"

"If you had seen the Academy, you would understand."

"Then by all means, if we must hurry, then let us hurry."

Gerard spun his ring with his fingers, then took it off.

"Lord Taren," he said, before the lord could get too far away.

Lord Taren turned around.

"What is it Gerard?"

"I just wanted to say thank you, before I forget."

He held his hand out, ring clenched between three fingers.

"What's this?"

"Thank you for loaning us the ring and the clothes and everything."

Lord Taren smiled. "Oh, no. The ring is not a loan. It is a gift. You cannot very well go to your father without a ring and claim that you are married to this delightful young woman."

A gift.

"You are certain?" Gerard asked. He was having trouble believing it. "We can make another, given time."

"From what Demetrius has told me, you do not have time. And if there is one thing I've learned over the years, time is shorter than you think. My wife gave me that ring. I wore it every day, and I wore it even after she died."

Gerard shook his head. It was too much.

"No, I cannot take this."

"She would want you to have it. Fill the drake with more good memories. But remember what I said. Remember where your duty lies."

Gerard slipped the ring onto his finger. And in that moment, it became something more to him. It was a reminder of his marriage, but it was also a reminder of his promises to Lord Taren. Perhaps that's what the old lord intended.

"I will."

The old lord smiled. "Now, let us eat."

✼ ✼ ✼

LORD TAREN LED Gerard and Robert to the small building that he used to hold prisoners. It was made of the same stone as the rest of the manor, but it had bars in the small window in the front, and the stout wood door was banded with iron. A guard stood outside the door, hand on the pommel of his sword.

Gerard gripped his staff tightly. He didn't think there would be any trouble, but after last night, he didn't want to be without what protection he could provide for himself.

Robert had insisted on coming along to provide the shield from Trajon Jarl. They had left the others to prepare their horses, and Angela put up a shield to keep them hidden.

The guard stepped aside as they approached. Lord Taren pulled a key from his pocket and opened the door.

Inside, the building was split down the middle by a corridor. On each side of the corridor, a pair of cells, four in all. Three of them were empty.

"You don't use these much," Robert said.

"No. Most of the lawbreaking takes place in town, and the magistrate handles it. I can't be bothered with every petty crime. But if it's a crime against The Seven Kingdoms, or against me, then it becomes my duty. Men don't stay here long."

Gerard understood. Crimes that ended in the death of the prisoner or crimes that sent the prisoners to the king's prisons.

"You mark me, Taren, this is a mistake." Uncle Bryce's voice erupted at them from the back of the far cell.

"The mistake was yours, Bryce."

Lord Taren ushered Gerard and Robert past him, and then stepped outside.

"I'll leave you to talk to him, otherwise I fear he will be so distracted by me as to not tell you anything."

"It should only be a few minutes," Gerard said. He only had one question for his uncle.

Gerard edged forward, waiting for his eyes to adjust to the low light within the building. There were only two windows in the walls, neither of them within a cell. Their placement left the backs of the cells in near darkness. He wished he had brought a lamp.

"What are you doing here, Gerard? I thought you were running off with that dirty little farm girl."

Gerard gripped his staff so hard his fingers ached after only a couple seconds.

"She isn't a farm girl," Gerard said as calmly as he could. "She's an apprentice wizard, and she's my wife."

"Bah, she's beneath you, Gerard. Our family has the royal blood of Risuk in it, and that girl? That—apprentice? What is she? Just some urchin from the fields of Dominand."

Gerard's chest tightened. His jaw ground his teeth.

He stepped forward into the darkness, toward his uncle's cell.

"Say that again, and you won't have to wait for Lord Taren to judge you," Gerard said.

"You don't have the guts. You never did. That's why you ran away to play at being a wizard. You don't have what it takes to be Maracane."

Gerard felt a hand on his shoulder. It pulled him backward a little.

"Gerard, don't," Robert said.

But he wanted to do something to prove to his uncle that he wasn't weak. He shook, trembled. The whole time, from the moment his uncle arrived at the Academy until now, the man had looked at him as if he were something less. Gerard needed to show him otherwise.

"You're going to listen to him? He's just as low born as that girl you *married*."

He shrugged himself away from Robert's hold, and then slipped into the vew and put a light to his staff. Lamps. Why had he thought about lamps? He was a wizard. He didn't need a lamp to light a room, and he didn't need his uncle to tell him who he was. He didn't need that from his father, either.

He made the light brighter, bright enough that he had to blink a couple times while his eyes adjusted.

His uncle shrunk back away from him. He looked like he hadn't slept. His hair, always somewhat long, hung down in wet strands. His clothing was wet, too. He'd been doused with something, probably to clean him up a bit before his trial.

"Uncle," Gerard said, trying to keep his voice steady. "I must know something before I go home."

His uncle laughed. "You're still going home?"

"Yes, I need to pay my respects to my brother, at least."

Bryce stood tall for a moment, then stumbled toward the bars. "Fine. What's your question?"

"How did Eric die? You never told me."

"I did tell you. He died when brigands attacked his caravan."

Gerard took a step forward, but stayed out of his uncle's reach.

"But that doesn't tell me how. Who were the brigands? Where were they? Did he die fighting?"

"I understand that he died with his spear in his hand, just the other side of the border with Stradetra."

"Who were the brigands, Uncle?"

His uncle threw up his hands. "How am I supposed to know?"

"I had thought you were with him when he died. Why else would father have sent you? He has other couriers he could have sent. He could have sent a letter."

"He sent me to make sure that you came home."

"Father sent you for me as punishment. You were with Eric when he died, weren't you?"

His uncle pursed his lips, pulled them sideways a bit, looking up to the roof of his cell. His head tilted to the side as if he were deciding how to answer, or as if he were listening to someone.

"I was," he said.

Gerard felt the tears, knew they wanted to come, but he held them back. He needed to know.

"Could you have saved him?" Gerard asked.

"He had an arrow through his throat."

Gerard sighed, though not loudly. He hoped his uncle hadn't heard it. "Who were they, Uncle?"

"Brigands. Just brigands. Why do you want to know?"

"So I can do what you didn't," Gerard said.

He knew, if his uncle had brought back the heads of those that killed Eric, his father would not have sent his uncle for him. His father would probably have named his uncle as successor.

"How are you going to do that?"

"I'm a wizard, Uncle, don't you remember?"

His uncle smiled.

"You won't find them."

Gerard stood for a moment, contemplating how much pleasure he would get if he hurled a fireball through the bars.

In the end, he decided it wouldn't be nearly enough.

He spun on his heel and left his uncle behind. It was enough that he knew the man was going to die.

CHAPTER 17

THE SQUAT, WINDOWLESS building in front of Trajon Jarl housed yet another Guild wizard. Buried among the apple trees of southern Dominand, it was far from the nearest road, and far from the nearest town. The sunlight filtered down through the leaves and the fruit that hung from the branches.

By the strength of the wards placed around the building, Trajon knew the ability of the wizard inside was considerable, though not formidable. Not to him. It would not be long before he slipped past the wards and into the laboratory. It would not be long before he held the wizard in his hands, drained the blood from him for use on another day.

It would have been so much harder if they didn't hide from each other, if the Guild hadn't gone so far in restricting the blood arts.

The Academy was the proof. He hadn't had the time to drain the four masters at the Academy. It was such a waste, but he'd had other goals there.

But since the night at the Academy, he had done very well for himself—the wizard inside the laboratory would make number eight.

He smiled at the thought.

How many Guild wizards were there now? They'd numbered roughly a hundred last year, before the Guild split. A third of those that had lived either scattered or came to him.

And with the eleven he'd killed in the last four days, soon to be twelve, how many were left? Forty-five? Fifty at most.

It had been a good four days.

As soon as that boy led him to Thiobulus, as soon as he took that old man's blood, there would be no one left who could stop him, no one to keep him from what should have been his.

Not even the sad little Emperor of Mrongil.

If only he could have persuaded Robert. That boy had no idea what he could be capable of. His shield was impressive, flawless. Every probe turned away. He hated knowing he would have to destroy that boy and waste his talent.

Trajon shook the thought away, to be dealt with later.

"Time to get on with it," he said in a quiet voice.

He dipped into his cloak and felt around among the several vials he carried. Each vial leaked a little energie through the glass and into his fingertips, a signature, unique to the person it had come from. When he found the vial he wanted, he withdrew it from his pocket. He worked the stopper free with one hand, poured a deep red drop of its contents into the palm of his other hand, then stoppered the vial and slipped it back among its brethren.

He dipped a finger into the drop of blood and spread it around in a slowly growing circle until it covered the palm of his hand with a sheen of red.

He reached out to his left, where he knew his staff leaned against the trunk of an apple tree, and placed his palm on the smooth wood. The blood made the bond between him and the staff, infused his every intention, wrapped every weave with the energie of a wizard long dead.

Trajon spun those energies out of the staff and formed a Knife and a Wedge—the Knife to slice the threads of the ward in front of him, the Wedge to push his way through.

Anticipation built in him. His muscles grew tight, like they always did, ready for action. He did not expect trouble, but since that day two-hundred three years ago, when the other members of the newly-formed Guild of The Seven Kingdoms stripped him of everything he had, he prepared himself for any eventuality. He would not be caught off guard again.

He readied the Knife, took a step forward.

Master.

Trajon stopped.

Master, help.

Trajon felt his upper lip curl involuntarily. *That fool normal. A waste of blood.*

He undid his Weaves, let them fall apart. The fool would pay for it later. His blood wouldn't be quite as useful as the blood he'd caused Trajon to waste, but if there really was trouble with the boy, there was nothing to do but waste it.

Well, not entirely wasted.

Trajon licked the blood from his hand, savoring the taste of iron and salt as he absorbed the energie. It wasn't enough for a proper dose, but every little bit helped. Every little bit added just that much more time to his life.

When the hand was free of blood, he wiped it dry on his cloak. He pulled out the Speakstone and found the fool's vial of blood.

A drop on the Speakstone was enough to tell that Bryce was out from under the cover of the boy's shield. He could feel the strength of the connection through his hand. He put the stone to his forehead.

Why do you need my help?

I'm sorry, Master. I'm in a cell. They're going to put me on trial, then execute me.

Execute you?

I killed a wizard.

Not the boy.

No. A retainer of the local lord.

The retainer of a local lord. Unlikely to have been important or dangerous. And now the fool was stuck in a cell. Trajon didn't care if the fool was executed. He felt an urge to jump to the cell and do it himself. But if he gave in to the urge, he wouldn't have anyone to lead him to Thiobulus.

Trajon wanted to vomit.

You are a fool.

Trajon cut their link.

He put the Speakstone back in his pocket and pulled out the Telanderal. He wiped a little of Bryce's blood onto the Telanderal, picked up his staff, and sent his energie through the stone.

Trajon hated the blackness of the in-between. It wasn't like a portal, where the two places connected so that it was like stepping through a doorway. The black of the in-between sucked at you, made time appear to take forever, yet no time at all. He worried what would happen if he somehow got stuck in the in-between—would he go mad? But it had never happened. He'd never heard of it happening.

The jump ended. He stumbled a little. The stone beneath him was uneven, and his foot landed in a small drain culvert.

"Master," said a familiar voice. "I..."

"Shut up. You've cost me some good blood, and I aim to take its measure from you. Your stupidity deserves as much."

"What? Please don't kill me." His voice quavered.

Trajon slapped the man across the face. It felt good, even though it made his hand sting. He wanted to cut the man open, but circumstances prevented that, at least for now.

"I'm not going to kill you, but to get you out of here, I need blood. And when I get you out, you're going to follow that boy, as far as he goes."

"They won't let me travel with them any longer."

"Find a way. Lead me to Thiobulus, and I will forgive many things."

"Yes, Master."

Trajon set his staff aside, then pulled out the small, thin knife he kept. He pulled out Bryce's vial, too.

"Give me your arm."

"I thought you said…"

"I said I needed blood to get you out of here, and the only blood in here is yours. You've failed me, but I'm giving you a chance. Hold out your arm."

Bryce's arm came up. It trembled.

Trajon took it, pulled it straight. The flesh was hot in his hand. He took the knife, set the tip of the blade against Bryce's wrist.

I'll give you a chance, you fool. A chance to serve me the way I should have made you serve in the first place.

"Don't move."

CHAPTER 18

ROBERT COUNTED THE days, five of them, as they rode north, and wondered when the attack would come, wondered when Trajon Jarl would hunt them down and act on his threats. He knew he'd done a good job keeping the shield up, and Angela had done well, also. He just couldn't get the aftermath of the Academy out of his head. He kept imagining Trajon Jarl tracking them down, despite the shield.

It hadn't happened yet.

The first day, about four hours into their ride, he had looked back to discover a large column of smoke rising from what he thought was Lord Taren's manor. He had quickly jumped to the conclusion that Trajon Jarl had found them, that he was on their trail, but Demetrius reminded him that Lord Taren was going to execute Bryce, and that the smoke likely stemmed from Lord Taren's burning the body afterward.

Robert still couldn't get the fear out of his head. It didn't help that, despite what Demetrius said, the man pushed the group a little harder afterward.

Gerard and Nina had frightened the rest of them the first night after they snuck away from the campsite. Robert had woken up to find them missing, but when they they returned, a bit sheepishly with large grins on their faces, it came out that Angela had encouraged them to go.

Over the next three days, they hadn't seen any evidence that gave weight to Robert's fears.

By the fourth day, his fear had faded somewhat.

The ride north presented them with a series of hills that stood ever higher. They passed through tiny settlements that were much like Bird—places to pass the night or gather for a drink. Trees began to appear, at first like lonely sentinels, but later on, they clumped together like they were seeking protection. The trees all leaned away from the mountains of Risuk, as if they were afraid of them.

Near the end of the third day, they crested a hill and came to a stop. In the distance, at least two day's ride, Robert caught his first glimpse of Risuk. The tops of the mountains were still white, and blended in with the haze of the late afternoon sky. The slopes seemed purple, though he knew that couldn't be the case. Gerard had said on more than one occasion that the slopes were covered with trees.

"They're so tall," Robert said. The mountains looked like a giant wall.

"They're taller than you think," Gerard said. "The tallest of them are never free of snow, and the air is so thin it is difficult to breathe."

Demetrius urged them to push on, and after a few moments more, the six of them descended to the valley below.

Every night, Robert spent more time working with Shane, trying to help him master the Weave. Shane was improving, but still each night, he let himself get distracted, and the Weaves fell apart.

It frustrated Robert. Maintaining the Weave during the day, with only half a night's sleep each night, was exhausting him. Angela tried to take the Weave for longer and longer periods, but it wasn't enough, and she too was showing the strain of sleepless nights.

By the fifth day, the road no longer climbed up and over the tops of the hills. The hills had grown too tall and too steep. Instead, the road met up with a river, then meandered along with it through a valley which led them on a path north between the hills.

Just after mid-day the valley grew littered with giant stones, many larger than a man. A pile of these stones forced the road to bend away from the river and traverse a hillside.

"I've never seen stones this large," Robert said.

"Sometimes," Gerard said, "when the mountains shake, giant boulders are flung from the their flanks. They bounce and roll their way into the valleys."

"The mountains shake?" Robert asked.

"Sometimes," he said. "They are treacherous. They don't want the weak living on their flanks, so they test us."

"You make it sound like you think they are alive."

"Some say so. The older women, they believe it."

"You don't," Robert said.

"Who's to say?"

Demetrius turned in his saddle. "There are places of power, here in Risuk. The land bleeds molten stone. I have seen it. Whether the mountains are alive, I cannot say."

The road wound past another large outcropping of stone. On the other side of the outcropping, the road narrowed as it clung to the edge of a steep hill. The road descended as it went, then switched back so that it ran practically underneath them. Robert felt like he could have leaned over and spit on the road below.

But it wasn't the road below that captured his eye. It was the town, very nearly a city. It had claimed the valley below between the river and the near cliff face they were descending.

Walls of thick stone surrounded the town. Robert could see every house from the road, many of them more than two stories tall with steep roofs and tall chimneys. Looking down, he could see the people walking the streets. From his vantage point, they looked much like ants as they wandered through a maze.

"Treading Valley," Gerard said. "We are on the border of Risuk."

"We're staying here tonight," Demetrius said.

Robert didn't like the idea. The bed would be nice, but he felt the pressure of Trajon Jarl hanging over him. He needed to find Thiobulus soon.

"Why? We have a whole half of the day before night time."

"We need to purchase more appropriate clothing for the trip into Risuk."

"Why?"

"Two reasons. It may be summer, but as you go higher into the mountains, the temperature drops. If we must go very high, we could find ourselves freezing to death at night."

Robert looked up, and from here, the snow that topped the tallest mountains nearly sparkled in the summer sunlight.

"You mean we might have to travel through snow?"

"I don't think so, but we should be prepared. Like Gerard said, the mountains are treacherous."

"You said two reasons," Angela said.

"The second is that wizard's aren't very well liked in Risuk."

Robert looked over at Gerard. Gerard had never mentioned that.

"Why?"

"During the Unification wars, Risuk did not have the number of wizards that the other kingdoms did. The ones they did have turned against them."

Robert looked at his friend and wondered if a dislike of wizards had spurred his father to send Gerard to the mines when Monteous expressed interest in Gerard.

He decided to change the subject. Talking about these things out in the open didn't feel right.

"Demetrius," he said, "we should be able to find clothes quickly and move on. We don't need to stay the night for that."

"True, but there is another reason to stay."

"And what is that?"

"Here is where I start my search."

"For Thiobulus?" Robert asked.

Demetrius nodded. "He has been known to visit Treading Valley. It will be useful to know if he has been through recently. If he hasn't, we can probably skip coming back."

"If he has?" Gerard asked.

"If he has, then we will have decisions to make."

"If he has," Robert said, "we should follow the trail from here."

Gerard opened his mouth, but Demetrius spoke before any words came out.

"If he has been through here recently, it does not mean we should start looking for him here, Robert. And I think it would do little harm to escort Gerard and Nina home. But like I said, we'll make that decision when we know more."

Robert wanted to protest more, but kept his mouth shut. Demetrius was right that it wouldn't matter until they found a trail to follow, and a memory of the man just disappearing in front of him surfaced. If Thiobulus used that trick often, he wasn't likely to leave a trail to follow.

When they reached the valley floor, Robert saw the walls of the town from a new perspective. They were built from the giant stones they had passed in the surrounding valleys, stacked upon each other, three or four high. A formidable defense. Robert imagined that only a wizard could have built them. A strange thought, considering what Gerard had said about how the people in Risuk viewed wizards—unless the walls were built before their wizards turned on them.

They weren't defended, though. Not even one guard stood outside a rusted iron gate that looked like it hadn't been closed in years.

"Do they close the gate at night?" Robert asked.

"No," said Demetrius. "There are guards that patrol, of course, but they want travelers inside the walls. Since the Unification of The Seven Kingdoms, there has been little need for defense. Treading Valley is a border town only in the histories, now."

The buildings inside the walls all had highly sloped roofs, all covered with wood planking.

"Why are the roofs so tall? I noticed them from the road, above, but down here, they seem even taller," Robert said.

"In the winter, the snowfall can be deep, and it doesn't melt quickly. The steep roof helps the snow slide off to the ground. If it didn't, they would collapse under the weight."

"How much snow?" Angela asked.

"As tall as a man, sometimes," Gerard said.

Robert had thought the snowfall they saw last winter had been deep. He couldn't imagine so much that he could not see over it.

"How do they go anywhere?" he asked.

"Lots of digging, unless a wizard is about," said Demetrius.

Woe to any wizard who happened by, Robert thought. Removing that much snow from the whole town would not be easy.

"How do the wizards help? It seems it would be a lot of work."

"Remember how I said they weren't well liked?"

Robert nodded.

"Well, they mostly don't help."

"Then why mention it?"

Demetrius laughed. "Because if you happen to get stuck here during the winter, they'll want you to help."

As they rode through the town, Robert noticed people watching them. The looks weren't quite unfriendly, but the townsfolk definitely seemed suspicious of them. Angela, Shane, and Nina still wore their apprentice robes, and four of the group were carrying staves. Robert felt exposed under their stares.

Demetrius led them to an inn, the Laughing Drake, and the five of them waited outside with the horses while Demetrius entered and negotiated for their rooms. Robert kept an eye out, watching the people of the town as they passed on the street.

Their stares were beginning to make him feel uneasy. In some cases, he thought he saw malice in the stares. He wanted off the street. He wanted to hide his staff, the staves of the others. He wished Demetrius would hurry.

He glanced down the street the way they had come. A man stood at the corner of a building, half hidden behind a stack of barrels. He was staring at the group of them. With the distance, Robert thought the man looked like Gerard's uncle.

But that couldn't be.

He climbed up the steps of the inn to get a better look. From the top step, the man looked even more like Gerard's uncle, but there was something different, too. He didn't look healthy. His face was whiter than Robert remembered, his hair, too.

"Robert," Gerard said. "What are you doing?"

Robert glanced down at Gerard.

"Come up here. There's a man back there that looks like your uncle."

Gerard came up to stand next to him.

"Where?"

Robert turned back to look and point the man out, but he had disappeared. Robert scanned the other people on the street, but none were the man he had seen.

"Where, Robert?"

"He's gone," Robert said.

"It couldn't have been him," Gerard said. "Lord Taren would not have let him go."

"Of course not," Robert said in an effort to make sense of it. There would be many people that looked and dressed like Gerard's uncle did in Risuk, and from a distance, a resemblance was possible.

But Robert still worried. The man had looked too much like Bryce, even with the changes in his face and hair color. He hadn't any idea what would do that to the man, but he remembered the smoke they had seen behind them that first day, and he remembered the ruins of the Academy, and he remembered the oddly bloodless body of Master Wendell.

Demetrius emerged from the inn. He had a smile on his face.

"Take the horses round back to the stable, then come inside and eat."

Robert took one look back down the street, hoping the man would reappear, but was greeted with only unfamiliar faces.

Maybe he was just tired, but he decided he'd tell Demetrius about it just the same.

DEMETRIUS SAT AT the table, watching over the young wizards while they ate a meal of elk haunch and rabbit-berries. Exhaustion lay plain on Angela's face, and Robert wasn't doing much better. Keeping the shield up had taken a toll on them, but it would be days, at least, before they could ease up.

Demetrius could get them more sleep, however. They could take a day or two for that, he thought. It would give him time to find any traces of Thiobulus.

He was thinking about Thiobulus, wondering what the man would think when Demetrius appeared, when Robert put his fork down and addressed him.

"Demetrius. Outside, while we were waiting, I thought I saw Gerard's uncle down the street, like he was following us."

Demetrius tried not to react in a way that would alarm them. While it was unlikely Bryce had escaped and was following them, he'd seen stranger things happen, and that column of smoke they had seen the first day after leaving Lord Taren's could have been something other than Bryce's burning body.

"You're certain it was Bryce?" he asked.

Robert shook his head. "I only saw about half of him, before he ducked out of sight when I looked away. His coloring wasn't right either. He looked pale."

"It could be someone that resembles him. We *are* in Risuk," Demetrius said.

"That's what the others said. But I thought you should know."

"I'll keep an eye out," Demetrius said.

He plopped one of the tart rabbit-berries into his mouth. The berries were tiny, but the flavor exploded on his tongue. One of his favorite things to eat in Risuk. It was unfortunate they didn't travel well.

Robert watched him for a moment, and Demetrius pretended at a lack of concern that he didn't feel. Once Robert turned back to his food, and the conversation at the table turned to other topics, Demetrius allowed himself to turn the possibilities over in his head.

He didn't like his conclusions.

While it could have been anyone, and it could have been the result of fatigue, Demetrius could not put the possibility aside that it was indeed Bryce. If Trajon Jarl had somehow become aware that Bryce was with them when they separated, Trajon could have found him. From the tales Demetrius had heard from Thiobulus, and even from his own experience, there were things that a wizard using proscribed Weaves and Works could make a person do, and Trajon had been a master of those.

He wanted to go out, search for Bryce, verify that Robert was just hallucinating, but Robert and Angela needed sleep and rest, and he didn't dare leave without them. He could not be sure that the *gifts* Thiobulus had given him would protect him against Trajon Jarl. He certainly knew that they wouldn't hide him.

When they finished their supper, Demetrius suggested that Robert and Angela could let each other sleep a couple hours extra before swapping their turns maintaining the Weave. They could all use the time to get extra rest.

And while they rested, Demetrius would work out how to search for Thiobulus, and for this ghost that Robert had seen.

CHAPTER 19

THE DAY WAS warm, though cooler than the past few. Thin, high clouds had moved in overnight. They didn't do much to block the sun, but they seemed to hold a promise of at least a few days of respite from the summer heat.

Robert was glad of it, too. As soon as Robert had awoken, Demetrius had pulled him from the room, made sure he ate, though it was lunch and not breakfast, and then took him out onto the streets to find clothing for them all.

"Where are we going?" Robert asked.

"The market district. I'm hoping we can find a merchant with clothes already made. I don't think we want to wait around to have them made for us."

No, Robert didn't want to wait at all, though he would like another night of decent sleep. It would help with the rest of their trip into Risuk.

While they walked through the town, Robert couldn't keep himself from looking for Bryce. He had a constant feeling someone was watching him, but each time he looked around, *everyone* was watching him, and not a one of them was the man he was looking for. It was the staff, he knew, that drew their attention.

At one point, he looked at Demetrius, and saw that Demetrius's eyes were constantly shifting, watching the crowd, looking for danger. Of course, Demetrius always seemed to be watching everything.

When they reached the market district, it was far different than the one he was familiar with in Dominand City. In Dominand City, the market was split into two streets that ran parallel to each other. It was crowded and difficult to walk through. You had to watch your back, or the pickpockets would pick you clean of everything you had just purchased.

But the market in Treading Valley had a central square, with room for hundreds of people. There were a dozen shops on each side of the square. The shops weren't open to the air, like they were in Dominand City. They were closed up, a sign hanging over the front door declaring what they sold. There weren't any hawkers in sight, and while the square wasn't empty, you could move through it without coming within two horse-lengths of anyone if you chose.

The center of the square had a raised platform, a stage.

"Do they hold plays on the stage?" Robert asked.

"Not the kind of plays you might see in Dominand," Demetrius said, "but yes, they do have actors that perform on holidays. Come, let's get this over with."

Demetrius walked toward the far side of the square, leading Robert to a shop fronted by a sign engraved with the image of a coat and needle and thread. Robert followed Demetrius, but looked back over his shoulder at the stage.

"I would like to see the kind of plays they perform," Robert said.

Robert liked plays, liked seeing the actors and watching the stories unfold. It seemed a sort of magic, how they fooled the mind into thinking what it saw was real, that the story was important. The backdrops they used gave him a way to see the other lands, places he had thought to never see.

But here he was, looking at a stage in another land.

"Perhaps, if they stage one in the next couple days," Demetrius said.

They reached the shop door, and as Demetrius pulled it open, Robert took one last look at the stage and saw the whitish figure of Bryce again.

"Demetrius," Robert said, "I see Bryce."

"Follow me in." Demetrius said, with no trace of urgency in his voice. "Try not to look like you've noticed him."

They entered the shop, and let the door close behind them.

Demetrius went to the window and looked out between a pair of mannequins wearing heavy clothing, to peer through the leaded glass of the shop.

"Hello," said a smooth, high pitched voice. "How can I help you?"

Robert turned to find a man taller than him, thin, and obviously not a native of Risuk. The man's black hair was combed to the right and greased with something so that it didn't fall into his eyes.

"A moment, please," said Demetrius.

"Do you see him?" Robert asked, turning back to the window.

Robert had to wait a tense moment or two for an answer.

"Yes," Demetrius said. "I think you are right. It does seem to be Bryce."

"What's he doing?"

"Standing and watching."

Demetrius extracted himself from the window.

"How could he have escaped?" Robert asked. "Lord Taren wouldn't have let him go, would he?"

"I don't think Lord Taren would have let him go free. Lord Taren and Master Lamen were close. Master Lamen was with Lord Taren for nearly thirty years."

"Then how is he here?"

Demetrius ignored his question and turned to the shopkeep. "We are going north, into the mountains. Would you happen to have the appropriate garments we would need? There are six of us, four men, two women."

"I will need your sizes," the shopkeep said. "I do not keep enough in stock to fit you all, but with your sizes, I can have them made for you by the end of the week."

"We don't have that long," Robert said, then took his own peek through the window.

A few more people wandered through the square than before, but Bryce stood where Robert had first seen him. He stood still, much like a statue.

"My friend here is right. We only have two days."

"Two days? I need measurements, time to purchase the cloth."

Bryce turned his head, like he had seen something out of the corner of his eye, or was talking to someone next to him. But he soon turned back, his eyes focused on the shop again. Robert wondered if Bryce could see him in the window.

"You can measure us here and get started. Later this evening, you can meet us at the Laughing Drake Inn and take the measurements of the rest of our group. You have friends, suppliers. You should be able to get what you need quick enough," Demetrius said.

"But that will cost extra."

"The Guild will take care of it," said Demetrius.

"The Guild?" the shopkeeper asked. His voice sounded full of vitriol. "Guild credit is worthless here. I won't see another one of you for weeks, and I'll need money now, if you want these items in two days."

"How much?" Robert asked.

"To get started? Fifteen Crowns. That's just for you two."

The amount startled Robert, and he pulled out from the window to look at the man.

"That's robbery," said Demetrius. "I see items in your shop that you could sell us. Eight crowns is more than enough."

"Those are just for showing what is possible. They are not for sale. Thirteen crowns for the two of you."

"Ten crowns," Demetrius said, "and twenty more for the others. If you don't like it, we'll visit your competitors."

The man winced when Demetrius made his threat. "There is no need for that," said the shopkeep. "Thirty crowns should be just fine."

"It's still robbery," Robert said. He had never heard of Monteous spending more than a crown or two for their robes and other items. He had more than enough crowns in his pouch back at the inn, but the price the shopkeep was asking would severely deplete it.

"No, Robert," Demetrius said. "It's acceptable for what we are asking."

The tailor pulled a string from his coat pocket and walked up to Demetrius. The string had a series of knots tied at regular intervals. "Let's get you measured."

Robert peeked through the window again, and Bryce was still standing in the same place. He apparently wasn't moving until they left.

"Demetrius," Robert said. "Why would Bryce be following us?"

"Perhaps he's hoping to catch Gerard and Nina alone at some point," Demetrius said.

Robert turned away from the window. The tailor pushed Demetrius's arms up and wrapped the string around Demetrius's chest.

"That's what I'm talking about. Why isn't he back at the inn? Why is he watching you and me?"

Demetrius turned his head to look at Robert. Demetrius's eyes had a dark look to them, one that seemed angry.

"Keep an eye on him. Let me know if he leaves."

Robert turned back to the window and looked outside.

This time, Bryce was gone. Robert scanned the whole of the square, the shadows around every storefront, but saw only the citizens of Treading Valley.

"He's gone," Robert said.

"Are you done?" Demetrius asked the tailor.

The man scribbled one last note, and then pulled the string from Demetrius's neck.

"I'm done with you."

"Stay here," Demetrius said. "Get measured, and then head back to the inn."

"Where are you going? Aren't you afraid Trajon Jarl will find you?"

Demetrius put his hand to the door and pulled it open.

"I'm afraid Trajon Jarl already knows where we are."

Demetrius slipped out the door and let it shut behind him.

A shiver crept through Robert's muscles.

"Arms up," said the tailor.

ANGELA LAY ON the bed, her hand clutching her staff, and stared up at the rafters. The bare beams were painted a dark red color, the color of a fire-drake, Gerard had said. To Angela, it looked closer to the color of blood.

Shane sat by the window, looking out on the street. He'd been quiet for days, hardly speaking, and not speaking to her at all, which she thought strange.

Gerard and Nina sat in a corner of the room on a pair of pillows snuggling with each other and talking in quiet voices. Angela tried not to look at or listen to them. It only made her wish she had the same time to spend with Robert, but with their sharing of the shield weave, one or the other was always occupied. They could never just forget everything except each other. She wished she could have gone to the market with him, but she needed to stay with the others, keep a shield over them.

And if she paid any attention to what Gerard and Nina were doing, she knew she'd start to resent it.

After breakfast, as they sat at the table toward the back of the common room, Demetrius suggested that the four of them retire to their room and stay there until he and Robert came back from their trip to purchase appropriate clothing for the group. Angela had been happy to follow Demetrius's suggestion, but Nina asked why they all couldn't go. Demetrius told them to look around the room.

Angela hadn't had to. She had already noticed that the people of Treading Valley were not very friendly to them at all. The other guests eating in the common room had seated themselves as far away from their group as possible, and kept glancing at them as if they were diseased. Angela had been waiting for a fight to break out. It hadn't happened.

"Oh," Nina said.

"It will be worse outside, at least until we get you new clothes."

When Demetrius and Robert left, the rest of them went up to their room without any further complaint.

Angela wished she had a book, a love story or something, where two lovers, after much adversity, came together.

It was what she imagined for her and Robert. It was what she saw in Gerard and Nina.

"Angela," Shane said.

"What?"

She shifted herself a little on the bed so she could see Shane better.

"Why do you think I'm having so much trouble learning to maintain the shield? Robert keeps trying to teach me, and I sometimes think I'm getting better, and then it just falls apart."

Angela sat up. It was a good idea, anyway. She was still tired enough that she might fall asleep laying down.

"What does Robert say?" she asked.

"He says that I'm distracted."

"You are distracted," said Gerard.

"Stay out of this Gerard," Angela said.

Gerard scowled at her, but Angela ignored him.

To Shane, she said, "Do you think you're distracted? There have been a lot of changes, lately."

She tried to put it delicately, and wondered if she succeeded. She remembered the days and weeks after Monteous died. She hadn't realized she'd come to love the old wizard so much. She had been upset when they kidnapped Monteous, but a part of her had still known he was alive. Seeing his body burn upon that pyre had sealed any futile hope he would come back. Even wizards didn't come back from the dead.

"I guess so," Shane said. "But I want to help so badly."

"What do you think is distracting you?"

Shane stood up and came over to the bed.

"Do you mind if I sit here?" he asked, indicating a spot next to her.

"No." She did, but she wasn't going to refuse him.

"Sometimes," he said in a softer voice, "I still think about Master Wendell. I'm holding the Weave, and Robert's instructing me, and then Robert says something that reminds me of Master Wendell."

"I know how that feels," Angela said. "I was a wreck for weeks after Monteous died."

"What was it like being his apprentice?"

Angela couldn't decide how to answer the question. The only thing she had to compare it to was the Academy, and that was so different as to not be comparable at all.

"I'm not sure how to answer that," she said.

"I mean, Master Wendell used to say things about him, talk about how he had the ear of the king, that he got all the best contracts from the Crown. Was that true?"

"I wouldn't know," she said. "The king never came to our laboratory, and while he had a lot of work that we helped him with, he rarely told us who it was for."

"He let you help?"

"Often. The last thing we helped him with was the portal that led to his abduction. I made the solution. Robert made the focus."

"I heard Robert opened a portal on his own," he said. "Master Wendell told me that wasn't possible, that no apprentice could have done it. He said it was just rumors and lies."

"He didn't do it completely alone," Angela said.

"I knew it."

"I made the solution. Gerard helped him make the focus. But when it came time to open it, Robert *did* do that on his own, and he did it the same day he and Gerard made the focus. Even Monteous didn't try that. It drained Robert."

"You're not putting me on, are you?"

"She's not," Gerard said. "I was there. You can ask Demetrius, too, when he gets back."

Shane went silent, and turned away from her.

Angela watched him and wondered what he was thinking. She remembered the vehemence he'd displayed after she spurned him back at the Academy. That seemed to be gone, but she couldn't be sure what had replaced it.

Without turning to face her, Shane said, "No wonder you like him."

Her first instinct was to become indignant, and indeed, fury at him ran through her. How dare he say she only liked Robert for his ability, for his power.

But that faded quickly, and she hoped Shane hadn't seen it on her face.

She didn't have to imagine how alone he was feeling right now. The loss of his master, the Academy, his place in the world. She knew how he was feeling. She had felt the same way when her parents blamed her for the actions of the man that had used her, blamed her and discarded her.

It was Monteous at first, and then Robert, who had been kind to her.

"I don't love him because of what he can do," Angela said in as caring a tone as she could manage. "I loved him before he could do what he can now. He was kind to me when I came to Monteous, and he's always been there for me, even when others haven't."

"Hey, now," Gerard said.

"Go back to nuzzling Nina," Angela said. "I didn't say anything about you. I could, though, if you want."

Gerard made a face at her, but did take her advice and went back to paying attention to Nina.

"He once told me that he often got distracted," Shane said.

"He did. He couldn't complete any difficult task at all. The littlest things would make him lose his concentration."

"You?"

Angela laughed, then thought about it. Maybe she had been part of it. Robert had never told her so, but that didn't make it untrue.

"Maybe so," she said.

And then she realized what Shane was saying.

"Wait," she said. "Am I distracting you?"

He turned back to face her. "Not all the time, but sometimes..."

His eyes were looking at her face, circling around her own eyes. He wouldn't bring them to meet hers.

"I do like you, Shane. More than I did when we were at the Academy..."

"But you love Robert."

"I do."

Her arm wanted to reach out and comfort him, but she held it back. She didn't want to give him any hope.

"I just feel so alone," he said.

"I know. We'll solve that, but first, you have to learn how to focus, even when I'm in the room."

He laughed. "Sure. Like it will snow in the summer."

"Gerard," Angela said.

"What?"

"Those mountains we're going to, does it snow in the middle of summer up there?"

"Sometimes," he said.

Angela offered Shane a smile. "See? You ought to be able to focus while I'm next to you. Go get your staff."

"Why?"

"We're going to solve this problem. Maybe I can teach you. Maybe if you're listening to me, you won't be distracted by me."

Shane looked dubious, but he got up and retrieved his staff from where it leaned against the wall.

"Okay," she said as she slipped into the vew. "Start the Weave. I've seen you do that much."

If this worked, if she could teach Shane, then they'd all be better off. He needed something to take his mind off his loneliness. She hoped an accomplishment might do the trick.

✹ ✹ ✹

AS SOON AS the tailor finished, Robert peered out through the window again, seeing neither Demetrius nor Bryce.

He was about to slip out the door when he heard the tailor politely cough.

"My crowns?" the tailor said.

"I don't have all thirty, just six," Robert said, dipping into his pocket.

"I'll take what you have," said the tailor. "If you do not have the rest when I visit your friends this evening, I will not take their measurements."

"I have the rest at the inn," Robert said.

He pulled the six Crowns from his pocket and handed them to the tailor.

"That will get me started, I suppose. The rest tonight."

Robert didn't know why the tailor repeated what they'd already agreed on, and he was in a hurry, so he left. He had to see if he could track down Demetrius.

He knew he should head back to the inn, but he had to know about Bryce. He had to find out why Bryce was watching Demetrius and him, and not watching Gerard and Nina. And he had to find out why Demetrius thought Trajon Jarl had already found them.

Robert had put together that Demetrius thought Bryce might be working for Trajon Jarl, but Robert couldn't believe it. Why would Gerard's uncle be working for Trajon Jarl? Why would Trajon Jarl need *him*, of all people?

It didn't make sense, and yet, it did. Bryce had been at the Academy when Trajon Jarl attacked it. Bryce had killed Master Lamen for no apparent reason. And Bryce had never been friendly with any of them.

All that explained why it was plausible Bryce could be working for Trajon Jarl, but it didn't explain why, nor did any of it explain why Trajon Jarl would need him.

Robert worked his way across the square to the spot where he had seen Bryce standing. There was nothing to find. Low cut grass surrounded the tree, but the grass had sprung up since Bryce had left, as if he hadn't stood there at all. Not even a broken blade.

It wouldn't have mattered, anyway. There were enough people walking through the market square that any tracks Bryce might have left would soon be lost.

"How can Demetrius track a man when the man doesn't leave any sign?" Robert asked himself.

He scanned the square, trying to learn if, from this new perspective, he could discover anything that might help him find Bryce or Demetrius, but all he saw were shops, people, and side streets.

For once, he wished he had not spent all his time indoors with Monteous learning to control himself and energie. He wished he'd spent time in the rest of the world like Demetrius had.

Robert gave up searching and decided to head back to the inn. He wouldn't find either of them.

As he left the market, he let his eyes drift over the shopfronts, wistfully. He'd given all his crowns to the tailor, and had nothing left with which he could get something nice for Angela.

Watching Gerard and Nina every night since they were married had been like a tiny splinter in his finger. Inflamed, but impossible to get out. When he was awake, Angela slept, and when she was awake, he had to sleep. When they were both awake, they'd been traveling and had little time to talk.

It didn't help that he'd finally figured out that it was Angela that distracted Shane most of the time. Shane had a hard time taking his eyes off her. Robert didn't blame him. Robert couldn't take his eyes off her either, or, he hadn't been able to when he was Shane's age. He'd managed to master himself since then.

He would have mentioned it to Shane, but thought the embarrassment of being discovered might make his problems worse. He didn't want Shane to think he was jealous, either.

But he'd have to figure out something, soon, or hope that Thiobulus would take them all in.

Robert turned down an alley that he and Demetrius had used to get to the market square. It was thin—two people could pass side by side within its confines, but a cart would never fit. The height of the roofs blocked most of the light.

He didn't notice he'd walked into the shadows, intent as he was on solving the riddle of Shane.

He felt strong arms wrap around him, bind his own arms tight to his body. Robert smelled smoke, and a hint of decay, like the man who held him had been sleeping in garbage.

Robert tried to turn, but whoever had him only squeezed harder, making it tough for Robert to breathe.

"You'll stop squirming little wizard, if you know what is good for you." The voice, cracked as it was, sounded familiar. It sounded like Gerard's uncle.

"Bryce," Robert said with what little breath he had left. "What are you doing? How did you escape."

"Now is not the time for stories. Save your questions. My master needs an answer, and it is past time to give it to him. He says you are good at hiding, but you can't hide from me, you see. What will it be?"

The voice did belong to Bryce, but there was something wrong with it. The words didn't seem right.

Robert did not need to ask who Bryce's master was, but he wanted to stall, and it wouldn't hurt to have his deduction confirmed.

He slipped into the vew.

"Who is your master?" Robert asked.

"You know who he is. The master wizard, the one who will rule."

Trajon Jarl. It could not be anyone else.

Robert found the energie he wanted in the stones around him and in the light at the end of the alley.

He directed it through the staff, then sent a tiny bolt of fire from the tip of the staff to the hands holding him.

Bryce laughed, each contraction within him only tightened the grip he had on Robert.

"Fire will no longer work on me, little wizard. My master has seen to that."

"Just leave us alone, Bryce. You don't really want to do this," Robert said. "We won't send you back to Lord Taren."

"Lord Taren? That silly lord is dead, his whole manor burned to a cinder. He should have never put himself in my way," Bryce said.

The revelation was a shot to Robert's stomach. Lord Taren hadn't put himself in Bryce's way. Robert had led Bryce to him.

Focus. Think about that later.

Robert calmed himself, and tried to think of other options. He could try lightning, but he would likely hurt himself in the process. Wind would be ineffective, he suspected.

"Have you been working for Trajon Jarl all along?" Robert asked, trying to delay until someone else entered the alley, or until he could think of another way to free himself.

"You wizards think you're so smart. My master will wipe you off the land. You will pay for your aggressions, for your arrogance. Answer my master's question. Will you join him, or will you pay the price like the others?"

"Robert!"

Demetrius's shout caused Bryce's grip to loosen a little, allowing Robert enough freedom to spin around and break from it.

A knife sprouted from Bryce's side just as Robert fell away and tumbled to the ground.

Bryce growled, turned, and ran down the alley and into the sun where he disappeared around a corner.

"Are you hurt?" Demetrius asked.

Robert shook his head.

"He's working for Trajon Jarl," Robert said.

"Get back to the inn," Demetrius said. "Stay out of alleys."

Then Demetrius dashed off after Bryce, leaving Robert to climb to his feet on his own.

He had taken a bruise or two in his fall, but they didn't bother him. It was something Bryce had said. Something about aggressions. That and the looks he received as he left the alley. People were standing there, watching. He hadn't seen them, but they had seen him, and they weren't going to come to his rescue.

And for the first time, he worried that the people of Risuk didn't just distrust wizards, but that many of them actively disliked wizards and would do anything to see the Guild fall.

The eyes he felt on him became all the more malevolent as he pondered what Bryce said. Once he returned to the inn and made his way to their room, he was happy to shut the door behind him.

CHAPTER 20

GERARD JUMPED UP when Robert entered the room and slammed the door behind him. Everyone else in the room turned to look at Robert, too. Robert's clothes were a mess, there was a rip on his right arm.

"What happened, Robert?" Gerard asked, at once excited and concerned by the prospect of a break from watching Shane struggle with the shield.

"It was your uncle," Robert said.

Gerard's breath caught in his throat.

"How is that possible?"

"I don't know."

Robert strode across the room and looked out through the window.

"Demetrius and I saw him in the market square, and we were watching him while we haggled with the tailor. But he disappeared."

Gerard went and stood next to Robert. He peered out through the window, too, but saw no sign of his uncle. Just the citizens of Treading Valley going about their day.

"Demetrius saw him, too?" Gerard asked.

"Yes. We looked away, only for a moment, and he disappeared again, just like at the steps. Demetrius went after him."

"That's why he's not back," said Angela.

Robert shook his head, but didn't turn away from the window.

"No," said Robert. "While I was walking back to the inn, your uncle attacked me. He had me. I couldn't do anything. Demetrius found us, somehow, and threw a knife at him. Bryce ran. Demetrius followed him."

Angela came over, put her finger through the hole in his sleeve. "Are you all right?" she asked.

"I'm fine. I'm worried about Demetrius."

"Why didn't you go with him?" Gerard asked. "Aren't you worried about Trajon Jarl finding us?"

Robert stepped away from the window and sat down on the bed. His shoulders slumped, and he stared at the floor.

"Trajon Jarl already knows we're here. Your uncle..."

Gerard waited a moment, but it didn't seem Robert would finish.

"He tracked my uncle here?"

"No," Robert said. "Your uncle is working for him."

Gasps filled the room, but not a one of them was Gerard's. He stayed silent, shut his eyes tight, tried to make sense of what Robert had said. But it just didn't make sense. His uncle was a good man, even if he didn't much care for wizards. And Gerard knew he didn't.

"I don't believe it," Gerard said. "He doesn't like wizards. Why would he work for one?"

Most of his family didn't like wizards.

"He told me he wanted to see the Guild destroyed."

That made a little sense, but it didn't seem like his uncle at all. But one more thing didn't make sense.

"How is he even alive?"

"I don't know, but he seems different. His voice, it's rough, cracked. He's as pale as if his skin had never seen the sun."

"Why did he attack you?" Angela asked.

The room went silent while they waited for Robert to answer.

"He wanted my answer," Robert said and then looked up. "He wanted to know if I would join Trajon Jarl."

"So what do we do?" Gerard asked.

The door swept open and Demetrius entered the room, closing it behind him.

"Stay hidden," Demetrius said. Unlike Robert, Demetrius was calm as always. "We still need those clothes, and I must still look for Thiobulus."

"But he knows where we are," Robert said.

"Once the tailor finishes with us tonight, I'll find us another inn, and we'll stay there."

"Aren't you worried about Trajon Jarl? Bryce knows where we are."

Gerard wondered the same thing, though he still had a problem with the idea that his uncle was working for that vile wizard.

"It does pose some concern, but I think Trajon Jarl has another agenda."

"What do you mean?" Gerard asked.

"I think, if Trajon Jarl wanted you dead, Robert, you would be dead already. I think he's waiting for you to do something, or he wants you running so that you aren't in his way."

"What could he be doing?" Gerard asked.

"Murdering wizards, I suspect, just like Master Wendell and Master Lamen."

Demetrius put his hand back on the door latch.

"Where are you going?" Angela asked.

"I'm going to try to find a trace of Thiobulus. And if I can find your uncle, Gerard, I'm going to kill him."

Robert stood up. "You didn't kill him?"

"No. He tossed my knife aside and disappeared. Not even a trail of blood." Demetrius seemed like he was about to say more, then stopped.

"I thought you could track him."

"Working for Trajon Jarl appears to have given him some advantages. I'll find him, though."

"He's immune to fire," Robert said.

Demetrius looked at Robert quizzically. "Are you sure?"

"I tried to Weave fire into his hands to make him let me go. He just laughed at me."

Demetrius swore. "I had hoped that wasn't the case."

"What?" Gerard asked.

"One of the reasons Trajon Jarl was expelled from the Guild two hundred years ago was because he refused to give up the use of the proscribed Weaves. One of the Weaves he mastered was reanimating and controlling the dead."

A shiver ran through Gerard, and he caught the same movement in everybody else in the room.

"That's not possible, is it?" Robert asked.

"Are you saying my uncle is dead?" Gerard asked at the same time.

Demetrius nodded, an answer to both questions.

Angela snuggled herself up against Robert. Gerard felt the same need for comfort; only Nina was still sitting across the room. Her eyes were wide with horror, but when she saw him looking at her, they seemed to fill with sympathy.

He didn't need that, though.

"What that means, though," said Demetrius, "is that he's not immune to fire. He just can't feel it. If you make the flame hot enough, he will burn. You do have a defense."

That relaxed Gerard a little, but not nearly enough.

"What else can Trajon Jarl do?" Shane asked.

"More things than I can recount to you right now. We'll talk about it later. Now, I must see if I can find Thiobulus. Keep an eye out. Don't let Bryce near you."

Demetrius slipped out the door before anyone said another word.

Gerard looked around the room at his friends, and he didn't know how to feel. His uncle. Was his uncle responsible for the destruction of the Academy? His family? What about his father? Was his father working with Jarl, too?

"Should I even go home?" he asked himself aloud.

Everyone looked at him.

He felt they all knew what he was thinking, but not a one of them answered him.

NINA FELT TRAPPED in their room, much like the rats she used to trap back on the farm. She sat up against Gerard near the window, but the window was far too small to have a good view. Gerard's uncle could easily slip past their notice and be at their door and through it before they had any idea he was near.

She glanced at her bow where it sat just within reach, a quiver of arrows against the wall next to it. If she had enough warning, she could put a pair of arrows through him before he crossed the room, but if what Demetrius had said were true, she doubted arrows would stop Bryce. Demetrius's knife hadn't stopped him.

The whole idea that Bryce lived, but didn't, chilled her. What else could this Trajon Jarl do that she had no idea was possible? She wished she knew what had happened to Lord Taren. He'd been so nice to her, between loaning her the clothes and giving them the ring for Gerard. She couldn't wish anything bad on the man. She felt that if anything had happened to him, it was their fault.

And Bryce, Bryce had been there with them. They had brought him. He'd been alive, but Robert seemed to think Bryce might have been working for Trajon Jarl even then.

She could not help wondering what she had put herself in the middle of. Her father had tried to warn her that a wizard's life was not a safe life, but her father had lived adjacent to that life for as long as Nina could remember. Her father didn't hate wizards, he respected them. He was friends with some of them.

"Gerard," she whispered.

He looked at her with his sharp green eyes, the eyes that had drawn her to him that first night last winter.

"What about the rest of your family? Will they hate..."

"Shhh. Everything will be fine, I'm sure of it," he said. He didn't sound sure of it. "My mother will love you."

"What about your father?"

"My father had plans for me. He won't be happy at all, but I don't think it will be because you're a wizard."

She snorted. "Hardly a wizard. Are you sure? Everyone here seems to dislike us."

She reached out and took his left hand. The strength in it, though not that of a farmer like her father, felt good to hold on to. She couldn't help toying with the ring on his finger.

"Most of the people of Risuk distrust wizards. During the Unification, our wizards left us to join the Guild. They went and fought elsewhere, even while Risuk was under siege from Stradetra. We know how to hold a grudge."

"That was two hundred years ago," Nina said. "Surely things have changed."

"They have," Gerard said. "A hundred years ago, a wizard didn't dare set foot in Risuk, or he would be mobbed and killed."

"Why did you want to become a wizard, then?"

"I didn't, at first. It was the better of my choices."

"I'm glad you changed your mind," she said and smiled.

He smiled back, then bent over and kissed her. It made her heart flutter every time.

"If I hadn't changed my mind, I would never have met you," he said.

She kissed him, wishing as she did so that there was somewhere more private to go.

And then, she wished she hadn't thought of it, because it brought back all her worry about what had happened to him.

"Do you think Lord Taren is still alive?" she asked.

"What? I hope so," he said. "Why are you asking that?"

"I was just thinking I wanted time alone with you, like that first night after we left Lord Taren's, when we snuck away from the others. It led to thinking about the smoke we saw, and then about your uncle."

"My uncle," he said and turned away from her to stare out the window.

She waited while he watched, wishing she hadn't brought them back to that subject again. Gerard hadn't had an easy life. She wanted to make it easy for him from here on, but the world conspired against her.

She glanced across the room. Robert sat next to Angela, but Angela slept. The two of them needed the rest. She wondered how much longer they could keep it up. If only she could help, but she knew there wasn't much she could do. She'd slipped into the vew a dozen times to look at the Weave of their shield, and it was far too complex for her, even if she were capable of directing that much energie.

She had even watched when Shane tried to hold the Weave. He could form it, but up until Angela had helped him, he had not been able to hold it for more than a few minutes at a time. He lasted longer with Angela's help, but it still wasn't enough. Eventually, Shane's Weaves fell apart.

"I wouldn't be surprised," Gerard said, "if my uncle murdered my brother, or arranged for the brigands to attack the caravan."

"What?" Nina asked.

"He was there," Gerard said while still looking out the window. "He was there when my brother died. My uncle said Eric took an arrow through his throat. Maybe he did. But maybe my uncle put that arrow there."

"Why would he do that?"

Gerard turned toward her, and she caught a tear in his eye. He wasn't crying. He wouldn't do that, but she could tell he felt like it.

"I'm not sure," he said. "Maybe he thought that my father would turn the business over to him with Eric dead. If he thought my father hated me, that he would never bring me back... With what my uncle said about Trajon Jarl being his master, I could believe anything of him."

"But you don't know," Nina said. "Maybe Trajon Jarl got to him after..."

"Maybe he did, but it makes me wonder, and it makes me worry."

She knew then where his thoughts were heading. Even with what Gerard's father had done in driving Gerard away, Gerard still wanted to make his father proud, and if he could believe that Bryce could kill his brother, then he could believe Bryce capable of anything.

She pulled him to her, put his head between her breasts. "Your parents are fine," she whispered, hoping she wasn't lying to him. "They're fine."

DEMETRIUS RETURNED RIGHT about the same time the tailor arrived to take measurements. Demetrius looked more ragged than he normally appeared. Robert wanted to ask him why, but he felt uncomfortable questioning Demetrius with the tailor in the room.

So Robert took Demetrius out of the room, down to the dining room, and sat him down with a pint of mead. Robert ordered a glass of milk. He couldn't afford to let the shield Weave come apart from the swimming head a pint of mead would give him.

Robert's staff drew attention, but kept people seated at a distance.

The innkeep must regret letting us stay.

After Demetrius took his first sip, he set the mug down in front of him and said, "Nothing."

"Nothing?" Robert asked.

"I couldn't find a trace of either Thiobulus or Bryce."

Robert slumped back in his seat. A sliver poked him in the shoulder, but he ignored it. The news from Demetrius was not what he'd hoped.

"What do we do now?" he asked.

"I will keep looking until we have our clothes. Just because I didn't find a trace today doesn't mean the trace isn't there. I may not have been talking to the right people, or was not in the right part of town. I don't know. When Thiobulus used to come here..." Demetrius looked down at his mead and stopped.

"What? What were you going to say?"

Demetrius sighed.

"When Thiobulus came here, to Treading Valley, he would stay in this inn. I had hoped to find a trace of him here, but I found nothing."

"When did Thiobulus come to Treading Valley?"

Demetrius took a long pull from his mead, then set the mug back on the table. He shut his eyes. He looked reluctant to answer the question.

"Demetrius?"

Demetrius kept his mouth shut, but he opened his eyes. They wandered, looking everywhere but at Robert. It was unnerving behavior from a man who had not showed fear once in the time Robert had known him. Robert wondered what could make the man afraid to answer the question, or perhaps it was something in the room.

Robert turned and looked, but there wasn't anyone in the room besides patrons of the inn.

"Demetrius, answer the question."

"A hundred years ago," Demetrius said. Then he promptly took another long drink of his mead. It had to be nearly gone.

Robert wasn't sure what to think. It didn't make sense.

"A hundred years ago? This place doesn't look a hundred years old." And then Robert thought of something else. "How do you know it was a hundred years."

"The inn was rebuilt after a fire about twenty years ago," Demetrius said, ignoring Robert's last question.

"How do you know, Demetrius? You make it seem like you know Thiobulus. You say you know how to find him. You say you know he was here a hundred years ago. How do you know?"

"I knew him," Demetrius said. His eyes were looking past Robert, though.

"You knew him? Why didn't you tell me?"

"It was a long time ago."

"Dammit, Demetrius. Stop being evasive. You knew him. When? How?" Robert knew he should have stopped there, but he couldn't. "I thought

I could trust you, Demetrius. I'm trying to find this wizard and I know almost nothing about him, but you say you knew him? Why didn't you tell me before?"

Demetrius toyed with his mug, running his finger up and down the side.

Robert waited for him.

"I didn't say anything," Demetrius said, "because you would find out eventually. I didn't need to tell you."

"What would I find out?"

"That I worked for Thiobulus before I worked for Monteous."

"How long ago?" Robert didn't want to ask the question. It had to have been a long time, judging by his comments about the inn. It would make Demetrius older than he seemed, but Robert needed to know who the man was—who they both were.

"Two hundred years, give or take. I've lost count."

Stunned wasn't the word for what Robert felt. He wasn't sure what he felt. Two hundred years. From about the time Trajon Jarl was kicked out of the guild and exiled.

"How?"

Demetrius stared into his mug.

"Please, Robert. Let it lie."

"Demetrius, wizards can live long lives, but I've only heard of two that have lived so long as you are claiming: Trajon Jarl and Thiobulus Soake. And you're claiming to be nearly their age. I can't let that lie, Demetrius. How is this possible? You aren't a wizard."

"No, I'm not a wizard. I am something else," Demetrius said. "I'd rather you hear what I am from Thiobulus himself. He'll tell you if you ask. He might tell you anyway."

"But..."

"Please, Robert. I will tell you if you persist, but it is a painful thing for me, and I don't want to think of it. I also would not be able to answer all the questions you will have. Thiobulus can."

Robert sipped the last of his milk, wishing it was mead.

"One last question, then, and I will leave it be."

Demetrius looked up at him.

Robert watched Demetrius for a moment. He didn't look like the competent man Robert knew him to be. He looked scared, vulnerable.

"Did Thiobulus do this to you, whatever it was?"

Demetrius nodded.

"And you don't like it."

"No, I don't."

"But you've lived a long life, longer than anyone but Trajon Jarl and Thiobulus Soake." Robert said.

"There was a price to pay," Demetrius said.

"What price?"

"Please, Robert."

"All right. I'll ask Thiobulus."

"Thank you."

They sat there, Robert staring at the milk he no longer wanted, Demetrius staring into his empty mug.

It was hard not to keep asking questions of Demetrius. He had so many of them, but he didn't want to make Demetrius upset, either. Demetrius was the only one he knew that could find Thiobulus.

"I've been wondering about something else," Robert said.

Demetrius looked at Robert without lifting his head up.

"Why do you think we'll find Thiobulus in Risuk if they don't like wizards? Why would he come here?"

"Because he knows no other wizard wants to come here."

Which made a sort of sense. But it still seemed an odd choice. It meant that Thiobulus had chosen to exile himself, much as he had participated in exiling Trajon Jarl. But it fit with what Thiobulus had told him when they met in the snow by the river: *Guild politics. You'll be better off if you stay well clear of them. I certainly do.*

But that meeting also told Robert one other thing. Thiobulus wasn't a complete exile. He spent time enough in the rest of The Seven Kingdoms to know who Monteous was, and to be in some tiny town at just the moment to see Robert in action.

Robert had to wonder if Thiobulus had arranged to be in Ferry Town at just that moment, if Thiobulus had known what would happen.

But if Thiobulus *did* know, then why wasn't he making it easier to find him now that Robert had a real need.

"No more questions, Robert?" Demetrius asked.

He had a lot of questions, but he didn't want to annoy Demetrius. He needed the man, and he felt like he might have pushed too far, earlier. As much as he was surprised that Demetrius hadn't left to tell the king about Trajon Jarl, Robert felt like he might never find Thiobulus without Demetrius's help, and he had no desire to turn him away.

So he shook his head.

But he would keep a close eye on Demetrius and try to slip in a question now and then that might tell him more about Demetrius's relationship with Thiobulus.

Unless they found Thiobulus before he had his answers. Then he'd have to hope that Thiobulus would answer his questions.

CHAPTER 21

ROBERT SPENT THE next two days worrying that Trajon Jarl would appear, burn down the Laughing Drake, and kill them all. They tried to move to a different inn, but the other two inns in Treading Valley would not take them in. Once the innkeeps saw who and what they were, their rooms were suddenly full.

Demetrius hadn't appeared particularly bothered, but it ran Robert's nerves to their breaking point, and everyone else seemed worried, too. Not a one of them liked being cooped up in their room.

Of course, Demetrius wouldn't be bothered. While the rest of them waited for the tailor to finish their clothing, Demetrius spent those two days on the city streets, looking for any indication that Thiobulus had passed through more recently than a hundred years ago.

He came back empty-handed each day.

He found no trace of Bryce, either.

When Robert speculated that Bryce had left, Demetrius disabused him of the idea.

"Bryce will not give up until Trajon Jarl does, or until his body is destroyed," Demetrius had said.

On their third morning in Treading Valley, word came from the tailor that their garments were ready for them. They packed their things and eagerly left the Laughing Drake.

The tailor had prepared two sets of clothes for each of them. One set was lighter and would help them blend in with the people in Risuk. Robert's set included a pair of dark breaches, a shirt made of a thin wool died light blue, and a light coat to match the pants. These he put on immediately.

The other set had thick, fur lined pants and a heavy coat that came down to his knees. This coat had a fur-trimmed hood that Demetrius said would keep the worst of the snow off him.

"We have to worry about snow?" Angela had asked.

"We could be in Risuk for a while, and if Thiobulus is hiding in the mountains, we are certain to encounter snow," Demetrius said.

"You will need the heavier coat when we get into the mountains, anyway," Gerard said. "Even during the summer, it can get cold at night."

But it wasn't cold that day, and they packed their heavier clothes onto their horses and left Treading Valley. Robert was disappointed they had been unable to find any sign of Thiobulus, but he was glad to be moving again. With the threat of Trajon Jarl hanging over him, staying in one place had been nerve-wracking, especially since he had spent most of the time worrying about Bryce, too. He knew Gerard's uncle was out there, somewhere.

"Bryce will follow us, won't he?" Robert asked Demetrius.

"Until we kill him or Trajon Jarl calls him off."

"Which isn't likely, is it?"

"No," Demetrius said.

"Where are we going next?"

"We'll escort Gerard home, and then we'll go on to the last place I knew Thiobulus lived."

"Where is that?" Gerard asked.

"Beyond your father's home, near Broken Thunder Ridge," said Demetrius.

"Up there? Even we don't go there, Demetrius. It's too dangerous. Ice falls, rock slides. The wind up there blows constantly."

"I suspect that is why he chose it."

"And the real reason for the winter gear," Angela said.

Demetrius nodded.

"How long will it take us to get there?" Robert asked.

"A week to Gerard's home, another four days to the ridge, assuming the weather holds."

"That's why you hoped to find a trace of him here," Robert said.

"I would have preferred not to go to the ridge."

Robert agreed. It didn't sound like the kind of place anyone would want to visit, which was probably the point. Thiobulus had isolated himself from the world so that they couldn't find him, even if he sometimes went out in it.

The path out of Treading Valley traced the river as it wound through ever taller hills. The hills thrust up on either side of the river, occasionally with multicolored rock faces exposed where the river had cut into them.

"Are we in the mountains yet?" Robert had asked once when the cliff faces hung above them and the hills were taller than any hill he had ever seen.

"No," Gerard said. "We're still in the foothills."

And then the road climbed the side of a hill to avoid a massive, ancient rockfall. The view in front of him opened up and showed him the southern face of the mountains—a wall of stone and trees, capped with snow and ice. When he had seen them before, Robert had felt awed by them, but now, the mountains were close enough that he could see the individual trees. The mountains blocked out the sky, and stood three to four times again the height of the hills they were traveling through. He understood why Gerard had called their current perch a hill.

They continued on, and the road descended back into the river valley.

As they traveled, the trees grew taller and closer together until they all but blocked the sky from their view. Once in a while, they found a hole in the tree cover, which afforded them a view of the mountains towering above them. With each successive opening, Robert could do little but marvel at how tall the mountains were.

The wind picked up as the day progressed, eventually growing strong enough to slow their progress. Robert had to shield his eyes from dust and the tiny little needles that the wind stripped off the trees. Once, he glanced up and noticed that the branches all bent south, and the north side of most of the trees was barren.

When asked about it, Gerard said, "The wind blows south off the mountains nearly every day and the branches grow with it, or they break off."

At twilight, they found a spot to camp off the road, among the trees. The mountains loomed over them, now. It seemed they rose straight up from the foothills. They weren't more than an hour away, Gerard told them, but Demetrius wanted to wait until daybreak to enter.

"When we get there," Demetrius said, "you'll see that the river and the road lie in a ravine that winds its way through the pass. The sides of the ravine keep the lower part of the pass dark for much of the day. The road climbs rapidly once we cross the threshold, and the temperature will drop as we climb. I'd rather wait until we're rested before we attempt it."

So they made camp and ate a meal of hot stew that Gerard and Nina prepared. When Robert saw that Angela had finished her meal, he handed off control of the shield to her, and rolled up in his bedroll for the night.

He had thought the looming mountains, their bulk black and oppressive against the stars, would keep him awake. But as he lay on the hard ground hoping to sleep, it wasn't the mountains that bothered him, but the thought that they hadn't seen Bryce in four days.

Eventually, after everyone else but Angela had fallen asleep, he gave up on getting any sleep of his own. He rose from his bedroll and went to Demetrius's side. He reached a hand out to shake Demetrius awake, but Demetrius rolled over and looked at him.

"I'm already awake," he said.

"I'm having trouble sleeping," Robert said. "I can't help thinking that Bryce would have tried something by now."

"Go to sleep, Robert. I know your worry, and I'm keeping an eye out."

"But your eyes were closed."

"At night, I hear things before I can see them. Go sleep. We have a long climb tomorrow."

"I'm watching, too, Robert," Angela said.

She'd been listening.

Robert went to her and hugged her, gave her a small kiss, felt her warmth against him in the rapidly cooling night air.

"Go to sleep, Robert. I need sleep, too," she said.

"Right," he said.

He went back to his bedroll, laid his head down, and tried not to think about Bryce.

Sleep did not come quickly.

WHEN SHE LOOKED up through the trees, in one half of the sky, Angela could see stars. An enormous wall of mountains, a gigantic black mass, blocked the other half of the sky. It was eerie, like part of the sky had gone missing, like something had eaten all the stars.

The nights were colder here than they had been south of Treading Valley. She was glad for their new clothes. She used the thick coat she had been given like a blanket across her shoulders. It kept her warm enough that she wasn't shivering. She didn't close it up, though. It was still too warm out for that, but it wouldn't be for long.

The hours after the others went to sleep were her least favorite of the day. It was getting harder for her to stay awake as the nights without a full rest piled up. The stay in Treading Valley had helped, but it wasn't enough.

She worried every night that she would fall asleep before it was Robert's turn to take the Weave.

But the Weave wouldn't protect them from Bryce.

She wanted to talk to someone. Demetrius had said he would still be awake, but he looked for all the world like he was asleep.

"Demetrius?" she whispered.

Demetrius sat up, his shape touched only a little by the dying light of the coals left over from supper.

"What is it, Angela?"

Angela moved and sat down next to him so she wouldn't wake the others while they talked.

"You and Robert were talking about Bryce. I had thought we might have lost him," she said.

"I don't think so," Demetrius said. "I don't know where he is, and I would have expected to see him by now, but he's still out there. Unless Trajon Jarl is using him for some other task, I have to believe he is following us."

"Why would he follow and not attack? He attacked Robert, didn't he?"

"It seemed like an attack, but he didn't actually hurt Robert. Trajon Jarl is playing a game, and Bryce is one of his pieces on the board. I expected to be attacked long before now. That we haven't been worries me."

Angela looked past Demetrius to the road. The sound of the nearby river and the high-pitched droning of the crickets filled the silence.

"What should we do if Trajon Jarl attacks?" she asked.

"Run," he said. "You can't hope to defeat him."

"What about Robert?"

"Robert needs to know what Thiobulus can teach him to have a chance. I don't know if Monteous could have survived an encounter with Trajon Jarl."

Angela shivered, and snuggled deeper into her coat.

"Why do you say that?"

"Trajon Jarl was a master of proscribed Weaves and Works, and he is at least as strong as Monteous in his ability to control all the other energies. He was the reason the proscribed works became proscribed."

Angela couldn't help checking on the Weave, verifying that it was still intact and that she hadn't let any of the threads slip. It wouldn't matter against Bryce, though.

Bryce.

"Demetrius? What if Trajon Jarl's purpose for Bryce is to follow us?"

"It would make holding the shield pointless," Demetrius said. "And if he's out there watching us, you and Robert are wasting your energie on the shield, and you'll be far less capable of protecting yourselves."

Demetrius stood up. "I'm a fool," he said.

"What are you doing?" Angela asked.

"I'm going to find him, and I'm going to make sure that Bryce doesn't follow us any further."

"He knows where we're going," Angela said.

"I'm not worried as much about whether Trajon Jarl knows our destination. I'm worried about him knowing where we are right this moment."

Demetrius looked around the campsite, then out into the forest.

"One other thing," he said. "Wake Gerard. Make him stay up with you and keep watch for Bryce. If I find him, he may come your way."

"Should I wake the others?"

"No. Robert needs his rest. Too many of us up and about might wake him."

Angela nodded and went to Gerard's side, carrying her staff and her coat with her. She started shaking him awake.

"Gerard," she said. "Wake up."

Gerard started to stir.

"Demetrius," she said, still with a soft voice, "What do we do if Bryce comes here?"

Demetrius didn't answer. She looked up, and he was gone.

"Why are you waking me up?" Gerard asked.

Angela started explaining it to him, all the while looking out into the trees.

DEMETRIUS BEGAN HIS search by backtracking their trail to the road. When he reached the road, he followed its edge, looking for points where the terrain would force Bryce back to the road in order to continue following them.

From what he remembered about these creatures that Trajon Jarl created, they couldn't just disappear. They left trails, especially in the wilderness. In the city, it was easier for them to hide among the refuse and the detritus. The cobblestones didn't take footprints. But on the road, which was often just dirt, and in the forest, the creature that Bryce was would leave prints and broken branches and other signs in its wake.

Demetrius didn't need the help that the moon gave him when it rose, but he was thankful for it anyway. The light would make his job a little easier.

About a mile down the road, the cliffs to his right squeezed the road right up against the river on his left. He started his search there, checking both sides of the road, looking for footprints that led off of it and into the forest. He searched for broken branches, stones that had been disturbed, anything that might give him a trail to follow.

He followed a couple false trails where travelers had left the road to camp before he came across a fresh trail that led into the forest.

He followed it, thinking at first it would be another false trail, but his hopes rose when the trail turned north along the road about a hundred feet into the trees.

Whoever, or whatever, had made the trail hurried their pace once they were off the road, as if they were trying to catch up with someone.

Demetrius had traveled about two thirds of the way back toward their camp when he came upon an old, gnarled tree that sprouted stumps of long broken branches. Moonlight shone on a bit of white at the tip of one particularly pointy stump. At first he thought it was clothing, and he bent in closer to get a better look.

It wasn't clothing at all. A chunk of flesh, white and bloodless, had been ripped from something as it hurried past. It had the stink of decay. Another day in the summer heat would turn it putrid.

Bryce.

It had to be the traitor's trail.

Demetrius pulled out his knife and followed the trail. He moved a little slower than he had, not wanting to stumble across Bryce if the man had come to a stop. He knew he was getting close to the campsite and that Bryce might stop at any moment to avoid being seen.

Then Demetrius noticed that the crickets nearby had stopped chirping. The rushing crash of the river still echoed in the distance, but the forest around him had gone still.

He sniffed the air. His nose wasn't quite as perceptive as his ears. The sweet smell of the rock pines came to him, carried along on an undercurrent of decay.

Demetrius took hesitant steps, eyes searching constantly for Bryce. He hid behind trees where possible, slipping from one to another in quick flits of speed.

He skirted a giant tree that could have hid two of him behind its trunk, and stopped.

Twenty feet down the trail, Bryce crouched behind a tree that had fallen to the ground long ago. Bryce faced the campsite, watching the apprentices. Demetrius could see them from where he stood, shadows in the clearing.

Gerard was awake and standing next to Angela, but they were facing the river, away from Bryce. If Bryce decided to charge them, they might not see him until too late.

Demetrius checked the wind. What little breeze there was blew in the right direction—down the mountain and away from him. It wouldn't carry Demetrius's scent to Bryce. But it carried Bryce's putrid stench to him.

Demetrius couldn't wait any longer. There was a risk, there was always a risk, but he had the monster in view and anything or anyone with a link to Trajon Jarl threatened them all. He just had to hope Bryce had not seen him leave and hadn't the hearing to know what they had talked about. It was difficult enough for Demetrius to judge the hearing of people who did not have his gift, let alone the abilities of something already dead. From where Demetrius stood, he could have heard every word, had Gerard and Angela been speaking. If the creature Bryce had become was breathing, he would have heard it. But he could not know if Bryce would hear him.

So Demetrius took silent steps toward Bryce, hoping Bryce wouldn't turn around, hoping the creature didn't realize he was missing from the campsite.

Fifteen feet. A few more steps. Eight feet. Another step.

Bryce turned around. Branches and sticks hung from its hair. A chunk of flesh was missing from its arm, probably the same chunk Demetrius had seen hanging from the tree. The wound Demetrius had given him back in Treading Valley gaped open.

"Demetrius," Bryce said, dragging out his name. Its voice was hardly a voice at all, but a rasp.

Demetrius launched himself, aiming his knife for the thing's neck.

Bryce ducked out of the way. The knife scored a hit on the shoulder, but missed the neck. Again, it was faster than Demetrius had imagined it could be.

Bryce turned on Demetrius as Demetrius fell to the ground. He kicked Demetrius in the ribs, causing pain to flare throughout his ribcage. Demetrius did his best to ignore the pain.

He jumped up, spun with his knife in his hand, tried again for the neck. His aim was low. The knife sliced through Bryce's already ripped shirt and across his chest.

That's not good enough.

It wasn't. Bryce ignored the cuts and pressed forward.

Demetrius ducked a fist that Bryce threw at his head and struck at Bryce's leg with his knife, slicing out a chunk of flesh.

Bryce brought his knee up and smashed Demetrius in the face. Demetrius fell over backward with the blow and his eyes watered. He wanted to check his nose to see if it was broken, but he didn't have the time.

He swept a leg underneath Bryce, knocking him to the ground, then rolled away until he came up against a tree.

He stood up.

It wasn't fair having to fight someone who didn't feel pain.

Demetrius waited and tried to catch his breath while the thing got to its feet.

He heard a branch crack, and then another.

He turned just in time to see Gerard stop running and level his staff at Bryce.

A gout of white flame lit up the night and smashed into Bryce.

Bryce silently faced Gerard as the flame ran through his clothes and turned Bryce into a flailing torch. The flame was hotter than anything Demetrius had experienced.

Bryce started moving toward Gerard, even though his flesh had begun to burn and melt.

Demetrius chased after him.

The flame licked the branches that hung low, catching some of them on fire.

Gerard backed away from Bryce, but continued to keep the flame on him.

Bryce reached out with his right arm, and then the flesh fell from the bone in a lump. The rest of Bryce's flesh followed, and then his bones fell to the ground, twitched a few times, and stopped moving.

The smell of burnt flesh permeated the air. The crackle of burning pine trees sounded from above.

Gerard stopped the flame and let the remains of Bryce burn on their own. Demetrius saw Gerard only had eyes for the burning pile of flesh and bone that had been his uncle.

"Gerard," Demetrius said, pointing at the burning branches.

Gerard looked up.

"The trees?"

The fire in the trees went out, allowing the dark of the night to return. Gerard went back to watching his uncle burn.

"Are you all right, Gerard?" Demetrius asked. It could not have been easy for Gerard to kill his uncle, despite what his uncle had done.

"I'm fine," Gerard said. "He really was dead already."

Gerard must have seen more of the fight than Demetrius thought.

"Yes."

"So now, Trajon Jarl won't be able to find us?" Gerard asked.

Demetrius looked down at the pile of melted flesh. The flames were quickly dying without Gerard to feed them.

"I don't think we should count on that," Demetrius said.

CHAPTER 22

ROBERT KEPT HIS head bowed against the wind and rain from a storm that had blown up out of nowhere, trusting his horse to follow Demetrius's along the road. Keeping his head down was the only way he could keep his hood from blowing off and exposing him to the downpour. The road was awash in rainwater as it drained down the sides of the cliffs that rose straight up into the clouds above them. The river raged to their right from the sudden rainfall.

He wanted to turn to see how Angela was doing, but he didn't have a free hand to keep the hood atop his head. He focused all the strength he had left into maintaining his hold on the reins of his horse with one hand and keeping a hold of his staff with the other so that he could maintain the shield. If they could just find shelter, he could check on her, but Demetrius had told him there was little shelter to be had for a couple more miles.

For three days, they had run. Three days since Gerard had destroyed his uncle with fire.

Robert had come awake in the night, just as Gerard was lighting up the forest and his uncle with a flame bright enough to make Robert think for a moment that morning had come and Angela had forgotten to wake him up, or worse, fallen asleep.

But once he found his bearings, the light had waned, and he jumped up and grabbed his staff. He went to stand next to Angela at the edge of their camp and stared out into the forest at the source of the light.

"What's going on?" Robert asked.

"Demetrius found Bryce," she said. "Gerard went to help him."

The light came from a fire Gerard had set.

The firelight died out completely, and minutes later, Gerard and Demetrius returned to camp.

"You're awake," Demetrius said. He looked exhausted, and was holding a hand to his face, checking his nose. "We should mount up and get back on the road."

"Now?" Robert asked.

Demetrius's hand came away from his nose. In the moonlight, it was hard to tell, but Demetrius's nose looked crooked.

"If Bryce was trailing us for Trajon Jarl, then there is a good chance Jarl knows where we are, and a good chance he knows Bryce is dead. Jarl won't be long in coming here."

Robert nodded and went to wake Shane. Gerard was already waking Nina.

None of them had slept long. By the stars and the moon, no more than an hour or two.

And they found themselves riding into the mountains in the middle of the night, the blackness of the canyon walls crowding out the light from above—exactly what they had hoped to avoid. Gerard Weaved a light at the end of his staff so that they could see their way.

Robert waited to take his turn with the Weave until after midnight, as he would have done if they had slept, but Angela did not get any sleep that night, nor did she get much sleep over the next two nights. None of them did.

Demetrius kept pushing them down the road as fast as they could navigate it.

They napped for a few hours each night after the first, but it was not enough.

Robert was wearing down, and Angela spent most of the time while they rode slumped against the neck of her horse.

Shane had offered to take the Weave from them so they both could sleep for once. Even though Robert knew Shane had worked with Angela, and Angela had assured him that Shane could help for an hour or two, Robert hadn't felt comfortable accepting the offer.

And then the storm had come up at the dawn of the third day, relentlessly battering them, slowing their progress so much that Robert worried they would be one more day on the road than they had planned.

Demetrius said when it started that the storms often came up in the summer, and that they would usually clear up in an hour or two, if not faster. Gerard had confirmed it.

But for whatever reason, this one wasn't clearing up.

Ahead of Robert, Demetrius guided his horse around a boulder in the middle of the road. There was no room for the horse between the boulder and the cliff face. There was little room between the boulder and a ten foot drop to the river below.

When Demetrius had navigated around it successfully, Robert directed his horse to follow the same path.

He could feel the nervousness of the horse underneath him. Robert felt the same way, but he hoped the horse didn't notice.

Carefully, the horse made its way around the boulder. When they were clear of it, Robert sighed and imagined his horse doing the same.

Demetrius had pulled up a bit down the road to watch, and Robert reined in his horse next to him.

The next to try to skirt the boulder was Angela.

Robert noticed her head was down. She wasn't looking where her horse was taking her.

"Angela!" Robert called out.

Between the rush of the river below and the pounding rain, he wasn't sure she could hear him.

Behind her, Gerard was trying to get her attention, but she wasn't moving. Her chin was against her chest, one arm hanging off the side.

"Angela!"

She didn't stir.

Her frightened horse was going to try to make it on its own.

Robert jumped down from his horse and started to make his way back to her, intending to take her horse's reins and lead it around the boulder. He barely registered Demetrius taking his own horse's reins.

Angela's horse put its first step to the right of the boulder, then its second.

Robert burst into a run, but he saw he wouldn't get there in time to lead it.

Half-way around the boulder, the horse looked up at him.

Its hind quarters were in between the boulder and the river, and its front legs had made it. Robert let himself relax.

The road under the right hind leg shifted a couple of inches. A look of panic entered the horses eyes, and it tried to push off the road and jump forward.

But the push from its hind legs only finished what the boulder and the rain had started.

The road gave out underneath the hindquarters of the horse, and it slipped down, carrying Angela with it, into the raging river below. The horse screamed as it fell.

Robert rushed forward, ready to try anything to save Angela, but her body had already tumbled out of sight.

"Noooo!"

He ran to the edge, almost slipping into the river himself on the loose rock generated by the slide, and scoured the river with his eyes, but all he saw was the gray of the water as it crashed against stones and flowed swiftly away from him.

"Angela!"

In that moment, all Robert could think was that if he had let Shane help, Angela wouldn't have been asleep on her horse, and she would have done something to keep the horse from panicking.

"Angela!" he cried again.

But the river boiled below him, all dirty water, and no Angela.

Robert had failed her, and she was gone because of it.

THE SHEETS OF rain that fell from the sky separated Shane from the others. At the rear of their party, he'd fallen farther and farther behind while he tried to keep his skittish horse from bolting on him.

He was wet, cold, and alone. Robert had Angela, Gerard had Nina, and Demetrius didn't seem to need anyone. Their shared experience in trying to rescue their old master last winter had bonded them together. Shane was outside that group, and he hadn't figured out how to break in.

It did not help that Risuk was anything but welcoming. The looks he had received from the people of Treading Valley had frightened him. They were the same looks he had seen given to beggars and thieves on the streets of his home kingdom of Stradetra.

He had worked so hard with Robert to master the shield Weave, and even harder with Angela, thinking it would be his way to acceptance within their group. He needed it. He wanted to go on and learn from Thiobulus. He didn't want to be sent back like the useless child his father had claimed him to be.

He would be a good wizard, he knew it.

If only they would give him a chance.

If only he could master that Weave, Robert would see.

A shout from ahead caused him to look up. He could not see the rest of the group. They had disappeared around a bend in the road.

The rain pelted his face, and he almost looked back down, but his eye caught sight of something floating in the water. No. Something struggling. A horse.

Whose horse?

He searched the river, but it was flowing fast. The horse would soon pass him.

And then, bobbing up out of the water as it rushed past a boulder, he caught sight of a black-haired head in the water. Then the arms moved.

Angela.

His breath caught in his throat, his body locked up.

And then she slipped past him in the river.

He pulled his staff out from where he had lashed it against his horse, then spun the horse around in the road and chased after her. The horse accepted his direction without balking, as if it, too, knew of the danger.

He could do this. He could save Angela. He just had to catch up to her.

He kept his eyes on her as best he could, allowing the horse to navigate the road on its own.

A roiling set of rapids forced her underwater and his heart skipped a beat.

She came up, moments later, her arms thrashing in her attempts to stay above water.

Shane knew she was exhausted, though, from their forced ride and the time she spent keeping the shield in place. She would not last long in the water.

The river flowed faster than the horse could run, and Shane began to despair that he would ever catch her.

He tried to reach out to her with a Weave in an attempt to slow her progress, but the movement of the horse and the distance between them proved too much for him.

He didn't stop chasing, though, in the hopes she might fetch up against a boulder or catch a branch of a tree before she succumbed to the wrath of the river.

Raindrops assaulted his eyes as he rode. The hood of his coat flipped off. He pressed forward anyway.

And then, he saw the edge of a falls ahead of Angela. He pushed his horse harder. He tried to remember what the falls had looked like when he passed it going the other way, but he'd been keeping his head down and out of the rain, not looking at much of anything.

As she came up to the edge of the falls, the water eddied and swirled around the rocks that lined the top. Angela reached out a hand and caught the edge of a boulder. Even through his rain blurred eyes, Shane could see she didn't have a good grip on it.

He pulled up on the reins of his horse, bringing it to a stop.

He slipped into the vew, focused all his energie, pulled what energie he could from the raging river, and reached out with a dozen threads in a Weave much like the platform he had used to carry Nina and Gerard from the Academy. This time, however, he wrapped it around Angela.

It was difficult. He could feel the water pulling at her, and across the thirty feet or so that separated them, it strained his ability to maintain control over the threads.

But he had done it. He was doing it.

He started to lift her up, out of the water.

Focus.

He let everything else go except his concentration on the Weave. The rain no longer bothered him. The wind was as a light breeze, easy to ignore.

Out of the corner of his left eye, he noticed Angela's horse floating down the river. It looked dead. It would knock Angela over the falls if he didn't get her out of the river.

Focus.

He lifted her, and slowly she came free from the water that was trying so hard to pull her over the falls.

Angela's horse spun as its shoulder glanced against a boulder.

Angela's torso came free of the river. Her legs were the only part of her that remained below the surface.

A horse rode up behind him.

Shane strained to maintain his concentration, every bit of his effort focused on lifting Angela from the river.

Angela's horse floated ever closer.

Angela was free above her knees.

He wouldn't make it in time. The horse would hit her.

Shane bent his will again. Focus. Hold on to her.

The horse struck Angela's feet, tugged at her, straining his Weave. And then it passed beneath her, and over the falls.

And he still had her.

Shane saw threads reach out from someone next to him. They surrounded Angela as his had.

Shane didn't release his threads, though. He wouldn't risk it.

Together, they brought her to the road and set her bedraggled body down without even a bump.

Shane undid his Weave, then turned to see who had helped him.

Robert.

Gerard, Nina, and Demetrius were behind him.

Robert jumped down from his horse and ran to Angela, leaving his staff to fall to the ground.

Shane looked up.

The shield was gone.

He wove the shield as Robert and Angela had taught him and set it in place.

Shane was tired, but satisfied with himself. He had saved Angela. He had a reason to be with them, a reason to stay.

Even if Angela might never be his, having a place was enough.

CHAPTER 23

A DAY AND a half after they rescued Angela from the river, Gerard led Nina and the others through Blisterwind Pass and into the town that carried its name. The town covered the lower slopes of the mountains that still towered above them, streets and homes were terraced into the sides of the mountains.

There were a few more terraces than he remembered, new homes with their steep wooden roofs, but other than that, it was much the same—the ever-present smoke from fireplaces filled the valley, the shops along the main road and their carved signs that hung from wrought iron poles, and the cleared land at either end of town where the excess snow could be piled up until summer came along to melt it.

Gerard kept his head down, though. He wasn't ready to deal with any of the people that might recognize him. They all knew where he'd gone, what he'd gone to become. His father had shouted at him in the middle of the street as he'd left with Monteous.

They passed a farrier and a blacksmith. The sound of a hammer striking iron rang out from the back. A clothier had the front of his shop open. During the winter, it would all be shut up, with only a path to the door carved through the snow.

After they passed the town hall, Gerard led them to the right and up a ramp to the next terrace, where they turned to the north again.

From the terrace, he could see across to the other side where the homes of the wealthier residents dotted the mountainside.

His father's home was among them, two floors and a dozen rooms, it blocked the view of homes from the terrace above.

At mid-day, however, his father wouldn't be home. He would be at his warehouse, if he wasn't with a caravan.

But he wouldn't be with a caravan. He would be waiting for his son to come home.

And he would be disappointed if Gerard went home and saw his mother without coming to him, first.

Gerard glanced back at Angela. She was riding behind Robert. She looked better than she had after first coming out of the water. They had found a small, covered spot along side of the road where Gerard had started a fire and warmed them all up. They had stayed there until the rain stopped and Angela no longer shivered.

The large wood doors of his father's warehouse stood open with three wagons, piled high with barrels, in front of them. A half dozen men were unloading the barrels into the warehouse. Gerard didn't recognize even one of them. It wasn't surprising. His father didn't pay much for the warehouse help, and there were always new helpers, young men needing work.

Gerard dismounted.

The others looked like they were going to dismount, too.

"Stay here," he said. "I need to see my father alone."

He looked up at Nina, and she smiled at him. He returned the smile and fidgeted with the ring on his finger.

He wasn't looking forward to telling his father about Nina, and he wasn't sure how to explain his uncle's death, but doing those things without his friends around would give his father time to yell and scream.

Gerard stepped in through the door, carrying his staff with him. The men unloading the wagons gave him curious, dark looks, but when he stared back at them, they turned away.

The warehouse was full of goods. Gerard guessed there was time for one more caravan before the snow started to fall, and his father was preparing for the trip.

"Gerard!"

A deep, rolling voice rang out through the warehouse. Gerard turned and found the voice's owner. He didn't look any different than the last time Gerard had seen him. A large belly, a gray beard that hung over his chest. Now, he was shorter than Gerard by a hand. Gerard hadn't expected that. The last time he had seen Hendy, his father's warehouse foreman had stood a foot taller.

"Hendy," Gerard said, putting out his hand.

Hendy ignored the hand and threw his arms around Gerard, squeezing him tight in a hug. He may not have been as tall as Gerard remembered, but his arms were just as strong.

"You've grown."

"You shrunk."

Hendy laughed and released Gerard. "Perhaps that's so. You're here to see your father?"

Gerard nodded.

"He'll be happy to see you. Where's your uncle? I thought he was fetching you home."

Gerard did not know exactly what to say. He thought he should tell his father first, but he did not feel right keeping it from Hendy, either. Hendy had been upset enough when his father sent Gerard to the mines to question him in public. It had almost cost Hendy his job.

"Something happened," Gerard said, "while we were on the road. I'd like to tell you, but I think I should tell Father first."

Hendy's smile fell. "Understood. He's in the back. You know, Gerard, that staff suits you. Your father won't like that."

"He won't," Gerard said.

"You're not staying."

"No. I came to pay my respects to Eric, and to see Mother, but I'm not the person I was when I left."

"No, you aren't."

Hendy reached out and shook Gerard's hand. "Good luck, Gerard."

Gerard left Hendy to his work and wound his way through the barrels and crates to the back where the accounting room was.

He rounded one last stack of crates and found his father standing at the door to the counting room.

They stood facing each other. Gerard took in his father, saw the lines on his face that had not been there before. His hair had turned gray but was still as thick as ever. His eyes moved up and down, obviously trying to see what Gerard had become, but they held a sadness that hadn't been there before.

Eric.

Gerard suddenly didn't want to tell his father anything. He didn't want to disappoint him and didn't want to tell him about Uncle Bryce.

"You've grown," his father said.

"You sent me away when I was thirteen," Gerard said, immediately hating the way it made him sound bitter.

"I did."

His father's nose twitched, and his fingers clutched into a fist and released repeatedly.

Gerard could not think of what to say next. The man in front of him had sent him to work in the mines, had cast him out, but had called him back, though only when his brother had died.

"You heard about Eric?" his father asked.

"Uncle Bryce told me."

"So you aren't here on your own, then. Bryce found you?"

Gerard nodded.

"I didn't know if he would. Where is he?"

So quickly. Gerard only brought more pain for a man who was obviously grieving for his son. Now, he had lost his brother. How was he supposed to tell his father that his brother had been in league with a two hundred year old wizard that intended to take control of The Seven Kingdoms? How was he supposed to tell his father that he suspected Bryce had been complicit in his Eric's death?

Should I even tell him at all?

"What's eating at you, Gerard? He's not here, is he."

"No, he isn't."

"That coward. He probably told you to come home and ran off. Well, I'm grateful he did tell you, at least."

"No," Gerard said, shaking his head. "He didn't leave." Gerard couldn't say it.

"Then where is he?"

Gerard walked over to his father and said, "We should go into the counting room."

"Why?"

"Please, Father."

His father grunted, but went inside.

A table in the center held the counting stones, a shelf on the wall held books of records. His father was meticulous when it came to keeping track of his business.

Gerard shut the door behind them.

"All right. We're here. Where is Bryce?"

Gerard knew this was where his whole homecoming would unravel. He took a wooden chair and sat down, but kept one hand on his staff. The seat was hard, but he needed that. He leaned forward so that he didn't look like he was relaxing, no matter how much he wanted to. He hoped his father would take the cue and find a seat for himself, but he made no hint that he would move.

"He was executed," Gerard said. His father didn't need to know what happened after.

His father's eyes shrunk to slits.

"Executed? You must be mistaken. Bryce was a scoundrel, but he would never do anything to have himself executed."

"We were staying the night at Lord Taren's estate in Dominand. He slit the throat of one of Lord Taren's men." He didn't need to know the man was a wizard, either.

"What reason would your uncle have to cut a man's throat?"

Gerard studied the books on the shelves. Leather-bound, numbered for each quarter of each year, going back before Gerard was born. He pondered how to tell his father the truth, or if he should tell him at all.

He stood up.

"Father, I think coming here was a mistake. You want me here to replace Eric, and I can't do that."

His father's mouth hung open, though it moved up and down as if he was trying to speak.

"I'm going to go up to the house, say hello to Mother, and then we'll be on our way."

It would be for the best, too. All he would achieve by staying was the creation of more heartache and turmoil. It would have been better if he'd never come at all. His father was hurt by losing Eric. He'd be hurt even more knowing that Gerard had precipitated the event that caused the loss of his brother.

He switched his staff to his left hand, and turned to head out the door.

"Stop!" his father shouted. "You can't just come in here, tell me your uncle died, and then leave without an explanation."

Gerard spun on his heel. Whatever emotion had caused him to try to save his father anguish burned away in the anger he'd stored up since his father had forced him to leave.

"And why not? You gave up your right to tell me what to do when you sent me away to the mines. You and Uncle Bryce. It's been eight years, father. Eight years without any contact from you, and then I get a message from you that it's my *duty* to come home and take Eric's place? I am no longer the boy you sent away. I am no longer yours to command."

A wave of red flooded his father's face.

"You are still my son and you still have a duty to this house."

"My duty to this house ended when you sent me away."

"I sent you away to become a man, not to become a stinking coward of a wizard."

Gerard's muscles clenched tight enough to cause him to shake. He spun a Weave to run fire up and down his staff, almost without thinking.

"Gerard!" His father shrunk back from him, stumbling against the table.

"The only cowards I know hide up here and pretend that the only important things happening in the world happen in Risuk." Gerard couldn't stop himself. "You want to know why Uncle Bryce was executed? He slit the throat of a wizard, and he slit the throat of that wizard just because he was in the way and wasn't expecting it."

His father recovered from his initial shock, and then took a step forward. He kept an eye on the flaming staff, but he didn't shrink from it.

"The only cowards I know of in Risuk are little boys that flee their duty to their family. If he slit the throat of a wizard, then the wizard probably deserved it. He shouldn't have put himself in Bryce's way."

Gerard stood his ground.

"Do you know who killed Eric, Father?"

"Of course I know. What does that have to do with your impudence right now?"

"I asked Uncle Bryce what happened. He told me brigands put an arrow into him. Do you know what Bryce said when I asked him what he'd done about it? Nothing. He said nothing, father, and it wouldn't surprise me if Bryce had set the whole ambush up."

"He would never..." His father stopped in the middle, obviously trying to think through the implications.

"No? He wouldn't have Eric killed in the hopes that you would give him Eric's duties and his share?"

"Why would he do that?" his father asked.

"Why would he kill a wizard in cold blood?"

"You tell me. You obviously know the answer."

The door opened behind him and Gerard spun around. It was Hendy's hand on the latch, but he ushered Nina into the room and shut the door behind her.

"Who is this?" his father asked.

"Gerard," Nina said. "Why is your staff aflame?"

Gerard extinguished it. Hendy was smart. Gerard couldn't allow himself to be angry at his father in front of Nina—not yet. He wondered how Hendy had discovered who Nina was.

"Just showing my father," Gerard said.

"That nice man Hendy said you were fighting in here," she said.

She was doing an enviable job impersonating a lady, though her clothes were more common.

"No, we weren't fighting," he said at the same time as his father.

Gerard glanced back at his father, who was visibly trying to settle himself.

"Aren't you going to introduce us?" Nina said, stepping between Gerard and her father.

He sighed.

"Nina," he said. "This is my father. Father, this is Nina."

"It's good to meet you, Nina," his father said. "How do you know Gerard?"

Nina took Gerard's hand in hers and pulled him to her side.

"I'm his wife," she said, spitting out the words as if she was issuing a challenge.

Gerard waited for the rage to burst out of his father, but his father did something completely unexpected.

He found a chair, sat down in it, and took several deep breaths.

"Your mother tried to tell me," he said. "She warned me that you wouldn't be anything like the boy you were when you left. If you'll excuse me, I need to get back to work."

"Father?"

"No, no. Please. Go see your mother. She'll be happy to see you." He looked deflated, like all the energy had left him, like all his hopes had fled leaving him empty inside. He pulled himself close to the table and started counting with his stones, but Gerard thought he was just counting to count.

Gerard felt Nina squeeze his hand, and then she pulled him to the door.

Gerard wanted to say something to his father to help him understand, or to make the loss less, but words wouldn't come.

CHAPTER 24

A
NGELA STILL SHIVERED inside, despite spending the day riding close
behind Robert, wearing dry clothes, and generally feeling warm
since they had dried her out following her plunge into the river.
She had been so close to tumbling over the falls and losing everything.

When she splashed into the water, submerged at first by the weight of
her horse until she had frantically disengaged herself, she had thought
her life had come to an end. She had not been swimming since before
becoming Monteous's apprentice, and it was all she could do to keep her
head above water. The water had been terribly cold, too, leaching the heat
from her body. She had been so exhausted, between the extended effort
to help maintain the shield and the more immediate struggle to keep
her head above water, that she hadn't realized that she was numb until
much later—after the fire Gerard made had warmed her to the point of
burning. Even if a trip over the falls had failed to kill her, she wouldn't
have survived much longer in the water.

The ensuing time spent riding behind Robert almost made it worth
the dunking and the shivering. He had doted on her since they pulled
her out, not letting her get far from him, or go very long without asking
if she needed anything, or if she was cold.

She knew it wouldn't last—the search for Thiobulus would take her
place with him again, soon, but she was enjoying his attention and
closeness.

The house Gerard led them to was larger than the houses surrounding it, though not quite as large as the home she had grown up in. She
suspected if more room existed in the crook between the two mountains,
Gerard's father would have built a more impressive manor.

An iron fence guarded the property, though no gate barred their entrance. An opening in the fence led to a courtyard that was surrounded by a manicured garden which seemed out of place in the mountain town. Perhaps Gerard's boast of his father being a lord of Risuk was true.

Which would put Gerard in an interesting position, being both a wizard and a lord. By law, one could not be a wizard and become a lord. Gerard's father had to know that law. But maybe it didn't apply if an apprentice had not yet become a master. Or perhaps, in this land that did not respect wizards, the issue had not even entered his mind.

Gerard led them into the courtyard. As they were dismounting, the front door opened. A woman with straight, silver hair cut short of her shoulders stepped out. She wore a deep blue dress, thick with many more layers than Angela had seen anywhere else in The Seven Kingdoms, but its cut was striking, easily the equal of the gowns her mother had worn. The woman had the same wide nose as Gerard, and looked to be nearly as tall.

Her eyes searched the group for a moment, before settling on Gerard. She took a step, then another, then raced down the steps.

"Gerard!" she said. A smile formed on her face, and tears came to her eyes.

Gerard handed the reins of his horse to Nina and dropped his staff just in time to accept the embrace of the woman.

"Mother," he said.

She pulled him tight, but he held his head up.

"It has been so long," she said. "I never thought I would see you again."

Gerard said nothing. He just stood rooted to the ground, enduring the embrace.

Angela felt herself swaying and took hold of Robert's arm. Her shivers seemed to be growing stronger, but she could not take her eyes off of Gerard and his mother.

The scene made her think about her own homecoming that she would never allow to happen. Would her mother be so happy to see her that she would deign to embrace the daughter she had all but thrown out? Or would her mother refuse to have anything to do with her? She knew what her father would say. She didn't ever want to see him again.

After learning more of where Gerard had come from, she had begun to realize how similar their upbringing had been. He could have been the man that had taken advantage of her and set her on the road to becoming a wizard if he had not been set on that road himself.

Now, though, she wouldn't trade her road for anything. She wouldn't trade Robert for her family or the wealth they had.

Gerard's mother stepped back from the embrace, then looked them all over once again.

Her eyes lit on Demetrius first.

"You. I know you. You came with that wizard and took my son away."

"Mother," Gerard said. "It was not like that, and you know it."

"He did take you away, Gerard."

"Father sent me away to the mines, and you know it. I chose to leave with them, instead."

"If you only had the sense..." She stopped herself. Her eyes settled on Angela. Angela felt their probing on her skin. "It does not matter, I suppose. You are home now. Tell me who these others are, Gerard."

"They are my friends," he said, and then pointed at Angela and Robert. "This is Robert and Angela. They were apprentices under Monteous with me. Robert has passed all the tests to become a master of the Guild. They just haven't admitted him yet."

"It is good to meet you Misses Maracane," Angela said. She would have curtsied, but she couldn't let go of Robert. Her legs were so weak she thought if she let go, she would tumble to the ground.

Gerard's mother nodded to her, but said nothing, as if the knowledge that Angela was a wizard had made her not worth the woman's time.

"The one behind them is Shane. I met him at the Academy."

"The Academy?" his mother asked.

"I'll explain later. This," he said while sliding his arm behind Nina to bring her forward, "is Nina."

Gerard's mother looked her up and down.

"Is she a wizard, too?"

"No," Gerard said. "She's my wife."

Angela didn't know what she had been expecting. Gerard had been so adamant at the Academy about not bringing Nina home with him that Angela had thought Nina wouldn't be welcome at all, but after Gerard's mother stepped back for a moment, she rushed forward and embraced Nina much like she had embraced Gerard.

"You are so beautiful," she said. "Your red hair I could wish for my own." Then she turned to Gerard. "I can't believe you didn't bring her to meet me before you married, Gerard."

Gerard spluttered, shocked at his mother's reaction. "There wasn't time," he finally said.

A violent shiver overtook Angela. She lost her hold on Robert and fell to the ground. She found herself looking up at the deep blue sky. It was beautiful with the clouds gone.

"What's wrong with her?" Gerard's mother asked.

Angela was surprised she could still hear. Her whole body was shaking.

Robert knelt down next to her.

"Are you all right?" he asked.

"She fell in the river during the storm," Gerard said.

Feet rushed over to her. A hand laid itself on her forehead.

"She's burning up! Why didn't you say something? Come, get her inside."

Hands pushed themselves between her back and the paving stones of the courtyard. They lifted her up. She saw faces, but they were blurry—not like the sky, which was so sharp and blue.

ROBERT STOOD OVER Angela's bed, just like he had a little over a half year earlier when she had been trapped in her mind by a proscribed Weave, but this time, he couldn't do a thing but wait for her to get better.

He wanted to lie down next to her and keep her warm, but he was exhausted. It was all he could do to stay awake and keep the shield in place. Climbing onto the bed would just be an invitation to fall asleep.

Gerard's mother, Abigail, had sent for a healer. When the healer arrived, she fed Angela a tonic, and then told them there was little else she could do but let the illness run its course.

Robert did not feel like they had time for that.

He hadn't noticed that he had dropped the shield when he helped Shane pull Angela from the water. He was so concerned about Angela that he'd forgotten about it for nearly an hour. When he remembered, he swore. He slipped into the vew to put the shield back up, but discovered a shield already there.

Robert looked to Shane, who hadn't said a word. Robert had no idea how long the shield had been down, and that concerned him. But Shane had proven that he'd somehow overcome his inability to hold the shield, so Robert let him continue to maintain it. He did, however, keep an eye on both the shield and Shane, watching for signs of fatigue.

Robert took the shield back from Shane in the alcove where they had all dried off, but they had traded it since. Robert had to concede that maybe Angela was the better teacher.

"Robert," Angela said.

She moved her hand to the edge of the bed, reaching for him. He took it. Her skin was still hot to the touch.

"How are you feeling?"

"Better," she said.

"You still feel hot," he said.

She smiled, but it seemed forced. Her eyes had a gray cast to them. "I'm still shivering under here," she said.

He could feel it, too. Small tremors in her hand.

He tried to tell himself that it wasn't his fault, that he had no choice but to have her help him with the shield, but he didn't believe it. He could have taken the shield more, he could have let her sleep more. She wouldn't have been exhausted enough to fall asleep on her horse.

"Stop thinking that, Robert," she said.

"What?"

"That it's your fault. It's not."

"I wasn't thinking that," he said.

"You weren't?" She raised an eyebrow.

They had hardly spent any time together in the last six months, yet she knew him well enough to know what he was thinking.

He reached out and touched her forehead with his palm, felt the heat there, then slid his hand down to cup her head.

Her fall had frightened him. For a short moment, he had thought Trajon Jarl had found them and was going to destroy them all right there between the river and the cliff face. But that hadn't happened.

It did make him realize, one more time, that he couldn't lose her.

"You get better," he said.

"I am," she said. "You told me the healer said I would be fine in a few days."

Robert knelt down on the floor, the padding of his thick Risuk style pants softened the pressure of the hardwood floor against his knees.

He brought her hand to his lips and kissed it.

"She did say that," he said, "but this reminds me too much of last winter when I found you succumbing to that Weave. I can't lose you, Angela. I'd have nobody left."

"You would have Demetrius," she said.

Robert cocked his head to the side and grimaced.

"He doesn't count," he said.

She squeezed his hand.

"Don't worry," she said. "I'll be fine. I just need to rest and drink that foul concoction the healer gave me."

There was a knock at the door, and then the door swung open, squeaking on hinges that needed oil.

Robert turned his head and saw Demetrius in the doorway. He had his coat on, and must have been out in the town. Robert wished Demetrius wouldn't go on his own.

"I've found him," Demetrius said.

Robert stood up, still holding Angela's hand. "Thiobulus? Where?"

"Come with me," he said.

Robert looked back at Angela. He wanted to stay with her.

"Go, Robert," she said. "I'll be fine."

"Okay," he said, and laid her hand back by her side. "I'll be back as soon as I can."

"I know," she said, then closed her eyes and turned on her side, away from him.

He followed Demetrius out the door.

"First," Robert said, "I need my staff."

IN A ROOM just down the hall from where Angela was recovering, Nina sat with Gerard and his mother and sipped at her kava. It was strong and bitter on her tongue, enough so that she had to work at not making a face when she sipped. She would have put it down had it not come from Gerard's mother. Abigail seemed to have taken a liking to her, and Nina didn't want to insult her by turning down the kava.

Which reminded her of the conversation she'd had with Gerard while his mother was attending to Angela.

"Don't let her know your father is a farmer," he had said.

"Why not?"

"She won't respect you."

"How can you be sure, Gerard?"

"Please, just play at being a merchant's daughter or something. I don't want her to know I married a farmer's daughter."

Nina froze. She couldn't move for a moment. She couldn't believe what Gerard had just said.

Then she came back to herself, and she stomped on his foot.

He yelled "Ow!" then danced around on his uninjured foot for a moment. "Why did you do that?"

"Are you so ashamed of me that you don't want your mother to know who my parents are?"

"No," he said.

"You haven't forgotten that Monteous came to my father for help on more than one occasion. Are you trying to tell me that my father didn't have Monteous's respect?"

"No."

He stopped hopping, tempting Nina to stomp on his foot one more time, but she had heard footsteps in the hallway.

"She didn't seem to be upset that you married me," Nina had said in a near whisper. "I think she might surprise you in other ways, too."

And then Abigail had entered the room and urged them to sit. She poured out cups of kava while they took their seats.

Nina and Gerard sat on a small couch covered in dark gray leather. Once they were seated and the kava passed around, Abigail sat down across from them with her own steaming cup.

"You know your father won't like that you've married her," Abigail said.

Gerard nodded. "He already knows."

"He knows? He had plans to marry you to Lord Tanger's daughter. I suppose he tried to shout at you so loud you would be convinced to give her up," she said.

"He didn't shout at all," Nina said. "All the shouting appears to have happened before I entered the room."

Abigail smiled. "I can imagine. I suppose he grew upset when you told him you weren't staying."

A look of surprise crossed Gerard's face.

"How did you know I wasn't staying?"

Abigail laughed. It was warm and hearty, and Nina knew she would come to like this woman, had she the time to spend with her.

"Gerard," Abigail said, "I know you thought I supported your father in his choices when you were a boy, but I did not. I knew all along that you would chose to go with that wizard whether I liked it or not. I can't say that I am happy you went, either, but it is clear that you grew up while you were away, and it is clear to me that you will not stay here long. You would not be happy running your father's business, nor being Lord Maracane, even if the law allowed you that privilege."

Abigail's grasp of the situation shocked Nina. Nina wondered how the woman had managed to figure all that out in the few hours they had been at her home. She hadn't even exchanged more than a few words with Gerard while getting Angela settled and calling for the healer.

"Father was livid. I think he wanted me to come home and take Eric's place."

"Of course he did, Dear. I warned him."

"I really thought you would take his side," Gerard said.

"You were thirteen when you left us, Gerard. Thirteen year old boys do not see much of what goes on in the world unless it is right in front of their noses. I support your father in the things he chooses to do because I must. He is Lord Maracane, and to refute his decisions would undermine what power he has. In private, though, I do tell him when I think he is wrong. He does not always listen."

Nina laughed. "Neither does Gerard."

Abigail smiled. "Nor would I expect him to. As much as his father doted on Eric, Gerard has always been more his father's son. Bear-headed, strong willed, and incapable of taking anyone's advice."

Out of the corner of her eye, Nina saw that Gerard had a bit of a frown on his face.

"I don't know if he's all that bad," Nina said. "I've worked with bulls that were more difficult to control than Gerard."

Gerard turned his head toward her, and his frown deepened, but Nina didn't let her eyes stray too far from Abigail. She wanted to impress this woman, but she wasn't going to lie to her to do it.

"You worked with bulls?"

"Yes," Nina said. "I worked with the cattle and trained horses on my father's farm."

"Then how did you and Gerard meet?"

"It's a bit of a story, but the part where we met, Gerard and Demetrius came to take shelter at my father's farm from a snow storm."

Abigail smiled. "I find it hard to believe Gerard would take shelter from a snow storm."

"We were not dressed for it," Gerard said, "and we had to get the horses some shelter."

"Not dressed for it? Gerard..."

"In Dominand, they do not have the clothes for the kind of storm they had last winter," Gerard said. "It was unusual."

"I suppose. What were you doing out in it?"

"They were trying to rescue Monteous," Nina said.

"Rescue him? He's a wizard. The Senior Wizard, isn't he?"

Gerard's eyes looked down.

"He was," Nina said. "But..."

"No, Nina," Gerard interrupted. "I don't think we're supposed to talk about it."

Nina thought it over. Master Brin had told them to keep quiet about what had happened. The Guild did not want any rumors getting out that the Guild had split.

But with Master Brin dead, as well as every other master they knew, Nina wondered if it mattered any longer. And Gerard's father was a lord. They had told Lord Taren. Why not his parents?

"Gerard, I think... I think we should tell her everything. They need to know, if only so they can prepare."

Abigail's eyes thinned to slits. "Prepare for what?"

Gerard sighed. "Mother, if you think I'm bear-headed, you don't really know Nina. After Demetrius and I left her home, she rode out after me against her father's wishes."

"What are you trying not to tell me, Gerard?"

"He doesn't want to tell you that the Guild split apart, Monteous is dead, and a very powerful wizard who was kicked out of the Guild more than a century ago is now killing every wizard he comes across in an effort to make The Seven Kingdoms vulnerable to invasion."

Abigail sat back and set her kava on a delicate looking side table. She tilted her head just a little, then looked at Gerard.

"Is this true?"

"Yes," he said.

"It sounds too far fetched to be true, but I can not imagine why you would make something like this up. I guess we'll have to tell your father. He will not like it. But you are here, now. You are properly out of it."

"We're not," Nina said, not wanting Gerard to bear all of the burden. "This wizard is looking for us."

"Why is he looking for you?"

"He wants Robert to join him."

"Nina," Gerard said.

Nina was about to continue, but Abigail stopped her.

"Gerard is right. I don't need to know all the details, but your father does. He needs to know everything that you know. You should have told him when you visited him."

Gerard scowled.

Nina knew he hadn't planned on telling them at all, but decided it would be imprudent to say so.

Instead, she took another sip of her kava. It wasn't quite as bitter as the last. Maybe she could learn to like it if she had enough time. Maybe she would have time when it all was over.

CHAPTER 25

D EMETRIUS TOOK ROBERT outside, then led him through a maze of
side streets that wound their way up the side of the mountain until Robert could look down and see nearly the whole of the town.
Eventually, Demetrius led Robert to an ale house called The Seven Cups,
an obvious play on The Seven Kingdoms.

When they went inside, Robert changed his judgment of the place, deciding that the name of the place was an accurate description of what was
on the inside. The ale house was small. It had four tables arranged around
a hearth, and he suspected only seven cups to serve all of the patrons.

Three men sat at one table, already deep into their cups. Their talk
echoed around the room, their laughter banged off the walls.

Away from the hearth to the right, a portly man with a balding head
and squinty eyes stood behind a bar that could seat at most three people.
He held a towel in one hand, an empty mug in the other.

"Why are we here?" Robert asked.

"Thiobulus was here less than two weeks ago."

"Does that mean we're close?"

"It might. Come with me," Demetrius said.

Demetrius walked across the room and took a seat at the bar. Robert
followed him, but remained standing.

"Back again, eh?" the bartender asked. "You want a mug of our finest?"

"No," Demetrius said. "I'm looking for some information."

"Ah, that comes at a dearer price than my ale." The bartender chuckled
and set the mug and towel aside.

"What price?"

"Depends on the information."

"I'm looking for a friend. He's been here within the last two weeks."

One of the men at the table said something that Robert didn't quite catch, then banged his mug against the table. The bartender looked over at him.

"Don't break my mugs, Sam," the bartender said, "or I'll dump you in the river."

Robert wondered how the bartender would accomplish that. The man at the table was easily a foot taller than the bartender.

The bartender reached down and filled a mug.

"I'll be right back," he said, then left Robert and Demetrius there at the bar.

"How do you know Thiobulus was here in the last two weeks?"

The look in Demetrius's eye told Robert that Demetrius did not want to divulge his secret, and Robert began to wonder if it was part of what Demetrius hadn't wanted to tell him back in Treading Valley.

"People leave a trail," Demetrius said, surprising Robert. "If it's fresh enough, I can follow it. Every person's trail is unique."

"Is it like the hunting hounds?" Robert asked.

Demetrius chuckled. "You're comparing me to a dog, now. It's not like that at all," he said.

Robert noticed the bartender returning. "Is it part of what Thiobulus did to you?" he asked quickly.

Demetrius nodded.

"Could you find Trajon Jarl?"

"Trajon Jarl," said the bartender as he returned to his place behind the bar. "I'm afraid I don't know who that is."

"He's not who we're looking for," Demetrius said.

"Then who is it you're looking for?"

"An older man named Thiobulus."

The bartender smiled, showing off a set of crooked teeth. "Oh, the wizard," he said.

Robert blinked, surprised that the bartender would know Thiobulus was a wizard.

"You know him?" Robert asked.

"I do. He comes in here about once a month for a keg of ale, then just disappears with it. Been doing it for years. That'll be five crowns. For another five, I'll give him a message the next time he comes in."

"What do you mean he disappears?"

"Well, he comes in through the front door, pays me for the ale, heads down to the cellar, and never comes out. When I look, he's gone, and so is a keg of my ale. He never takes more than what he's paid for, so I don't ask him questions."

"Can we see the cellar?" Demetrius asked.

"Sure. Another five crowns."

"You want ten crowns for that?" Robert asked.

"Of course I do. I know all you wizards have more coin than you know what to do with. Thiobulus is a good customer. I'd hate to see him take his business elsewhere, so, ten crowns, just in case he does."

Demetrius had already dug out the crowns and slapped them on the bar.

"Right then," the bartender said. "See, young man? Your friend here knows how this works. The cellar's right through this door. Don't be taking any liberties with my kegs, now."

The door the bartender pointed at was right behind the bar.

"Your kegs are safe," Demetrius said.

The bartender opened the door, and let them through.

A few steps down, the cellar grew dark.

Robert Weaved a light at the end of his staff, bright enough to show them the area around them.

The steps, dug into the stone of the mountainside, descended beyond the strength of his Weave light.

As Robert and Demetrius traveled down the steps, Robert's light revealed that at the bottom, they opened up on a large room. Every wall was smooth, untouched by any tool that Robert could see. Casks of ale and wine were stacked against the walls.

"I wonder how he built this," Robert said.

"It was probably built by a wizard," Demetrius said. "Risuk did not always loathe them. Now hold that light up so I can see."

Robert held the tip of his staff up near the top of the cellar. It was obvious the cellar was empty but for the two of them and the kegs of ale. There was no other way out but the door at the top of the stairs.

Demetrius searched the floor, walking it piece by piece with his head down.

Robert decided he should help and started looking for signs of a portal. After a few minutes, he gave up. He couldn't find any indication Thiobulus had used a portal. He would have had to leave the focus behind, at least, and there was none. Unless the bartender was complicit in Thiobulus's use of a portal, and hid the focus for him after he left... But no, the bartender had appeared baffled as to how Thiobulus vanished with a full keg of ale.

It completely confused Robert, too.

"How could Thiobulus just disappear from here with a keg of ale, and not have a portal?"

"Maybe he didn't," Demetrius said. "Perhaps he stopped time like you said he did when you met him, and just walked out."

Robert hadn't though of that, but it was a possibility. He couldn't imagine the old man carrying the keg up the stairs, but then, he wouldn't need to carry it by hand. He could have floated it on a Weave.

"Did he?" Robert asked. "You can see his trail, right?"

"He didn't walk out," Demetrius said. "Not up the steps, at least."

"Then where did he go?"

Demetrius came to a stop at the back wall. He looked from side to side along the base, then slapped the stone wall with his hand. The smack, smack echoed throughout the room.

"He went right through here," Demetrius said.

Robert slipped into the vew again, looked around the room. There weren't any Works that he recognized. There weren't any Weaves.

"There isn't anything special, here," Robert said.

"It's a dead end. I guess we'll have to go the long way."

"The long way?" Robert asked.

"Yes, and we should leave tonight."

Robert slid out of the vew at that. He almost let the light Weave go.

"What about Angela? We can't leave her here."

"She'll be safe, Robert. Shane has proven he can hold the Weave. Between Shane and her, the two of them can keep them all safe until we are away. I don't think Trajon Jarl will bother with them if he doesn't know where you are."

"How can you be sure?"

"I can't, Robert, but I think time is growing short. You need to find Thiobulus, and we can't wait here while Angela recovers."

Robert tapped his staff on the stone floor of the cellar, making a clack, clack sound.

"Why are you pushing me to hurry? You didn't even want to come this way."

"I feel that time is growing short. I think the only thing that has kept us alive is that your Weave made it inconvenient for him to find us. I have no doubt that Trajon Jarl could find us if he wanted to, if there wasn't something more important for him to do."

Demetrius stepped away from the wall.

"I've been thinking about something else, too," he said. "How many wizards has he killed in the last two weeks? How many more will we lose if you don't learn how to stop him?"

"You think he's killed more?"

"I am certain of it," Demetrius said.

The thought startled Robert, but he remembered the letter, the conversations with him. He'd tried hard to put them out of his head and had succeeded, but when he thought back, he realized Demetrius was probably right. If Trajon Jarl wanted to destroy the Guild, what better way to do it than to kill each wizard when they were alone in their laboratories, spread all over The Seven Kingdoms? Monteous had often gone weeks without talking to another wizard.

"Do you think Master Lamen's warning found someone? Perhaps the Guild knows and is already working to thwart him."

"Ask the question this way, Robert. Should we take the chance that no one received Master Lamen's warning because Master Lamen died before he could send it?"

"We should hurry, then." He didn't like it. Angela would not like being left behind. Neither would Gerard or Nina, or even Shane.

But he didn't see how he had a choice.

GERARD'S FATHER RETURNED home just before sunset.

Gerard stumbled into him only moments after leaving Angela's room. In his excitement at learning that Demetrius had returned with news of finding Thiobulus, he completely missed that his father had stepped in front of him at the bottom of the stairs. The resulting collision nearly sent the two of them tumbling to the ground.

"Watch where you're going," his father said as they separated.

Gerard was too excited to let his father's grumbling get him down. Demetrius had found Thiobulus. It wouldn't be long before they could stop running and hiding.

"Sorry, father," Gerard said, outwardly contrite. Inside, he wanted to chase after Robert and Demetrius.

"Come with me," his father said before walking down a hallway that led to his study.

Gerard had little choice. He didn't want to anger his father by ignoring him, and his father would think he was being ignored if Gerard did what he wanted and chased after Robert.

His father's study had not changed much in the years Gerard had been away. There were more books, more papers, but the desk was the same, if a little worn. The spear his father had used to kill his first bear hung above an expansive leaded glass window. His father had already taken a seat behind his desk. Two other chairs waited, empty, across from him.

"Sit," he said.

Gerard took the seat closest to him and settled in. The back was as hard as he remembered, but instead of banging his head on it as he had when he was a child, his shoulder blades now took the brunt of the chair's back.

"I've figured out why Bryce killed that wizard," said his father. "He was trying to keep you from marrying that girl. Why?"

"How do you know that?" Gerard asked. "I could have married her before..."

"The ring on your finger is distinctive. I have seen it on the finger of Lord Taren a time or two. Now answer my question."

"He seemed to think you would have been angry with him."

"He was right. I would have been angry with him. He wasn't supposed to let you do something so stupid as to marry some country girl."

"Nina is *not* a country girl," Gerard said. He had to work hard to keep his voice level. He was glad he didn't have his staff with him.

"She is surely no lady of the court. Her hands have seen hard work already. Why did you marry her?"

"I love her." He wanted to defend her against his father, but he was right. She did grow up on a farm.

"Enough to give up all of this?" His father spread his hands wide as he asked his question.

"Yes," Gerard said. "I can't have it, anyway."

"What do you mean?"

"I'm a wizard. Wizards can't be lords."

"You are not a wizard, yet. And the law states that you can't be a lord and a member of the Wizards' Guild. Even so, it is not the title of lord that provides my wealth and keeps this family where it is. Being a wizard might make things easier."

Gerard closed his eyes and leaned back in the chair. He would not get angry with his father.

"Do you know why my friends came with me?" Gerard asked.

"Your friends? I thought you only came with the girl."

So Hendy hadn't told his father about the others, and his father hadn't seen anyone in the house, yet. With Robert and Demetrius out looking for Thiobulus, and Angela laid up in her room with Shane keeping her company, it wasn't surprising he didn't know the others were there.

"Yes. There are three other apprentices with me, as well as Demetrius..."

"I remember that name. He worked for the wizard that convinced you to disobey me."

Gerard opened his eyes again. His father's face had gone red. "Father, forget about that. It's long past."

"I won't have him in my house."

"Mother has already let him in and given him a room."

Gerard's father stood up. "Where is he," he said. "I have some words for him."

"Sit down. He's not here right now."

His father blustered and remained standing, unsure how to take Gerard's instruction, but did sit down after a moment. He was breathing heavy, though. It surprised Gerard. He hadn't thought his father cared that much.

"When he returns..."

"Do you want to know why he's even here? Why we're all here?" Gerard asked.

"Why?"

"Wizards are being murdered."

"Good."

"I'm a wizard, father."

"Not yet."

Gerard rolled his eyes and decided to ignore that. "A powerful wizard that was involved in the Unification, but was later exiled, has come back. He's trying to destroy the Guild."

"You haven't said anything yet that concerns me," he said.

"He wants to destroy the Guild in order to leave The Seven Kingdoms open to invasion," Gerard said.

At that, his father sat up.

"From whom?"

"I don't know. Demetrius thinks Mrongil was behind an attempt last winter."

"Last winter? Wait. How are you involved in all of this?"

"It's a long story, father."

"We have time," he said. "I need to decide if I should gather the Council of Lords."

Gerard was surprised. His father seemed to have forgotten about their personal troubles. Gerard's surprise must have showed on his face.

"You think, Gerard, that just because we don't like wizards or the Guild in Risuk, that we would let The Seven Kingdoms come to ruin because of it? You should be ashamed for thinking it. Whatever our opinions of the Guild is, we are loyal to The Seven Kingdoms. The Seven Kingdoms has been good to Risuk, and going back to the way it was before the Unification is not something any of the lords want to see."

"I'm sorry," said Gerard. "I just assumed..."

"You assumed that because I don't like wizards, and I didn't like that you ran off to become a wizard, that I would sit here and let The Seven Kingdoms be invaded. You assumed I would just sit here and do nothing. In our positions, mine as a lord, yours as a wizard, we can't afford to make assumptions. Now tell me your story."

Chagrined, Gerard told his father about Monteous, how he'd gone missing, how they'd found him, and who had abducted him. He explained his own role in the events that led up to Monteous's death, and the eventual creation of the Academy.

His father's expression did not change while Gerard told his tale. Gerard didn't know if that was a good sign, or bad, but he continued to tell the story of all they had gone through since the Academy burned.

Until he got to the part where his uncle killed Master Lamen.

"Why do you stop?" his father asked.

He did not know how to tell his father that Uncle Bryce was a traitor. He knew he had to, he just couldn't.

He tried, though. "Uncle Bryce..." He stopped.

"What about him? Is this where he killed that wizard?"

"Yes."

"You've already told me about that, and I figured out why," he said. "Get on with the story."

"There's more to it, father."

"More?"

Gerard took a deep breath, then nodded.

"Well, what is it?"

"After we left, we discovered that Bryce was a traitor."

His father's nostrils flared. "A traitor? I don't believe it."

"I asked him how Eric died, father. He was evasive."

"That doesn't prove he's a traitor, Gerard."

"What reason would he have to skirt the truth if brigands killed Eric like Uncle Bryce claimed? Why would he fear to tell me?"

His father picked up a black pen that lay on the desk and started tapping it between his fingers.

"But that's not everything," Gerard said. "He attacked Robert while we were in Treading Valley."

The pen tapping stopped. "You said Lord Taren had him executed for killing that wizard."

"I did. He should have been. We don't know what happened, because we left before the execution. But when Uncle Bryce attacked Robert in Treading Valley, he told Robert he was working for Trajon Jarl."

"You're certain?"

Gerard nodded.

"Then he's still alive. Where is he? I'll get the truth out of him and kill him myself, if I have to."

Gerard hung his head. "You won't have to." The image of his uncle's body melting in the fire he created came back to him.

"Why not?"

"You won't believe it," Gerard said. He almost didn't believe it himself, despite having seen it. Monteous had never taught them that something like what Trajon Jarl had done to his uncle was even possible.

"Gerard."

"Demetrius told us that Uncle Bryce was already dead, that Trajon Jarl had somehow brought him back."

"You're right. I don't believe it."

"He followed us all the way to the entrance of Blisterwind Pass. Demetrius backtracked the trail and found him. He was hiding in the forest, watching our camp. I heard Demetrius and Uncle Bryce fighting. I went to see if I could help."

"What happened?"

"Demetrius cut him with a knife. I saw the knife go in, come out. Uncle Bryce didn't react. He didn't bleed. There wasn't any blood. I..." How could he admit to his father what he had done? He knew Bryce was dead, that Trajon Jarl had done something to him, but his father and Uncle Bryce were brothers.

"You what?"

"I set Uncle Bryce on fire," he said. "The hottest fire I could make. He didn't scream at all. Even as he died, he didn't scream."

The two of them sat in silence.

There had been enough to deal with between them without this. But Bryce had done what he had done, and Gerard had only been defending himself and his friends. He hadn't done anything wrong, but he was not sure his father would see it that way. If only his father had been there.

"I don't like this, Gerard. I don't like it at all. A traitor in my own family."

"What? I thought you would be angry with me."

His father set the pen down.

"I am angry, Gerard. I'm angry that you didn't lead him here so that I could see what he had become for myself. I would have liked to put his neck in a noose, but you took care of that.

"I'm also angry at myself," his father continued. "Bryce was a little too eager to track you down after giving me the news of Eric's death. I should have seen it, I guess, but I grieved for Eric. I still grieve for him. When he suggested that he should be the one to find you and bring you back, it only made sense. I started to make plans. I should have known he had plans of his own. I wonder how many other malcontents Trajon Jarl has subverted."

It all fell into place for Gerard.

"Uncle Bryce didn't plan for me to survive the attack at the Academy. If I had died, he would have been next in line to inherit your title. I had thought you sent him to get me because you were angry with him, but he wanted to be sure."

His father nodded. "It seems that way."

The sound of the front door opening, then slamming shut reverberated throughout the house, even to where Gerard and his father sat.

"Demetrius and Robert must be back," Gerard said.

His father stood.

"Come, I need to talk to Demetrius, and I'd like to meet these friends of yours before I call a Council."

Gerard's mind swirled with possibilities. His father had become something other than the man he'd known growing up, and different again from the man he had first come home to. Gerard had to wonder if his father had changed, or if he himself had changed and grown since the day his father all but kicked him out.

ANGELA WAS ALREADY tired of lying in bed. She still shivered, despite the three thick blankets that covered her and the fire that burned in the hearth. The concoction the healer made her drink seemed to be working a little, but she wondered if the healer was as good as Nendra had been. She certainly hadn't been as friendly.

On top of her misery, it seemed like hours since Robert left with Demetrius.

The thought that they had found Thiobulus so quickly after arriving here had Angela excited. She wanted to know if they would be going, soon. It would mean their journey was almost over.

"I wonder what Thiobulus is like," Shane said.

He was sitting in a chair by the fire, holding his staff in one hand, a cup of kava in the other. He was stuck with her, maintaining the shield since she could not do it herself. As much as he had struggled maintaining it before she fell in the river, it now seemed easy for him.

But if Demetrius really had found Thiobulus, it could mean that none of them would have to maintain the shield. They could all get more sleep.

"I have no idea," Angela said.

"Do you think he will help?"

"Of course he will," Angela said. But she wasn't sure she believed it, even though Robert seemed convinced he would help. "Robert said Thiobulus told him to come to him for training. Even Monteous told Robert to seek Thiobulus out."

Another shiver wracked her body. She wished they would stop.

"It just seems that he's been hiding here for so long, almost as if he has little interest in the rest of the world."

"Robert saw him in Dominand last winter. That is hardly hiding."

Shane tapped his staff against the floor two times.

"I suppose. It will be nice to stop running," he said.

"It will."

"Is this what it was like when you were searching for Monteous last winter?"

"It was a lot colder last winter," she said, despite another shiver that wound its way down her arms.

"That's not what I meant."

"I know."

She thought about it, worked her way through her memories of those two weeks.

"Back then," she said, "we had help. Demetrius, Lord Ivron, they both helped us."

"Demetrius is with us now," Shane said.

"It's not the same." And it wasn't. This time, it seemed to her that Demetrius deferred to Robert more than he had the previous winter. And Ivron wasn't around. She missed him and his wife. Marena had made her feel so comfortable, and had helped her get over her fear of telling Robert the details of her past.

The difference, this time, was that she didn't feel like she and Robert had grown any closer. The threat to their lives hung between them like a veil. A thin wall that could be seen through, but not pierced.

She envied Nina in that way. There wasn't anything keeping her from Gerard any more. Gerard had decided he wanted Nina more than he wanted to make his father happy. Watching them together brought an ache to Angela's heart.

Robert had been better in his attention to her right up until Demetrius came into the room with news of Thiobulus. And then he had left. She had told him to go, but it didn't take much. She knew she was being selfish, but she had wanted it to be harder.

She heard the thumping of boots outside her door, right before the door opened.

Robert entered her room. He still wore his coat, as if he were leaving again.

"Did you find Thiobulus?" she asked. She tried to push herself up in the bed, but she felt so weak. She could not manage more than a few inches before Robert rushed to her side and pushed her back down into the bed by her shoulder.

"Stay down," he said. "You need your rest."

She conceded, and slipped back under her covers.

"Did you find him?"

"We found where he had been, and we know he's somewhere nearby."

Angela felt confused. He didn't seem excited about their discovery.

"What's wrong, Robert? What happened? Is Demetrius all right?"

Robert sat on the edge of her bed, still with a wistful look in his eye.

"Demetrius is fine. He's downstairs with Gerard's father. I guess Gerard told his father about Trajon Jarl and the Guild. They're discussing what Gerard's father should do about it."

"Then why do you look sad?"

Robert tried to smile, then. It didn't work so well.

"Robert, tell me," she said.

"I'm trying," he said. "I don't want to, though."

"Why not?"

"Because I wanted you to come with me."

Angela pushed herself up in bed this time before Robert could stop her.

"What do you mean you wanted me to come with you?"

But she knew what it meant. They weren't going to wait for her to get better.

"Demetrius and I are leaving tonight. We're going to find Thiobulus."

"You're leaving me here alone?" she asked, panicking. "I don't know these people."

"Not alone. It's only Demetrius and I that are leaving. Shane, Gerard, and Nina will stay, too."

She felt a little better knowing she wouldn't be alone, but he was still leaving her.

"You're leaving me here?" Shane asked. "I can help you."

Robert turned his head away from her, and she silently cursed Shane. If Robert was going, she wanted to memorize his face so that she could dream of it while he was gone.

"I need you to help Angela. You need to keep the shield up until she's better."

"If you're going to be gone, why do we need to keep the shield up?"

"There is no way to know who Trajon Jarl is looking for, if he's even looking any more. If he finds Angela, he might do something to her to get at me. If he finds you or Gerard or Nina, he might do the same. We don't know what his plans are."

Angela thought Shane seemed satisfied with the answer, even if he wasn't satisfied about being stuck here with her. He sat back in his chair again, rubbing the wood of his staff with his thumb.

"I don't have a staff," she said. She wished, not for the first time, that she hadn't lost hers in the river. "Not even a wand. When I get better..."

"You can borrow Gerard's or Shane's, if you need one," Robert said.

"You can use mine," Shane said, surprising Angela.

But she spared little time thinking about it. The staff wasn't actually important. She knew she was stalling. She didn't care.

"When will you be back? You will come back for me, won't you?"

"As soon as we find Thiobulus," Robert said, "I'll send word, somehow. I'll let you know how to find us."

"You swear it?"

He leaned over and hugged her—the fur trim on his coat tickled her nose. The whiskers on his cheek scratched her ear.

"I don't want to go just as much as you don't want me to go, but we don't have a choice. Every day that we waste is a day that Trajon Jarl could get lucky and find us and kill us all. I can't let you die."

"You need to shave," she said, trying not to cry. She hated that he was right. He couldn't afford to waste time because she was bedridden.

He sat back and rubbed at his face.

"I guess I do," he said.

"I wish I hadn't fallen in the river. I feel like I ruined everything."

"You haven't ruined anything," Robert said, "and it wasn't your fault at the river. It was my fault. I pushed you too hard."

She put her hand on his.

"No, Robert. You didn't push me. I was just trying to keep up with you."

His face came near to hers, then their lips touched. It had been days since she'd tasted his lips. She wished she wasn't ill so that the taste of sickness didn't taint that taste.

Then Robert parted from her and she was left with only the feel of those lips on hers.

He turned to Shane.

"You can do this, right?" he asked. "I'm trusting you to keep her safe."

"I can do it," Shane said.

"If you get tired, give the shield to Angela for a couple hours so you can take a nap. All your effort will be for nothing if you fall asleep."

Angela hoped she could handle it. She thought she could if needed. Her head was clear enough.

More footsteps in the hallway, and then Demetrius stood at the door.

"Are you ready?" Demetrius asked.

Robert bent down and kissed her again, deeper this time. She imagined he was taking a memory of her for himself.

When their lips parted this time, he stood up.

"I love you, Angela," he said.

"I love you, too."

He stepped out through the door, and shut it behind him.

She wished Shane would leave the room.

She wanted to cry.

CHAPTER 26

ROBERT HAD A hard time keeping his mind on the road during the first night away from Angela. Even though she was with Gerard and Nina and Shane, if Trajon Jarl found them, they had no way to protect themselves. Robert wanted to be back there protecting her, but he knew that even he could not stand against Trajon Jarl.

Which was the only reason he had left her. The only way to protect her was to find Thiobulus and hope the wizard could teach him something he could use against the monster that had been chasing him and haunting his dreams for the last two weeks.

"They will be there once we've found Thiobulus, Robert," Demetrius said.

"How long?" Robert asked, ignoring the fact that Demetrius had figured out what he was thinking.

"Two days' ride."

Two days of keeping the shield up and in place. Two days of no sleep. He'd already had a hard ride that day, and held the shield for much of it. With the rest of them left behind, he didn't have to keep it so big, but it would still be a strain. His biggest worry was that the lack of sleep might do him in, first.

"Is that with time to rest?" Robert asked.

"No. That's if we don't stop. Four days if we rest for the night."

Demetrius had just crushed Robert's thought that they would shorten the trip by riding straight through.

"On horseback?"

"Most of the way. We will have to abandon the horses for the final leg of the trip."

Which would only make him more tired.

"Maybe we should have stayed, given ourselves time to rest," Robert said.

"We went through that, already."

"You're not worried that I will fall asleep and drop the shield?"

Demetrius looked at Robert with his piercing eyes. "Do you have a better idea?"

"No." He couldn't bring Shane—it would expose Angela and Gerard to Trajon Jarl. Staying until Angela was better left them vulnerable in Gerard's parents' house. Jarl had to know where they were going. He couldn't imagine that Bryce had kept that a secret from his master.

"Then stay awake, whatever it takes."

The road wound its way through the mountain peaks, working its way ever higher. The air was thin enough that at times, Robert felt like it took several breaths to get enough air into his lungs. It was cold enough that he had to wear the thick coat they had bought in Treading Valley.

Once they passed beyond the easy reach of the lumbermen in the town, the trees grew taller and wider than anything Robert had ever seen. Their black shadows blotted out the moon and the stars so that only slivers of the night sky were visible above them. If Robert had walked up to one of the trees and tried to wrap his arms around it, his arms would not have extended even half way around the tree.

Just before dawn, Demetrius turned down a smaller road leading East. The trees stood closer together, crowding the road that snaked its way between them. A cart could not pass along the road. Their progress slowed considerably.

"Where does this take us?" Robert asked

"Around Grappling Peak. There is an iron mine on the far side, and a small village that supports it."

"How do they get the iron down this road? It won't fit a cart."

"There is a larger road that leads from the mine, beneath Broken Thunder Ridge, to the lowlands," Demetrius said. "This road is only used for travel between towns."

"Are we going to the mining village?"

"No. We turn off before then."

About mid-day, the temperature had risen enough that Robert had to remove the heavy coat. It was still cool, compared to the Dominand summer days they had left behind, but it was too warm for the coat.

"You'll be putting that back on, before long," Demetrius said.

"Why?"

"The sun will start to set behind us and the air is so thin it won't retain the heat."

They came upon a small clearing where someone had carved a large stump into a table and benches. Demetrius brought them to a stop and suggested that they give the horses a rest and some water.

"Water?"

"There is a stream that runs past this spot."

Demetrius pulled a small package wrapped in paper and a water pouch from the pack on his horse.

"Here," he said, handing the items to Robert. "Sit and eat while I water the horses. You look like you are about to fall over."

Robert took the water pouch and the package to the stump-table and sat down. He hadn't noticed while riding, but the walk proved to him that his whole body was weary. Tired of maintaining the shield, tired from lack of sleep, tired from worry. Demetrius was right. He needed to eat.

He spilled the package and the water pouch onto the table in front of him. He switched his staff from his right hand to his left. Both of his hands ached from holding the staff nearly non-stop since they'd left Nendra's. It seemed they might permanently be stuck in a curled position. He couldn't wait until he could set the staff aside for a day or a week.

Out of habit, he slipped into the vew to check the shield. It was still there, keeping him hidden from Trajon Jarl. Out of the corner of his eye, he noticed another Weave, this one around the package Demetrius had given him.

He picked up the package with his free hand, flipped it over and over, and couldn't figure out what it was. The Weave didn't seem dangerous, and he didn't think it would be, having come from Demetrius. It was woven into the paper, and looked like a protection Weave.

Robert pulled at the paper, unwrapping what was inside, and discovered three flat pieces of dried meat.

He picked up one of the pieces, turned it back and forth in his hand, but couldn't figure out what it was. He sniffed at it, but didn't recognize the underlying smell, though it had a strong pepper smell.

He bit into it. The first taste jumped into his mouth, spicy and sweet at the same time. Another bite. His energie started to flow through him again, undimmed by his fatigue. Even the fatigue seemed to have lessened.

When he finished the meat, he swallowed a good bit of the water. He no longer felt as tired as he had, and his energie had been renewed enough that he thought he could hold the shield without faltering.

Demetrius returned with the horses as Robert set the water pouch on the table.

"What was that meat, Demetrius?"

Demetrius smiled. "Do you feel better?"

"I do."

"The meat is from a bear."

"It was more than bear," Robert said. "There was a Weave throughout that wrapper."

"Monteous gave me that paper," Demetrius said. "It is supposed to preserve whatever you put in it for months."

"It seems to do more than that," Robert said. He picked up paper and examined the Weave. It hadn't diminished. "It seemed to make that meat more potent than it should have been. My energie is nearly back to what it should be, as if I had slept all night. I don't feel as tired as I should."

"The only thing it's ever done for me is ease my fatigue," Demetrius said.

Robert went to hand the paper back to Demetrius, but Demetrius refused it.

"You keep it," Demetrius said. "It seems you'll get more out of it than I do, and I have another one."

"That's why you didn't seem worried about me falling asleep."

The corners of Demetrius's mouth rose a fraction of an inch.

"Thank you, Demetrius."

Robert folded the paper carefully with his free hand, then went to slip it into the pack on his horse. He'd have to find more food to put in it, soon.

As his hand went into the pack, it rubbed up against another piece of paper, and he pulled it out.

It was the letter Angela had written him at the Academy. He turned it over. It still had Trajon Jarl's message on the back. He flipped it over again and read Angela's words one more time. They gave him some comfort, so he slipped it back into the pack. He'd keep it with him until he saw her again.

True to Demetrius's word, the road climbed higher, and the temperature fell toward evening so that Robert had to don his coat again.

The trees thinned out, allowing him a view of the snow-cap atop the mountain only a few hundred feet above them.

Robert followed Demetrius through the night, wondering just when they would have to turn off and abandon the horses. His horse had been good to him, and he didn't like the idea of abandoning her to bears or mountain lions or whatever else might live nearby, but he didn't see he had much choice. Without her, he could never have made it this far.

Just before dawn, Demetrius led them to a small meadow next to a stream.

Demetrius dismounted, and Robert followed his lead.

"What are we doing?" Robert asked.

"We'll tie off the horses here with long enough leads that they can reach the water and still eat. Once I've delivered you to Thiobulus, assuming he's here, I'll come back and take them to Blisterwind Pass."

That Demetrius was thinking of the horses made Robert feel a little better about leaving them. However, the idea that Demetrius would leave him with Thiobulus frightened him. He'd come to depend on Demetrius's presence.

"You're going to leave me with him? Why?"

"You won't need me, and the others will need my help to find this place."

"And if he's not there?"

Demetrius reached into his pack and pulled out a long rope.

"Then we'll have a problem."

WITHOUT HIS STAFF, Gerard felt vulnerable in a way that he had not felt since his first days as an apprentice. He'd given it to Angela the morning after Robert left in search of Thiobulus. She needed it to spell Shane while Shane rested. Angela could have used Shane's staff, but she had argued that Gerard didn't need his right then. He thought she had other reasons for not wanting to use Shane's staff, but she had been right. He didn't need his staff.

His father had sent runners out the night before to the nearest lords, and already, the three that lived within a day's ride had come to visit. The first had arrived that morning, and Gerard's father had suggested that Gerard hide the staff. They didn't need to provoke the lords after the news he had sent them.

Gerard had agreed.

His father said there would be six of them, all told, and once they arrived, Gerard would have to tell them the story.

Gerard wasn't sure that was a good idea, but his father said he trusted these men, and that he was certain they would not have rolled over for Trajon Jarl like Bryce had.

Which meant, to Gerard, that they all had a healthy hatred for wizards.

Gerard spent the morning with Nina, hiding in the room next door to Angela's so that she didn't have to project the shield very far. It seemed like that need might never end.

"I hope Robert finds Thiobulus quickly," he said.

He wished Robert had not left him behind, but he knew why he had to stay. Robert wanted him to protect Angela as best he could. Of course, if Trajon Jarl showed up, Gerard had no idea how to do that. His first experience with that vile wizard had shown him just how much he couldn't do.

"Demetrius knows where he is," said Nina.

Her head was nestled in his chest. He stroked her hair with his fingers.

"Demetrius thinks he knows. But if Thiobulus isn't there, then what? Angela and Shane can't keep up the shield forever. One of them will wear out and make a mistake, and then Trajon Jarl will be right on us."

"You worry too much," said Nina.

He couldn't dispute her, though holding her and feeling her weight against him helped keep his worries in check.

"What if Jarl does show up?"

"We'll kill him," she said.

"How are we supposed to do that?" he asked, remembering the scene outside his window at the Academy right before Jarl had turned and sent a fireball at him. What chance did they have against a man that had defeated all four masters at the Academy?

"He'll die from an arrow through the throat. He's still a man."

Gerard wasn't so sure. He had no idea how wizards lived to more than two hundred years, like it seemed both Trajon Jarl and Thiobulus had done, but it wasn't natural. Wizards did have longer lives; he knew that. But none of the wizards in the Guild were that old. Not even Monteous. Master Brin had been approaching a hundred, and he hadn't looked like he would live another ten years before Trajon Jarl cut his life short.

Gerard didn't express his doubts to Nina, though. He didn't want to frighten her, just in case she was right and an arrow through the throat would kill him. Fear destroyed more attempted Weaves than anything, and he doubted shooting arrows was any different.

He did love her spirit, though. Nina wasn't afraid of much at all.

And if Shane and Angela kept the shield up, they would be safe. Trajon Jarl wouldn't be able to find them, and Nina wouldn't need to put an arrow through his neck.

He shivered.

"What's wrong?" Nina asked.

"I don't know. I was just thinking about how Angela and Shane are keeping us safe, and I suddenly felt like we are missing something, and we aren't safe at all."

She lifted her head up and looked at him. "Do you think so?"

"I don't know. It's just a feeling."

"Father always told me to trust my feelings," Nina said.

"That's how you ended up with me," Gerard said and chuckled.

She punched him in the shoulder. "I'm not joking. If you really feel like we aren't safe, then you have to figure out why you feel that way."

"I don't know what it is."

"Maybe you should talk to your father. He might have an idea."

"No," Gerard said. "Not right now. I've seen enough of him for now. I'll keep thinking about it. Maybe it will come to me."

Nina laid her head back down on his chest.

It felt as good as before, but he couldn't take any pleasure in it. He kept searching for the splinter that had wedged itself in his mind. It wouldn't let him leave it alone.

TRAJON JARL CURSED Bryce Maracane one more time. He hadn't counted how many times he'd cursed the man, but he had cursed him every day since the fool got himself killed a second time.

Ever since, Trajon had been stuck in the tiny little windowless lab with a single workbench and a dearth of proper Works, constantly scrying for any sign of Robert and his apprentice friends with little luck. The lab only had the one room and a single hard-backed chair to sit in. It smelled of dust and ruin even before he had destroyed the wizards that were Working in it.

The constant scrying had only proved frustrating. There was one moment when Robert's shield had dropped and he had found the young apprentice, but the shield had gone back up only moments later. There hadn't been enough time to do anything but understand Robert and his friends were in a canyon next to a river, and that it was raining.

Trajon figured they had to be in Risuk, on the way to that apprentice's father's home. That weasel Bryce had said they were going there before looking for Thiobulus.

Trajon thought about going, waiting for them, then following Robert and that creature Demetrius until they found Thiobulus, but he had other things that needed doing.

The Guild was in a panic, now, huddling together like the sheep they were. They knew Trajon was killing their members. Thirty-three at last count. Too many had disappeared to keep it a secret, and it seemed Robert had somehow sent them a message. Maybe it was that wizard Bryce had killed.

Trajon supposed he should thank Bryce, were he still around to accept his thanks. Having the wizards group together would only made it more exciting for him, and more satisfying, when he proved to them that he could not be stopped.

He took in a satisfied breath, and the stench of death hit him again.

Trajon looked up from the water of the borrowed scrying bowl to the bodies of five wizards piled against the far wall. Their limbs all hung askew, where they were still attached, their faces melted and sloughing off their skulls. He hadn't been able to drain them all of their blood. He'd had to kill them, first. Exciting, but wasteful.

No. He wouldn't thank Bryce.

If he could have raised Bryce's body again, just so that he could kill it himself, he would have.

He didn't have time to sit and watch for an opening that would tell him where his prey was hiding.

He knew where they were going. He could trail them from there. It would interrupt his plans for the Guild, but killing Thiobulus was far more important. The Guild could wait.

Trajon knocked the scrying bowl from the workbench, sending the water flying to splash upon the dead wizards.

He gathered his things, few as they were, and put them into the pockets of his robe.

He fished out the Telanderal, Weaved the image of that canyon he had seen into it, and prepared for the jolt that using the Work always gave him as he was in one place, and then another.

The rain had stopped. The river next to him flowed free, lower than it had been in the scrying bowl.

Now he knew where he was.

And he knew the apprentices were ahead of him.

He walked north, while he awaited the inevitable wagon that would pass by. He would ask for a ride, and he would soon find himself in Blisterwind Pass.

A smile crossed his face.

He was close to finding Thiobulus, close to exacting his revenge on the man that had imprisoned him for so long.

CHAPTER 27

ROBERT'S LEGS FELT like they were filled with stones. Every muscle in his body cried out for rest, but Demetrius pushed on. He wanted to reach their destination before nightfall.

At mid-day, Demetrius let him rest for a few minutes and gave him the other wrapped bit of bear meat that he had. It helped, but not as much as the previous day. Robert needed sleep. He knew he was dangerously close to draining himself.

"Are there any more of those?" Robert asked, pointing at the now empty paper. He knew there weren't, but asked anyway.

"No."

Robert pulled himself to his feet, using his staff for leverage.

"We should get moving, then," he said, though it went against everything his body wanted at that moment. Even with the infusion of energie, he felt out of sorts.

The trail followed a seemingly random route up and down the side of the mountain. For a time, it followed a creek that, when Robert sampled it, turned out to be nearly as cold as winter ice. From the creek, the trail led up again to where the forest thinned out from the altitude. At that point, without any obvious reason, it crossed over a ridge in the mountainside and led them back down the mountain and into thicker forest again.

Several times, he stumbled over rocks and almost lost control of his staff. He quickly slipped into the vew when this happened to make sure the shield was still in place—it was, but the threads looked more and more ragged each time he inspected them. He tried to tighten them up, but that spent even more precious energie.

After they turned up the mountain again, Robert noticed that his vision was starting to blur. Even while he walked, his eyelids tried to droop.

Once, he found himself stopped, just staring up at Demetrius as Demetrius climbed up the trail. Demetrius turned around, but Robert closed his eyes, just for a moment. They were so heavy. Just a short rest.

Then someone grabbed him by the shoulders and shook him.

"Robert, don't go to sleep," Demetrius said.

"I'm not," Robert said. "I'm just resting my eyes."

"Come on, Robert, there's only a little farther to go. Just up this bit of the mountain, and over a ridge. Once we're there, you can rest."

Robert tried to sit down to rest his legs. "Just a few minutes," he said.

"No, Robert. You don't want Trajon Jarl to find us."

Trajon who? He couldn't remember who that was. Demetrius thought he was important.

Demetrius took his hand, pulled Robert with him up the trail.

Robert gave in and went with him.

Demetrius's help made it only a little easier.

Robert's eyes kept closing. He opened them, and they'd stay open for a few steps before sliding closed again.

Demetrius led him, stumbling, up a rocky slope. There were only a few thin, stumpy trees battling to survive amongst the rocks.

When they crested the ridge, a mountain top panorama opened up in front of Robert. Through his blurring vision, he could see a thousand other mountains, a sea of white-capped stone edifices. For a moment, his mind drifted back to the chase through the snow and ice to find Monteous.

His body started to shake.

Demetrius took his arm and guided him over the top of the ridge.

Robert's foot slipped out from under him.

His leg gave way, and he lost his grip on the staff.

And then he slid down the slope, rocks digging and cutting through his breaches. He tumbled over, then rolled. He rolled and rolled, then thumped to a stop. Pain like he had never imagined broke through his exhaustion and flashed up from his arm into his neck.

Where was Demetrius? Robert tried to look for him, but couldn't see him through the tears the pain brought to his eyes.

He tried to shift his body in hopes of relieving the pain, but he couldn't move, even a little. He had nothing left.

Movement from up the slope drew his eye, but he couldn't make out the detail. The sky seemed to be growing darker. Was night falling? He didn't know.

He only wanted the pain to stop.

And then he remembered his staff.

He didn't have it.

He slipped into the vew and looked up.

Through the blur and haze of pain, exhaustion, and tears, he could find no trace of a Weave. The shield was gone.

He closed his eyes against the pain . . . and couldn't open them again.

GROWING UP, GERARD had never been allowed to attend a gathering of the lords. His father told him he would never have the need to attend, since he would never inherit.

But now, he sat in the room with five other lords, not counting his father. The sixth one, a Lord Engram, had not yet arrived.

Gerard wasn't sure what to make of the lords. The five of them looked and acted like a bunch of old men who had nothing better to do with their lives but argue.

They had done nothing but argue since Gerard told his story two hours earlier.

His father had been right to keep him from the gatherings, but not for his father's reasons. These lords bickered even more than the wizards of the Guild.

Gerard found himself musing that it was amazing The Seven Kingdoms had lasted as long as it had. He couldn't help but contrast them with Lord Ivron Meningale, who had helped them find Monteous and defeat Orliss last winter. Ivron was nothing like these men. He had taken action to defend The Seven Kingdoms. He had risked his own life to help four apprentices.

Then, the thought came to Gerard that maybe it wasn't the entirety of The Seven Kingdoms that was ill-served by its lords, but only Risuk. Perhaps the wizards of Risuk had left with reason. Maybe they left because the lords of Risuk couldn't stop bickering like little children.

He felt the smile cross his lips, but was too late in erasing it.

Lord Graminer, a particularly bitter and unpleasant man, noticed it.

"You smile, young Gerard. Do you find something funny?"

The man's nose hooked down like the beak of an owl, and a thick white mustache hid his lips. He held himself straight, but could not hide the bend in his neck, the veins on his temples, or the thinning hair on his scalp.

"Was I smiling?" Gerard said, hoping to pass it off as something other than mockery.

"You most certainly were," said Lord Graminer.

"Then it was inadvertent, Lord," Gerard said.

"Leave him alone, Graminer," said his father.

Lord Graminer turned away from Gerard to face his father.

"I cannot believe that you would suggest I ignore him," Graminer said. "He's your heir, now. He should be paying attention to these discussions, not daydreaming."

"I am not the heir," Gerard said and then wished he hadn't.

"So you are going to slink back to those wizards that got us into this mess?"

Gerard stood up, the anger coming to him easily. "You have no idea what you are talking about, Lord Graminer. If the Guild did not exist, The Seven Kingdoms would have been overrun long ago. I cannot be the heir because I am a wizard. It is against the law, and you should know that."

That Graminer was willing to ignore that Gerard was a wizard only served to fuel his anger. It made Gerard wonder if Graminer would side with Trajon Jarl, just like his uncle had, in order to eradicate the Guild.

"Gerard, sit down," his father said, but Gerard hardly heard him through his anger.

"If it weren't for the wizards, Risuk would still be a sovereign country," said Lord Graminer.

Gerard ached for his staff. He slipped into the vew and started to gather energie from the wood around him. The staff would have been more effective, but he could still show Lord Graminer that wizards were not cowards, nor were they traitors.

"Gerard!"

His father's shout broke through to him, and he slipped out of the vew to find that his father was also standing, his face red with anger.

"Sit down. And you, Lord Graminer, I suggest you keep your opinions about wizards to yourself. That goes for all of you. Whatever we were, that was two hundred years ago, and we are a part of The Seven Kingdoms. If The Seven Kingdoms falls, we fall with it. This wizard that Gerard told us about won't spare us, nor will Mrongil."

Gerard sat down, reluctantly. He wished he could just leave the room, but he couldn't now, even if his father would let him. It would only give credence to Lord Graminer's claims, and Gerard wouldn't allow himself to be party to that.

Lord Graminer would not be dissuaded so easily.

"You hold no power, here, Gentran," he said with his finger pointed in a crooked fashion at his father. "No more than the rest of us, and I have a right to be heard."

His father sighed. "You are correct, of course, but that does not give you the right to disparage my son or the Wizards' Guild. The Guild is under attack, as is The Seven Kingdoms. You heard what Gerard told you, and you heard about my brother. There may be others like Bryce among the lords of Risuk, for I cannot believe that my brother is the only person close to power that this Trajon Jarl has subverted."

"You think he has subverted lords already?" said Lord Regnarm, a short, pudgy man with a bulbous nose and gray hair that still held its curl.

"That's ridiculous. No lord of Risuk would stoop to working with a wizard," said Lord Graminer.

"I would not have thought my brother would fall in with one, either," said his father.

"Are you sure you can believe your boy?"

Gerard seethed. He imagined wrapping a Weave around the man and hanging him from the rafters.

"He has no reason to lie to me," his father said. "He wasn't there when Eric died. He didn't come here on his own, but at the behest of my brother."

Lord Graminer harrumphed.

Lord Regnarm cleared his throat. "I propose that this is too much of a problem for the six of us to solve here. We should send a rider to Lord Henfelgar and have him convene a Council at the earliest date."

A Council. Gerard couldn't believe it. It took weeks for riders to work their way through the mountains.

"We don't have time," Gerard said. "It'll take weeks, won't it? Trajon Jarl could have murdered every wizard in the Guild by then. We need to send warnings to the lords."

"You forget yourself, young wizard," said Lord Graminer.

"I..."

"Quiet, Gerard," said his father.

A knock at the front door echoed into the room.

The sun had nearly set.

Who would be knocking at the front door?

Gerard felt a shiver run down his spine.

He stood up when his father did.

"Don't answer it, Father," Gerard said.

"Why not? It's not like your uncle is at the door."

His father started to leave the room.

And then Gerard realized the mistake he had made. Trajon Jarl didn't need to find them. Bryce could have told him where they were going, and his father's house was easy to find.

Gerard raced after his father and pulled at his arm.

"Father, don't."

"Gerard, it is probably Lord Engram just arrived. Release me."

Gerard loosened his hold on his father, and his father strode to the front door. Gerard followed at a distance, aiming for the staircase. If it was Lord Engram, he could pretend as if he needed to relieve himself. But if it wasn't, if his fears were true, he would be that much closer to Nina and his staff.

He couldn't believe what a fool he had been. Even if it was Lord Engram, he knew they would have to leave. He had put his mother and his father in danger.

His father's hand gripped the latch and pulled the door open.

At first, Gerard couldn't get a look at the person beyond the door, because his father blocked the way. Gerard reached the stairs and put his foot on the first step.

"Hello," said a voice Gerard didn't recognize. "Lord Engram sent me. He could not make it."

"Ah," Gerard's father said, stepping aside to let the man in. "What is your name, sir?"

Gerard got a good look at the man who stood outside the door before the man saw him at the back of the room. His skin was pale, his eyes dark with a reddish tint. A wisp of black hair peeked out from beneath his cowl.

Gerard's next step up the stairs missed and landed hard on the step below it's target. The sound of it rang out through the room.

The man looked up at the noise and saw Gerard. He smiled. It was a smile Gerard would never forget.

"My name is Trajon Jarl," said the man. "You might know of me."

CHAPTER 28

"**N**INA!"

The first time she heard Gerard shout, Nina rolled over on the bed that she had been resting on. Even having a full night's sleep the night before had not been enough to restore her body.

"Nina!"

The second time, she heard the panic in his voice.

She rolled out of bed, grabbed her bow and the quiver of arrows standing next to it. She slung the quiver over her shoulder, pulled out an arrow and knocked it before opening the door of the room.

For a moment, she felt silly, like she was overreacting. Her first thought had been that Trajon Jarl found them, but Shane had been keeping up the shield, and Angela helped when she could. He couldn't have found them.

"Nina, ru..." Something cut Gerard off, but Nina knew what he'd been telling her. *Run.*

The door to Angela's room opened, and Shane stood there with his staff. Behind him, Nina saw that Angela was struggling to get out of bed. She already had Gerard's staff in her hand, but she was in no shape to do anything.

"Get Angela out of here, Shane," Nina said as quietly as she could.

"What's going on?" Shane asked.

"I don't know. Just hide her somewhere."

"You think it's..."

Nina nodded.

"I can help."

"No," Nina said. "We can't fight him."

Shane squinted and drew his brows together. "Then what are you doing?"

"What I can," she said.

She knew she should be helping Shane escape with Angela, but she couldn't leave Gerard. Not so soon after he married her, not before they had a chance at a life together.

She reached out and pushed Shane back through the door before pulling it shut.

"Robert." A deep, cracked voice sounded throughout the building. It made Nina shiver, but she wasn't going to let that stop her.

"Come down here, Robert. I have your friend."

Jarl did not know where Robert was. He wasn't omniscient. He hadn't penetrated the shield. Nina took a little comfort knowing that, though the knowledge did not calm her nerves any.

She edged forward, thankful she was in her bare feet. They would keep her silent on the wood floor of the hallway as long as the boards did not creak under her.

"Your friends are not important to me, Robert. If you come down, I'll let them go. I just want to talk with you."

"No Robert!" Gerard's shout echoed up the stairway, and Nina knew Gerard was trying to give them some time to escape. "Don't come down here!"

Then Gerard cried out in pain. Jarl had hit him, or worse. She tried not to imagine.

She reached the end of the hallway. She wanted to stick her head out to survey the foyer, but she kept it back, kept herself hidden. There was too great a chance Trajon Jarl would be looking up and would see her.

She had only one shot. Jarl would throw a fireball at her the moment he knew she was there. She wished she could remember how she had saved herself and Gerard the first time, but it had been instinctual.

She aimed her bow down, about the angle where she expected she might find Jarl if she was looking over the railing to the floor below. She drew the arrow back.

"Robert," said Jarl. "Don't make this hard on your friends. I can use you all. I can teach you things the Guild would never have taught you in a thousand years."

Nina spun out from her place against the wall, aimed her bow over the railing.

Below her, Gerard was on his knees in front of Trajon Jarl. Gerard's father was there, too, but he was lying on the floor, his skin pale, like Master Wendell's had been when they found him. Nina knew instantly that he was dead.

She adjusted her aim for Jarl's head and his strangely dark eyes.

She released her arrow.

It burned up in a flash before it even left the bow. Her bowstring snapped and the bow's limbs sprung to their natural position sending a shock up her arm. She cried out from the pain.

Something gripped her around the waist, lifted her into the air and brought her toward Jarl and Gerard. It had to be a Weave.

"You must be Nina. You really should have listened to Gerard, you know."

She slipped into the vew like she'd been taught. She could see the threads that held her, but she could do nothing about them. There was far too much energie in them for her to handle.

Jarl set her down in front of him and kept his hold on her.

"Where is Robert?" he asked. "Is he up there, too?"

"Don't tell him anything," Gerard said.

Jarl's booted foot kicked Gerard in the back, knocking him to the floor.

"Be quiet, apprentice."

Jarl turned his attention back to her.

"Now, tell me where Robert is, or you'll end up like this one, here," Jarl said while pointing at Gerard's father.

Nina didn't believe that Jarl would just leave them be, but she didn't know what else she could do. She had never imagined he could set the arrow on fire and burn it to ash after she loosed it, but before it left her bow completely.

"He left," she said.

"Where did he go?"

"He didn't tell us." She hoped he wouldn't hear the lie.

"HE DIDN'T TELL us," said the red-headed girl.

If Trajon had been so inclined, she was pretty enough to take with him, and full of the kind of spark that he liked in his women.

But he had not been so inclined since escaping his prison to learn that his wife was long dead. Since that rueful day, he had spent every moment plotting his revenge against Thiobulus and his cronies.

This girl, though, she meant something to the boy on the floor. He could use that.

"He didn't tell you," he said. "That is not so good for you."

Her heartbeat sped up, the beat of it thumping in his ears. The boy's heartbeat echoed hers. There were five other heartbeats in the room to his left, all beating furiously in fear. Trajon would not be surprised if one of them just fell over and died. Old heartbeats. Worthless men.

"He... he was looking for a wizard named Thiobulus," she said.

"Nina!" shouted the boy.

Trajon thought about kicking him again, but the idea wasn't all that satisfying.

"I know that," Trajon said.

Making them squirm was far more satisfying, and the boy, the boy he could use.

Someone opened a door upstairs. He heard another pair of heartbeats that he had briefly heard earlier, just before the girl tried to shoot him.

"There are two other friends of yours upstairs. Please call them down."

He snugged the Weave a little tighter on the girl to give her some incentive.

She didn't say anything.

"I can squeeze you until you die," he said.

She glared at him with hate in her eyes. It made him smile.

Then the little bit of blood that was still in him, the blood that matched the blood that he used to write the letter to Robert on the back of that amusing love letter, the part that he continually monitored with the back of his mind, stirred. The letter became visible to him again.

And Robert was nowhere near him.

But Trajon had the direction.

He threw the girl to the ground.

He had to leave, and leave now, if he were to have any chance of finding Robert before Thiobulus corrupted him.

He wished he had a scrying bowl so that he could get a better idea of where Robert was. Then he could just use the Telanderal to go right to the young wizard, but in this place, he knew he would find no scrying bowls.

He had a distance, though, and he had a direction. He just had to get close enough.

He shoved Gerard to the ground.

If only he had time to question them more...

But if Robert was leading him to Thiobulus, there would be time once the old wizard was dealt with.

He whirled and stormed out through the door into the twilight.

There will most definitely be time.

CARRYING ROBERT UP and down the slopes of the mountainside wore on Demetrius. He hadn't had any sleep, either, and he needed some. His gifts did not extend to the ability to go without sleep for days on end. He did need less sleep than most, but he was fast approaching his breaking point.

Every muscle in his body ached. His hands were raw from catching himself on rocks each time he fell underneath Robert's weight. They would heal quickly, given a chance, but he wasn't giving them that chance.

His stomach had a hole in it, too, and that hole was growing. He wished he could stop to eat, but with Robert unconscious, he knew it was only a matter of time before Trajon Jarl found them. He had to get Robert to Thiobulus before that happened.

And, as much as he didn't want to see his old master, he needed the wizard, and found himself wishing Thiobulus would appear over the next ridge to help him carry Robert to safety.

But he trudged on, step after step, climbing over the rocks. Night had fallen. The stars and a newly risen moon were his only light. He thought he had less than a mile to go—over one more ridge that loomed black in front of him, then up the mountainside to a small, quite hidden, cave entrance.

The air had cooled, chilling the sweat on his arms, but he wasn't at all cold, not after carrying Robert on his back.

"If only you weren't so heavy," he said.

Only the birds heard him.

He stumbled as he reached the top of the ridge and fell flat on his stomach. Robert's weight was not enough to crush him, but it made breathing hard, especially with the thin air. The rock dust caught in his nostrils with each inhale, further impeding his ability to breathe.

He pushed himself up, stumbled over the ridge, then slid down the other side. The rope that he'd used to tie Robert to him broke, and they separated. As Robert fell away, his staff, which Demetrius had threaded in between them, cracked Demetrius on the head, sending a burst of pain through his skull.

The slide down the hill bumped and bruised Demetrius. Sharp rocks poked and sliced at him as he slid past.

When he finally came to a stop, he groaned and set his head down, relieved that there wasn't a drop-off below them.

After a moment, he turned over to push himself up.

Then a light bloomed above him on the slope.

"You were far less clumsy the last time I saw you, Demetrius."

Demetrius looked up.

Thiobulus stood above him, the light shining from his staff. Thiobulus hadn't changed in the fifty or so years since Demetrius had last seen him. His beard was still white and trimmed to just below his collar, his hair was mostly missing, but for a tuft behind each ear.

"The last time you saw me, Master," Demetrius said, unable to call Thiobulus by name, "I was not carrying a full grown man on my back after two days without sleep."

"Why were you carrying him? A full grown man should walk on his own."

Demetrius frowned. One of the things that he had grown tired of during his years with Thiobulus was the wizard's penchant for asking questions to which he already knew the answer.

"We need to get him inside. He was keeping a shield over us to hide from Trajon Jarl. He slipped and fell, knocked himself out. Trajon Jarl might find us here."

"We are safe," Thiobulus said. His voice had gone cold as the air around them. "If Trajon chooses to follow you here, that will be his last mistake."

"Are you certain?" Demetrius asked. "He defeated four wizards at the Academy, and killed most of the apprentices, too."

"Have you started losing your memories, Demetrius? Did I do my work that poorly? I know everything that Trajon knows. The men that call themselves wizards these days are a shadow of what we once were. They play at being wizards, and it would not surprise me if Trajon would be able to best a dozen of them. Your own self would have a better chance against Trajon than those wizards of the Guild."

"But Trajon escaped the prison you put him in, Master," Demetrius said.

"He did. Forty years ago."

"Forty years?"

"I knew the moment he broke free, Demetrius. I have searched for him all these years, but he hid himself well. He would have been weak to start, but he's had all these years to gain his strength back. It won't matter. We imprisoned him once, we can do it again."

Demetrius wondered about that, but kept his thoughts to himself. It had been a close thing the first time, and Thiobulus had the help of others nearly as powerful as himself. And Demetrius knew there were things that Trajon Jarl was more than willing to do that Thiobulus would never do, even to save the world from destruction.

"Well," Thiobulus said. "Enough of that. Where is your burden?"

"The rope broke, Master, and he tumbled away."

"You don't need to call me 'master' anymore, Demetrius. I am not your master, and haven't been for sixty years. That boy is your master now."

Demetrius didn't think he could stop calling Thiobulus 'master', and he didn't think he could start calling Robert that, either. But he knew that if he didn't try, Thiobulus would make him, one way or another. In that regard, Thiobulus was just like Trajon Jarl. They would do whatever it took to get their way.

"Shall we go find him?" Thiobulus asked.

"Yes, Thiobulus," Demetrius said with difficulty.

"That's better."

CHAPTER 29

ANGELA'S HEAD ACHED, her eyes didn't want to open very far, and now, she was out in the cold again. She wasn't ready. She knew she was ill. Her nose would not stop running, no matter how many times she had blown into the handkerchief Gerard's mother had given her. She was loathe to use it anymore, too. It needed a good washing.

Shane had hurried her out of the bed, and made her dress. While she dressed, Shane slipped the door open. They could both hear Gerard shouting, as well as the loud, disturbing voice of Trajon Jarl.

Then they slipped out the window, onto the roof above the front steps of the house. Shane Weaved a platform for them, and lowered them to the ground.

Angela was glad he did it. She was in no condition to jump.

"What next?" she asked Shane. She felt she should have known, but her mind just wouldn't work.

"The horses," Shane said. "I'll get them. Hide in the bushes."

Shane ran off, leaving her standing by herself, cold and miserable, leaning on Gerard's staff.

The door banged open behind her, and she turned to see a man step out onto the porch. She recognized him, but her mind worked too slowly to put a name to him.

"There you are," he said.

She knew the voice. Trajon Jarl.

He smiled, just like he had in the hallway back at the Academy.

"I don't need these others," he said, "but you..."

She tried to run, but tripped almost immediately and fell into a bush that scratched at her skin with sharp thorns.

"Oh, don't run this time," he said.

He seemed to glide down off the porch to come to her side.

She slipped into the vew and tried to pull the energie together to strike at him with fire, but she was still too weak and tired. The energie slipped out of her grasp no matter how hard she tried.

"Oh, I don't think so," he said.

He reached down and took her by the arm. His hand was cold. If it hadn't moved, she would have said it felt lifeless. He pulled her to her feet, then pulled Gerard's staff from her hand and cast it aside.

He put his own staff in the crook of his arm, then reached into his pocket and withdrew a small bit of stone and wood. In the vew, she could tell it was a Work, but she had no idea what it did.

She struggled against him as best she could, but her struggles were fruitless. She was too weak, and each movement of her head made it ache worse.

Jarl rubbed the Work with his finger. She could see the energie he was pouring into it, but it was in a pattern she had never witnessed.

"What are you doing?" she asked.

"We're going to find your lover," he said.

She heard the door bang open again. She couldn't move her head to see, but she heard Gerard yell, "Leave her alone!"

Trajon Jarl said, "I don't think so." Then he laughed.

The world shifted, and Angela no longer stood in front of Gerard's house.

She now stood on a forested mountainside with a vile wizard intent on destroying the only life she thought still possible for her.

Tears threatened to come. She tried to hold them back, but with Trajon's cold hand on her arm, she didn't succeed.

"Why are you crying, Angela?"

There wasn't any hint of concern in Jarl's voice.

She didn't answer.

"There's no reason. We'll find Robert, and the two of you will come with me, and I'll teach you everything that the Guild does not want you to know."

"Never," she said through her tears.

"Oh, I think you will change your mind." He sounded amused. "Now, come with me. I do not want to do for you what I did for Bryce, but I will if you cause me trouble."

Angela shuddered, and Jarl laughed.

"Come along, now. We must hurry if we are to find your Robert."

He pulled at her arm, and she stumbled along behind him. After a few moments, she managed to get her feet under her. When she did, he let go of her arm.

"Do not try to run. You will not get anywhere," Jarl said.

She knew that. Without a staff, she couldn't do much to him. She would bide her time, try to get better, and hope for an opening in which she might kill him. If she couldn't kill him, she'd at least try to warn Robert, but she needed more energie than she could handle right then.

If only that healer's concoction would start to work.

✺ ✺ ✺

GERARD BLINKED IN shock. Jarl and Angela just disappeared, vanished like they had never been there. If his staff hadn't been lying on the ground as evidence, he might have thought he'd hallucinated the two of them.

He stepped over and picked up his staff, Weaved a light at the end of it, and searched the ground.

There were footprints in the dirt.

They had been there.

And disappeared.

The sound of horses came to him. He looked up and saw Shane riding into the courtyard on one while leading another.

An urge to yell at Shane for leaving Angela alone erupted inside Gerard, but he capped it. Angela wasn't in any shape to walk anywhere. Shane hadn't had a choice.

Nina came out to stand next to him.

"What happened?" she asked. She was rubbing her head.

"Jarl took Angela. They just disappeared."

"Disappeared? Is that even possible?"

"It must be. I saw it happen, and it wasn't any sort of invisibility Weave like Angela could do. Their footprints are right there," he said pointing at two sets of prints among the other scuffs in the garden dirt, "but they don't lead anywhere."

Shane jumped down from the horse and ran over to him.

"Where is she?" Shane asked.

Gerard went through the same quick conversation that he'd just had with Nina.

"What do we do, then?" Nina asked. "What do we tell Robert when he returns?"

Gerard didn't know. How could they even find her? They couldn't without knowing where Jarl was going.

He heard a scream from inside the house.

He ran through the door and found his mother cradling his father in her arms.

Gerard dropped his staff, ran to his mother, and put her arms around her. In his fear for Angela, he had forgotten about his father.

"I'm so sorry, mother," he said.

She sobbed in his arms. Every shake of her shoulders shook him, too.

He could feel the presence of someone behind him, but he ignored it for the moment. His mother needed him, and he needed her. He hadn't thought he cared much for his father since he'd been away, but knowing he was gone, knowing he was partly responsible, ripped at Gerard even more than the death of Monteous had.

"What happened?" his mother asked in between sobs.

"The wizard, he found us. He did this," Gerard said.

"Why? Why would he do this to Gentran?"

"To put pressure on me to tell him where Robert was."

"Why... why didn't you..."

He had a tightness in his throat.

"I didn't know," he said.

His throat grew tighter.

He would not allow himself to cry. Not when his mother needed him. He had to be strong for her.

A hand came to rest on his shoulder. He thought it was Nina, but the voice that came from behind him was Lord Graminer's.

"Come, Gerard. Let these others help your mother and father. I need to speak with you." His voice was not the angry, insulting voice that he had used earlier, but was instead filled with a warmth and compassion that Gerard would never have imagined the man could possess.

Gerard turned to look, and saw Graminer and the four other lords standing, waiting to help. To a man, they looked shaken, nervous. Nina and Shane had apparently followed him in, as they stood off to the side of the door

"Later," Gerard said. "I need to help her."

"We don't have time to wait, Gerard. Whether you like it or not, you are now Lord Maracane, and we must speak."

"Go, Gerard," his mother said.

"No, mother, I'll stay with you."

His mother spun her head toward him, and through eyes that had bled enough tears to stain her face with makeup, she commanded him to listen. "You do your duty, Gerard. Go with Graminer. If you would honor your father, you will listen to me."

"Yes, mother," he said. He could not deny her. Not right then, especially not when he knew she was right.

He hugged her tight to him, and then let her go and stood on balky legs that shook beneath him.

Nina rushed up to him and handed him his staff. He used it to steady himself.

"Come, Gerard," Lord Graminer said, and led Gerard back to the sitting room where they had been arguing just before Trajon Jarl appeared.

Nina and Shane followed.

Graminer put his hand up, as if to stop them.

"This is for Gerard, only," he said.

"I am his wife," Nina said.

Graminer turned to Gerard. "Is this true?"

"Yes," Gerard said, wondering if Lord Graminer would deny her, anyway.

"Then she can come. The boy cannot."

"But..." Shane said. His shoulders slumped, and a look of panic crossed his face. Gerard could only guess at what was going through his mind, and his guesses all had to do with being left alone.

And he would be left alone, if Lord Graminer had his way. A young apprentice wizard that was also a lord could hardly be wanted. One that wasn't would be sent home.

But Gerard wasn't about to let Lord Graminer have his way, and he still owed Shane for helping to save his life at the Academy. He would probably owe Shane until one of them died, and maybe longer.

But he needed a plan. He needed to move forward. What would his father have wanted from him? He wouldn't have wanted Gerard to sit around while his murderer escaped. But there were other considerations, too.

"No," said Gerard, knowing that he had been silent far too long. "I need you to get another horse ready, and get us all packed."

"Where are we going?" Shane asked.

"You can't leave," said Lord Graminer.

Where are we going?

They couldn't follow Trajon Jarl. That was impossible. But why would Trajon Jarl just leave them all alive and walk out the door without saying a word, and then why would he abduct Angela? It didn't really make sense unless he knew—

"Robert," he said.

"What?" asked Lord Graminer.

"Trajon Jarl knows where Robert is. That's the only reason why he would leave so abruptly. It's also the only reason he would have abducted Angela."

"I'll get them ready," Shane said, and disappeared through the front door.

"You can't leave, Gerard. Your people need you," Lord Graminer said.

Gerard stepped into the sitting room, and sat down where his father had recently been sitting.

Lord Graminer followed him in, and tried to shut the door on Nina, but Nina pushed her way through before he could.

"Lord Graminer," Gerard said after the door finally shut. "You wanted to talk to me about my duty to my people and my duties as a lord, isn't that right?"

"Yes," he said and sat down across from Gerard. "You must take your father's place, at least for the short term."

"But I am a wizard, am I not? Doesn't that flout the laws?"

Nina took a seat in a chair next to Gerard. He was glad she was there.

"You are an apprentice. The law states only that one cannot be a member of the Guild and be a lord. It does mean that lords generally don't have training as wizards, but that does not make it unlawful."

"But you don't like me."

"What I like and don't like is not of import at this moment. I'll be happy to see you renounce your lordship once this crisis is over. Now..."

Gerard shook his head. "Wait. If I am now lord in my father's place, shouldn't I do what my father would have wanted done?"

"He would want you to take his place," Lord Graminer said.

"He would want me to catch his murderer and have him executed. He would want me to eliminate the threat to Risuk, and to The Seven Kingdoms, if it were at all possible."

Lord Graminer raised a hand as if to point at Gerard in anger, then he let it fall and sighed. "Your father would want those things done, yes, but they do not need to be done by you. Your father's men-at-arms can do those things. It is a lord's place to direct his people to do the things that need doing."

"Pardon me, Lord Graminer," said Nina, "but isn't it a lord's place to protect his people?"

Graminer's eyes looked up toward the ceiling. "Yes."

"Are there more qualified people in Risuk right now to undertake the task of tracking down his father's killer?"

"Yes!"

"Did you see what Trajon Jarl did to my bow?" Nina asked.

Lord Graminer nodded, but grimaced.

"Trajon Jarl can do the same thing to swords. He can bring the dead back to life to fight for him. He can jump from one place to another on a whim. Do you think any of Lord Maracane's men could fight this man? Do you have any wizards of your own?"

"You two are no better. You could do nothing against him."

"With respect," Gerard said, "I was without my staff. But you are right. I could do nothing against him then, and even with my staff, I would be able to do little against him. Our only hope lies in finding Robert and warning him, and hoping he has found Thiobulus already."

"Men-at-arms can do that," Lord Graminer said.

"Can your men-at-arms track at night?" Nina asked.

"No. You're saying that you can?" He looked skeptical.

"Yes," Nina said. "And we can see things they can't."

Gerard kept his mouth shut. He wasn't much of a tracker, himself. He knew Nina could track nearly as well as Demetrius, but he'd never heard her boast that she had tracked something in the dark of night.

Lord Graminer's shoulders slumped, and he looked tired of the argument.

"Very well. You need to designate a successor, first, should you not come back."

"Take care of it, Lord Graminer. I will not be coming back, except for my father's funeral." Gerard said. "And the longer you make me wait here, the less chance we have of finding Robert before Jarl does."

"But..."

"What would you have done had I not returned and my father died anyway?"

"We would have found a cousin of yours," he said, "or some other relative."

Gerard stood up and held his hand out to Nina. It was time to leave. "Then do that. Pretend I never came home. Pretend Jarl already killed me, because he could have tonight. He could have killed us all."

CHAPTER 30

THE SMELL OF bacon and potatoes brought Robert back to life. It was slow going, though. His body felt scraped raw in places, but he had no recollection of how it came to be that way.

The last thing he remembered was climbing up the side of the mountain while following Demetrius near the end of the day. He had been so tired.

He was still tired, but he was far less tired than he was hungry.

He sat up.

"The apprentice wakes," said a voice from behind him. It sounded like he should recognize it, but his head was still foggy from sleep.

He turned his head so he could see the speaker.

A man sat at a table across the room. He wore a deep red robe, nearly a wine color, had long white hair that was as thick as a younger man's, and a long, drawn face that was sharp from age. Robert had seen him for a few moments once before, during the aftermath of a bloody battle by a river during the search for Monteous. And then he had disappeared.

Demetrius sat across from him, sipping at a steaming cup of kava.

"Thiobulus," Robert said.

"You learned my name. That is a start. But you are only one for two. You were supposed to find me on your own. I am not sure having Demetrius lead you here counts."

Panic rose up in Robert. He couldn't afford to have Thiobulus turn him out.

"I..."

Thiobulus put up his hand. "Do not make excuses, Robert. Excuses are unbecoming in a wizard. Sit with us. I can hear your stomach growl, even at this distance."

Robert swung his legs out of the bed, and he took his first good look at his surroundings. The room was fairly large, and well lit. There were windows on each of the walls that let in the light, but they were foggy and he couldn't see through them. The walls were lined with shelves where the shelves would not block the windows. It looked much like a laboratory, with a workbench near the far wall, but it had a subtle difference. It lacked the Works and the tools for creating them.

"You are wondering if this is a laboratory or a library," Thiobulus said.

"I am," Robert said, amazed Thiobulus knew what he was thinking. Early in his apprenticeship, Robert had asked Monteous if it was possible to read minds, and Monteous told him it wasn't possible.

"It is both," said Thiobulus. "You are wondering if I read your mind in some fashion?"

Robert shifted his gaze to the old wizard. "I was told that was not possible."

"Well, you don't have to worry. I was not reading your mind. The question is a common one among people that have seen this place. Come eat." Thiobulus flicked a finger and a chair pulled itself out from the table.

Robert could have done the same thing, but not with the same insignificant gesture.

He stood up, and as he walked to the chair Thiobulus intended he take, he asked, "How many have seen this place?"

"Two."

"Two?"

"Yes," Thiobulus smiled. "Demetrius, and now you."

Robert stopped with his hand on the back of the chair.

"Sit," Thiobulus said. "You must eat if you are to start your training today."

"Training?" Robert asked as he sat down in the chair.

The table in front of him had a plate filled with potatoes, chopped and seasoned with a mountain herb he had never smelled before. Atop the potatoes, four slices of bacon. Demetrius had a plate in front of him that was nearly empty, but Demetrius had not looked up from it during Robert's entire exchange with Thiobulus.

"That is why you are here, is it not?"

And then Robert remembered Trajon Jarl, and realized he did not have his staff. He searched the room for it in a panic. He found it, after a moment, standing against a bookshelf near the bed he had slept on.

"You do not need your staff, Robert."

"But Trajon Jarl..."

"He will not bother you. He can not find us here."

Robert did not feel comforted. Thiobulus's lack of concern about Trajon Jarl troubled him.

"Didn't Demetrius tell you his plans?"

"In excruciating detail, but we will discuss that later, after you have eaten. You nearly drained yourself projecting that shield and trying to go without sleep, you know."

Robert did know. He could feel it in every muscle. Food *would* help.

He picked up the fork and started picking at the potatoes, eating around the bacon. He would save that for last. The herbs on the potatoes gave them life, but did not sear his tongue. After a couple bites, he decided he'd have to ask about the herb, figure out how to grow it back in the garden behind Monteous's laboratory. Behind *his* laboratory. It was Monteous's no longer.

"Why are you still here, Demetrius?" Robert asked around bites. "I thought you would go get the others once we arrived."

Demetrius shook his head.

"Others?" said Thiobulus. "No. I will not train others. I will train you. You will decide if others can be trained."

"Why not?" asked Robert.

"They are not ready."

"How do you know?"

"I have seen them, of course, like I saw you by that river. They are not ready to give up the Works, the crutches that they still need."

"Crutches? Works help focus energie. Some Weaves are impossible without them."

Thiobulus smiled, then pushed his chair back and stood. "Think on it, Robert. When you have finished eating, we will begin."

Thiobulus left the room, and Robert found himself alone with Demetrius.

"Is he always like this?" Robert asked.

"Yes," Demetrius said. "He does what he wants, and only what he wants. It was always possible he wouldn't help us with Trajon Jarl."

"Why didn't you tell me?"

"Because it was possible he would help. It's still possible, but if he helps, it will be when he chooses to help."

Robert picked up a piece of bacon and chewed it. It crumbled in his mouth, and the flavor alone suggested it would help restore his energie. It didn't have quite the same effect as the bear meat Demetrius had given him, but it wasn't far off, either.

While he chewed, he tried to figure out how he felt about his situation. He knew he should be furious at Demetrius for misleading him, but he also knew that Demetrius had never said Thiobulus would help—only that he could. And it wasn't just Demetrius. Monteous had sent him, too, but not because of Trajon Jarl.

No, he had misled himself into thinking that Thiobulus would help, that all he needed to do was find Thiobulus, and Thiobulus would fix everything.

He should have known that wouldn't happen. Thiobulus could have helped with Monteous, but had left Robert at the side of the river without lifting even a fingernail to help.

After he finished a second piece of bacon, Robert looked at Demetrius. Demetrius seemed different, here—withdrawn, almost fearful, or perhaps just resigned. He was not the same dynamic man that refused to give in as he had been just before Robert lost consciousness.

"Demetrius," Robert said, then stopped. He didn't know how to ask, or if he even should. The last time he had broached the subject, Demetrius had told him to ask Thiobulus.

"What?" Demetrius asked.

Robert decided to ask another question entirely. "What about the horses?"

"Thiobulus and I went to retrieve them while you slept," he said.

"The horses couldn't make it up that trail," Robert said, and then realized he was being stupid.

"Never mind," he said. "With Thiobulus around, the horses didn't need to use the trail, did they?"

"You're learning," Demetrius said. "Perhaps you should finish your meal and go find out what else Thiobulus can teach you."

Robert attacked the rest of his potatoes, hoping whatever Thiobulus wanted to teach him would be useful against Trajon Jarl.

IT DID NOT take long for Nina to realize they might have made a mistake. In town, and even near the edge of town, there were too many tracks to make any sort of tracking possible. She followed two sets of horse prints from the stable, saw that one of them had a distinctive chip out of one of the horseshoes. Finding that mark among the myriad prints left on the roads in town verged on impossible.

Eventually, she gave up trying to follow that track through town.

"What's North of here?" she asked Gerard.

His face was illuminated by his staff. He looked tired, angry, and a little bit desperate. She wondered if she might be projecting her own feelings on to him.

"More mountains. There are a couple roads that lead off from the main pass."

"Do you think they could have gone that direction? I remember Demetrius saying something about Broken Thunder Ridge."

"That's possible. Broken Thunder Ridge lies along one of the roads in that direction. There are also more possibilities if that's not where they went."

She knew that, having just traveled through the south only days earlier. There weren't any other roads to the south of them until just before Treading Valley. The mountains rose up too quickly and too steeply for any side roads.

"Then lets head north," she said. "I can search that road, and all I'll need is one track to know we're going the right way."

Assuming we're following the right horse.

She climbed back up on her horse, adjusted the borrowed bow on her back, and set off to the northern entrance of the town with Gerard and Shane behind her.

The edge of town wasn't much better, though there were a few more distinct prints, but none were the print she was seeking.

"This is hopeless," she said. "I don't know what I was thinking. It's been two days."

"What do we do, then?" Shane asked.

"We can't quit," Gerard said.

Nina agreed with him, but she had no idea how to proceed. It frustrated her. She was used to being able to track anything through the forest that surrounded her father's farm. But this was different.

"There are just too many conflicting tracks," she said. "And the wagons come by, they obliterate everything."

"Well, what do you want to do," Gerard asked. "I was never much of a tracker. I could hunt down goats and other small animals near here, but if my brother wanted to lose me in the forest, he would."

Nina sighed. Why did it have to be left up to her?

"What about you, Shane?"

Shane shook his head. In the dark, beyond the ring of light that Gerard's staff cast, Shane was a shadow. His face had been drawn and he had talked little ever since they set out. Nina knew he blamed himself for leaving Angela to fetch the horses. Nina had tried to tell him it wasn't his fault, that Jarl had just turned and left without any obvious provocation or reason.

So the tracking was left to her.

"We're not going back?" she asked.

"No," Gerard said.

"Then I say we keep on until we get to one of these side roads you talked about. Maybe Robert and Demetrius turned down one of them, and maybe that one won't have so much traffic."

It was all she could hope for if they weren't going to give up the search.

And she did want to help Angela and Robert.

She just worried they were wasting their time searching for two-day-old tracks.

ANGELA TRUDGED UP the mountainside, followed and prodded along by Trajon Jarl. She felt cold and dizzy, but the man behind her did not seem to care. He met every protest with a stinging slap of air in the middle of her back.

She stared up the mountainside. Jarl had pushed them up above the tree-line. She had a good view of the snow above her. In the moonlight, it reflected a pale glow that was mesmerizing. Everything else was shadow.

She tripped over a rock and fell to her knees, which banged against yet more rock.

"Get up," Jarl said.

Her head swirled. She just wanted to close her eyes and go to sleep.

Another slap of air against her back pitched her over onto her face. She just managed to get her arms out and avoid cracking her skull on the exposed stone, but a stone sliced her cheek, anyway. The sting of it made her want to tear up.

"Why are you doing this to me? I'm ill! I can't go on," she said.

She hoped it came out right. Her tongue felt thick. She needed a drink of water.

"Ill?" Jarl asked.

"Yes," she said slowly. She closed her eyes against the new pains she had acquired. Sleep would make them go away.

But Jarl didn't let her sleep.

He knelt over her, then rolled her over.

A sharp rock bit into her back.

Jarl put his hand to her forehead.

She felt something inside, a tingling near his hand, spreading out through her body.

"Well, it seems you are telling the truth."

Then he muttered something to himself that Angela heard as, "This won't do."

The tingling in her body intensified, almost to the point of pain. She wanted to cry out, but the needle pricks Trajon created within her wouldn't allow her to breathe more than enough air in to keep her lungs from complaining. There was nothing left to make sound with.

And then the feeling abruptly stopped. Jarl removed his hand.

"What did you do to me?" she asked.

She took stock of herself. She no longer felt colder than she should. The pains in her knees, so new and fresh, were gone. She could no longer feel the sting of the slice in her cheek.

She sat up.

"What did you do?" she asked. She knew what he had done, she just wanted to hear it. She couldn't believe it.

"I healed you. Get up."

"How?" She was stunned. "Wizards can't heal," she said, quoting Master Monteous, Master Brin, and every other wizard she had ever asked about the possibility.

"No," Jarl said. "Wizards *do not* heal. At least, not wizards who are members of the Guild. Get up, or I will make you get up."

"You won't hurt me," she said, feeling defiant. "You just healed me."

Jarl laughed, his guffaws echoing across the mountainside. It took him a minute to get his laughter under control.

Once his mirth faded, he said, "I have ways to make you feel pain without hurting you. It is the same as healing, only reversed."

Angela stood.

"How is it possible that you can heal me?" she asked.

"All those proscribed Weaves and Works of the Guild? They make it possible. The healers use them to heal you, if they are any good. Walk." He prodded at her with a hard push of air, but not enough to make her stumble.

She decided to cooperate for the moment. She wanted to get answers to her questions, and hoped her cooperation would keep him talkative.

"If they use proscribed Weaves to heal, then why aren't they members of the Guild? Doesn't that make them wizards, too?"

"That would be logical," Jarl said. "But when the Guild decided to proscribe those Weaves and Works, they created a separate guild for the healers. They knew they needed that ability, but they refused to teach those women any other uses for their power."

"Women?"

"Originally, all the healers were women, all the wizards were men."

She had a hard time believing that. It didn't make sense.

"That's not true, any more."

"No, it is not. When the number of Guild members started to fall, they could not find enough men to replace them. They had to bring women back in, but there are not many of them, are there?"

"There were quite a few at the Academy," Angela said, "before you killed them all."

"Regretful, but necessary," he said. "I can not allow the Guild to regain its strength."

"Why?" Angela asked. Trajon Jarl was not at all what she expected. "All because they expelled you?"

Silence hung in the air between them, broken only by the crunch of their footsteps on a thin layer of loose dirt.

When Jarl did answer, his voice contained a tinge of anger. "They did not just expel me," he said. "They imprisoned me. One hundred-fifty years. My family died. Everyone I knew, dead and buried before I could escape. And all because I disagreed with them. The Guild is not to be trusted."

The anger in his voice brought Angela back to herself and her situation. She was being forced across the top of a mountain because Jarl was trying to find Robert. She had heard that same anger back in Gerard's house.

"How can I trust you?" she asked. "You threatened my friends, killed my masters, did that horrible thing to Gerard's uncle."

Trajon Jarl chuckled. "Whoever said you could trust me? I want Robert's assistance, and I will do anything I must to get it."

"Why do you need his assistance?" she asked, trying not to tremble.

"Do not twist my words, apprentice. I said I *want* his assistance. I do not need it. If he does not want to join my cause, I will kill you both. There is no room in this world for wizards opposed to my wishes."

She couldn't stop herself from shuddering. She knew Robert would never give in to Jarl. She hoped he wouldn't do it to save her life.

"They didn't just expel you for using proscribed Weaves."

"Smart girl. No, they did not," and then he chuckled again. "I am the reason the Weaves are proscribed."

With that, he pushed at her again, forcing her forward into the cold of the mountain night. She had to find a way to escape. She couldn't let herself be used as a pawn to coerce Robert into helping Jarl.

Even if I have to die.

As soon as she thought it, she wondered if it were true. Would it be so bad? But she didn't have to think hard to understand that it could be. Trajon Jarl could easily do to her what he had done to Gerard's uncle, and she knew she didn't want to become one of those things.

Dying was far more attractive.

CHAPTER 31

ROBERT STOOD NEXT to Thiobulus, who had taken a seat on a fallen tree. It was still cold, with the sun barely above the horizon, but the sun was bright and promised that the day would bring warmer weather as it went on.

"The trick to managing all those Weaves without a Work," Thiobulus was saying, "is to realize that all Weaves are interconnected. They all have a starting point, and that point is within you, but it is not within you, either."

"I don't understand," said Robert.

"Enter the vew, and tell me what you see."

Robert allowed the focus of his eyes to blur, and then brought it back in the way that Monteous had taught him so long ago. "I see the energie around us," Robert said. He wished he knew where Thiobulus was leading him. He couldn't see how it mattered, or how it would help against Trajon Jarl.

"And what is it doing?"

"In the air, it flows with the currents. In the trees, it flows with the sap."

"Why does it flow, do you think?"

Robert pondered the question for a moment, but could not come up with an answer he thought would satisfy Thiobulus. He didn't think it would be smart to suggest that it just flows because that's what it does. Monteous had never mentioned that it mattered. It was just there for the taking.

"I don't know," he said.

Thiobulus snorted. "You're not thinking."

"I'm trying," Robert said. "I just don't..."

Right then, Robert decided Thiobulus was right. He wasn't thinking about what Thiobulus was doing. He had Trajon Jarl on his mind. He pushed Jarl to the back of his mind, and decided to focus completely on Thiobulus.

"There you go," Thiobulus said. "Now you're ready to learn."

"What? Do you know what I was thinking?"

Thiobulus laughed. "No, but I could see the energie in you as you pushed whatever you were thinking about aside. The energie shifted with it."

Then Robert realized the answer to Thiobulus's previous question.

"The energie is all connected," Robert said, "even without being woven into a thread."

Thiobulus clapped and smiled. "Yes. Now you see."

"But how does knowing that help?" Robert asked.

"It helps because the energie is all around you to be used, and since it is already connected, you do not need to Weave it together through you, or through a Work. Once you know the pattern of a Weave, you can use the energie within you to control the energie outside of you. You can impose the Weave upon the energie around you without having to Weave it."

Robert thought back to the Weave that Thiobulus used to seemingly stop time for his friends when they first met by the ferry. The Weave had been so complex that Robert hadn't been able to find an individual thread in it to start unraveling it.

"The Weave you used on us at the ferry last winter. You told me to not even bother trying to unravel it."

"Yes, I did say that, I suppose."

"I looked for a thread to pull. I couldn't find one. I thought at the time that I couldn't find it because of the complexity of the Weave, but there wasn't an endpoint to that Weave, was there?"

"No."

"You imposed the Weave on the energie surrounding us. It was so quick."

"Yes. Once you know how it is done, it does not take much time to impose a complex Weave because you do it all at once. There are no knots. There are no loose ends."

"The shield I was using. I could have created it once, and it would have stayed in place."

Thiobulus nodded. "There are limits, of course. It would not have moved with you. You would have had to pull it along, but that would have used far less of your energie than maintaining it the whole time."

Thiobulus stood up.

"In fact, I want you to try it right now," he said.

"Create the shield?"

"Yes. Create it above us. It should be fairly easy for you to do. But instead of going through the steps to create it one thread at a time, look at the energie around us, find what you need, and make it go where you want without bringing it through you."

"How?"

"Just reach out for the energie you need with your mind. Remember that it is all connected. It will do what you want."

Robert searched around him, found the energie in the air, the snow, the trees, and the earth that he needed for the shield. He imagined the completed Weave above him. He felt awkward without his staff.

"You know how to draw the energie to you," said Thiobulus. "Instead of drawing it to you, push it where you want it to go."

Robert heeded Thiobulus's instructions. He reached out as if he would pull the energie to him, but instead of pulling it, he tried to push it where he wanted it to go. It was like pushing a cart through thick mud, at first. It didn't want to move for him.

"That is right," said Thiobulus. "I can see it moving. It will be hard at first. You are so used to pulling it in that it will feel wrong to do otherwise."

The energie moved quicker after a few moments. The Weave formed slowly above them. Pushing the energie grew easier. It was like having a thousand tiny threads at his direction, pushing and prodding at the energie to make it do what he wanted, but there wasn't any of his own energie at use. He could do it for days on end without tiring, without draining himself.

Suddenly, the energie he was controlling snapped into place, and the shield was fully formed above them.

"Good," said Thiobulus. "A little slow, but well executed. Now, you are still connected to it. Let it go free."

"Will it remain in place?"

"Yes."

Robert released his hold on the energies of the shield, and to his surprise, it did remain in place.

"How is it that the Guild does not know of this?" Robert asked. "How did Monteous not know?"

"Monteous knew, but the rest of the Guild does not. We have kept it a secret."

"Monteous never did anything like this," Robert said.

"No, he could not."

"Why not?"

Thiobulus took a seat on the fallen tree again. "It takes a special mind to be able to do it. I tried to teach Monteous, but he could never grasp it."

"Why not?"

"I do not know."

"Then why did he send me here?"

"Ah, the letter. Demetrius told me about it. He wrote that, did he not, before you overcame your issues with focus?"

"Yes. How did you know?"

"I talked with Monteous on occasion. I am guessing he sent you to me because he thought I might be able to help you with your focus, and it seems there were plots afoot within the Guild that he wanted you kept out of."

Robert looked up at the Weave. It was still there, keeping them hidden, even though Thiobulus claimed there was no need for it. He knew, now, he could keep himself hidden wherever he went with little effort.

"Then why teach me?"

"Do you forget that I saw you at the ferry? You were imaginative in your use of Weaves, trapping them from across the river so they could not move or shout out. You did not want to kill those men, did you."

"No." He hadn't wanted to at all, but they hadn't left Ivron and his men much choice.

"That is why. I will one day pass away, and with Monteous gone, someone needs to know."

"Because I didn't want to kill those men?"

"When we formed the Guild after the Unification, one of the driving ideals was that wizards should not kill if they do not have to. That is what sets us apart from the likes of Trajon Jarl and his ilk."

Trajon Jarl. Robert had all but forgotten about him during the lesson.

"Master Thiobulus, keeping the shield above me with little effort will help, but I had hoped you might teach me how to fight Jarl."

"I just did," Thiobulus said. "How do you create fire?"

"You draw the energie from the sun, from any flames around you, from anything that could produce heat, and then you…"

Robert stopped and contemplated the implications. If he just pushed that energie to where he wanted the flames, created the Weaves in place, fire would just spring up. He could create fire far more quickly. He wouldn't have to throw it. It couldn't be dodged.

"You understand?" asked Thiobulus.

Robert nodded. "You create it in place. There wouldn't be threads to block. There wouldn't be anything to dodge."

"You do understand. That is good."

"Another question," Robert said. "How do I defend against the proscribed Works and Weaves? I can not see them."

"That, too, is just a trick, and it is not an especially hard one to master. Go into the vew."

Robert was already in the vew. He hadn't left it.

Thiobulus stood up. He pulled a small knife from his robe, then he held up a finger.

"Now, you see the energie running through my finger, yes?"

"I do."

"Describe it to me."

"It's gold, and it runs up and down your skin. It's ordered, not random like most people."

"Good."

Thiobulus brought up the knife and drew it across the pad of his finger. Blood oozed out and ran down the length of the finger until it dripped to the ground.

"Do you see anything different?" Thiobulus asked.

"No," Robert said. "You're bleeding."

"Yes I am. Now, slip out of the vew, and then back in again, only this time, watch the blood while you do it, and go slowly."

Robert did as he was asked.

First, all the energie he had been seeing disappeared.

He then allowed his eyes to fall out of focus, before slowly bringing them back toward the level of focus that would let him see energie.

When he was about half way to the normal vew, with the rest of the world still out of focus, he saw a flicker in the red stain that was Thiobulus's blood. Particles of energie, smaller than he had ever seen, ran through and around the blood. They were red, too, almost as red as the blood, but they shined like any other energie did.

"What do you see?"

"Energie, and it's red, almost like the blood. It's so small."

"You see it then," said Thiobulus.

"Yes."

"Now you know the trick."

And then Robert watched the energie coalesce into threads, and start pulling the wound together. In moments, the finger had healed.

Robert fell out of the vew in amazement.

"How? How did you heal yourself?"

Robert watched as the blood that had leaked from the wound disappeared, leaving Thiobulus's skin clean. There was no sign the cut had ever happened.

"This is the problem with the dogmatic stance the Guild has taken against the healer's Weaves. Things that should be easy to do, no longer are."

"Are you saying healers use proscribed Weaves?"

"I am saying that, and more. I am saying that The Seven Kingdoms could have a lot less suffering were its wizards allowed to use these weaves."

"But I thought Trajon Jarl was kicked out for using them?"

"He was imprisoned for using them to control people."

"How?"

"How was he imprisoned?" Thiobulus asked.

"No. How did he use it to control people?" Robert asked.

Thiobulus looked up, then down the slope into the forest. After a moment, he turned back to Robert.

"Walk with me. We need to be heading in," Thiobulus said, and then turned to head back to his home in the cave.

Robert hurried to walk next to him.

"The energie of the blood runs throughout a person's body. It is intertwined with the parts of the body in a way that keeps us alive and facilitates the mind's communication with the rest of the body."

"But what about the other energie within us? The energie we use in making Weaves?"

"That is different. Your body feeds off it. You collect it from your surroundings. If you lose all of it, of course, you will also die. The difference is that you do not consume, or replenish, the blood energie from an external source. Your body creates it when it creates blood, and if you take the energie from the blood, the blood turns black and useless. The energie is not useful for long, either, unless it is bound into a Weave."

"Or a Work," Robert said, thinking back to the Work bound into the staff he had used to kill Orliss and the Weave that had killed Wallace.

"Exactly. Back to your question. Since it is bound so tightly to the blood, an unscrupulous wizard can take a bit of a persons blood, and then use that to Weave a thread between them, thereby giving him control of the victim's body, and even his thoughts."

"Even if he's dead?" Robert asked, but he knew the answer.

"It is, in some ways, easier if the victim is dead. There is little resistance."

They had reached the entrance to Thiobulus's cave. Robert could not see it, but he knew that a Weave had been created to make it look like solid stone. The Weave would even hold the weight of someone that tried to walk across it.

Thiobulus made a thin opening in that Weave, and stepped through it. Robert followed him in, and the Weave closed behind them.

"So," Robert asked. "How do I protect myself against Jarl?"

"It is obvious, is it not?"

Robert thought about it as they walked down the passage. He didn't even notice the lights above as they came on ahead of them and winked out behind them. He had already examined the Weaves that made it possible on his way out.

"Do I just take the energie from his Weaves and make it do something else?"

"That is the idea of it, at least. You do want to get to the energie in the threads before the Weave is fully formed. Unfortunately, it is difficult to watch both the blood energie and other energies at the same time."

"You mean I have to figure out what he's going to try to do, and watch for that, and hope he doesn't try something else."

Thiobulus nodded as they entered the room where Robert had first woken up.

"That is one strategy."

"What other strategy is there?" Robert asked.

Thiobulus walked across the room to a bookshelf and started pulling books from it.

"The other strategy is to take him down before he can do anything to stop you," Thiobulus said, already with several books in his hands.

"What are you doing?" Robert asked.

"What?" Thiobulus asked as he pulled out another book.

"What are you doing with the books?"

"Oh, I am leaving," he said. "It is time for me to go."

"Go? You can't go. I thought you were going to teach me."

"I have taught you everything you need to know, Robert. Teach yourself the rest."

"You haven't taught me any new Weaves. I thought..."

"There are always new Weaves, Robert. I could show you Weave after Weave, but the real masters do not know Weaves. They know how to make energie do what they want, learning the patterns that create specific effects. You will learn them as you work. Be creative."

Robert walked over to stand beside Thiobulus as he picked another book off the shelf.

"Tell me," Robert said, "how did you get from the cellar of that alehouse to here?"

"You know the Weave to get to the Guild hall?"

"I do."

"It is the same principle."

"You have a work, here, that is the same as the works at the hall?"

"Of course not," Thiobulus said. "I do not need a Work. I know this place. I can cause energie to form the Weave I need here, no matter where I am."

"But how?"

"You have created a portal. You know the Weave to the Guild hall. Is it really that hard to connect the two? Now, I really must be going."

He turned away from Robert, carrying his books toward a door at the far end of the chamber.

Robert looked around. He realized then that Demetrius wasn't in the room. He had been so preoccupied with Thiobulus that he hadn't even noticed.

Robert raced after Thiobulus and touched him on the shoulder.

Thiobulus whirled around, and for a moment, Robert thought he saw anger and fear intermixed in Thiobulus's eyes.

"Do you know where Demetrius is?"

"I sent him on an errand. He should return soon. Now..."

"One last thing before you go," Robert said, resigned to the fact that Thiobulus wouldn't help him with Trajon Jarl.

"One more question, and no more."

"What did you do to Demetrius?" Robert asked.

Thiobulus seemed to deflate. "Ask him."

"He won't tell me. He said to ask you."

Thiobulus stared at Robert, his eyes hard, his gaze sharp as a blade that Robert would have sworn he could feel scraping against his skin. Robert refused to look away.

"All right," Thiobulus said. "Let me put these books down, and I will tell you, but after that, I am leaving."

"Fair enough," Robert said.

GERARD KNEW HE was failing. They had not found a print in miles, and it was already mid-day. Every time Nina looked back at him, the circles under her eyes were one more shade darker. She needed sleep. They all needed sleep.

They had traveled deep in the mountains. Giant bloodwood trees surrounded them, looming over the path, threatening to dislodge the weary travelers from their horses with low hanging branches. The farther they traveled, the slower it seemed the trees would let them go.

In spite of the trees, Gerard tried to push the pace. He felt they had little time left if they were going to find Robert and Demetrius before Trajon Jarl did—before Jarl did something to Angela.

Robert had left her there, in his parents' house, and it had been Gerard's duty to protect her from something like this. And he had failed. He couldn't fail Robert or Angela again, despite having no idea how he could be of any help.

He just hoped that Robert had found Thiobulus already. He hoped they would not find Robert and Demetrius dead somewhere along the side of the road.

The only thing they could do was keep going, keep searching.

They had been lucky the previous night to find a print from the cracked shoe down the side road that led to Grappling Peak. He knew the road did not have any other side roads. At the very least, if they got to Grappling Peak and found that Demetrius and Robert had not entered it, they would know they had to turn back, and that Thiobulus was in the mountains between where they were and Blisterwind Pass.

They had found additional tracks for a mile or two after turning down the road, but since then, nothing.

The road widened enough that there was room for two horses to ride side by side. Shane took the opportunity to ride up next to him. Gerard wished he hadn't.

"Maybe we should turn back," Shane said. "Maybe we missed where they turned off the road."

Gerard shook his head. "Nina doesn't think so."

"She's tired, Gerard. Maybe..."

"She didn't miss anything," Gerard said.

Shane's eyes widened, and Gerard realized he had let some of his frustration through.

"Look, I don't think we missed anything. Demetrius said it was about two day's ride, and we haven't ridden even half of that."

But Gerard couldn't remember if Demetrius had actually said two days' *ride*. So much had happened, and he was so tired, he knew he could be mis-remembering. Demetrius could have said two days' travel, which could mean that it was only a day's ride and a day wandering through the wilderness.

"I don't remember," Shane said.

Shane's eyes had circles under them, too.

"Look," said Gerard. "We're all tired, but we have to keep going. If we get to this evening and haven't seen another track, then we'll talk about doubling back, but not until then."

Shane frowned, but didn't say anything.

Gerard pushed his horse to catch up with Nina.

"See anything else?" he asked.

"I would have said something," she said.

Gerard wasn't surprised with her tone. She'd grown increasingly ill-tempered as the day wore on.

"Do you want to rest a bit?" he asked. "There's a place to sit and rest up ahead with a stream nearby for the horses." He had stopped there many times with his brother and father. The table and benches that someone had carved out of a stump made for a nice place to camp for the night under normal circumstances.

Nina looked at him, then bent down over her horse's neck and patted it.

"They need water," she said. "Maybe we'll find something there. Robert and Demetrius must have stopped to rest at some point, right?"

"If they stopped anywhere," he said, "it would be there. You have to see it."

A slight smile creased her face, and she looked at him. "Then let's stop there." The circles under her eyes were even darker than he had thought.

They had to travel a little farther than Gerard remembered, but he recognized the area around it just before Nina set her eyes on the clearing for the first time.

When she saw it, Nina put her hand up, indicating she wanted them to stop. Gerard pulled up, and Shane came up next to him before bringing his own mount to a halt.

"What's going on?" Shane asked.

"We're going to rest for a short while," Gerard said, "but I think Nina wants to check the area for tracks first."

"You think they stopped here?" Shane asked.

Gerard nodded.

Nina climbed down off her horse, her movements slow and deliberate, with only a hint of the exhaustion they were all feeling.

Gerard climbed off his horse and walked up next to her, leading his horse.

She handed him the reins of her horse.

"I want to look before we trample through," she said.

Gerard nodded. She was so much better at it than he. She had tried to point out to him what to look for, but she always saw tracks before he did. The few times he pointed something out that he thought she hadn't seen, inevitably, he had been wrong.

Gerard stood and watched as Nina worked her way across the road, then up into the clearing and around the table and benches. She knelt down behind the table then quickly stood up again. She wore an excited look on her face. She quickly went back to the road, and walked down it a little farther, head bent toward the ground. She knelt down again, then came back, smiling.

"They were here," she said.

Gerard felt an urge to push on, but the dark circles under Nina's eyes had not disappeared. She needed to rest, and they all needed food and water, including the horses.

Gerard led the horses up into the clearing, then went to their packs and pulled out the berries and strips of goat his mother had given them. He set the food on the table.

"Sit and eat," he said to Nina. "Shane and I will water the horses."

Shane grimaced and stared at the food. He had obviously thought about eating first, and was disappointed with Gerard. He grabbed a strip of goat from the table, and then followed Gerard down to the side of the stream without saying a word.

The smell of the goat, peppered the way he remembered from his childhood, made Gerard's mouth water, and he wished he had done the same as Shane.

He watched Shane eat and the horses drink. He wondered, again, if he was doing the right thing, if he should have stayed and helped his mother instead. Yes, Nina had found their trail again, which narrowed the area they had to search significantly, but if they didn't find another trace, what would they do? It was near noon, already. Were they already too late?

He heard the crack of a twig out in the forest, on their side of the river. His first crazy thought was that his uncle had somehow come back to follow them, but he quickly put the idea aside. He'd seen his uncle burn until there was little left.

"Stay here," he said to Shane in a whisper. "If something happens, take Nina and run."

Gerard slipped his staff from thong that held it to his saddle.

"What are you doing?" Shane asked.

"There's something out there," Gerard said.

"What?"

"I don't know. It could be a bear, or a goat, deer, or a bird. Or it could be Trajon Jarl, now be quiet."

Holding his staff in front of him, he took steps toward the edge of the clearing. He wished he had Demetrius's ability to move quietly through the forest, or even that of his brother. The dirt and rock crunched under his boots. Whoever or whatever was out there would be able to hear him, he knew. The stream flowed past them too slowly to make much noise, which was why he had heard the stick break in the first place.

He stopped at the edge of the clearing and stared out into the brush and trees. He looked for any sign of movement, but all was still. Even the wind, which was a near constant among the peaks of Risuk, was absent.

"What do you see?" Shane asked.

Gerard turned his head and shot what he hoped was a disdainful look at Shane, but he said nothing. He didn't want to give themselves away, but he knew the damage was probably already done. Whatever was out in the forest had to know they were there.

Gerard turned back to peer into the forest again, and just as he did, a dark shape reared up out of the brush right in front of him, reached out, and grabbed him by the shoulder.

CHAPTER 32

THIOBULUS LED ROBERT to a small chamber off the main room. When they entered, the ceiling lit up, bathing the room in a soothing warmth that reminded Robert of mid-afternoon sunlight.

Robert slipped into the vew, saw the Weave across the door with a thread that led to a Weave on the ceiling. From outside, anyone checking for Weaves would see it and think that it looked like a trap.

"Sit," Thiobulus said.

There was an old, rickety wooden chair off to one side of the room that looked like it would fall apart if Robert sat in it. Thiobulus had already taken a much nicer chair that sat in front of a desk for himself.

Robert wondered at the presence of a second chair for a wizard that preferred to remain aloof.

Robert went to the chair and gingerly sat in it. He discovered that its construction was far more solid than it looked. The chair did not shift at all under his weight.

"So," Thiobulus said. "You want to know about Demetrius."

Robert nodded.

Thiobulus took a deep breath and put his arm on the desk. He tapped his fingers three times as if he were pondering what to tell Robert.

"Demetrius was near dead when I found him, a victim of a battle. I recall he had several wounds, none of which, individually, would have been life threatening. Taken together, he would not recover from them. Indeed, I thought he was dead already, until he turned his head toward me."

"What battle was it?" Robert asked.

"One of the Unification battles. I cannot remember which, and it does not really matter.

"I took him home with me and went about healing him.

"At the time, I was also trying to fight wizards like Trajon Jarl, wizards who used the healing arts to kill people . . . or control them.

"Before I healed him, I asked Demetrius if he would serve me, if he would fight these men with me."

"He agreed," said Robert.

Thiobulus looked down at his sandal-clad feet. His toes showed through the ends, gnarled and dirt stained.

"You must understand something. He would have died had I not found him. He would have died had I not done some of the things I did."

"What did you do?"

Thiobulus looked up and stared into Robert's eyes. "I made a weapon of him."

The stare made Robert uncomfortable, and he tried to look away, but the bright blue eyes held him fast.

"I don't understand," Robert said.

"I threaded energie through him, embedded Weaves in him as if he were a Work. I enhanced his senses, I strengthened his muscles and gave them a quickness that no normal man could possess. His body will heal itself rapidly, as long as his head is not separated from his body and his heart remains within it. He can see in near darkness, he can hear people talking from as far as he can see, and he can smell as well as a dog, if not better."

Robert imagined being able to do those things, to be able to see in the dark, to know when someone was sneaking up on him.

"I don't see how that is such a curse as Demetrius thinks it to be."

Thiobulus stood up from his chair and then started pacing across the room.

"Those things aren't. He used them for me, and he used them well, and he has had the benefit of them all these two hundred years. It is the other things I did that make him hate being near me."

Thiobulus stopped for a moment, looked up and out through the doorway, but then resumed his pacing as if he had never stopped.

"What other things?"

"I bound him to me," Thiobulus said. "He could not go against my wishes. He could not betray me. He could not leave."

"I don't understand."

Thiobulus stopped pacing. He held up a withered hand in front of him. Robert noticed for the first time how ancient his hands looked, the meat nearly gone from them. They were still steady, though.

"I bound a weave into him that made it impossible to do those things. I used the blood energie, just like the wizards I was fighting. I did not go as far as they. I left him with free will, I kept him alive, but he could not go against my wishes."

Thiobulus pointed right at Robert.

"He can not go against your wishes," the old wizard said.

Robert sat up straight.

"My wishes?"

"While I trained Monteous, when I realized he would eventually become the Guild's Senior Wizard, I transferred Demetrius's contract, which is what I call that Weave, to Monteous. At some point before he died, Monteous transferred that Weave to you."

"Why didn't Monteous tell me? Why didn't Demetrius?"

"I can not answer for them," Thiobulus said.

Robert couldn't grasp all that had been done to Demetrius. Two hundred years of serving first Thiobulus, and then Monteous, without any choice.

"Why didn't you remove the contract once you defeated Trajon Jarl?" Robert asked. "Why didn't you free him from it?"

Why didn't Monteous?

"After awhile, I couldn't see how I could do without him," Thiobulus said.

"But you gave him to Monteous like he was a cow or a horse to be bought and sold."

"I was leaving the Guild," Thiobulus said. "Monteous needed his help."

"But..."

"No," Thiobulus said, waving Robert to silence. "You are right. It can not be justified. I have learned that through all these years."

"Then why don't you remove the Weave?" Robert asked.

"It is not within my power," Thiobulus said.

"Why not?"

"It is the weave that regenerates his body. Removing it will bring about his death within a year."

"Why?"

"His body has lived beyond its years. Once the Weave is removed, his body will quickly fail."

"You are sure of this?"

Thiobulus nodded.

He wished Demetrius was with them. He would have liked to ask Demetrius about his opinion.

"Does Demetrius know about what would happen?" Robert asked.

"No. I have not told him."

Thiobulus looked at his books. Robert could tell Thiobulus wanted to escape.

"So you're going to leave it to me to tell him?"

"You do not have to tell him. That is your choice."

Robert stood, his anger rising up within him.

"How can you do that? How can you not tell him yourself?"

"He does not want to be around me."

Robert understood that. He no longer wanted to be around the wizard, either. It made him wonder. If Thiobulus could do this to Demetrius, if Monteous could perpetuate it, what other lies had the two wizards told? Did that mean that Trajon Jarl might not have been lying when he insinuated there was more to the tale of how Robert came to live with Monteous?

"You are going to tell him before you leave," Robert said.

Thiobulus looked up from his long investigation of the floor.

"I have been a wizard ten times as long as you have been alive, apprentice. You do not tell me what to do. When..."

A loud rumble interrupted him. The mountain shook underneath them.

"What was that?" Robert asked, even as the rumble was subsiding.

"One of my traps, I think," said Thiobulus. "Something has triggered it. Come with me."

He went to the door of the room.

"I thought you were leaving," said Robert.

Thiobulus looked to his books.

"If I help you with this," Thiobulus said, "you will tell Demetrius yourself?"

"What is this?" Robert asked.

"I suspect Trajon Jarl has found us."

Robert shuddered. Thiobulus wasn't leaving him much of a choice. Face Trajon Jarl alone, or tell Demetrius that he would die if he were freed from his bonds.

"That isn't fair," said Robert.

"I don't care about fair," Thiobulus said. "I have my reasons. Do you want my help, or not?"

It wasn't much of a choice. And he thought Thiobulus would try to leave without telling Demetrius, if he had any chance. Robert wondered what his reasons were, but could only imagine he thought Demetrius might kill him if Thiobulus told him. Robert knew he would want to kill Thiobulus if he were in Demetrius's place.

"Yes," Robert said. "I need your help."

"Then come with me," Thiobulus said.

The old wizard rushed through the door, and Robert chased after him. It wasn't until they entered the giant laboratory that Robert began to wonder how Trajon Jarl found them despite Thiobulus's assurances that they were safe.

Thiobulus had a lot to answer for.

ANGELA'S LEGS NO longer wanted to hold her up. The constant travel up and down the side of the mountain, across ridges and ravines, had worn them out. She wasn't used to such effort. She had begged Trajon Jarl to stop more than once, but he kept pushing her onward. The fate he had threatened her with kept her from protesting too much.

She still had not come up with a plan to escape, either, and she felt that every moment she didn't try made her escape ever less likely. But he kept her in front of him at all times—she was never out of his sight.

If only she had a staff.

But she had thought about that a thousand times, and each time, decided it wouldn't matter if she did. She had seen what Trajon Jarl could do to a full wizard with a staff at their disposal. She wouldn't stand a chance.

He directed her up the mountain again, right up near the snow-cap. It was cold there. She was glad she had put her coat on before climbing out the window, but she didn't think it would keep her warm forever.

"Where are we going?" she asked.

"There is an entrance up there," Jarl said, pointing ahead of her.

She couldn't see it. It was all just mountain rock and low grass.

"Where?"

"Thiobulus has hidden it," Jarl said. "You are not much of a wizard if you can not see it."

Angela slipped into the vew. Still she could not see anything.

"There's nothing there," she said, stopping to rest.

He put a hand to her back and pushed her forward.

"Keep moving."

She lifted her foot up and took another step, then another, inching higher up the mountain.

"There are more ways to see than the vew," Trajon Jarl said.

"You're talking about seeing proscribed Weaves," she said, letting herself fall out of the vew.

"That is one of them."

"Thiobulus wouldn't use one of those Weaves," Angela said.

"Don't be so certain about what Thiobulus would and wouldn't do. He and I worked together during the Unification. I know what he is capable of.

"However, you are correct to a point. He did not use one of those Weaves here."

Angela wondered if it was a Weave that was similar to what she had used to hide Robert from Orliss's henchmen so long ago—a Weave that mimicked the scenery around it. But if it was her Weave, she would have seen the cave entrance. It would have hidden a person standing there, though.

No. This was something else. She couldn't see it, but Trajon Jarl could.

"All right," Jarl said. "Stop here."

Angela did, grateful for the chance to rest. She knelt on the near frozen ground. The snowline was only feet above her head. Before them, the face of the mountain stood near vertical.

Trajon Jarl dipped into his pocket and pulled out a small Work. She caught a glimpse of iron and a bright blue glass, but it disappeared into the palm of his right hand.

He held that right hand out in front of him, aiming for a spot in the center of the mountain face.

She slipped back into the vew. She saw a few threads of energie stretching out from Jarl's hand to the solid stone in front of them, but she thought he used more threads she couldn't see. The hairs on her arms tingled from the energie.

After a moment, the rock face disappeared. Thiobulus had masked it, but Trajon Jarl made the mask disappear. The failing mask revealed a tunnel entrance that didn't look natural. It had a perfectly flat floor, but the walls and ceiling were rounded. Thiobulus had to have done the work himself. Angela guessed the amount of energie Thiobulus would have had to expend would have been enormous.

And keeping it hidden like that, the entrance was probably a Work of its own.

The thought reminded her of the Work that Trajon Jarl had used to uncover the tunnel.

"Why did you have to use the Work?" Angela asked.

"Thiobulus set a nasty trap for anyone that entered," he said. "I removed it."

"What did the Work do?" She hated that she asked, that she might learn anything from the man, but she had to know.

"So, you want to learn?" Jarl asked. Then he laughed.

Angela didn't answer the question, at first, but then realized that doing so might help him lose his suspicion of her, and might give her the opportunity to escape. She *did* want to know the answer.

"Please, tell me," she said.

He laughed again.

"Fine. The Work eats the energie in a Weave and disperses it throughout the surrounding area without triggering a collapse."

That was the source of the tingling she had felt. It couldn't have been anything else. But she should have been able to see the energie as it was expelled from the Work.

"I didn't see any energie coming out of it," she said.

"You *were* watching. Well, the energie just disappears. I do not know where it goes."

But she suspected he had just lied to her. He did know. He just wasn't going to tell her.

"Lesson's over," he said. "Go on in."

"Me first?" she asked.

"Of course. Just in case I missed something," he said.

Angela cursed herself. She shouldn't have waited to try putting Jarl at ease.

She stepped forward, into the gaping hole of the tunnel.

As they walked, the tunnel grew darker around them. She kept waiting for Trajon Jarl to Weave a light, but he did nothing. Eventually, she couldn't see any farther.

She stopped.

"It's too dark," she said. "I can't see."

"Keep going. Your eyes will adjust."

He pushed her in the back, and she stumbled forward.

She decided to Weave her own light. It wouldn't have to be bright.

She held out her hand and slipped into the vew.

Energie swirled around her. She saw Weaves throughout the tunnel, and she couldn't imagine what they were for.

She drew in some of the free energie, sent it to her fingertip, wrapped a small light Weave around it. The corridor appeared in front of her again.

She heard a rumble from the ceiling in front of her.

"What did you..." Trajon said.

The light on her fingertip winked off.

The rumble in front of her became a roar just before dust and rock hit her in the face, pushing her back into Trajon Jarl. They both fell to the floor. She landed atop him among the floating dust.

She reached out with her hand to push herself up, and it came to rest on something that felt like cold, dead flesh.

She recoiled from it, and scrambled away.

She looked back up the tunnel toward the entrance. She couldn't see it. She didn't care.

Angela ran in that direction, and smacked into a wall of stone.

"You stupid girl," said Trajon Jarl.

A Weave lifted her from the ground and tossed her against the wall. Her face smashed into the stone, and she thought she heard a crack in her skull. Red hot fire flared in her nose, making her eyes water. The rough wall scraped her cheek as she slid down, but she hardly noticed.

"Now they know I am here."

The corridor lit up, and she turned away from the wall.

Through her watery eyes, Trajon Jarl looked like a monster, his flesh gray with dust, and his forehead scrunched toward the bridge of his nose in rage.

Through it all, she had managed to stay in the vew, and she could see him drawing the energie into him. He held another Work in his hand, the one he had used to take them from Gerard's home.

He moved toward her. She scrunched back against the wall as far as she could, but it would not yield.

He reached out with his gray hand, grasped her wrist. His hand was as cold. She realized she had put her hand on his arm when she had tried to get up. There was no warmth in the man at all.

"What..."

He slapped her, the tips of his fingers brushing her nose as they went by, causing the pain in her nose to flair again. The slap on her cheek was inconsequential. She couldn't help herself. She started to sob.

Jarl stopped drawing energie.

The world shifted.

Angela was in the dark again.

Underneath the pain and the sobbing, she came to realize she felt a quiet bit of satisfaction. If Thiobulus and Robert were anywhere nearby, they were now warned.

GERARD PICKED HIMSELF up from the ground and dusted himself off. He was glad Nina hadn't seen him fall backwards when Demetrius jumped out of the undergrowth.

Demetrius retrieved Gerard's staff and handed it to him.

"You didn't have to jump out at me," Gerard said.

"I didn't want you to accidentally torch me," Demetrius said.

Demetrius wore a bit of a smile on his face. The whole incident caused Gerard to think back to the first time he had met Demetrius, just after Monteous had been abducted. It had happened in almost the same way, except that time, it had been dark out.

"I wouldn't have set you alight if you had just called out to me. What are you doing here?"

"Looking for you," Demetrius said.

"How did you find us? Wait..." Gerard looked around for Robert, but Demetrius appeared to be alone. "Where's Robert?"

Demetrius stepped out of the underbrush.

"He's with Thiobulus, and to answer your first question, Thiobulus sensed you here, somehow. He sent me to you."

Gerard heaved a sigh of relief. At least Robert was safe.

"What are you doing here?" Demetrius asked. "You were supposed to be back at your parent's home."

Gerard would have kicked himself in the head, were it possible. In his scare, he had forgotten about Angela.

"Trajon Jarl came to my house. He took Angela."

The smile on Demetrius's face disappeared completely.

"Where'd he take her?"

"He was asking after Robert. He wanted to know where he was. He caught me right away," he said. There was no shame in admitting it. "Then, he caught Nina. He was trying to force me to tell him where you were, but we didn't know, exactly."

"I am surprised you live," Demetrius said.

"Right after he threatened to kill Nina if she didn't tell him where they were, he knocked us across the room, then turned and left."

Demetrius suddenly grew so tense that Gerard could see it in his shoulders. "What time of day was that?" Demetrius asked.

"Just about nightfall last night."

"Damn," Demetrius said. "That was about the time Robert fell."

"Robert fell?"

"He's fine, but the shield must have fallen apart. He should be fine with Thiobulus, but now Trajon Jarl knows where to look. And he has Angela with him?"

Gerard nodded.

"He's going to use her against Robert," Demetrius said.

Gerard ran back to his horse, leaving Demetrius behind.

"Nina!" he shouted. "We have to ride!"

Then he turned to Demetrius. "Where's your horse?"

"We don't have time for horses. Get Nina and bring her here. Get her horse, too."

"Why?"

Demetrius fished in his pocket, and eventually brought forth a piece of paper. He held it out, and Gerard took it.

"What is this?" Gerard asked, but he'd already started to figure out what it was. Dark black ink described a Weave.

"It's a Weave that will take us back to Thiobulus's laboratory. Can you weave it?"

Gerard didn't know. It had a lot of the energies in it that he was less adept at.

"I can try," he said.

He looked around and found that Nina had not come at his call. A surge of fear ran through, and he ran to get Nina.

He found her asleep at the table, a half eaten strip of goat meat between her fingers. Just looking at her sleep brought his own need for rest to his mind, but he knew he didn't have time. Angela didn't have time.

He put his hands on her shoulders and shook her until she roused. "Come on, Nina," he said. "We've got to go. Demetrius is here."

"Go? Demetrius?" she asked.

She moved her hands, and the meat fell to the table. From behind her, Gerard couldn't see her face, but she didn't seem to be waking up too fast. She had gone into deep sleep rather quickly.

"Yes, Demetrius is here to take us to Thiobulus," Gerard said.

"I'm coming," she said.

But she stayed right where she was.

He pulled on her arm, until she relented and stood up.

He gathered up the food, handed the half eaten piece of goat to Nina, and then held her as he walked her back to the stream, the horses, and Demetrius.

By the time they reached them, Nina was fully awake.

Gerard pulled out the paper that described the Weave and took up his staff.

He ran through the sequence a couple of times in his head, before he slipped into the vew to try it for real.

It didn't seem like it would take much energie, which left him hopeful that it wouldn't tire him any more than he already was.

He turned to face the edge of the clearing, intending to place the Weave right along it.

He took a deep breath, let it out, then started gathering the energie he needed. He spun it out through his staff, forcing it to take the shape from the drawing. It looked very similar to the Weave that Monteous had spun to take them to the Conclave where the Guild met to govern itself. When he was done, and spun the last thread out, a portal formed, just like he had seen when Monteous spun his. Only that one had been dark. This, he could see through to the far side of a room that was lined with bookshelves.

"Go through," Gerard said.

Demetrius led Gerard's horse into that room, whatever it was. Gerard hoped Thiobulus didn't mind horses in there. Then Shane led his horse through, followed by Nina and hers. The room looked large enough.

Gerard took a breath and stepped through. Once he reached the other side, he released the Weave and the portal collapsed behind him. And then he heard a rumble, as if rock were falling down the side of a mountain. The floor shook.

And moments later, an old man ran into the room, with Robert following close on his heals.

CHAPTER 33

ROBERT NEARLY TRIPPED while coming to a halt. Thiobulus's laboratory was filled with horses and his friends.

Demetrius stood in the center of the room, holding the reins of Gerard's horse. Nina and Shane had their own horses, and Gerard was standing next to the one blank spot on the wall, holding his staff as if he had just used it.

He quickly realized that the errand Thiobulus had sent Demetrius on must have been to bring his friends, but unless they had left right away—

Wait.

"Where's Angela?" he asked. He couldn't see her.

Maybe she's still in bed, sick, but why would Gerard leave her there? Why would Shane?

Thiobulus came to a stop, too. "What are you waiting for, Robert? We do not have time."

Gerard looked confused. They all did. All of them except Demetrius.

"Demetrius? Where's Angela?" Robert asked.

"Robert!" Thiobulus shouted. "Trajon won't wait."

But he had to know where Angela was.

"Where is she?"

"Jarl took her," Demetrius said.

"Took her?"

Robert couldn't get his head around what Demetrius had said. How could Jarl take her?

Thiobulus ran over to Robert and grabbed his arm in a surprisingly strong grip. He pulled Robert off balance.

"I'm not taking him on without you, Robert."

"How did he take her?" Robert asked as he fought to regain his balance.

But his thoughts quickly shifted after he asked the question. "Never mind," he said.

It wasn't important how Trajon Jarl took her. It was only important to know what he would do with her, and he knew that already. Trajon Jarl would use her against him, and Robert knew in the darkest places of his heart that it would work. Robert would not let anything happen to Angela if he could prevent it.

"We have to go," he said.

Thiobulus grunted, and then rushed to a doorway that Robert had not been through before.

Robert rushed after him. "Where does this lead?"

"To another entrance," Thiobulus said.

"How many entrances does this place have?"

"Six, if you count the portal."

Thiobulus paused with his hand on the door, and looked at Robert.

"You must know a few things about Trajon Jarl," Thiobulus said.

"Tell me."

"Always be watching for the blood weaves. He will use them. He is a master of Works. He invented many of the ones that are in use by the Guild today. He is sure to have access to Works you have never seen."

"Anything else?"

"Do not trust anything. If you see him Weave the obvious, he has already Weaved another that will come at you from behind."

Robert felt a presence at his side, and he turned to find Demetrius standing there.

"What are you doing?" Robert asked him.

"I'm going to help," he said.

Robert thought back to what Thiobulus had told him. Thiobulus had made Demetrius what he was so that he could fight men like Trajon Jarl. Only Robert could not be sure, any more, why Demetrius was helping. He had thought it was because Monteous asked Demetrius to help, and maybe because they had become friends. But now, he couldn't help thinking that Demetrius didn't have a choice in the matter.

"You don't have to," Robert said.

Demetrius lifted an eyebrow, as if to say, "Try and stop me," but he didn't say the words.

Gerard and Shane rushed across the room at that moment.

"What are you two doing?" Robert asked.

They looked at each other for a moment, then Gerard said, "We're coming, too."

Another rumble ran through the mountain.

"We do not have time for this," Thiobulus said, and pulled open the door. The corridor beyond was dark.

"You two get Angela free. Don't do anything else. Take her and Nina to safety." Robert looked back at Nina, surprised she wasn't coming, too. She was standing near the horses, but everything about her looked exhausted. He wondered for a moment if she might collapse before they came back. "What about Nina?"

"She's exhausted," Gerard said. "She spent all night trying to track you and Demetrius down."

Thiobulus grunted, then entered the corridor, and just as Robert expected, the ceiling above lit up as he entered.

They ran down the passageway, Thiobulus leading them. He ran faster than Robert thought possible for the old man. The passageway curved to the left, so that they could only see about fifty feet in front of them.

Around that curve, they came upon a rockfall that had sealed off the passage.

"That's what caused the shaking?" Robert asked.

"Yes," Thiobulus said. "Be ready. Shall we find out what is inside?"

Robert readied himself, as much as he could. He slipped into the vew and looked for energie sources to use, but he had little idea of what to prepare for. Was Trajon Jarl waiting inside? Was Angela all right?

At the last second, he remembered to use the other method Thiobulus taught him to watch for proscribed Weaves.

Thiobulus Weaved threads of blue energie, tapped from the air around them, throughout the rockfall. They appeared in an instant, and then constricted. The rockfall in front of him shifted, then exploded into a shower of dirt and dust. It left a huge mound on the floor. Dust filled the air, but not enough to choke him, or to block their vision of what lay beyond.

And what lay beyond was another rockfall. The space between the two, where Robert had expected to find Trajon Jarl holding Angela hostage, was empty.

NINA FOUND A chair and sat in it. Her back ached, and she felt a deep desire to sleep. She could not remember the last time she felt so exhausted. Maybe right after she woke up from draining herself, but then, she had used up her energie protecting Gerard. This time, she had done little but ride her horse for most of the night.

It was true she hadn't slept since the morning of the day before, the few minutes in that clearing hardly counted, but she'd gone three days without sleep before, and had never felt as tired.

It didn't help that her stomach seemed to be revolting against the goat that Gerard had given her.

All she wanted to do was rest—sleep for just a few hours.

But she knew she could not rest, not with Trajon Jarl nearby. Not when Angela was in danger.

She sat with her borrowed bow in her lap, ready just in case, even though Trajon Jarl had already proved the bow to be ineffective. She hoped she could somehow surprise him with it, even still, as she was no match for the man's Weaving.

She watched the horses for a time. They wandered through the room, looking for food, but she knew they wouldn't find any. They seemed calm enough, but she worried what would happen if Trajon Jarl burst into the room, or if something else frightened them.

There wasn't much she could do about them, though. There wasn't anything to tie them to—only bookshelves, and a workbench.

As she sat, her eyelids grew heavier until she could not keep them open.

I'll let my eyes rest, just for a moment.

Just one moment.

❋ ❋ ❋

ANGELA FIRST FELT Trajon Jarl's rough hands on her arm, right before the sting of a knife punctured her wrist.

She screamed and tried to pull away, but Trajon Jarl held her fast.

And then she felt his lips on the wound, and a tongue, a slimy tongue, licking it, licking her blood.

The revulsion within her was so strong, she pulled hard enough to break away from him, but it sent her tumbling backward to the ground. On her way down, her head collided with the floor, and it sent sparks flashing across her vision.

"I should have done that before," Jarl said. "You taste so . . . fresh."

"What? What did you do, you vile..."

"Now, now. None of that," Jarl said.

And Angela found she could no longer say the things she wanted to say. She could think them, but she could not make her mouth form the words, or the air push up through her throat to vocalize them.

Her body stood of its own accord.

"Yes, that is much better. Now, I think it is time we find Thiobulus and your lover."

She felt her foot take a step, and she tried to resist, but her body moved, no matter how hard she tried to stay still, to stay where she was.

"What did you do?" she asked, but the words did not come out. She only heard them in her head.

Somehow, he had taken control of her body.

Horror welled up in her as she took step after step without volition, as her mouth refused to form the words she wanted to say, as she realized that Trajon Jarl could make her do anything he wanted.

She tried to slip into the vew, and it worked. There was still something she could do. The energie around her was there for her to use. She could wield it against him.

She tried to reach out for it, to draw it within herself, but the energie refused to cooperate. It stayed where it was, tantalizing her with potential, but frustratingly unwilling to do anything for her.

Trajon Jarl laughed. "Even that," he said, "is under my control."

She wanted to cry, to close her eyes and not see the energie anymore, but she knew it wouldn't help. She had waited, so long ago, for her parents to come to her rescue at the party where she had lost everything, and they never came. She had to help herself, if she wanted to save Robert. She knew he would give in to Trajon Jarl if he thought it would save her.

And she could not allow that to happen.

She forced down the terror and the fear and the revulsion. She squelched the desire to shed tears.

There had to be a way to get control of herself back.

Somehow, her blood had given him power over her.

But she still had far more of her blood in her than he did.

She just had to figure out how to use it before Trajon Jarl found Robert, or Robert found them.

Ahead of her, light seeped around the edges of a door that was not shut tight.

She ignored it.

What she wanted was inside of her. It had to be her energie that he was using. She had long ago learned how to protect her energie from another wizard stealing it. But she had never understood that a wizard could use it against her, and certainly not to control her.

She wished she could turn the vew inward, to see within herself, but that was impossible.

The door was getting closer.

She closed her eyes. With Trajon directing her walk, she didn't need to see where she was going.

He had to be using a proscribed weave to control her, but she didn't know how to see them. She cursed the Guild for not teaching their apprentices these things until after they were accepted as masters. They had made her vulnerable. They had made every single apprentice vulnerable.

If it was a proscribed weave, then it had to be woven from threads of energie. And if it was using energie, she could see it. Robert had told her about seeing the threads of the proscribed weave that killed Wallace outside of the room where Orliss's henchmen had held Monteous prisoner. They had become visible to him right at the last moment.

And Wallace had been able to see the Weave.

Why?

What had he done differently?

It had to be a trick of the vew. A different way of seeing. If only she could figure it out before Jarl used her against Robert.

She felt her body come to a stop, and she opened her eyes.

The door stood slightly ajar in front of them.

"I can feel you thinking, you know," Jarl said. "I like that feeling, the fear that people have. I like it when they fight against me, searching for a way out, a way to regain control."

It almost made Angela stop. She didn't want to do anything to give him pleasure, and for a moment, she thought that denying him pleasure would be a form of fighting. But a twitch in the corner of his eye, seen in the barest of light from the room beyond, belied his statement.

He didn't want her fighting him.

She closed her eyes again.

But they opened right back up.

"You will want to see this," he said.

He pushed the door open, then forced her to walk into the room ahead of him.

The room looked like a giant laboratory. There were more books on the walls than she'd seen even at Monteous's laboratory. Momentarily, it made her miss the old lab, the less complicated time that she had thought complicated.

But this laboratory was different.

There were three horses in the laboratory. They were loose and seemed skittish, though not yet frightened enough to bolt and hurt someone—not that they had anywhere to run to. She recognized them, too. They belonged to Gerard, Nina, and Shane.

They were here, somewhere, in this labyrinth of Thiobulus's.

Then her eyes swept over the sleeping form of Nina. She had a bow in her lap, but it would do her little good.

"Listen," Trajon Jarl said. "I will tell you the trick."

"What trick?" Angela was surprised that her mouth moved for her.

"I know the Guild does not teach you how to use their proscribed Weaves. They do not even teach you how to see them, do they?"

"No," Angela said, surprised her mouth was free to speak.

"Well, here is the trick. Go into the vew."

It felt wrong to do what he asked, but she did it anyway. Perhaps this would be her opportunity.

"Now, slowly slide out of the vew. Focus on your friend, focus on her skin, on what is inside."

Angela did as she was told, letting her eyes lose their focus on the energie around her, but concentrating her sight on Nina.

And then everything popped into vew again. But this time it was different. The energie around her was still there, but there were additional energies running through Nina's body, and in the bodies of the horses. It throbbed and ebbed, almost like a heartbeat.

"Good," Trajon Jarl said. "You see it, don't you?"

"Yes." It was as if a whole new world opened up to her.

There was something else, too. In Nina's abdomen, another flicker of energie, different from Nina's.

Trajon Jarl laughed behind her.

Nina woke at the laughter, and Angela watched as Nina climbed out of her sleep.

Nina looked up at Angela. She didn't seem to quite recognize her right away.

And then Nina's eyes popped open and she reached for her bow, but it was too late. Angela saw the threads string out from Trajon Jarl to snatch the bow and toss it against the far wall.

"Now," Jarl said. "I have two of you."

Angela wanted to scream, but her mouth and her lungs wouldn't cooperate. Jarl had taken control again.

She turned her newly found vew inward and started looking. Maybe that was the answer. She had to do something to escape now that Jarl had both her and Nina, and Nina's recently conceived child.

CHAPTER 34

"WHERE ARE THEY?" Robert asked, panicked. He had expected to find Angela and Trajon Jarl, but the now crushed rock wall exposed only air and dust.

"I do not know," Thiobulus said. "Wait while I look."

Robert was in the vew, he saw the energie form into threads and enter the Weaves that ran the length of the passage way to provide light. He studied the weaves, the threads. They were nothing like he had seen Monteous use.

But waiting and watching proved difficult. Every few seconds, he found himself wanting to ask Thiobulus if he had found them, but he kept the questions inside each time.

He caught looks from Gerard and Shane, questioning looks, but Robert didn't dare inquire about them, for fear of interrupting Thiobulus.

Only Demetrius looked calm, but he was rarely anything but calm.

"Back!" Thiobulus shouted, startling them all. "Back to the laboratory."

The old wizard broke into a sprint. Robert chased after him, but found it hard to keep up. Something far greater than just the threat of Trajon Jarl had spurred Thiobulus into action, and Robert feared to find out what it was.

They ran so fast, he didn't dare turn his head to see if the rest of them were following. He knew they were, he could hear their footsteps behind him, but those footsteps were slowly receding.

Thiobulus burst through the door to the laboratory. Robert entered not a second later, and had to turn to the side to avoid running into Thiobulus, who had come to a stop just inside the doorway.

Robert looked his way, but Thiobulus seemed frozen in place.

"I am glad to see you Robert."

Robert knew the voice and turned away from Thiobulus to scan the room for its owner.

He found Trajon Jarl standing just to the left across the room, his hand held out in front of him, pointed at Thiobulus.

Robert entered his newly learned variation of the vew and found a thick red rope of energie reaching out from a tiny little work in Jarl's hand to encase Thiobulus. Other energies, air, spirit, water, were all intertwined throughout the rope.

"Robert, look," Gerard said, having come up behind him.

Robert looked where Gerard pointed. Angela stood, still as a statue, not ten feet from Trajon Jarl. She had a look of terror on her face. That she didn't run confused Robert. Next to her, Nina looked similarly distressed, though she was seated at the table.

"Run, Angela!" Robert shouted.

But Angela didn't run. Her cheeks twitched, as if she wanted to say something, but that was the only movement she made. Her lips remained firmly closed.

"She won't be running anywhere," Jarl said. "Not unless you give me your allegiance, Robert."

Robert saw energie move out of the corner of his eye.

"No, Gerard, don't do it," Robert said.

But when he turned, he saw that it wasn't Gerard, but Shane that had drawn in the energie. He spun out a thread of lightning that flashed across the distance between him and Trajon Jarl in the time between one blink and the next. The lightning glanced off of Jarl and crashed into the ceiling, startling the horses with its roar. Stone rained down from above, adding to the din.

Jarl retaliated with a blast of air that knocked Shane up against the wall behind him. The crack of his skull against a bookcase echoed throughout the room as Shane's body fell limply to the floor.

Robert's mind flashed back to seeing Monteous's youngest apprentice, Wallace, fall to a malicious proscribed Weave during the search for Monteous.

I won't let that happen again.

"Now, Robert, are you going to join with me, or must I kill you as I have every other member of the Guild."

Every member?

Robert didn't think that was possible. He couldn't have killed them all, not in the time he had. Unless Jarl had started earlier than Robert knew. Shane's master was already dead when they went to him for help.

But he couldn't have started much earlier, or Robert would have heard about it. The Guild would have told Demetrius.

Robert examined the rope of energie that held Thiobulus. He wished he knew if it were doing more than just holding him. The rope pulsed and throbbed as if a battle were going on inside of it.

"If they're already dead," Robert said, stalling, "then why do you need me? Just let us go."

Robert reached out for that energie, but the rope rebuffed him. The energie was bound tightly into the rope, and he could not disrupt it.

He needed another plan. He wished Demetrius would try something, say something.

Robert glanced behind him. Only Gerard stood there, and he looked exhausted. Demetrius was missing.

"You have one thing wrong," Jarl said. "I don't *need* you. I *want* you. I want you at my side."

Did Demetrius run off? Robert couldn't imagine the man would do that to him. But he couldn't imagine where Demetrius had gone to, either. He had been sure Demetrius was right behind him as they ran down the corridor.

"Why?" Robert asked.

Robert reached out for air and spirit energies. He took energie from the stone around him, too. He imagined the pattern of the shield in his head, planned it out to the last thread.

"Because you have just as much reason to hate the Guild as I do, Robert."

"No," said Robert, denying it. He didn't hate the Guild, even if they hadn't allowed him to join.

"No? They keep you at arm's length because they are afraid of you. They are afraid of what a young wizard like you might do were you to become Senior Wizard. Not to mention that, as a Guild member, you would be able to find out what truly happened to your parents."

"I know what truly happened," Robert said. "They died in the uprising."

Robert coerced the energie he had gathered to form the Weave he had built in his mind, and in the instant it came together, he smashed it down through the rope of energie holding Thiobulus.

The rope shredded, like Robert hoped it would. The energie, newly released, spilled out in a rush, blasting everything around it.

Robert found himself on the ground, laying on top of lumpy flesh. Gerard. Robert's bones ached from the collision, but he didn't have time to concern himself with aches.

He looked to his left, and saw that Thiobulus was free of Jarl's weave, but he wasn't moving.

Robert rolled off of Gerard and crawled to Thiobulus. He put his hand up against the wizard's mouth and nose. A slight puff of air, hardly a breath, told Robert Thiobulus still lived.

It wasn't enough, though. He needed Thiobulus to wake up, to help him. He had to know what Jarl had done to Angela.

Jarl. Angela. Robert looked toward where they had been.

Jarl was just struggling up from the floor where he'd landed after being thrown by the blast of energie.

Robert could not see Angela at first. He found Nina, still in the chair, although the chair had moved across the room. The blast had knocked Gerard's horse from its feet in front of Nina, and it was struggling to stand.

But Angela had gone missing.

"Angela!" he cried out.

She didn't answer.

It all seemed to be moving so slowly.

But Robert knew he didn't have much time.

He took the energie from the air, wrapped it around Trajon Jarl, and threw him across the room to crash into a shelf filled with books and a few long disused works. Jarl fell to the ground amidst swirling papers and broken glass.

"Angela!"

Gerard's horse managed to get to her feet. She looked unsteady and frightened. Her nostrils flared.

Between her legs, Robert caught sight of Angela's still form. He couldn't tell if she was alive and still under Jarl's control, or if she wasn't moving because she was dead.

He checked on Jarl again, but the wizard hadn't moved. Robert wrapped a Weave around him, on the chance that Jarl was feigning unconsciousness, then ran across the room to carefully skirt the frightened horse and kneel at Angela's side.

"Angela?"

She didn't move, but her chest rose and fell. She was breathing.

"Angela?"

She still didn't move. Her eyes stayed closed.

Out of the corner of his eye, he caught Gerard running to Nina. His face wore a frown, his brow, furrowed.

"Nina!" Gerard called out.

Robert glanced up at Nina. She was still sitting in the same position she had been, but her eyes were open.

What was wrong with them? What had Trajon Jarl done?

Robert returned his attention to Angela. He reached out and brushed a lock of hair from her face. Her skin was warm. She was alive, the breathing proved that.

"Angela," Robert said. "What did he do to you?"

Her eyes popped open. They seemed to see his face, but her lips didn't move, her cheeks didn't lift as he would have expected.

"Angela?"

Her eyes shifted.

"Can you hear me?"

She didn't answer. She made no move to sit up.

He was in the vew. He couldn't see any threads surrounding her. Not even proscribed Weaves. Her own energie, the energie he could see, looked to be in its familiar pattern, and not the somewhat chaotic mess of a normal person. Her blood energie seemed odd, sort of stuck in place, but he didn't know if that was normal or not. The pulse of her heartbeat still echoed throughout her body.

Robert stood. He faced Trajon Jarl, and walked toward him.

Whatever Trajon Jarl had done to Angela, he would pay for it.

A hand grabbed his leg, pulled it out from under him, and he fell to the floor. His head smashed against the stone and a bloom of pain forced him to shut his right eye.

He looked back with his still open left eye. The hand that had pulled him down belonged to Angela.

She had moved just enough to grab him. She looked like she had folded herself in half to do it, her torso bent at an odd angle. He could not see her face.

He tried to pull his leg free, but her grip was too strong. She wouldn't let go, and he didn't want to kick too hard for fear of hurting her.

It didn't make any sense, either, unless...

He remembered Gerard's uncle.

Did Jarl do something like that to Angela?

He looked back at Jarl. The wizard had come around and was staring right at Robert. There was a trickle of blood on Jarl's temple that had run down to his slash of an eyebrow.

"Robert, it is a shame it had to turn out this way," Jarl said, "but your girlfriend is quite delightful. She obeys my commands so very well."

"Let her go!" Robert said.

The corners of Trajon Jarl's mouth lifted.

"Oh, I don't think so. I think I'll keep her."

FROM THE MOMENT they started down the tunnel toward what he thought would be a confrontation with Trajon Jarl, Demetrius had hung back. He was not meant for a frontal assault on that wizard. He was meant for more subtle attacks. The gifts Thiobulus had given him were designed to let him work from the shadows, and if the truth were told, he preferred the shadows.

When they discovered that Trajon had escaped, Demetrius had cursed silently, his hopes for a swift resolution dashed against the stone of the mountain. The group turned around, and again, Demetrius hung back.

He could not survive confronting Trajon Jarl out in the open. He needed to come at the wizard from behind, if at all possible. But the wizard would be looking for that. It was how he and Thiobulus had trapped Trajon the first time.

As they raced back to Thiobulus's laboratory, Demetrius pondered the possibilities.

He didn't think Trajon would have left once he learned he had been discovered. Trajon had too much at stake to leave he and Thiobulus alone. And he knew the wizard wanted to see Robert at his side, or dead. The boy had too much potential to let twist on his own.

He also didn't think Trajon would try hiding any more. He would have found a place where he could control the confrontation. Demetrius ruled out the laboratory almost immediately. It was too large, with too many opportunities to surround him.

Would he be waiting for them to come out, waiting outside a tunnel? It was possible.

Demetrius tried to think of other rooms, but they all were too far out of the way, with too little chance of the confrontation happening at all.

Reluctantly, just as Thiobulus burst through the door into the laboratory, Demetrius concluded he'd been wrong, and the laboratory was the only place Trajon Jarl would have gone.

But it was too late to save Thiobulus.

Robert ran through the door, too, followed by Gerard and Shane.

Demetrius hung back amongst the shadows. The door stayed open, giving him a view of the room as Trajon Jarl greeted Robert.

Just over Robert's shoulder, Demetrius caught sight of Angela, standing still as a statue.

Demetrius shuddered, recalling the battles of the Unification, the constant fights against men who were not in control of themselves, but instead were under the control of wizards like Trajon, made to fight beyond what their bodies could handle.

And now, Trajon had Angela. Trajon wouldn't hesitate to use Angela against Robert, to break her against Robert.

Demetrius wanted to rush out and warn the young wizard. He wanted to rush out and stick his knife in Trajon's eye so that it sunk to the hilt into the wizard's brain. He even took a step in that direction.

But he took control of himself. Rushing out would endanger him, Angela, and Robert, not to mention the others. He had to stay hidden, wait until there was a moment he could use to slip out of the tunnel.

He knew there would be a moment. He needed it.

Even if it was almost too late, all he needed was to slip a blade into the back of Trajon's neck, and the wizard would fall. It was something he regretted not doing when he had the chance nearly two-hundred years earlier. He wished he could have disobeyed Thiobulus.

He shook his head to clear the thoughts.

That was then.

So he waited, listening to the heartbeats of the people in the room. Robert's was racing. They all were.

Robert turned and said, "No Gerard, don't do it."

But Gerard didn't do anything.

Shane let loose with lightning, surprising everybody but Trajon Jarl, who effortlessly blocked it, then sent Shane crashing up against the wall.

Demetrius readied himself, thinking that it all might turn into chaos, but Robert remained calm on the outside, and tried to bargain with Trajon Jarl.

Demetrius ran through a number of curses in his head. He needed them to move away from the door. He needed Trajon's attention diverted.

"Now, Robert, are you going to join with me, or must I kill you as I have every other member of the Guild," Trajon said.

Demetrius knew the wizard was boasting. He hadn't had the time. It probably wouldn't take him much longer, and then any protection The Seven Kingdoms had against the predations of Mrongil or any of the other rival countries would be gone.

"If they're already dead," Robert said, "then why do you need me? Just let us go. Let us all go."

Robert's question surprised Demetrius a little. They had talked about it. For Trajon's plan to succeed, he would want to build up his own Guild. A promising young wizard like Robert could be a great weapon in Trajon's hands.

But Demetrius knew Robert well enough. Robert wouldn't go along with it.

But why was he asking the question?

Then Demetrius realized Robert had to be planning something. He hoped Robert was planning something. He just hoped it wouldn't get them all killed.

"You have one thing wrong," Jarl said. "I don't need you. I want you. I want you at my side."

Demetrius caught Robert glance behind him, looking for something. He hoped Robert didn't see him. He didn't want Robert to give him away to

Trajon Jarl. Demetrius knew Thiobulus's gifts should work to help Robert not see him, but Robert had surprised him more than once, and Robert wasn't the only one. The gifts did not always work.

"Why?" Robert asked.

"Because you have just as much reason to hate the Guild as I do, Robert."

"No," said Robert.

Demetrius silently urged Robert to hurry. Whatever he was planning, he was taking too long. Thiobulus could be dying inside whatever Weave Trajon had placed him in, and while the old wizard's death would not bother Demetrius too much, it wouldn't help their situation, either. They needed Thiobulus. And if Trajon Jarl had killed as many wizards as he boasted, they would need Thiobulus to help reestablish the Guild.

Trajon spouted the same nonsense about Robert's parents that he had tried to plant in Robert's mind back at the Academy.

Robert denied it again.

"They died in the uprising," he said.

Demetrius could not tell what happened then, but the room erupted in a burst of wind, knocking everyone outside the door to the ground. The wind rushed past Demetrius. It wasn't just wind. It made his skin tingle, almost like a burn. The hairs on his arms stood up. The force buffeted him, nearly pushed him over, but he managed to keep his feet.

Once it was past him, Demetrius rushed out into the room. A quick survey of the room dashed his first plan to drive a knife in Trajon's throat as the wizard was already starting to recover.

Demetrius found a low cabinet up against the far wall, somewhat behind Trajon Jarl, but not directly, and raced over to it. He knelt and pressed himself against it, using his gift to conceal himself from any searching eyes.

Trajon Jarl struggled to get up from where he had fallen.

Demetrius pulled his knife out and prepared himself, intentionally slowing his heartbeat, bending his legs just enough so that he could spring across the space between them. He just needed Trajon to move forward a few steps, enough so that Demetrius would truly be out of his sight, and then Demetrius could take a chance.

Demetrius checked on the others.

Robert had crawled over to Thiobulus, and then he looked up. A moment later, he cried out for Angela.

He must have seen her.

Suddenly, Trajon flew across the room to smash against the wall of shelves and fall limply to the floor. Books fell from the shelf above Trajon to land on the wizard.

Demetrius silently cursed his luck, and cursed Robert. Trajon was now twenty feet farther away, and had a clear view of Demetrius.

Demetrius knew he had to move. His gifts wouldn't conceal him from Trajon should the wizard open his eyes and look right at him.

But where?

Robert ran to Angela's side, and was trying to wake her up, to get her to respond.

Futile while Trajon lived.

Demetrius spied one of the horses, somewhat nearer Trajon Jarl. It was frightened, but not yet panicked.

Gerard ran across the room to Nina. He'd have no better luck than Robert.

But it gave Demetrius the chance to slip over to the horse. Once the horse shielded him from view, he approached it slowly, not wanting to frighten it any further.

He took the loose reins, rubbed his hand along its neck in an effort to soothe it. It took a few moments, but the horse's fright slowly ebbed.

He peaked over the horse.

Robert had stood up. Trajon Jarl twitched a little, but he hadn't opened his eyes.

Robert stepped toward Trajon. His eyebrows had come together, and his eyes burned with fury. His intent was obvious on his face.

Behind him, Angela moved.

Before Demetrius could shout a warning, Angela's torso bent awkwardly, and she reached out, grabbed Robert's ankle and yanked, pulling Robert to the floor.

Trajon's eyes popped open.

"Robert, it is a shame it had to turn out this way," Jarl said, "but your girlfriend is quite delightful. She obeys my commands so very well."

"Let her go!" Robert shouted.

"Oh, I don't think so. I think I'll keep her."

Trajon Jarl pushed himself up from the ground with his right arm. Robert had hurt him. There was blood on the wizard's forehead, his left arm hung limp at his side.

"No," Trajon Jarl said in response to something unsaid. "I want you to watch, Angela, as I teach Robert a lesson. Perhaps you will learn from it, too."

Angela must be trying to break free.

Trajon took a few steps forward, enough that Demetrius could come at him from the side.

It would have to be enough. Demetrius could not let this go on much longer. And maybe whatever Angela was trying would distract the wizard just enough.

Robert said something to Jarl, but Demetrius ignored it. It was unimportant. He focused all his thought on being quick, invisible, deadly. A few moments preparing himself while Jarl responded, distracted.

A ball of fire erupted from Gerard's direction, breaking Demetrius's concentration. Jarl squelched it and turned it on Gerard. Gerard cried out in pain from the flame, but there was nothing Demetrius could do.

"You'll have to do better than that, Gerard."

Demetrius cursed under his breath. He'd missed his opportunity.

Gerard's cries subsided quickly, and Demetrius looked over at him. Someone had healed him.

It had to be Robert.

Trajon was saying something else, but Demetrius missed it. He did hear Trajon's next words.

"You have three seconds to decide."

Demetrius had three seconds to do something. He knew in his heart that Robert would try something rather than give in.

"One," Jarl said.

Demetrius lifted the knife.

"Two."

Demetrius crouched, ready to spring.

Jarl's focus shifted.

"You couldn't," he said.

Demetrius slipped around the horse.

Angela said something that Demetrius, with all his effort focused on hiding himself, failed to catch.

Jarl stumbled.

It was his chance.

Demetrius took his first step toward the man he should have killed two hundred years earlier.

ANGELA PUSHED THE horror into the back of her mind. Her hand had reached out and pulled Robert down of its own accord—*no*—at Trajon Jarl's bidding. He had forced her to contort her body in a way that was completely unnatural, folding herself sideways, so that she could reach Robert. It had put a fire in her back, the muscles on her side were stretched so tight they felt like they might snap.

She had to do something, but she had looked and looked, and could not find a way to remove his control of her. There was not a Weave to dismantle that she could see. Not a Weave as she understood them, at least. This new sight Jarl had given her access to made her think there might be something else beyond the traditional Weave. She only had to figure it out. What else had the Guild failed to teach her?

She wished she could move her head. She had a view of Trajon Jarl, and she could just see the top of Gerard's head if she really strained to move her eyes, but she could not see the rest of the room. She could not see what had happened to Shane, and she could not see if Thiobulus was waking up.

The way Demetrius had talked about Thiobulus, she had thought him the key to defeating Trajon Jarl, but he had been as ineffective as any of the wizards back at the Academy.

She closed her eyes and again delved deep within herself, looking for the latch that would release her from Trajon's control.

"No," Trajon Jarl said. His voice pierced through her, interrupting her search. Her eyelids opened despite her wish to keep them closed. "I want you to watch, Angela, as I teach Robert a lesson. Perhaps you will learn from it, too."

She tried to shout at him, but her lips did nothing, her throat refused her command.

Trajon Jarl took a few steps forward. His left arm hung limp at his side, but his right arm held a Work in it. Another small thing that Angela did not recognize. She wondered, briefly, how many he carried with him, and then chided herself for letting her mind wander.

Robert tried to pull his foot away, but Angela's grip tightened. Everything about her felt strained. Robert didn't seem to put much effort into trying to escape—he obviously did not want to hurt her. But she wished he would kick her hand free. It could be healed, and she could endure the pain if they lived.

He did not kick at her, though, instead giving up.

"Please let her go," Robert said.

"Hmm," Trajon Jarl said. "I had thought you stronger than this, Robert. After you killed Orliss, I thought you had the stomach for doing what needs to be done. You could free yourself easily, yet you refuse to do so."

Angela couldn't close her eyes and look inside her, so she instead turned the vew on Trajon Jarl.

And there, she saw what she hadn't been able to see, because she had been looking in the wrong place.

There were patterns of energie in Trajon's body that did not match, nor did they mesh together. He seemed a patchwork of energies, a quilt made from the energie of others.

She wondered if there was any part of him at all that was still himself.

One of the patterns in the flow of his energie looked familiar to her, because she had been looking within herself. It was hers, a bright string of red diamonds held together with thin strands.

Just behind his eyes.

"I will never hurt Angela," Robert said. "I would die, first."

No, Robert.

She wished she could shout it.

"It seems she doesn't want that," Jarl said.

Robert looked back at her. She could see the confusion and pain in his eyes. She tried to tell him to kick himself free, but she remained mute.

And then she had an idea. If so little of her blood could be used to control her so completely, could she control that little bit of her blood that was inside Trajon Jarl? Could she make it do anything at all?

She looked to Trajon Jarl, but as her vision flashed past a cabinet to the left of the wizard, she caught sight of Demetrius, hiding. She looked back, and he seemed to have disappeared again. No, there he was. But she wasn't seeing his body, she was seeing his energie, and his energie hardly moved within him, static, waiting.

But waiting for what?

"How do you know what she wants?" Robert asked.

"I control her," Trajon Jarl said.

Angela gave up on Demetrius. She couldn't figure out why he wasn't attacking Trajon Jarl, why he was letting Trajon control her, and she didn't have any time. She had to see if she could do something to Jarl before he killed them both—killed them all.

She found the patch of energie within Trajon Jarl that was hers, again. She reached out to it, like when trying to draw energie into her body from other sources, and she could feel it. It recognized her, or her body recognized it. She tried to pull it back to her, but her hold on it failed.

"How is that possible?" Robert asked.

He was still trying to pull his leg from her grip, still fighting while trying not to hurt her. The only way he could escape would be to hurt her, or if she could somehow make Jarl release his hold on her.

Angela reached for her energie again. It was hers. It did not belong to Jarl. It did not want to be there at all. She knew it. She felt it. It wanted out. She tried pulling again, though gentler this time.

A gout of flame ripped through the air toward Trajon Jarl, and he blocked it without thinking about it. The flame caused her to lose her hold on her energie again. The flame had to have come from Gerard.

"You'll have to do better than that, Gerard."

Gerard cried out in pain. When she tried to see him, she could no longer find him. He had moved out of her field of view.

Robert pushed himself to his knees, then turned toward Gerard. A Weave formed just at the edge of her vision, and then disappeared. Gerard's cries subsided.

"Impressive," Jarl said. "It seems you had time to learn something from Thiobulus, after all. Still, whatever you learned will not be enough. Agree to join with me now, or I will kill her, and then I will kill you. You have three seconds to decide."

No! Again, she shouted only in her head.

Back to the energie in Trajon's head.

This time, she would not try to pull it free.

She reached out for it.

"One," Jarl said.

Jarl raised his good arm. He didn't need it to kill her, she knew. He could just stop her heart, or keep her from breathing.

Angela took hold of the energie, tying herself to it at several points.

"Two."

"I will..." Robert's words were distant, tentative.

Angela ignored them.

She focused on the energie and formed it into a Weave that resembled the platform Weave that had been the last she learned at the Academy.

Trajon Jarl's eyes locked on hers.

Her hand released Robert's leg. It didn't do anything else, but it had stopped maintaining her grip on him.

Her body straightened out a little, no longer maintaining the painful position Jarl had forced her into.

"You couldn't," Jarl said.

But she had.

"You don't control me," she said.

She pulled that Weave toward her, and it caused Jarl to stumble. The Weave didn't come free from him, but it didn't slip from her control, either.

"What have you done?" he asked.

She couldn't be sure what happened next.

An immense Weave spun out from the work that he had in his hand toward her and Robert, but another Weave slammed down in front of them and blocked it. The rope split into a thousand threads, all flailing harmlessly on the other side of the Weave that had come down.

Robert must have put it there, or maybe it was Thiobulus.

And then Demetrius flew across the room at Trajon Jarl, knife held to the side. A moment later, a single cut, and Trajon Jarl's head leaned off to the side, a giant chasm opening up in his neck where Demetrius's blade sliced through his throat. Blood spurted from the open wound in a wide arc.

Trajon Jarl's body crumpled to the ground as the blood energie spewed forth with the blood, the force that had held the wizard up, dissipating almost as soon as the blood left the body.

Angela's Weave unraveled on her as her own blood spilled out of Trajon's body.

She slipped out of the vew, unable to watch any more, and closed her eyes.

A hand came to rest on her forehead.

"Angela?"

She opened her eyes to find Robert leaning over her.

"I'm all right, Robert," she said.

CHAPTER 35

THE SMELL OF Trajon Jarl's blood was acrid, old. It assaulted Robert's nose, choked off every other smell, including the smell of Angela's hair.

Once it was clear Jarl was dead, Robert spun around and pulled Angela to him, hugged her tight, and her hair, black and thick as ever, fell across his face. Her body trembled in his arms, warm and soft and no longer burning with fever.

"It's over," he said. "Are you all right?"

"I'm fine," she said, weakly. She didn't sound like she was crying, though.

He could hear the others moving around, but he ignored them. Angela was all he cared about at the moment.

"Whatever happens," he said, "I will never leave you again."

"Don't be silly," she said.

"I should have been there. I should have waited until you were better."

She pulled away from him, put her hands on his shoulders, and stared into his eyes with a look of steel that he had never seen in her before.

"Robert, if you had waited, you would never have found Thiobulus, and we would never have defeated Trajon Jarl. I saw what you did. I don't know how you did it, but you learned something from him, and whatever you learned from Thiobulus..."

"Thiobulus," he said and turned to look.

Thiobulus hadn't moved since he had fallen to the ground. Robert watched for a moment and did not see Thiobulus's chest rise.

He got up and ran over to the wizard. Angela trailed along behind him.

He slipped into the vew, tried to see the wizard's energie, but there was nothing there. He touched the old man's cheek with his finger tips, but the cheek was already growing cold.

Robert slipped to his knees. He didn't feel like crying, exactly, but his chest hurt. Thiobulus had been about to run out on him, on them, but he hadn't run out in the end.

"I was too slow," Robert said. "I should have broken that Weave so much sooner."

"You don't know that," Angela said as she knelt next to him. Her arm slipped over his shoulders.

"I hesitated. I could have saved him."

"If you rushed the Weave and made a mistake, it may have done nothing at all, or could have made it worse," Angela said.

Robert knew she was right.

He heard Demetrius's footsteps approach, and wondered what Demetrius thought about Thiobulus's death. Would he be happy? Or would he be angry?

Demetrius stood over them for a moment, his clothes drenched in the foul smelling blood he had just spilled.

"I never thought he would die before I did," Demetrius said. His voice was bereft of any emotion. "I wondered what would happen to the Weaves he set in me, wondered if they would live beyond his death."

"You know why they do," Robert said, looking up.

"I do," Demetrius said, shifting his eyes to look at Robert. "You know, too, don't you."

Robert nodded. "I didn't understand why you changed your mind so easily when I insisted on finding him."

"You do now, though."

Robert stood so that he could speak face to face with Demetrius. Angela came with him. Out of the corner of his eye, he could see she was confused, but this wasn't something he could stop to explain to her.

"I do now," Robert said. "I would free you from your burden, if I could."

Demetrius's eyes lit with a guarded excitement. "You would do this?"

"Yes, but I can't."

Demetrius's excitement dimmed. "You can't?"

Robert closed his eyes. He didn't want to see the effect his next words would have.

"Thiobulus told me you would die were you to be freed."

In the silence that followed, Robert heard a groan. He opened his eyes and turned to see Gerard sitting up with Nina's help. His clothes and his hair were singed, and it looked like there were a few burns on his face. Robert knew it would have been much worse had he been unable to quench the fire. The weave to save Gerard came together so quickly that Robert had nearly lost it in surprise.

It reminded Robert that Shane had been thrown against the wall and hadn't risen from it. He looked in that direction and found that Shane had managed to rise and was rubbing at the back of his head.

"I should have been dead two hundred years ago," said Demetrius.

"And we would likely all be dead," said Robert, "if you hadn't intervened to help us out of Monteous's laboratory last winter."

"You would," Demetrius said. "Tell me, if I were to ask, would you release me?"

"And kill you?"

"If I asked."

Robert didn't like even thinking about the possibility. He considered Demetrius a friend, and he couldn't imagine killing a friend. Not after watching all those that had been close to him who had died. He had seen enough death.

But he also could not abide the idea that Demetrius was not free to do what he wished, either.

Thiobulus had done to Demetrius what Trajon Jarl had done to Angela. He'd only done it more thoroughly.

"If that is what you want," Robert said. "But if you give me time, I will try to find a way to release you that won't kill you. I don't want to see any more death."

"Then I shall wait. Besides," Demetrius said, "I still think you will have need of my help."

"Trajon Jarl is dead," said Angela.

"Yes," Demetrius said, "but The Seven Kingdoms' wizards are far fewer in number than they have been since the Unification. The Guild will need to be rebuilt if The Seven Kingdoms is to survive."

Robert sighed, put his arm around Angela, and pulled her close. He saw Nina across the way, ministering to Gerard, her hand caressing each of his wounds, a small but tired smile on her face.

He wanted that. He didn't want to be pulled away from Angela by duty, again.

"There's one thing I must do, first," he said.

"What is that?" Demetrius asked.

Robert turned to Angela. She was looking at him, her thin nose only two fingers breadth from his.

"I need to meet Angela's parents." He said it, knowing she didn't want to go back, but he needed to meet them, to understand better where Angela had come from. And maybe, just maybe, it might help to heal those wounds.

"No," whispered Angela.

"Why?" Robert asked.

"If I'm going to marry you, Dear, don't you think I should meet them?"

ON THE ROAD back to Blisterwind Pass, Angela spent most of her time riding behind Robert, conflicted.

Robert wanted to marry her, and her heart sang every time she thought about it. She could hardly keep the smile off her face.

But it inevitably led to her thinking about seeing her parents again, and her anger at them welled up and threatened to overwhelm her joy. She knew why Robert wanted to do it, that he thought whatever problems there were could be worked out, like Gerard had nearly done with his father. But she kept replaying the final conversation she had with her parents, just before she left with Monteous. They had said things she didn't want to remember, blamed her for being overpowered by that man at her father's party, blamed her for having her chastity stolen. Her father had said he didn't want to see her again, that she had ruined all their plans.

She forced her anger down, refusing to let it take over. Perhaps Robert was right. Maybe she should see them, now that she had become a wizard, now that she would be marrying perhaps the most powerful wizard alive. And knowing what lay ahead of them with the Guild and the possibility of war, she knew she might never have the chance to see if things could be better with them if she didn't take it now.

The group stopped again at the carved table by the stream.

Angela climbed off the horse, and caught a glimpse of Nina.

"I can't wait until we get back to your home, Gerard," Nina said. "I'm just so tired."

Angela smiled.

In the rush and fret of worrying about Robert's plans, she had forgotten about Nina.

She went over to her friend and took her hand.

"Gerard, may I have a word with your wife?" she asked.

She didn't wait for an answer. She tugged at Nina's hand until Nina came with her.

Robert had told her about the stream just over the rise, and Angela led Nina to it. The stream burbled along, the soft murmuring of the water and the light wind through the trees put her at ease.

"What's this about, Angela?" Nina asked when they finally came to a stop. "I'm tired, and I want to eat."

Angela hugged her.

"I'm so happy for you," Angela said, "for you and Gerard, and I'm sad you won't be able to come with us to Stradetra."

"Why won't I be able to come with you?"

"Because you and Gerard will have more important things to do," Angela said.

"What?"

Nina looked confused and perturbed. It made Angela smile.

"When Trajon Jarl had me under his control, he taught me to see proscribed Weaves. He taught me to see the energie used in them. When he brought me into the room, I saw you and your energie, and within you, I saw another little bit of energie that was not you."

"I don't understand," Nina said.

Angela hugged her friend to her and whispered into her ear.

"It was your baby."

Angela held on to Nina as Nina's legs stopped supporting her, and then Nina started to giggle.

Together, they slipped, giggling like young girls, to the grass.

They were still giggling when Robert and Gerard found them.

When Gerard asked them what was so funny, their giggles turned to laughs, and it was minutes before either Gerard or Robert could make sense of them again.

Angela soaked it all in, knowing that she would have to hold on to it in light of what she knew was on the horizon.

About The Author

Mark Fassett lives in western Washington with his wife, children, and cats. He's a fantasy and science fiction author whose novels include *Shattered* and *Questioner's Shadow*. He's also written several novellas in those same genres. In the past, he had extensive experience in the mobile game business and was involved with some of the top selling titles at the time of their release, including multiple *Duke Nukem Mobile* games and *Guitar Hero World Tour Mobile*.

Find Me Online

Blog — http://www.markfassett.com
Twitter — http://twitter.com/mark_fassett
Facebook — http://www.facebook.com/markfassett.writer
E-Mail — mark.fassett@gmail.com

Learn About New Releases

Visit http://markfassett.com/newsletter to join my mailing list and get notified about my newest releases! I don't send out daily or weekly updates on my cat, and I don't tell you about my personal tragedies. I only send out information about new releases, and nothing more.